I spent the later half of my twenties in the Service as a Marine. I served my country and felt proud to do so. Coming from where I came from I was just lucky to survive and get out of my neighborhood. Once I did that, I knew I was on to bigger and better things. It wasn't that I forgot where I came from, because I was proud of being from da South Side of Chicago. But I knew it was better for me to pursue my education further and go into the Service. In hopes of having a good career. I was from the Roseland section of da South Side. Was raised by both my parents before they divorced. Me, my older brother Sidney Jr, and my younger sister Savanah. We saw a lot of things growing up in the neighborhood we grew up in. You couldn't even imagine the things we seen from day to day. I guess that's why I always wanted to be successful and dreamed big. So, I could move out and get away from it all.

So after graduating from high school, I attended DePaul University. I studied Secondary Education and Teaching, got my Bachelor's and Master's Degree. Straight out of high school and onto college. It was how I wanted it and how it was supposed to be, in my mind. It was also something my mother always encouraged me to do. She saw the light in my eyes the rare times we would see nice things when I was a kid. She knew I was a dreamer, and she knew I always dreamed of buying her a nice big home off Lake Shore Drive. The things I always dreamed of put a smile on my mother's face and gave her hope while we were all growing up in our South Side neighborhood. We were all ambitious kids growing up in one of the most dangerous cities in the world. By the time I had graduated college, I was twenty five years old. I could've pursued a career in my field, but I felt like I had more life and energy to give to something else. So I decided to become a United States Marine.

I wanted to give my energy to the United States Marine Corps. That was also something I had dreamt of growing up. I didn't want to join the Army, Air Force, or Navy. I wanted to be a Marine. So I went in the Marines hitting the ground running. Went to basic training in San Diego, California. Which was a change for me weather wise, no more brutal Chicago winters. After going through basic training, I gave eight years of my life to the Marine Corps. And came back home to Chicago wanting to make a difference in my city. My name is Silas Jones, a black man and Veteran living in America. Wanting so bad to make a difference, and patiently waiting for my opportunity to do so. This is my life, and my journey to make a difference in this cold world we live in. Through education.

Chapter One "Home"

I was happy to be home from the Service, although I enjoyed my eight year tour of duty in the Marine Corps. It was good to be home around my family. Now before I went to the Marines and was fresh home from graduating college. I wouldn't have said I was happy to be home with my family. Because I went to DePaul, which was still in Chicago. So I really wasn't away from my family so to speak, until I went away to the Marines. When I first got home, I was still getting my check each month from the service. So I wasn't necessarily in a rush to find work when I first got home. Fatima and I was able to find a place in the Near West Side neighborhood in

Chicago. My mother and sister still lived on da South Side, but now in a better neighborhood than we grew up in. So I felt better about their safety nowadays as opposed to when I was in college and just about to go to the Marines.

Either way my older brother Sidney Jr. would hold the family down. My brother Sidney Jr. was like my hero in a sense growing up. He was three years older than me and always looked out for me. After our father Sidney Sr. left the household when Sidney Jr. was twenty, I was seventeen, and our little sister Savannah was fifteen. My older brother Sidney Jr. assumed the role as man of the house. He used to look out for me and our little sister when our mother worked two jobs. Which was most of the time. My mother wasn't the type of woman to want a man to take care of her and her children. She was always independent, and despite the fact her and my father eventually split. She never hounded him about paying support and taking care of his kid's when he should have as a man. And he did for the most part. Plus we were already of age. She never talk down my father, because all of our lives he was a great father to us. It was just after him and my mother split, is when his ties to his children became strained a little. I never had much animosity towards my father after him and mother split. I remember him telling me before he left that, sometimes things just don't work out. And he would always love us regardless.

My brother on the other hand, took the whole thing pretty hard when my parents split. My brother really looked up to my father and expected him to be around. That led my brother to start acting out, and he turned to the streets for a while. And drove my mother crazy. But my mother was no joke. If she had to go in the most dangerous neighborhoods in the city to get her children straight, she would. She was fearless in that regard. And it made my brother think. He didn't want his mother out in the streets in danger chasing after him. So he straightened out and had been doing well ever since. After getting home, I myself was patiently waiting for my opportunity.     Page 1

I had a few interviews here and there. Of course I had an impeccable resume, getting my Bachelor's and Masters in Secondary Education and Teaching. And giving the Marine Corps eight years of my life. I had never been to prison, or even as much as a parking ticket. I was what my brother used to call me sometimes when he teased me. "Good Boy". It was cool, because I took pride in making my mother proud. And just living a good life. I was to go meet with a friend of mines, he knew about a school that had a position that was open. And I was interested. So we met for lunch to discuss the opening. In Downtown Chicago at Lloyd's Chicago, since we both loved seafood.

"Silas it's a great opportunity to do what you told me you wanted to do. Lead young minds. But these kids, well some of them are troubled youth. I believe they're truly smart young people, just misguided. That's where you come in at, I believe this is the job that you're seeking" Mitchell Bates said.

"It does sound a little enticing from what you're telling me. I mean I will go to the interview, at the moment this is the only opportunity that I have anyway" I replied.

I didn't want Mitchell to feel some kind of way, being that he looked out and got me the opportunity. I was never the type to be unappreciative. So the fact he was a good friend of mines, I was at least going to check it out. So I agreed to with an open mind, and who knows this may just be the job for me.

"I'm glad you are bro. I told the Administrator that you were a strong, smart, and dedicated guy. That has natural leadership skills" Mitchell said.

"Thanks man I appreciate you, and appreciate the opportunity" I replied.

"So how's Fatima ? You guys been out lately ? Any Jazz Clubs in the city lately" ? Mitchell asked.

"No not lately, but she has been saying we need to get out soon. So we might be going this weekend" I replied.

Fatima was my lady of over four years, and we were engaged. She was the epitome of natural beauty. Beautiful black queen of the universe, she was bad. I don't just mean her beauty, her whole vibe was sexy. I knew from the time I met her six years ago when I had came home on a break. That I wanted to spend the rest of my life with her. She was not only beautiful and had a great personality, but she was smart. She had her Masters also in Sociology and was a Case Manager. That was also why we both clicked, we both liked helping people. It was in our hearts, and we could both tell that about each other almost as soon as we met.                    Page 2

Besides her natural beauty and incredible body. From her beautiful brown eyes natural black hair full lips nice size D breasts slim waist and her round thick ass. She just did it for me, from day one. I had to make her mines. But she didn't make it easy, they say the good ones never do. We were friends for a little over a year before we actually started dating. If it was up to me, we would've been dating immediately. But she made me wait. In the meantime I called myself being faithful to her by trying to wait, when we weren't even together. Needless to say, I got weak and dated a few chicks from around the way before we actually got together. Hey...I'm a man that had my needs at the time. Regardless of any of that, Fatima NEVER left my mind. As soon as she said the word, I was shutting everything down for her.

"Yeah me and Kendra was thinking about going too, so y'all let us know" Mitchell said.

"No doubt bro, you know we always get together. Even though it's been a while. We all been busy, me trying to find me somewhere where I feel I fit. And can make a difference. Fatima got her case work going on. So I just been plotting my next move" I replied.

I had two good friends. Mitchell who was married to his wife Kendra. They were married for over five years and had two children. And my homie Angelo from my South Side neighborhood. He was with his girlfriend Lauren, they were together for three years and had three kids between them. So each of us as couples were fairly new...but not new. I guess thats why we were all such good friends, besides the fact we were black power couples so to speak. All young, educated, and successful African American couples. And we were all from the inner city of Chicago. Mitchell was from the West Side of the Chi, I had met him from being in this Men's Group at the church that me and my lady Fatima attended. I have known Mitchell a lot less time than I knew Angelo. Me and Mitchell had known each other for about two and a half years. Fatima and I would go out with Mitchell and Kendra from time to time to Jazz and Comedy clubs in the city.

Either way we became cool from the start, and have been friends ever since. Mitchell and Angelo were like night and day though. Angelo was from da South Side and he would let you know it. But he was professional when he needed to be. A District Manager of a food chain. But when he wasn't at work, he was Angelo from the neighborhood. It was cool, because Mitchell being more of a professional and Angelo being a little more hood. Balanced things out for me. Because I was both of their personalities in one man. After Mitchell told me about that opening, I was really excited to see if it was the place for me. Don't ask me how I would know, to me I could just feel it. I had looked for work before within the city, with no luck because the options I had I didn't like. I knew once I found the place for me, I could set out to achieve what I want to achieve. Page 3

"Yeah I know what you mean. Speaking of Jazz, I have to fly to New Orleans at the end of the month. I have a Business Conference down there, so you know I will be hitting a few Jazz Clubs for sure. And where were you at yesterday ? You slacking on your gym time too bro" Mitchell said joking.

"Naw man, I just been trying to find my place, I guess I been a little off track and lost my focus on my workouts. This too shall pass, don't worry Mitch I'm good" I replied.

As much as I didn't want to admit that to him, I felt I could because after all he was a good friend of mines. Who else was I going to tell ? Angelo wasn't around. Plus in our Men's Group at church, we're taught to be open about our problems free from judgement. Our jobs were to help people, not ridicule them. So I had to take my own advice, the Men's Group advice and come clean to my boy about how I was really feeling. After having lunch with Mitch, I returned home. Fatima was still at work, her days were usually long so I decided to prepare her a nice dinner. But I started cooking a little later than usual. That was because I wanted to run her a hot bath. She loved those after coming home from a long day. I was giving my soon to be wife, what she deserved from her man. Fatima knew I could be romantic when I wanted to, plus I enjoyed her reaction to it. There is nothing like doing wonderful things for the person you love.

Fatima deserved it all. I was head over heels in love with this woman, it's exactly why I asked her to marry me. We had been engaged for two years now and the wedding was approaching in about five months. After running her a hot bath, I returned to the kitchen where dinner was cooking just nicely as I wanted. I had made us some steaks along with some freshly cooked baked potatoes and some broccoli. The kitchen smelled great because your boy is nice in the kitchen. As I was finishing up, my Queen Fatima was walking through the door. I couldn't help but go meet her at the door and embrace her as she came in.

"Ummm....smells delicious in here. Don't tell me, you made steaks?!! I love steaks, thank you baby. It was another long day, and paperwork up to my....." Fatima said.

Before she could say another word, I just grabbed her and pulled her close to me. And then kissed her before she could get that word out. She wasn't surprised, but then again she was. Because it was far from the first time I've done that. But she just didn't know I would do it right at that moment when she was in full venting mode. But that's why I did it.

"Your bath is ready and hot, the food will be done soon. Take your bath and relax, we should be ready to eat when you get out" I replied.  Page 4

"You're such a good man, I can't believe you're going to be my husband in a little over five months. Ok baby, I'm going to take my bath and then we'll have a nice romantic dinner" Fatima said hugging and kissing all over me.

I loved making my lady happy, especially after a long day. She deserved it. It was the least I could do, being that I wasn't necessarily employed at the time. I was still getting my check from the Service and I was highly qualified to get plenty of jobs. I had my Masters and Bachelors in Secondary Education and Teaching. I was just waiting for the right opportunity for me. And Fatima respected and supported my decision. One of the reasons I loved her so much. She could've been like a lot of women and dogged me out because I didn't have a job, or talked me down to her friends. And who knows, she might've left me. And could I blame her ? Regardless I believed my opportunity would come sooner rather than later. So I was confident that things would change for the better soon.

After taking her bath, Fatima came out in the kitchen with a little night gown on that barely covered her ass and sat down and we ate dinner. It was hard as hell for me to concentrate on eating my meal just looking at Fatima's sexy self. That milk chocolate skin looked so smooth as I could see her thighs when she crossed her legs as we ate. After dinner of course we couldn't get it in, not on full stomachs. So we decided to relax and watch some TV. Fatima and I didn't have any children, although we were planning on having some after we were married. And I know, we're late in the game as far as having children. Most of our friends had children. My siblings had children, my brother Sidney Jr. had three children. And my sister Savannah had two.

So we had a lot of privacy to have all kinds of wild sex all over the house when we wanted to. And we did on plenty of occasions. I mean we weren't necessarily young, but we weren't old either. I was thirty one years old, and Fatima was twenty nine. Later that night we had some of the best sex we had since we had been together. We woke up the next morning feeling incredible and not wanting to get out of bed. But we both had to, she had to go to work. And I had that interview today. So after getting up and both getting showered, we kissed and told each other we loved each other and went on our separate ways to start our days.

I'm not going to lie, I had somewhat mixed feelings about the interview although I had hoped it would go well. So I put on one of my best suits, I had about five of them. And went on about my way. The interview was on the West Side of the Chi not too far from where we lived. And so I was off. After getting there and waiting for about ten minutes, I was able to go back and get interviewed.
Page 5

I could sense from the time I got in there that it wasn't for me. Of course the gentleman who was interviewing me was impressed by my resume. And I could tell if I really wanted that job I could've had it. But it wasn't for me, I knew in my heart it wasn't. So I walked out of that interview that day, still feeling like there was an opportunity out there for me somewhere. I decided to drive to my mother and sister's home on the South Side. They lived in the Hyde Park section. When I got there, my sister answered the door.

"Hey Si....how you been" ? Savannah said answering the door and greeting me with a hug.

"I'm good, just came to see how y'all was. Where's mom" ? I replied.

"She's in there sitting in her chair watching TV" Savannah said.

"Hey momma, how are you ? You know I had to check up on my favorite girl" I said as I embraced my mother with a kiss and hug.

"Hey Silas, I'm good. Just sitting here watching some TV. You want some coffee" ? My mother replied.

My mother Lucy Jones was an incredibly strong woman. The first woman of strength that I ever knew in my life. She raised three children from da South Side of Chicago and for the most part, we all turned out to be decent human beings and stable productive adults. My brother Sidney Jr. had his time on the darkside growing up, but he was able to get his life together as time went on. My mother stayed on all our asses from our education to our personal lives. She wanted us all to be successful. She didn't want us to be just another statistic in Chicago streets. We all saw what was going on around us. A lot of kids we went to school with were getting murdered in the streets. My mother accompanied us all to countless funerals of our friends growing up. So she stressed we walked the straight and narrow, and become successful adults.

I admired everything about her. My mother was a beautiful woman also, brown skin woman who was naturally beautiful. My father Sidney Jones Sr. was also around and living in Chicago's North Side. He had a good relationship with us children. Although him and my brother didn't have the greatest relationship. Basically because they were so much alike. Even though they would both never admit it. They were both stubborn and bullheaded to a fault. I was more of a mix between my mother and father, my sister Savannah too. I made it a point to check up on my father also from time to time, so I would head to the North Side once a week.
Page 6

So as I was in my mother and sister's home in the Hyde Park section of the city, after a twenty three minute drive South down Lake Shore Drive. As always it felt good to see two of the three favorite women in my life. And like always. Me, my mother, and my sister had an interesting conversation about my current job search.

"Fatima is a good woman letting you pick and choose your place regarding work. I'm sure you're highly qualified for all the jobs you passed up already" Savannah said as we were all in the living room talking.

"She's fine with it sis, because I still get my money from the Service. So its not like I'm not bringing any money in the household. Plus we saved for our wedding. And you're right sis, she's a great woman that's why I put a ring on it" I replied sticking out my tongue at Savannah and smiling.

"You lucky you're my brother punk. I'm just curious though, what kind of job is the job for you? According to you ? Savannah asked.

"Somewhere as soon as I walk in, I feel right at home. I don't even have to meet my students yet. Just the feel of the school and the feel of the classroom. I can also tell by the School Administration. Are they willing to fight for these kid's education. This country talks a lot about education, but when you look beneath the surface. They aren't putting their money where their mouths are, in terms of first and secondary education. That's where I come in sis, I'm going to fight for it. If it takes everything I have" I replied.

My sister was a nurse at The University of Chicago Medical Center. She enjoyed her job, it was something she always wanted to do since she was a little girl. I was proud of her, but she and my mother were always critical of me and my older brother Sidney Jr. Yes our little sister was critical of the things we did. As opposed to the norm of big brothers being critical of their little sisters. She just cared a lot like my mother, and it was out of love. So I never took it personal. Whenever I was around them two, I always felt happy. My sister was a strong woman like my mother. She had been a single parent for a little over five years, raising her two children on her own. And being a fulltime nurse in the process. She put herself through school partly, she had earned some scholarships that helped pay some of her tuition. Three years ago she met a great guy name Tremaine Edwards, he stepped right in and assumed the role of the father figure for her children. They were together, and he also stayed at the house with my mother, sister, and my sister's two kids. It was a big house. They all had plenty of room.

Tremaine was a carpenter, very skilled at doing just about anything inside or outside of a home. Which was vital, especially with the big house they had. And it was just a great trade and career to have. There would always be jobs, especially in a big city like Chicago. Tremaine was a good dude too, he had a child from a previous relationship himself. He had a son, Tremaine Jr. My sister always made him feel apart of the family. And he was in our eyes. Blood or not. Tremaine treated my sister like a Queen, and that's all me and my brother could ask for as siblings. But back to my conversation with my sister.

"Well it's good that you at least know what you want. I'm sure you'll find it. Just afraid you might be letting some great jobs go past that some people would die for. Either way you know you always got my support bro" Savannah said as she gave me another hug.

"Now that's what I like to see with my children, supporting one another. Y'all all y'all got after me and your father are gone" my mother said as she sat in her chair smiling.

"Momma you know you and Savannah always been critical of me and Sidney Jr. We're both her big brothers, and she acts like she's the oldest. She gets that from you momma, but I know it's all love" I replied.

"That's right son, it's all love. We just care about you two a great deal. You two are our Kings and we want you two to do well. I'm proud of all my children. Savannah being a nurse, you both got your degrees which makes me very happy. And you being a Veteran returning home to make a difference. Makes me very proud son. Your brother getting his life together makes me happy for him, but I know he can do a lot better. I know the potential Sidney Jr. has" my mother said.

"Thanks mom, and that's true. I got a few other interviews coming up, hopefully one of them is for me" I replied.

"I hope so too son, you were born to be a leader. And I'm glad you have that passion in you to do so" Lucy said.

"Yeah good luck bro. Mom I have to get back to the hospital, there's leftovers in the fridge if you get hungry. Love y'all, see you later mom. Tremaine will be by soon. Later bro" Savannah said as she was leaving. Heading back to work an overnight shift.

After Savannah left I sat and talked to my mother a little longer. My niece and nephew would be home any minute now, as they were out with their friends somewhere. When my sister worked overnight, her boyfriend Tremaine would be home to check on my mother in between shifts when he was working.     Page 8

We all made sure both our parents were taken care of. Even though they had divorced many years ago, my mother kept her last name. My father had no problem with it. Because I believe regardless of all that they had been through with the divorce and all. They still deep down inside loved each other. I mean they were married for over twenty two years. When my father first left the house, they got separated. And remained separated for years before finally going through with the divorce. They got along enough to be around each other for family functions, such as my niece and nephew's birthday parties that my sister would have at the house. I knew my mother wanted grandchildren from me, because she would hint at it at times when I was around. But she also respected the fact that, Fatima and I had made the decision to have children AFTER we were married.

As I was leaving my mother and sister's house, my brother called me on my cell.

"What's good Si, what you up to" ? Sidney Jr. asked as I answered the phone.

"I'm good bro, just leaving mom and Savannah's house. What's good with you" ? I replied.

"Nothing much, wanted to see if you wanted to get together next weekend and go to a Bears game with me and my son. I got an extra ticket" he said.

"I'll see, I don't think I have anything planned. And I'm always down to watch my Bears play. But I will let you know in a few days for sure" I replied.

My brother loved the Bears and the Cubs ever since we were kids. I mean I never really got into baseball like that, but I loved the Chicago Bears. It had been a while since I was at Soldier Field. I just enjoyed the experience of being in a Pro Football stadium. I also loved the Bulls. I had the pleasure of finally getting to some games in recent years. We really couldnt afford to go as kids. For that reason alone I appreciated it more as an adult. Even took one of my nephew's to a Bulls game before. And I would be looking forward to going to another game with my nephew and brother.

"Ok let me know bro, you know these tickets aint cheap. So definitely let me know in a few days. So how's the job search going" ? Sidney Jr. asked.

"I had a few offers here and there, but you know me Sid. I have to find my place where I fit, for me to feel like I could do the job to the best of my abilities" I replied.

Page 9

"I hear you bro, I know you will find your way. You're smart, you always were. I had the muscles and you had the brains in the family" Sidney Jr. said laughing.

I just laughed a little and told him whatever. My brother Sidney Jr. was a smart man also, he just at times made the wrong decisions. But he was a good man, we all were good people who came from good parents. Even though our parents were separated for a time and then divorced, they always instilled good values in us from day one. It was why I knew from an early age that I wasn't going to be in the streets. It wasn't easy though, I had to fight several times on my way to school and from school. At times I carried weapons, it was just how it was growing up in the inner city. Of course they were gangs all over the city, I manage to dodge all of them. Dont ask me how, but I just did. I spent a lot of my time studying, and doing other productive things. And less time in the streets. The fights I were in, I was defending myself.

After talking to my brother on the phone, I went home and went on my laptop to look for more openings. Fatima was still at work so I had the time to focus on my search. I wanted to prepare dinner soon so it could be ready by the time she got home. I know what people are thinking, another bum living off his fiancée. Wrong....I had an eye on somewhere I think I would fit. There was a school that had a mix of students from all over the city, they were troubled children. I felt that was important, because I just didn't want to help South Side kids, but children of Chicago period. Even though I was from da South Side, I had relatives all over the city. So I was intrigued by the opening, I called and they set up an interview for me. I was for once excited about going into an opportunity. The first time since I had returned home, I felt really good about this.

The next day came and my lady Fatima was off. As I was sleeping, I could feel her touch in the morning. Right before I woke up, I could feel her kiss me lightly on the back of my neck.

"Good morning baby, I'm glad you're off today. It's good having you home" I said as I got up and rolled over. Still in bed, but awake.

"Yes....I'm glad to be off too. But I have some paperwork to do" Fatima replied.

There was no way in hell I was going to let my sexy lady do paperwork all day, not with me home with her. I was indeed going to take full advantage of the fact she was home. And in bed with me. She didn't have much on, a little night gown with nothing on underneath. I quickly took that off and took my boxers off, and within a few minutes we were heavy into action. Passionate sex in the morning, and then that action continued in the shower.
Page 10

After an intense sex session between us, I finished showering. My interview would be a few hours later. Having great passionate sex with my lady, and after getting out of a nice warm shower. I felt incredible and ready to claim my spot. I got dressed in another one of my best suits. Had just got a cut a few days ago, so my Low Cut Caeser was still looking nice. My bread was sharp as a razor. So I looked good, felt good, and was confident as ever. Plus my resume was impeccable. The difference with this place was, they didn't come looking for me. I seen an opening with them. So as long as everything looked good to me, and they would give me the opportunity. I was going to take it. So instead of taking my car and trying to maneuver through Chicago daytime traffic. I decided to take the L train from my house to the North Side where the interview was.

That always beat sitting in daytime Chicago traffic. After the ride I finally reached my destination, and got off at my stop. Walked a few blocks up the street and I reached this school. I knew then that I was at the right place. A woman greeted me as I walked through the doors. Very nice, as she asked me was I Mr. Jones? I smiled a little and nodded yes. She then led me back to the Principal's office. We walked back this somewhat long hallway and into the Principal's office. A tall Caucasian man with brown hair. He introduced himself as Mr. Edward Hunt, I introduced myself as we shook hands and both sat down. Him at his desk, and me sitting across from him. That was important to me, because I was always taught to do a firm handshake at an interview. And have strong eye to eye contact. Sit up straight and the whole nine. He was sitting right across from me, so I could look in his eyes. To see if he was really ready for a man like myself being on his staff. I had a strong character, and that was me at work as well as home.

"I see you have a very impressive resume. Bachelor's and Masters Degree in Secondary Education and Teaching. Spent eight years in the Marine Corps. Very impressive Mr. Jones.....I mean everything looks great to me. I would like to offer you the job, if you want it" Principal Hunt said.

I sat back in my chair and took a deep breath, just to keep him in suspense. And I replied. "Yes Principal Hunt, I will take the job".

He naturally was happy, I believe he had wanted to fill that position for a while. I had no problem taking it. The kids were a mix of kids from all over the city. That was something that intrigued me. Because like I said before, I'm from da South Side. But I wanted to help kids from all over the city. I wanted the effect and influence to be widespread. One student at a time each day. And you want each of them to improve each day, that was my goal going in. To improve on what the School District had done, which up until this point wasn't much.      Page 11

I got back on the L train and headed back home. Feeling optimistic about the opportunity. And knowing that next day I had to be ready to make a statement day one. That's right, I would be starting that next day. He gave me the option, and I thought why not start the next day. It's a challenge, and I lived for challenges. I had text Fatima the good news, as she was happy for me. And I'm sure she was glad I found the place for me finally. She knew I was sick of being home. And she knew I was more than qualified to be in the workforce. The timing was perfect, and I was ready. After getting home I just sat and watched some TV until Fatima got home. We were going out to eat tonight and celebrate on me.

So after she got home she quickly changed and we were off to dinner. We went to one of the many Downtown Chicago restaurants The Gage on S. Michigan Ave. Had a nice dinner and some vintage wine, as we were enjoying ourselves. Me and my Queen had a interesting conversation about what lie ahead for the both of us. Including our wedding, which was approaching.

"So did everyone get fitted for their tuxes Silas" ? Fatima asked me.

"Yeah everybody is good, and we all looked good. You wait till you see how handsome your soon to be husband and his groomsmen are going to look on our special day" I replied bringing her closer to me and kissing her on the cheek.

She playfully pushed me back a little as we were sitting in this round booth almost right next to each other.

"We're supposed to be discussing some important things baby, stay focused. So happy you finally found the place you would like to teach. I know you're excited about meeting your students tomorrow" Fatima said.

"Indeed I am, but I'm also going to lay down the law early and often. My classroom will not be taken over by no one. My classroom is for children that WANT to LEARN, and NOT children that want to WASTE my time. Seen it too many times, teacher's losing control of their classrooms. It's not going to happen to me" I replied.

"I know that's not something that I have to worry about with you. I knew that was one of the first things you would do, and you should. It's the right decision, they have to know who they're dealing with. I just hope you don't have to go overboard, and they receive it well. This IS Chicago you know....so" Fatima said holding her hands up as if to say you never know.

Page 12

"Baby I'm not worried about a thing, I'm going to be me as always. And do my best to lead to the best of my ability. That's all they can ask for, and that's all I can honestly give. Everything is going to work

out well. How's things going with you at your place of employment" ?
I replied.

"It's up and down like always. Lots of different cases to go over
and deal with. Some days I don't know how I do it, then I have to
remind myself of what my passion is. And has been most of my life.
I'm sure you will soon have those type of days, especially leading
young minds" Fatima said.

"I'm sure I will too. But the key thing is keeping a balance between
the good and bad days. I remember an older guy I was in the
Marines with, told me that one day. That always stuck with me
throughout my life. I'm ready Fatima, ready to do what the man
above put me on this Earth to do" I said.

"I'm happy for you babe, and I love you" Fatima said leaning over
and kissing me.

"I love you too baby, thanks for always supporting me" I replied.

We sat and continued talking and enjoyed our dinner. It was a
great night celebrating with my Queen. We got home at a decent
hour. I had a big day ahead of me the next day. I guess you could
say I was anxious. I could hardly sleep the night before, but when I
got up that next morning. I knew I was ready. I was going to be the
best History Teacher I could be. And although teaching would be my
job, it would also give me a platform for my vision. At the time no
one knew my vision but my Queen Fatima. I mean my mother and
siblings had an idea. But they didn't know the specifics. This was
really going to be a crash course of sorts. I hadn't met any of the
other staff. But I knew once they seen me and heard me speak, they
would notice me right away. I had no intention of being loud and
unprofessional, but when I speak I wanted them all to know that I

meant what I said. And I felt strongly about my beliefs, about how I taught and education in a whole.

Well within the guidelines of the School District of course. Either way, my students would know from day one. Who the teacher was and who the students were.

I decided to drive my car to the North Side High School. So before I left, my Queen Fatima gave me a kiss and hug. Wished me good luck on my first day and I was on my way out the door. Headed to my first day of what I believed would be a long journey, but a meaningful one worth the while.

## Page 13

After the short thirteen minute drive from our place, I had reached the North Side High School. Parked in the parking lot and commenced to get out of my car. I was dressed in one of my many suits along with my briefcase in hand. I strutted into the school with confidence and swagger. That said I belonged here, and I'd dare anyone to tell me different. I wanted people to get that feel from me from day one. As I walked in the school and past some rowdy kids that were loud in the hallway. I just glanced at them and kept walking. For now I wasn't worried about their loud disrespectful tone amongst their peers. I had to get to my classroom and get ready for my students. Surprisingly enough my classroom wasn't that hard to find. I found it and started to set up my board the way I wanted. I had another twenty minutes before my students arrived. So as I was setting up my board. An African American woman who I assumed was a teacher, came and knocked on my door as she was standing at the entrance to my classroom.

"Hello Mr. Jones, I'm Mrs. Williams one of the English teachers here at the school. Nice to meet you, we heard about you joining us. Welcome" Mrs. Williams said.

"Thank you, and I hope what you heard were good things. Thanks again, I'm happy to be here" I replied smiling.

It's always good to start and give off the vibe of a positive person. You can be positive and real at the same time, it just wasn't the time to show them something real yet. But I'm almost certain that time would come, and I would be ready to show them when it did. For her to come into my classroom and meet me meant one of two things. Either she was genuinely welcoming me to the school, or she was nosey as hell. Because she had heard so much about me, she wanted to see if it was really true. That's what I think when people say they heard so much about me. Five minutes before my class would be walking in. And I had just about everything set up, as a few students started walking into class.

And yes they were loud as ever walking into MY classroom, which was actually normal for Middle School and High School students. I was teaching History in High School. I let them all file into their seats, and let them be as loud as they wanted to be for now. After they all got in their seats. I got their attention, well not at first. Not until I yelled.

"Hey !!! I need all of your attention right now. My name is Mr. Silas Jones and I'm your History Teacher" I said. And then I was interrupted by this big kid that was sitting in the back.

"Who fucking cares" !!! The kid said yelling from the back. I didn't say anything, just looked where I heard it from and walked towards that direction. As I got to the back of the class, the other kids were laughing. I approached him like a man since he spoke to me in a man's tone.

"Stand up" !!! I said as the kid stood up. And when he stood up, I got right in his face. We were almost eye to eye, I was of course looking down on him a little. But not by much. He was a big kid, because I myself was a big dude. I was six three and about two hundred and fifty pounds. I was stocky, solid muscle. Since leaving the Marines I still kept my workout regimen by going to a local Chicago gym. So I was definitely in shape, and ready for whatever this youngin thought he had for me.

"I stood up, now what the fuck you gonna do muthafucka? Huh" ? !! He said.

"I'm not going to do nothing unless you put your hands on me. You put your hands on me young man, and I'm going to forget you're a student. And react to you like a grown man. You or anyone else in here will not interrupt my class again" !! I replied.

"Or what you bitch ass nigga ? You can't touch none of us, or you'll lose your job" he said.

I got even closer in his face and looked him directly in his eyes. At that point I was towering over him. With both my fists clinched and replied.

"Let me tell you something youngin. I'm a retired Marine. I got money coming in whether I have this job or not. So if you think I won't defend myself if you touch me, you're sadly mistaken. So try me....try me youngin" !!!

The whole classroom grew silent as I yelled so loud I believe the classroom across from me and down the hall heard me. And I wanted them to. So they would know I wasn't taking nothing from any of these kids. I was there to do a job, and I was serious about doing it. I had a mission to accomplish, and any child that didn't want to learn wasn't going stop me. I would show the kids that didn't want to learn and showed no effort to learn the door. I wouldn't rob any of my REAL students that wanted to learn of any time that they rightfully deserved. I would give my all to the kids who wanted to learn.

Needless to say the kid didn't really want anything, just showing out for his classmates. For what he thought was the "new teacher". What he didn't know was, I was far from new to this. I may not have been a teacher, but if I could deal with fellow Marines in combat. I could handle any high school kid.     Page 15

He must've been the hardest kid in the class, because after he sat back down in his seat. The rest of the class followed, and I got back to what I do.

"As I was saying before I was interrupted. My name is Mr. Silas Jones and I'm your History Teacher. I'm assuming that you all are here to learn, and if I'm assuming right you all will have a great experience of learning this course. I will do everything in my power to teach you to your full potential. We just don't want to be regular people, we want to maximize our potential and be the best we can be. So to each of you, why not shoot for an A in this course. Just getting a passing grade is minimal learning, which often times leads to minimal potential in other facets of your life. And could also lead into your adult life. What I'm saying people is, be the best you can be. That will bring the best out of me. Even though I'm going to bring the best out of each of you whether you like it or not. Here are your books, here help me hand these out" I said as I passed out textbooks and another student helped me.

At the time things were going smooth, and they were starting to understand me and what I expected from them. But it was still too early to tell how long things would stay that way. I was just setting the tone early so they all knew I wasn't scared of any of them. And some of the kids were in gangs in the city. I could tell by their tattoos, and I still didn't fear any of them. Plus I had a license to carry, so I carried my Nine Millimeter Ruger with me everyday to school. Of course I left it inside my car underneath the seat, but I had it with me. After getting the textbooks passed out, I passed out some paperwork that I was required to have them fill out for school records. Something I never agreed with from hearing friends complain about the same paperwork being filled out each year. But it was policy, so I did what I was told to do.

As they were filling out their paperwork, I sat at my desk and looked over some paperwork of my own. That's when I felt someone staring at me. So I picked my head up from the paperwork. And looked out my classroom door window, and a man was standing at the door staring in my classroom. Didn't know who he was, but after I stared out at him. He then preceded to walk away. Weird....but then again a lot of the outside world was weird to me. Often times I felt like I was in a world by myself. My thoughts, my vision for what I wanted for my students. And not only just my students, but the whole educational system period. I wasn't at all happy with the educational opportunities for children across this country from the inner cities. In any inner city in America it's basically the same ingredients laid out for you to fail. It's up to you to rise above and succeed at all costs. In the name of education. Most of my students and people that looked like me had to work that much harder to get their recognition and reach their goals of success.         Page 16

After they filled out their paperwork I needed to lay out the way my classroom workload would be for my students. I already had in my mind that I would have weekly quizzes to keep my students on top of their lessons. I knew they wouldn't like it, but it would make them better off for it. And prepare them to do well on their midterms, and final exams. It was my job as their teacher to prepare them for those exams and beyond. And without a doubt I was going to do so.

"Ok let me explain how things will go in this classroom as for as the workload. Each day of course you will have a lesson, and you will have a quiz each week on those very lessons you learn throughout the week" I said.

The kids then started moaning and whining, but I didn't care. They were going to have weekly quizzes like I had planned for them. There was always a reason for the madness with me. I didn't really think it was madness, but people who weren't me thought it was. As long as at the end of the day, all goals were accomplished. That's all that really mattered to me, was getting these kids to reach their full potential. It would be a challenge, but that's why I decided to teach. To lead young minds, and mold them into great adult minds and visionaries.

"So any questions before we get started" ? I asked.

A young lady raised her hand and asked a question. "Mr. Jones will there ever be a week without quizzes? Like can we get some incentives with this" ? She asked.

"Hmmm...well let me say this. If you all as a class collectively have consecutive good weeks. I may be inclined to let y'all go a week without a quiz. BUT that all depends on you all" I replied.

The students then clapped and started cheering, but I reminded them. That was IF they maintained their consistency with their lessons and their quiz scores. So it was all up to them if they earned it, only time would tell. But I was willing to be a little lenient IF they did well collectively as a class. This would motivate the ones who would normally not do their work, to actually do their work. That is if they didn't want to let the rest of their class down. After that question, I began to go over my lesson plan with my students. They all for the most part were listening, but as I was looking around the room. I could see a few students weren't paying me any mind. I put those students in my memory bank. And I let them THINK that they were going to get away with it. I continued teaching and doing what I do for my students that were paying attention and wanted to learn. But I definitely had something for the students who weren't paying attention, the next class we had together. Which would be the next day.      Page 17

I came home that day feeling pretty good, knowing that I only had to check one kid the first day. I was somewhat surprised it was only one. But something told me I didn't have complete control over my entire classroom yet. But trust me, I would. Only a matter of time. I got home after that first day of school. Fatima was working late, so I decided to go get some classic authentic Chi Town Deep Dish Pizza from Giordano's. She loved Deep Dish Pizza, we both did. I was home for about a half hour when my Queen Fatima got home.

"Hey baby, welcome home. Guess what I got us" ? I said.

"I can smell it. Ummmm.....smells like my favorite. Deep Dish Pizza from Giordano's. Thank you babe !! Was a long day, had a meeting today. Things are hectic at the job. But anyway, how was your first day" ? She replied.

"It was cool for the most part, had some kid try to test me. You know I figured that would happen. So I told him, I get a check from the military each month. I don't HAVE to teach. And if he put his hands on me, I'm most certainly going to defend myself as a man. This was while we were in each other's faces. After he noticed I wasn't backing down from him, he sat down. But I'm sure there will be another kid that tests me. I'm almost certain" I said smiling.

I didn't have to teach, but I enjoyed all aspects of teaching. From the actual teaching and instructions to dealing with the different personalities everyday. Before I actually started teaching, I had talked to different teachers to get their input. It was some similar input and some different. And that's what made it unique for me. I wanted to blaze my own trail in the teaching ranks. I had some ideas that were my own. Different methods of teaching and handling students. The only question. Was the school system in Chicago ready for me ? I knew that this country didn't value education like they proclaimed they did. You hear Politicians talk education all the time in their campaign speeches to get votes. Only to do the complete opposite when they get into office.

I never believed any of them, not since I was old enough to understand what they were talking about. My parents always taught me to never trust a Politician. So I decided, if I ever became a teacher. I would put my heart and soul into my teaching and giving kids the best education they could get. It was my vision, and why I took the job. Being a kid from da South Side of Chicago already had its disadvantages from day one. I was one of those kids that fought through it. Seeing me and my siblings friends get killed growing up. Gave us all a first class lesson up close and personal. I didn't want to be a statistic, I wanted to be an asset to society.

"Knowing these kids, I'm sure it won't be the last time either. Just be careful....and I know you can handle yourself. I still worry about you, this IS Chicago" Fatima said.

"I'll be fine. I feel really good where I'm at, and happy I found a place that I believe I can make a difference. It's still early, have to get my students used to me. Today was just a crash course of what's to come. But I'm excited baby, really excited" I replied.

"And I'm excited for you also my soon to be husband" Fatima said as she gave me a kiss.

Every time I was with my soon to be wife Fatima, I felt like I could take on the world. She was my Michelle to Barack, my Beyonce to Jay. She just gave me so much support, even when I was just collecting my check from the Service. When I finally got this teaching job, she gave me so much confidence to take this thing head on. And that was one of the biggest reasons that I had to make her my wife. I still remember the day we met when I came home on leave. I wasted no time. Besides the fact she caught my eye right away. I knew she was the one, and I had to have her. Wasn't easy, as I said before. But it was well worth it, once I finally won her heart. And we been going strong ever since. It's strange hearing a story like ours in this day and time. With so many marriages and relationships not working. We managed to stay together. No we weren't perfect, we had our share of issues amongst each other. But we knew we were better together than apart. We even split a few times and seen other people, but always managed to find our way back to each other. And we needed that to be honest, because we went through our rough times and survived them. That prepared us for this moment, of where we are right now. Less than five months away from our wedding day.

Fatima had been stressing me about getting the groomsmen fitted for their tuxes, and I finally did. My brother Sidney, my homie Angelo, and my associate from the Men's Group at church Mitchell. Would be my groomsmen. And my sister Savannah would be one of the bridesmaids, courtesy of my Queen Fatima. Along with Fatima's two sisters Mia and Destiny. I had my side of things taken care of, just not well enough for Fatima's liking. So she stays on my ass about getting my part done the right way. And it may have gotten my nerves, but I wouldn't have it any other way. I loved the fact that my woman would help push me to greatness. Rather than not care if I succeeded or not. Because ultimately, a woman who doesn't care about your dreams or motivating you. Isn't the woman you need to be with.

That was something I knew from day one, having a mother and sister in my life. Like I said before, my mother and sister were protective over me and my older brother Sidney. They always looked out for us, and made sure we were doing the right things. And anybody we were dealing with also, as far as they could see. Yeah they gave my Queen Fatima a hard time at first, until they got to know her. And she showed them just how much she really loved me. I mean I always knew it, but my mother and sister were a different beast in that regard. You had to show them, it wasn't about what you were saying. They could care less about what you were saying.

The next morning came, and as usual I got up extra early and took a shower and got ready. Went out to the kitchen and grabbed me some coffee before I left. Also had some toast. Before I left, I went back upstairs to our bedroom where my Queen Fatima was sound asleep. I stood by the bed and kneeled down and softly kissed her on the cheek and then was off to start my day. On the drive over to the school, there were a lot of things going through my mind. More than anything I was once again excited as if it was still the first day. But I knew today, I had to further sell my class onto the way that I taught and led my students. It had only been one day, it was definitely going to take a lot more than one day for these kids to buy into what I was selling. Not sure if they had ever had a teacher like me. That truly cared and wanted to challenge them and the powers that be. To give kids the best education they can get. Not only colleges, but first and secondary education. Those levels of education meant the most to me.

That's where it started before an individual could go to college, was first and secondary education. The country wasn't putting their money where they mouths were in that regard. Schools in inner cities got the worse education, including a lot in my city of Chicago. I felt compelled to get involved when I officially became a teacher. I always felt teachers had so much power and impact on the youth, besides a child's parents and of course their environment. It was the teachers who had a lot of a kid's attention. So the time I had, I wanted to make the most of it.

So as I stepped inside the school for my second day on the job, I was determined to make an impact right away. Got to my classroom about twenty minutes before my first class would arrive. Got my things in order and my lesson plan ready. Even had a little time to sit and relax before my students arrived. Another five minutes went by before the kids started to enter my classroom. As they did, I let them all get seated as I noticed the two students who weren't paying attention the previous day. That's when I motioned for the both of them to come and sit in the front of the class. And of course, they gave me a hard time, but it didn't matter. Because they were going to do what I told them to do, or be out of my class.

"Why do we have to switch our seats? We been sitting in these seats since we been in this class" the one young man said.

I looked over in his direction and I responded. "I gave you both your new seats, because yesterday I noticed you both were not paying attention. Almost falling asleep. Maybe you two couldn't hear or understand me well enough, so I thought I would move you two closer to me. Does that answer your question" ?

He just looked at me with this dirty look on his face and said. "This some straight bullshit"!!

That's when I walked towards him again, only this time I stood right in front of him while he was sitting at his desk. As I stood there, I looked him right in his eyes and asked him if he was done. So I could start my class. He just stared at me and said. "Fuck you and fuck this class"!!

"Ok you can exit my classroom, you will not use that type of language in my classroom. And you won't be disrespecting me the way you do anymore either. When you're ready to act like you have some sense, you can return. And that is ONLY if you apologize to your classmates for disturbing their learning experience. Let's go" !! I replied.

Even after telling him to exit my classroom, he still sat there. So I was thinking in my mind. Am I going to have to physically remove this kid? And if I do, will he swing on me and I have to defend myself? Either way, he was leaving my classroom for his disrespect towards me and his classmates. Just as I was contemplating that,

Principal Hunt came in the classroom with a tall African American student. That young man happened to be Deshawn Williams, one if not thee best high school basketball players in the city of Chicago. I had heard about him and saw a few games the previous season. He was a Senior this year and had a bunch of major Division One colleges after him hard. But he had also been rumored to have had trouble in the past with his personal life at home. I was a little surprised to see him enter my class. But hey....I was up for the challenge. Why not. After entering my classroom, Principal Hunt then pulled me to the side.

"You know who that is right"? Principal Hunt asked me.

I looked at him as if to say. Yeah I know who he is. So what. So I decided to take the high road and replied.

"Yeah I know who he is, well I heard of him. What's he doing in my classroom" ? I replied. Page 21

"Well he was taken out of Miss Summers History class, to be in your History class. We just think him being in here would be better for him" Principal Hunt said.

"I hope you don't think I'm going to give this kid special treatment because he's a basketball star" I replied.

Principal Hunt just looked at me and said. "He'll be fine here, I will keep in touch".

I had no response to that, I just gave the kid the seat that was vacated in the back. Regardless of him being a local basketball star or not, I wasn't giving him any special treatment. He would earn whatever grade he put the effort in to get, like the rest of my students. After all of the distractions had ceased, I finally was able to start my class. And for now, I let the student I was going to kick out remain in my class. He had calmed down after Principal Hunt came in. After being behind with my lesson plan, I was able to squeeze what I needed to in the time I had left with my class. The bell rang and class was over. As the students were filing out, I stopped Deshawn Williams to talk to him. Not as a fan, but as his teacher.

"Can I ask you a question young man? Why were you put in my class? What happened between you and Miss Summers" ? I asked.

He just looked at me and smiled. And then replied. "I mean I really don't know. She just had a tendency to call on me in class all the time, as if she was trying to prove a point. They're other kids in the classroom besides me, I felt like she was singling me out because I'm a basketball star. So I requested to be moved to another class"

"Oh so I guess Principal Hunt figured if he removed you from a Caucasian female teacher's classroom. Into an African American male's classroom, that you would thrive better. I respect Principal Hunt, and I hope what I just got done saying to you isn't true. Because he is sorely mistaken. My class may be even more challenging for you. You seem like a smart kid, and you will not get any special treatment from me. So I expect you to perform on a high level. The same way you do on the court. Understood" ? I said.

Deshawn just looked at me again, and was almost at a lost for words. I guess he was shocked that I wasn't impressed with his stardom. And I wasn't expected to be. I hardly knew the kid, and only seen him play a hand full of games. I knew he was good and everyone was talking about him. But that wasn't what I was focused on. So I had to check the temperature so to speak, to see if we understood each other.

"Yes understood" he replied.

"Ok well I'm looking forward to teaching you" I said.

Deshawn would be fine, and a great student to teach now that we got that out the way and an understanding I hoped. As far as the young man that had interrupted class that I had switched his seat to the front. He was mesmerized when Deshawn came into the classroom with Principal Hunt. After that he was no problem. I guess you could say that day Principal Hunt and Deshawn Williams saved that young man from my wrath. Because at that point I was about to kick him out of my class. Maybe Deshawn being in class will help keep the other students in line and make my job easier. Either way as a class we will succeed.

That happened to be my last class of the day I was just referring to. All my classes were unique in their own ways. They were a lot of bright students, who I knew were going to be successful. And then there were students who you had to push, and that was ok. Sometimes. It was apart of my job to get the best I could get out of my students. One thing that bothered me about my job since I had been there was, the lack of textbooks and the quality of the textbooks. I had told Principal Hunt that I wanted to speak with him at the end of the school day. As I was walking to the Principal's office, I ran into Miss Summers. She had stopped me as I was walking.

"Hello Silas Jones right" ? She asked.

I turned around and replied. "That would be me. And you would be Miss Summers ? Nice to meet you". I said extending my hand.

"Yes I'm Miss Summers. I've heard a lot about you Mr. Silas Jones" she said.

"Please call me Silas. And I hope it was all good things" I replied smiling.

"Oh they were, Principal Hunt had a lot of nice things to say about you. All of us were excited about meeting you" she said.

"I'm just a kid from da Southside of Chicago that's grown into a man. Trying to make a difference in a lot of people's lives through education. Doing my part Miss Summers....just doing my part. But I did want to ask you a question about Deshawn Williams. Why did he get kicked out of your class" ? I asked.

As soon as I said his name, this look of disgust came over Miss Summer's face. That's when I knew that Deshawn was more than what he was saying he was. And what I mean by that is, he was lying about what REALLY happened. It didn't matter now, because I was going to get the truth from Miss Summers.

"Silas he's an entitled High School basketball star with everybody at his feet. He never respected me or my classroom. And I was just fed up with trying to deal with him and teach my other students. It became stressful and tiresome, so I asked Principal Hunt to take him out of my class. I'm glad I no longer have to deal with him" she said.

"Hmmm.....is that right ? So he basically lied to me and told me a totally different story. I can't say I'm surprised because the time I was talking to him, I could tell he was the type to talk his way out of things. Now this confirms it. Don't worry about him Miss Summers, I will handle him myself. One thing I don't like is people who lie. I have to get going Miss Summers, thanks for the information I appreciate it. And nice meeting you" I said as I quickly walked away from her.

Trying to see if I could catch up with Deshawn. I had looked all over the school for him, but I believe he had already left. See my History class was last period for the class Deshawn was in. And I guess this could wait until Monday.

Meanwhile I had gotten back with my brother Sidney about going to the Bears game. I decided to go with him and his son, my nephew Chris. My brother Sidney was still like he was when we were kids about the Bears. Even as a grown man he was so excited to be at Soldier Field. And I can't front, I was excited too. We were all having a good time at the game.

"So how has the first two days been at school little bro" ? Sidney asked me.

"It's been ok. Looking forward to next week to get a full week in with the class. Had to lay down some ground rules. Of course, you going to have a few test you. And oh yeah....now I have the local basketball star in my class. Last period too. Deshawn Williams" I said.

And once I said that name, my brother knew exactly who I was talking about.

"Deshawn Williams!!? That young boy can hoop man, he got a bright future ahead of him on that hardwood bro. He's nice" Sidney said.

"Well don't be so sure of that. Without education he isn't going anywhere. At least he won't slip through the cracks with me, not under my watch. He was already removed from one classroom.

That's why he was placed in my History class. Plus he's already lied to me, and you know how I feel about liars. So its safe to say, me and this kid haven't gotten off to a good start. But I won't give up on him, I'd rather push him to his full potential. The worst thing I want to see is another young black male's talent wasted because of his attitude and not giving forth the effort" I replied. Page 24

"Can't argue with you there, wish I would've furthered my education. But at the time I wasn't in that frame of mind. But I'm proud that you and Savannah got your degrees and both successful. That's what mom wanted for all of us, and what I want for my kids" Sidney said.

"We all do bro, we all do. I'm sure whenever Fatima and I have children, we want the same for them and even more. Chris, me and your father used to go crazy over the Bears. We never could afford to go to any of the games as kids. So whenever they were on TV. We would fight your Aunt Savannah over the TV. You just had to be there" I said to my nephew Chris as we both laughed a little.

Chris was a good kid, all my nieces and nephews were good kids. All of us made sure they all pushed themselves in anything they did. And actually the real reason we came to the game was because Chris had made honors at school. His grade point average mostly stayed at and around 3.8 to 4.0. He was a very smart kid, and I loved being around him. He was naturally a Bears fan also, like his father. And he always loved hanging out with me and his father. We enjoyed every minute of the game, as the Bears beat the Vikings 21-17. It was the start of a nice weekend, and I was looking forward to Monday believe it or not. I had enough time off after coming home from the Marines. I was ready to get back to teaching my students.

The next day was Sunday and I awoke to the smell of some bacon, eggs, and grits. My Queen Fatima was in the kitchen making breakfast. As I got up and went in the bathroom to wash my face and brush my teeth. I went in the kitchen to my breakfast just getting done.

"Hey babe, you're up. Good I was just about to wake you up. Good morning" my Queen Fatima said as I came in the kitchen and gave her a kiss.

"Good morning, smells good as always. And I'm starving too. Had a great time yesterday at the game with Sidney and Chris. I always like hanging out with them, glad I decided to go. Plus the Bears won" I replied.

"That's good and I'm glad you guys had a great time. So what do you want to do today since we're both off ? I do have some paperwork to go over, but other than that my day is pretty free" Fatima said.

"Lets ride our bikes through Millennium Park like we do from time to time. It's been a while" I replied.

We rode our bikes together when we had the same days off sometimes.   Page 25

It was something me and my Queen Fatima enjoyed doing together. We rode our bikes all around the city of Chicago. It really helped that it was a nice Fall day and the sun was shining bright. Fatima was athletic like me with plenty of body, one of the reasons I was so attracted to her. Personal health is something we both took seriously and had in common. Neither of us hardly drank at all, sometimes on special occasions. The countdown to our wedding had begun, and we were now less than three months away from our big day. And as of the moment I was caught up on my wedding duties as a soon to be husband. My Queen Fatima had eased up on me now that I took care of what I had to take care of for her. As far as the preparation was concerned.

For now we were enjoying our Sunday ride on our bikes on this sunny Fall day. We rode through different parts of the city just loving and experiencing Chicago. One of the most beautiful cities in the world. Despite our crime rate and violence within the city, there were still plenty of beautiful and nice places to go see in the city. Those are the places I would like to think of when I think about my hometown. No I definitely didn't forget where I came from, da Southside was everything to me. But like I said before, I wanted more. I think of the families that still lived in the neighborhoods we came up in. How at times it was dangerous for us, and how much worse it was now. That always stayed in my mind, and drove me to be great. I wanted those kids in those neighborhoods to have the same opportunity and education. In a country of this magnitude, it should never be a restriction on great education for all kids who want to learn. Regardless of what neighborhood or section of any city in America that they came from.

That was the major part in my fight for education for all kids of every race. I could only speak from my people's point of view, because that's all I knew. And what I've experienced as a young African American male in this country. Not only did I receive less than adequate education on the first and secondary level. But I had to do my own research about different things that I wanted to know personally. Certain things they didn't teach me in public schools about MY own History and my people's History. Which I guess was the norm for most if not all American schools. When I wasn't learning public school education. I was doing my own research, plus I had what many people call now "woke" parents. They taught me what they knew about our History. Their pictures of Malcom X and Martin Luther King Jr, Nelson Mandela. And more recently, Chicago's own Barack Obama's picture on my parents walls. The previous three were all on our walls growing up.

After a nice ride through the city, Fatima and I was beat by the time we got home. We quickly got out of our sweaty clothes and took a shower together.        Page 26

## Chapter Two "Making Progress"

That next day was Monday, as usual I got up early and got myself a shower and got ready for my day ahead. Went downstairs and got my coffee brewing. As I turned on the small TV that Fatima had in the kitchen that she liked to watch while she cooked. I was watching the news and watching a local politician talk about what ? Of course education. You know the same ole same, classic politics about how much he cares about Chicago schools. I watched just to see if he would actually say something with substance, something different to keep me listening and not turn the T.V. off. I listened and listened, and just like I thought. Nothing. So like most times when I heard most politicians, I would give them a shot to hold my attention. If they didn't hold it by saying something that I really thought in my heart they would do. I would be done listening to them until they did.

I had little patience with the powers that be. To me and many others, we were tired of the same old story. Of hardly no opportunities for certain people. Of course that started with education. And once I could get myself in a good position to leverage first my city of Chicago, into providing better schools for inner city youth. The impact that Chicago would have on this country would be enormous. But it had to start right here, right now for me. Each day I had to make progress, and that started with my students. From their studies, to their test scores.

After having my daily dose of caffeine, I got my things and headed out the door. Got in my car and headed to the North Side. Arriving at school I went directly to my classroom and sat at my desk going over my lesson plan. My students wouldn't arrive for another twenty minutes. As I was sitting there, Mrs. Williams the English teacher knocked on my door which was open.

"Mr. Jones, you got a minute" ? Mrs. Williams asked.

"Hey....Mrs. Williams please call me Silas. And yeah, what's up" ? I replied.

"I wanted to talk to you about Deshawn Williams" Mrs. Williams said.

"Yeah....what about him" ? I replied.

"Well I just wanted you to keep an eye on him. He's really a good kid. And he's my nephew" Mrs. Williams said.

"Oh he's your nephew ? That's interesting. And why would you ask me to look after him? He won't get any special treatment from me, I mean no disrespect Mrs. Williams. But I'm just being honest with you" I replied.

"Silas I'm just saying he's a good kid that just at times needs some direction. He has an incredible talent as an athlete in basketball. The skies the limit for him, he's been a little spoiled because of his talent and a lot of people just see dollar signs with him. Maybe you can be that mentor to him to keep him straight. He's my nephew by marriage, he's my husband Larry's nephew. My husband's sister Roberta's son. She's been raising him on her own for a while now. Along with his three other siblings" Mrs. Williams said.

"I understand, and I have to get ready for my class" I replied as a few of my students started to enter my classroom.

I understood Deshawn's situation, and I felt for his mother being a single parent. My mother was a single parent for a time when we were growing up. But I also didn't want him to use that as an excuse like I had heard before from many others. I was still going to treat him like I treated all my students. And at times push him harder to reach his full potential. Especially now that I knew his story. I knew Deshawn was smart, he was just spoiled because he was a star basketball player. Like many before him. I didn't want Deshawn to be just a basketball star that slipped through the cracks. I will say that the standard had improved for student athletes. As far as requiring them to have a certain grade point average to be eligible to play. But my rules would be more tougher if I had anything to do with it. I expected excellence from my students. Because I myself expected excellence from myself when it came to teaching. I put a lot of pressure on myself when it came to teaching. I wanted every student in all my classes to succeed.

I knew realistically that was asking a lot from students who did so poorly the year before. But I would give all the effort I had to make an improvement. And so after talking to Mrs. Williams, I got on with my class. And speaking of the devil, Deshawn walks in class last and almost late. I just stared at him as he went to his seat.

"Ok now I want you all to open your textbooks to page one hundred thirty and I want you to read from page one hundred thirty to page one forty two. And after that we will talk about what you all have read" I said

I then returned to my desk. I would have a different lesson each day for my students, I never wanted my class to be predictable. It was a way to keep my students on their toes and keep them interested and intrigued. They never knew what challenge I would have for them each day.                    Page 28

I gave my students twenty minutes to read over those pages I announced before I got up from my desk and got the classes attention.

"Can someone volunteer to tell me and the rest of your classmates what you just read. That is before I have to call on one of you to tell me. Nobody huh ? ....Ok Deshawn. What did you just read" ? I asked looking over in his direction.

He looked a little shocked that I asked him, figuring I wasn't going to call on him in class like he complained Miss Summers always did. Calling him out by calling on him. But it was completely the opposite in our case. Miss Summers and I wanted Deshawn to succeed and not just sit in class going through the motions. He definitely wasn't going to be doing that in my class. And that's exactly why I called on him.

"We read about "The Great Depression" Mr. Jones" Deshawn said.

I can't say I was that surprised, but maybe a little surprised. He was right, which showed me that he actually read what I told him and his classmates to read. And I was happy he did, but regardless if he answered that question right or not. I was going to stay on him and keep him motivated to learn. I continued on with my class, asking my students different questions about what they had read.

As there were some right answers and wrong answers. My initial goal with this situation, was to see if they comprehended anything they had read. I was looking for effort and willingness to learn. Like anytime, there were ones who showed effort and others who didn't as much. Those were the students I would probably have to push to keep them motivated. As I said before, I wanted all my students to succeed. That challenge was up to me to take on, and I graciously accepted that challenge.

For the rest of class I continued to go over my lesson with them, and I told them all to remember some of the things they learned today. Everything they would learn throughout the week, they would be a quiz about on Friday. Each Friday they would have a quiz on what they learned throughout the week. Those quizzes would add up to have a part in their final grade in the class. It wasn't that I was being a hard ass teacher, I was just giving them refresher courses on what they've learned to keep it fresh in their minds. The quizzes would only enhance their learning experience.

I planned on giving them homework at various times also, not too much though. But enough to keep them on their toes for midterms and finals. After finishing my class that last period. I was a little tired, although I was still very much on point mentally. I had a few things I had to go over before I actually left for the day. As I was sitting there, I got a knock on my door which was opened.     Page 29

It was Principal Hunt. I motioned for him to come in, and he did.

"Silas I need to talk to you about something. My secretary just informed me that we ordered new History textbooks ? I talked with Miss Summers and Mr. Watson and they both said they didn't order any new textbooks. So it had to have been you that ordered them" he said.

"It was me who ordered them. Look Principal Hunt, if you want these kids to learn and learn on a high level. Then they need better books than they have. Those books we have are probably over thirty years old. And...I said before he interrupted me.

"No Silas, you can't just go around here ordering things without my consent. Or the rest of the faculty. You think I can let every teacher in this school order what they want ? I can't, we have a budget we must stick to. And if you want to continue working here, you must follow the rules and abide by School Policy. Is that understood Mr. Jones" ? Principal Hunt asked me.

I just stared at him for a minute before responding. You could only imagine the thoughts that were running through my head. But I kept my composure and remained calm. Because above all, this was my job and I enjoyed teaching. So I had to respond with the pride and dignity as the man I knew I was. But still keep it professional.

"I understand the policy Principal Hunt, but I don't agree with it. And I don't think it serves these kids right. It's not in their best interest. How about this. IF these young men and women's grades improve, AND test scores improve. The school pays for the textbooks. If they don't improve, then I pay for the textbooks out of my own pocket. Deal" ? I replied.

Principal Hunt just looked at me like I was crazy, he didn't know what to say. He couldn't believe that I would lay it on the line like that. But I was very serious about it. If that's what I had to do, to get my point across and get people to believe in my teaching. So be it. Who knows how much these kid's grades and education period could improve with new resources. But I had to first prove my point to Principal Hunt. Because I'm not going to front, Fatima would kill me if she knew I was spending our money on books the school would keep.

But then again, my Queen Fatima was always so supportive. She may have not cared if it meant for me to see my dreams of a better education for all come true. That's how much she loved me, and exactly why I was making her my wife real soon. So after looking at me like I was crazy, Principal Hunt responded. Page 30

"I guess I will take you up on your offer, and I hope you're right. This doesn't leave this classroom you hear? Strictly between us. I could lose my job over this. So you do what you say Silas Jones" Principal Hunt said.

"You got my word....and my word is bond" I replied.

I put Principal Hunt in a corner so to speak, to see just how far he would go as a leader of students and faculty. For something that was indeed positive and apart of the educational system. And the young men and women's learning experience. If i would go all the way for these kids and he wouldn't. How would that make him look as a leader ? He had to take me up on my offer, and I did all that without acting out. And maybe doing something that could potentially have me lose my job. I stayed calm and handled it with class. I could tell by the look on his face that he thought I was going to snap, but I didn't. And when I proposed what I proposed to him, he didn't know what to say. He was damn near speechless. I was smiling inside, almost laughing. I knew he had underestimated my intelligence and savy to get what I wanted. Without breaking the obvious rules. My intentions were not about myself, or to prove I was better. It was always about the kids.

So after ironing that out with Principal Hunt, I continued working on a few things in my classroom until I finished up and went home for the day. It was a productive day for my classes, I was happy about that. And I'm even happier to go home to my Queen. My Queen Fatima had gotten home earlier than me that day. So when I arrived home after my day, she was in the kitchen cooking up something that smelled delicious. I could smell it outside my door.

"Hey babe, how was your day ? I got home early so I decided to start dinner for my man" Fatima said looking beautiful as always.

"Hey...and it smells delicious. You can smell it outside our door. And you're looking beautiful as always" I said giving her a hug and kiss.

"Thank you babe. Sit down and relax, dinner will be done soon" Fatima said as I sat down and did just that.

It felt good to get off my feet for a little. I just sat in the living room watching a sports show until Fatima called me in the dining room to eat.

"Baby I have something to tell you. I challenged the Principal to buy us new textbooks. The ones we have are like thirty years old. Those kids can't learn on the level of learning now with that. So I told him I would buy them, and if their grades and test scores improved. Then the school would reimburse me" I said.     Page 31

"Oh really ? Well....I'm sure you can back up what you say. You always do, so I support you babe. All day" Fatima replied.

I couldn't do nothing but smile at her and give her the biggest kiss and hug. This woman is truly amazing. Always supporting me and having my back, that was priceless to me. To have a woman like Fatima by my side, I felt like I could do anything. Before I had even met Fatima I had been in several failed relationships, with very little support. It was almost too good to be true that a woman like

Fatima existed. Even from the beginning that was my thoughts of her. But as I got to know her more, I realized it was apart of her character. It was just who she was, and I loved who she was. Every inch of who she was.

"Thanks my Queen for being so supportive of me and my dreams. I love you very much, and I can't wait until you become my wife in a few months. I love you baby" I said to her.

"Love you too babe, and of course I'm always going to be supportive of you. We in this together for life right" ? Fatima said.

"You know it baby, for life" I replied.

We continued eating our dinner and just talking about our days. Casual conversation over some Veal, Asparagus, and mixed vegetables. And of course some dinner wine. It was those conversations that brought us even closer together. We weren't just lovers, we were very good friends. We could sit in the house all night and talk and enjoy ourselves. Without having sex or touching each other. And then they were the nights and days where we would have sex all day and night. That was the adventure about our journey. You never knew how we would be from day to day. We were spontaneous, something we both loved being. Our friends Mitchell and Kendra would always tell us that once we had children. Those wild nights would be cut to a minimum. And honestly we knew it. We just liked rubbing life without kids in their faces for friendly fun every once in a while.

Matter of fact, we were finally planning on going to a Jazz Club together like Mitchell asked. It was always good hanging out with them. They were where we were eventually going to be. They gave us a lot of insight on life as a married couple. And we soaked up all the information we could from them. Our conversations were always all over the place, but interesting to say the least. Mitchell and Kendra were both very well educated. Both graduating from traditional Black Colleges. Mitchell graduated from Morehouse and Kendra from Spelman.

The next day started like any other day. I got up early like I always do on school days. Showered and went in the kitchen got my coffee and watched the news, as much as I didn't like to. I mean I was a History Teacher so I think it would be good to watch the news every once in a while. So I did, even though I didn't like the direction the country was going in. I was just a History Teacher but somehow some way I wanted to make a difference in this country. For not just my students, but students from all over the country who wanted to learn. But I had to handle my class first, one step at a time. And one day at a time. I didn't want to rush the process, I knew it would take time.

I arrived at school and got to my classroom. A couple of my students arrived early, which surprised me a little. But it was good to see. I greeted them with a smile like I did everyday as I saw more of my students entering the classroom.

"Find your seats and turn to page ninety two in your textbooks. Page ninety two kids, find your seats and turn to page ninety two" I said as the rest of my students arrived in the classroom.

I always wanted to start my class with my students reading a portion of the lesson they were to learn that day. That would get them ready and engaged on what they were about to learn. I didn't do things the conventional way, because I wasn't a conventional type of guy. I didn't believe things should stay status quo, especially when they weren't working. All along the lines of the basic rules and guidelines of the School District of course. But I was open to any and every method it took for my students to succeed. And I know it seemed like I used every method each day to my students. I loved it, they didn't as much. Because they couldn't predict what my class would be like from day to day. Or what they were going to learn each day.

The spontaneous aspect of teaching, much like my relationship with my Queen Fatima. Maybe that's where my idea came from. Either way it worked for me and kept me excited about teaching. And the objective was to keep my students on point from day to day. Keeping them interested in what they learned. I had some good news for my students, that I think they would like. So I decided why not tell them now.

"I have some good news, that I think you all would like to hear" I said.

And then one of my student said. "No more quizzes on Friday".

"No...y'all are not that lucky. I wanted to tell you all that we're getting new textbooks. Brand new" I said.

Page 33

Wasn't a whole lot of cheers or excitement about it. A few students gave me the thumbs up and some smiled. Others looked relieved that they were finally getting new textbooks to better serve them and their learning experience. And I mean honestly, what could I expect from some young men and women that needed direction. Some needed to be motivated to learn, and I was up for the challenge. I knew what I signed up for. This would be my destiny, to lead and develop young minds.

After telling my students about their new textbooks to a lukewarm response, I was ready to move forward with my lesson plan. After having them read, I asked them questions on what they read. Like I had done our first full week together. I wanted to get them used to that. And some of my students had adapted well and were paying attention to the way I ran things in my classroom. Some of my students didn't know it at the time, but those new textbooks would do wonders for them. I couldn't wait until they came that next week. I sounded like a kid in a candy store, but I couldn't hide my excitement. It was just one step of many, in my journey to make good on the vision I had for education.

After that class ended, it was the end of the day. And as I was sitting at my desk getting my things in order before leaving for the day. I heard someone say my name.

"Mr. Jones could I have a word with you" ? Mrs. Williams said as she entered my classroom.

Mrs. Williams was of course the English Teacher. And the aunt by marriage of one of my more famous students basketball star Deshawn Williams. To be honest with you, I had no idea what she wanted now. Especially with her already pulling me aside asking for me to pay extra attention to her nephew. In which I told her, he would be treated like the rest of my students. And expected to put forth the same effort or more. Being that he was a young African American student athlete, he had to do more to really be successful in this world. As one of his teachers I wanted to prepare him for that, and that mindset going in.

"Yeah what's up" ? I asked.

"I heard that you got some new textbooks for your students. Many of us in this school have been wanting new textbooks for our students for a while now. How were you able to get Principal Hunt to agree to get new textbooks? We've been trying to convince him for years now" Mrs. Williams said.

I really didn't want to get into the specifics with her about me and Principal Hunt's agreement. But I had to say something before she made this bigger than it really was. So I had to think of something quick to say and change the subject.

"It's apart of an experiment that I discussed with Principal Hunt, he agreed and we're trying it out in hopes of it working for the good towards these kid's education" I replied.

Mrs. Williams just stared at me for a moment and looked as if she wasn't happy about me being the teacher chosen for this experiment. Especially with me being new at the school and all.

"Why wasn't this ever discussed with the rest of the faculty ? No one ever knew about an experiment. This is somewhat unprofessional on Principal Hunt's part" Mrs. Williams said.

"Mrs. Williams, with all due respect. Why does it matter ? If it works, we all get new textbooks and maybe even more new and better resources. This isn't about me, but about why we're all here. And that's to be the best teachers we can be" I replied.

"I guess you're right. I just thought that Principal Hunt would be more professional about it. It's not like him to keep things from us" Mrs. Williams said.

"Don't blame him. We kept it quiet to see if it works. We didn't want everyone to think that it was already in play that everyone would get them. We have to see the results first, then the powers that be would ultimately make the decision. You see Mrs. Williams, this is much bigger than Silas Jones" I replied.

After hearing that, she kind of calmed down. And wasn't so angry. I really was telling her the truth for the most part, it wasn't about me. But I was indeed going to lead the charge for an overall bigger goal. My colleagues didn't know it yet, but of course I did. I was slowly but surely making my mark. But this experiment so to speak had a lot to do with whether I would have a chance to even do that. A lot weighed on this new textbooks thing. If it didn't work, I would pretty much be finished. And it would pretty much be just left as a forgotten dream. But if it worked, I would continue my climb. And my superiors would start to believe in me. That was all I needed, it was all anybody ever needed to succeed. Was someone believing in them. But it always started within, with yourself. And I truly believed in my methods of teaching. And I believed as much as this country talked about education and how important it was. That it would never short change any school when it came to improving a child's education. On every level of learning.
Page 35

All the unwanted attention about some damn textbooks, and they weren't even here yet. But I knew once they did get here, I would get a few visits from my fellow teachers. Just being nosey to see how nice the textbooks were, and believe me they were because I personally picked them out of a catalog. Nobody else needed to know that but me and Principal Hunt. I definitely didn't want to be his understudy, because him and I had different views on education. Principal Hunt was more of the same ole same. Let the kids get by, even if they weren't learning anything. Push them through the Public School Educational System into a cruel world where they have no skills. No skills mean no jobs, no jobs can lead to criminal activity that could ultimately lead to prison or death.

As it was once said before, the system was set up for us to fail. I wanted to do something to change that. Whatever it took. I wanted to eventually have a child, and I didn't want to bring him or her into a world where they couldn't grow. Evolve and be who he or she wants to be. I talked about this with Fatima all the time, and she felt the same. We were both concerned about a world we would be bringing a child into. If the both of us or one of us could do something....something small to start some type of change. It would be well worth it ten times over.

That night after getting home, me and Fatima were to go to a Jazz Club in the city with Mitchell and Kendra. They had wanted us to go for quite some time now, so we finally agreed. Not that Fatima and I didn't like Jazz, we loved Jazz. And frequented several Jazz Clubs in the city. From Andy's Jazz Club to Jazz Showcase M Lounge to B.L.U.E.S. We been to them all. Tonight though we were at The Green Mill, a historic Jazz Club in Chicago. We all arrived together and sat at a nice table near the back. Mitchell and I both smoked cigars from time to time. I didn't do it as often as he did, but I enjoyed it every once in a while. This particular night, I was out on the town so I figured why not. After listening to the smooth sounds of Jazz, you know we had to have a conversation. What would it be like if four intellectuals couldn't have a conversation over cigars, drinks, and some smooth Jazz sounds.

"So how's things going at your school Silas" ? Mitchell asked.

"It's going good, and things are getting better each day. You know you're always going to have your mix of kids and their level of intelligence. But all I ask from my students is effort, give me your best. And fortunately for me they have" I replied.

"That's great man, it really is. I hope it continues for you, you're a natural born leader. And us men in the Men's Group knew that about you right away. We see how passionate you are about your beliefs and what you do" Mitchell said.

"Thanks....so how's the business world Mitch ? You don't talk too much about your job, how's things going with you" ? I replied.

"You know business is business, sometimes up and down. But things are going ok right now" Mitchell said.

I never really knew Mitchell's true place of employment. I just knew he was involved in the business world. And a mover and shaker in the city of Chicago. If you wanted things to get done, you see Mitchell Bates. He was a very successful businessmen and lived in a very nice home on Lake Shore Drive. Mitchell was a leader at church, and had formed the Mens Group we were apart of. He had also made some generous donations to the church ever since Fatima and I were going there. I considered him an associate and someone that was genuine. But I never got too personal about what he did. I felt like if he wanted me to know, he would tell me. But every once in a while I liked to mess with him about his career, and how he never talks about what he does around us. He would laugh it off every time. All I knew was he had just got back in town from New Orleans on business.

"So are you two excited with the wedding approaching ? I know y'all are. I remember when Mitchell and I got married. Those months before all we did was fight and have sex" Kendra said as she laughed.

"Yes girl, you know I'm excited. I have been waiting for this day since I was a little girl. I have been driving Silas crazy, making sure he has his part covered. And he has, my baby has been great throughout all this" Fatima said as she looked at me and gave me a kiss on the cheek.

"If I don't, she will kill me before we get married. But naw....Fatima has been great also. I'm truly blessed to have found my best friend and life partner. She has been so supportive of me in me finding my place where I wanted to be. I thank her for her patience, love, and support. She's my everything, and I can't wait to make her my wife" I said smiling at Fatima.

"That's beautiful....really is. We wish you both the best, and many years of happiness. Like anything else, marriage is work. But I believe you two will have a great and happy marriage. We can tell how much you two love each other. So let's make a toast to Silas and Fatima" Mitchell said as everyone raised their glasses.

"Thanks, we appreciate you both" I replied as I took a sip of my dinner wine.

Page 37

The smooth Jazz continued to play as we drank. Fatima and I had a great time out on the town with Mitchell and Kendra. We always enjoyed ourselves with them, they were very intelligent people who always had good conversation. That was always big to me. Someone who could hold an intelligent conversation was the type of people I wanted to be around. Those kind of people inspired me. It was the same thing when I first met Fatima. After seeing her and having a conversation with her, I was completely sold on the possibility of her becoming my wife one day. And it didn't take long to make that happen. I looked for the same qualities in friends, and people I kept close to me. When either Mitchell or Kendra talked, I always paid attention and was interested in whatever they had to say. Because more times than not, it always had substance to it.

 Despite my homie from the neighborhood Angelo being hood as ever, he was also very smart. Being a Regional Manager at a Food Chain, he had to be smart and be a leader. And Angelo was indeed a leader. Amongst the kids I grew up with from my neighborhood, Angelo was the leader of us all. Whenever we were all together, I was like the bridge between Mitchell and Angelo. They knew each other through me and that was basically the only time they were around each other. So as we're sitting there talking and finishing up our drinks. In comes Angelo and Lauren.

 "Ayyyeee....I didn't know y'all was going to be up in here. What's good Silas...Fatima. Hello Mitchell and Kendra, y'all know my lady Lauren. So how are y'all ? Can we sit with yall" ? Angelo asked.

 Of course bro, how you been" ? I replied as him and Lauren ordered the waiter to bring over two more chairs.

 "I'm good man, you know just working a lot. We're opening a new store in Springfield. And I been back and forth between there and here over the last couple of weeks. But that's the life of us Regional Managers. How y'all been Mitchell and Kendra ? You know I don't see y'all out unless yall with my boy Silas. But it's good to see yall" Angelo said taking a sip of his drink.

 Angelo was just sarcastic like that sometimes, especially with Mitchell. And it wasn't that he didn't like him. He just liked messing with Mitchell. Because Mitchell was always laid back, and always kept his composure. Angelo was more loose, being from da Southside. It's just what we did and how we were. We liked to have a good time, and we did for the most part when we were together.

Lauren always would tell Angelo to chill and leave people alone. But he would never listen. So it was a typical night for me with my childhood friend, an associate, and our women. Page 38

"We're fine Angelo, just enjoying a night out. And yes you do see us out with Silas and Fatima, because we know you through them. And it sounds like things are really busy for you as a Manager. Always a good thing, job security" Mitchell replied in his nonchalant way of a comeback.

It was always funny hearing them verbal sparring. Fatima and I just sat back and laughed, it was all in fun of course. We all sat there for another twenty minutes just talking and enjoying each other's company until it was time to leave. I had another day ahead of me tomorrow. After a night out, we got home around ten o'clock and went straight to bed. I usually didn't go out on a weekday during the school year, but Mitchell and Kendra insisted we go out with them because it had been awhile. So we decided to go out. And had a great time too, so we were glad we went.

Believe it or not, I didn't feel bad at all the next day. I mean I wasn't trashed, but I did have some drinks. Enough drinks that Fatima drove home. I got up early like I always did, today was Friday and it would be my classes first weekly quiz I would give. Since most of the kids had improved, and I didn't have any class interruptions. I let them have an extra week to study what they had learned so far. What they had learned thus far would be what the quiz would consist of. I was happy for two reasons. One. My students were going to take my quiz today, and I was eager to see how each of them would do. Two....it was Friday.

So as I stepped in my classroom and cut the light on and went to my desk, I just sat there for a minute before I went in my bag and got out my stuff. The textbooks would most likely arrive Monday. But for now I was putting all the quizzes on each student's desk. So they knew as soon as they stepped in the classroom, they would be welcomed by me and then they would take their quiz. I sat at my desk another five minutes before my students arrived. I greeted them with a smile, but as soon they seen the quizzes on their desks those faces changed. I had to laugh to myself for a moment as I turned towards the blackboard. I heard one of them say, "Mr. Jones...a quiz already" ?

"Yes. And I actually gave you all an extra week. We been together as a class three weeks this Monday. So good luck to you all on your quiz, and you will all have twenty five minutes to complete your quizzes starting now....go" !! I said as I walked back to my desk to sit down and wait for my students to finish their quiz.

I was excited to see how they all would do on their first quiz, but I also realized that this was their FIRST QUIZ. And I couldn't look too much into it. I just sat patiently and waited.

Page 39

After about twenty minutes I looked at my watch and told them that they had five minutes remaining. I looked at each of them as I scanned the classroom with my eyes, from one side to another.

"Ok....And stop !! Put your pencils down and stay seated. Deshawn gather each person's quiz including yours and bring them to my desk please" I said.

Deshawn looked a little shocked and hesitant to do it. I just looked at him. Until he finally got up and did what I asked. I could see he was still on his soapbox claiming basketball star. It was exactly why I called on him to do it. To show the rest of my students, that I didn't care who you were. If you wanted to pass in my class, you were going to work. No matter who you claimed to be. After he brought the quizzes to my desk, I had my students read a few chapters from their still old textbooks. As they were reading, I was grading the quizzes. Some teachers waited to they got home to grade tests or quizzes. I chose to grade them right there. I think I was more anxious than my students about the quiz results. I never made an facial expressions while grading them, not to give away what I was feeling until I gave them the results.

For the most part, the class did pretty well overall. But like anything else, there were some students who underachieved. Like I said, it was the first quiz so I tried not to look too much into it. But I would keep an eye on the students that underachieved from a distance. Gauging their progress as we moved forward.

"Ok class I have graded your quizzes, and as a class you guys and gals did pretty good. Although there are some students who can and will improve, we will move forward as a class. Anyone that needs any extra help, or don't understand. Please feel free to ask for help. There is nothing wrong with needing help, we all do at different times of our lives. The purpose here is to learn and grow as a student and class. Now...is there any questions"? I said.

One of my students raised her hand and said. "Will there still be a quiz next Friday" ?

"Yes there will be a quiz next Friday, and the Friday after that also. Focus on learning and studying, and those quizzes will become easy and second nature to you all" I replied.

Just then the bell rang and as the students got up and were about to leave, I had a few words for them before they left.

"I will give each of you the results of your quizzes on Monday. Have a great weekend and keep your minds sharp. Next week will be even more challenging" I said.

The weekend was here. And on this Friday night, me and my boy Angelo was planning on going to shoot some pool. So we went to one of our favorite spots in the city, Chicago Billiard Cafe. It was a spot we would frequent from time to time, and we liked it there a lot.

"So Angelo tell me something. Why is it every time you and Mitchell are around each other, you both have this sarcastic wit back and forth thing going on? What's that about" ? I asked.

"Man you know Mitchell thinks he knows everything, and deep down he looks down on me because I'm from da South Side. Probably looks down on you too, you just don't know it yet. I think he's a smart man, but I wouldn't trust him. I just co-exist with him because of you. Plus I hardly know the man" Angelo replied.

I got that Mitchell and Angelo had two different mindsets, and were completely different in the way they carried themselves. And the fact they coexisted because of me. But I wanted to bring my childhood friend and associate closer. With the wedding fastly approaching, they both were my groomsmen. So I wanted us to have a tighter bond so to speak. But another part of me, just wanted to leave it be and let it happen naturally if it was ever going to happen. Even though Mitchell came up on the West Side of da Chi, he was different. Angelo was definitely South Side to the tee. They both had careers where they had to show their professionalism. Mitchell carried that throughout his life, or at least for how long I've known him. Angelo was professional when he had to be, outside of that he was the same Angelo from da South Side of Chicago. So I summed it up as. Mitchell showed me the professional side. And Angelo would keep me humble and remind me of where I came from. Not that I forgot, I was proud of being from da South Side of Chicago. And it was good to have that balance in my life.

"I'm just glad y'all both coexist, because I value the both of you greatly. I think you're both smart men, it's always good to have people with intelligence around you. Plus y'all both are in my wedding, my groomsmen. I wouldn't just include anybody to be apart of my big day. One of the biggest days of my life" I said.

"Silas what you trying to say ? What you getting at man? I know dude through you, he's aight. But I can't say I'm going to be buddy buddy with the man" Angelo replied.

"Its all good. I guess I should be thankful for the relationship you two do have, it's not like y'all have came to blows or anything like that. So it's cool, I just wanted to make sure y'all was good with this wedding coming up.

We continued shooting pool and talking about any and everything from the wedding to our jobs. The old neighborhood and old friends that we knew that was murdered in the same streets we came up on. And how we was lucky to escape everything that was going on in our environment. I was fortunate to have good parents, even though my parents eventually got a divorce. They both instilled great morals and values in me, my sister, and my older brother. Angelo came from a single parent home. And he still stayed clear of the gang activity that was going on in our neighborhood and around the city. Just like I did. He always used to say that he didn't want to use being from a single parent home as an excuse as to why he couldnt become successful. He would be successful with or without a father. Angelo was just determined, we both were. I went away to the Marines and he went away to a Junior College. Got his degree in Management and went onto become a District Manager at a local food chain.

After being a Store Manager for over five years, he was promoted to Regional Manager. And with that he was making about $95,000 a year. He was very much a success story coming from where we came from. And I was personally proud of him, someone I've known since we were like seven years old. It was great seeing him have the success he's had. And no matter how much success he obtained, he was still the same Angelo from da South Side. And that's why he was my best friend. Even us being best friends, we definitely disagreed on many occasions. But we always maintained that respect for one another. Loyalty really meant something to us, we were old school Chicago dudes. And we always had each other's back. I knew when I introduced Mitchell and Angelo, that Angelo would be hesitant to really get to know a cat like Mitchell. But I hoped for the best, and after talking to Angelo this time I wouldn't stress it anymore.

I had a great time hanging with my boy Angelo, but it was time to get back home. My Queen Fatima was preparing dinner for us. And as soon as I came in our house I could smell it....mmmm.

"Hey baby, it smells great. Let me get cleaned up and I will be right back" I said as I went behind my Queen Fatima. Put my arms around her and kissed her on her cheek.

"Ok babe, hurry up because it's done. When you come back it will be served" Fatima replied.

I just loved that woman, and couldn't wait till she was officially my wife. My weekend was starting great, and I was loving every minute of it. Tomorrow which was Saturday, I was planning on visiting my father Sidney Jones Sr. On the North Side. But for now I was going to enjoy this dinner that my Queen had prepared for us. And just enjoy the rest of my night with the woman I love.    Page 42

That next day I got up and went out for a jog, yes I not only go to the gym. But I also jog sometimes on the weekend early in the mornings. I got my sweatshirt on with my hoodie and my sweats, put my hood over my head and went on my jog. Fatima was still sleep, I kissed her softly on the cheek before I left. I was out that morning for over an hour. I got back home, and by that time Fatima was up reading the paper and drinking some coffee when I came in.

"Hey babe, how was your jog? And do you want any coffee" ? Fatima asked me as I came in.

"It was cool, and yeah I'll take a cup. What you have going on today" ? I replied asking.

"Well I was going to go by the office for a little, catch up on some paperwork. Why what do you have planned for today" ? Fatima said.

"I'm going to see my pops and see how he's doing. It's been a little while since I've been over there since I've started my teaching job" I replied.

Fatima loved my father, my father was what many would call a ladies man. He knew how to talk to women and he was very charming. Probably too charming, and that's also probably why him and my mother's marriage didn't work out. I remember plenty of times hearing them argue about other women my mother had suspected my father was running around with. My father was always kind to Fatima, he knew that she was the love of my life. So going to see him without her, she was kind of bummed about it. But she understood that I wanted to have this time with my father. Especially with the fact that my father and older brother Sidney Jr. didn't have the greatest relationship. My brother held sort of a grudge against my father because of our parents marriage didn't work out. Now my father was never one to abuse my mother physically, but he did lie and was suspected of cheating. And that upset my brother. As much as it did they remained cordial over the years at family gatherings, such as my niece and nephew's birthday parties.

My sister and I never held our father's infidelities against him, and we never really got into it at all. We heard the rumors and heard some of the arguments over the years. Sidney Jr. had seen a lot growing up, and that was the main reason he felt the way he did about our father. From here on out I would stay out of it and let them handle it like men. They were both older than me, and in part both taught me how to be a man. So I felt like they should handle this situation like mature men, like the mature men that they taught me to be. I didn't know when it would actually happen, but I was hoping it would happen soon. Regardless I was on my way to visit my father, and spend some much needed time with a man I still loved dearly.   Page 43

As I got to my father's place, which ironically enough was the same area of the city where I taught at. The North Side. I knocked on the door and waited for about another ten minutes before he finally answered the door.

"Hey old man, how you doing? It's your youngest son Silas" I said smiling.

"Boy I know who you are, I made you. Get on in here and make yourself comfortable" my father said as we embraced with a hug.

"I just wanted to make sure you were still sharp Pop, testing your memory" I said smiling as I entered his home and sat in the living room.

My father was watching an Old Western, something he loved to do since we were kids. My father had a nice place. That was one thing about my father, he could always handle his own. Before him and my mother got divorced, he was a great provider for his family. He made sure we never went without the essentials in life. We were far from rich, and we weren't dirt poor. So we were kind of in the middle. Both my parents worked all our lives. When my older brother Sidney Jr. was old enough. He would look after me and our younger sister Savannah.

"I'm as sharp as I can be at my age. So what's new with you Silas ? I hear you're teaching in this area. How's that working out for you" ? My father asked.

"Its still early in the process, but so far so good. I'm just getting to know my students and laying the groundwork for my vision Pop. But I will say one thing, I got the school to invest in new textbooks for a better learning experience for the students. Those books we had were over thirty years old Pop" I said.

"Son half these inner city schools are the same. The people that could do something and improve these schools, they don't care. Mainly because of where these schools are located. When I went to school it was a lot worse. But I applaud you and others like you for trying to make it better. These kids need it Silas....you know that. You and your sister took advantage of all your opportunities and made good on them. That's what you have to do" my father said.

"Right and it's even harder if you're a person of color. I got this kid in my class by the name of Deshawn Williams. You heard of him ? Local basketball star" I said.

"Hmmm....I believe so. What about him" ? My father asked.

"He's just one of those kids that feels entitled because of his talent on the court, but he won't get any special treatment from me" I replied.     Page 44

"And he shouldn't, a lot of kids are like that these days. The environment they lay out for these kids nowadays has them like that, back in my day you worked for everything you got whether you were talented or not. You continue to do the work you do, and hope others caught on to what you were doing. You're a leader Silas, you had it in you since you were young. Go where your destiny takes you" my father said.

"You always were full of knowledge Pop. I indeed intend to continue my vision as long as I'm involved with education. Thats why I got in this field. To teach and help young minds develop into future success stories. You and my mother, as parents always wanted us to succeed. Thats what I want for these kids Pop" I replied.

"I know you do son, that's why I love what you're doing. And I'm proud of you and all that you do for this community. I know there's so much more for you to do, but I'm proud of the progress. Getting new textbooks was a big step, and the first step. It only proves to you to keep going and reach your goal" my father Sidney Sr. said.

"You're right, and I am" I replied.

I wanted so much to bring up my older brother Sidney Jr. in the conversation with my father. But I promised myself I would stay out of it. It was really hard, because I knew how stubborn my father and brother were. And how neither one of them would make the first step. I'm not sure if my sister ever tried, but I have in the past. So much that I had gave up after the last time, and chalked it up to they were both grown men. And if they really wanted to mend things, either or both would make the first step. I knew both my brother and father loved one another without question. But they couldn't let go of the past, well my brother couldn't. My father wanted to move on without any apologizes or explanations. And that's where my brother had an issue. After my mother and father divorced, my brother felt he didn't have to listen so much to my father. He was the man of the house now. That's what our father always taught us, protect your mother and sister.

After my father left, my older brother treated him like an outsider. He resented him for years. That anger turned my brother to the streets for a time in his life. But he was fortunate to live through it, and get his life together. Before he ended up going to jail for a long stretch or being killed in the streets. I was proud of my brother for doing that, because we were raised by good parents. Parents that instilled great values in us all, and what he did in the streets wasn't what they had raised. But it was great to see us all doing well now. Including my parents. My wedding was coming up, and I was excited to have all my family attending.

Page 45

"So how's your mother and sister doing Silas" ? My father asked.

"They're good Pop, thanks for asking. I know you and mom got this thing between y'all, it's good that you're being the bigger man about it" I said.

"Son I been being the bigger man for years now. And that also goes for your brother. I was a young man married with three kids, and I made some mistakes in my life that I didn't feel I had to pay for. For the rest of my life. Your mother and brother still feel I should pay for what I did years ago. I'm glad you and your sister have some sense. Some sense to know that just because a person makes a mistake doesn't mean you can't forgive them. I know me and your mother are going to be what we are. That relationship goes back a long way, before you all were born. Your brother has to be a man, and let that past hurt go. I'm not going to be here forever" Sidney Sr. said.

"Pop maybe all it takes is for you to apologize, maybe that's all he wants to hear" I replied.

"I never apologized to you or your sister, why should I apologize to him ? The only person I owed an apology was your mother. And I did that years ago" my father said.

It was clear, and we all knew my father was stuck in his ways. He didn't feel he owed my brother an apology. He felt my brother should've gotten past it. In his eyes we all should've gotten over everything by now. I knew my brother wasn't going to try to reach out. Because he was too much like my father. So as I previously planned, I stayed out of it and changed the subject. I sat there for another twenty minutes with my father until it was time to go.

Two days later it was Monday. And I was excited today for the fact that the beginning of my plan was about to be in motion. In the form of brand new textbooks. It was great because the kids would have a better learning experience with up to date textbooks. They weren't excited at the moment, but they would thank me at a later time. After leaving my house en route to the school, I thought about how I made the right decision by being at this school. It felt right, and already I've improved my students learning experience. Today was the start of a special journey and I was ready.

As I got to the school and walked to my room and went inside. Turned on the lights, sat at my desk got my lesson plan together and waited on my students to enter the classroom. As some started to do.

Page 46

As the rest of my students filed into the classroom, I was called to the office. I knew that was because my textbooks were here. So I walked up, and had one of my students walk up with me to help carry the textbooks back to the classroom. As soon as I walked in the office they were right there waiting for me. And Principal Hunt happened to be in the office as I was getting them. He just stared at me and gave me a head nod. I knew deep down that Principal Hunt wanted this experiment to fail. Basically for his own personal reasons. Plus the fact that if it worked, it would put added pressure on him to get the School District to buy more brand new textbooks. And that would kill his budget, and challenge the people who set that budget. The people in charge of funding first and secondary education weren't spending a lot of money in inner city schools.

They didn't care for the most part. They already had a stereotype of inner city kids, despite the fact that some of them were some of the smartest kids in the world. I felt like every kid deserved a chance to learn and better themselves educationally. We finally got back to the classroom as I had two of my students pass the new textbooks out.

"As I said to you before class, about having quality textbooks. Makes the learning experience so much better. They're finally here, and I hope you students enjoy them. And put them to good use by learning your lessons out of it. Yes Tonya" ? I said as one of my female students raised her hand.

"What is the difference between the old textbooks and these new ones ? When it comes to the actual lessons in it" ? She asked.

"Those could differ, especially with how old the old textbooks were. But as we get familiar with this one, you will notice the difference between the two. Just know having these now is great for many years to come. A new era starts today ladies and gentlemen, you're one of the first classes in this new era. Now let's make it count. Turn to Page 36 in your new textbooks please" I said as I officially started class with my brand new textbooks.

It felt good to get something accomplished, I felt refreshed and ready to teach. I knew from the time I got to this school, that the odds were against me when it came to my plans and vision. I knew most teachers and faculty were status quo, and were going to continue on with the norm. And I was anything but the norm. Regardless of the methods I used, the intentions were always the same. I was just happy to be teaching a class that was getting more and more used to me by the day. And that's what I wanted. It was also interesting learning each of my students. Yes....us teachers not only teach our students, but we learn from them also. Their strengths and weaknesses, their tendencies and what drives and motivates them. Page 47

I felt this was just the beginning of me doing just that. I didn't know if any of the rest of the faculty would be with me or not. And honestly I didn't care. As I was teaching, I could see some of my students were in awe of the new textbooks. And after teaching my first class with the new textbooks, I could say it was a success. It was way too early to tell how they would affect the students test scores like I had promised Principal Hunt. But so far so good. After teaching my class, I had some time in between classes. So I decided to go to the Teacher's Lounge. A place I didn't go very often, I usually ate my lunch in my classroom. As I walked in I ran into another teacher of color. I had seen him around but was not formally introduced to him. This day we couldn't help but run into each other. We were face to face.

"Hey how you doing? I'm Carl Maxwell, Science Teacher for over the last seven years here. I've heard about you but never got introduced to you. Nice to meet you man" he said.

"Hey Carl, nice to meet you too. And it seems like everybody has heard about me. Science Teacher huh ? Interesting" I replied.

"Yeah I've been here for a long time, seen some changes in this school. Not much for the good honestly speaking. I'm surprised a man like yourself with your credentials would be at a school like this" Mr. Maxwell said.

"Well I could have all the accolades in the world, it wouldn't matter for nothing if I didn't make a difference. I'm sure I could have a better job, but I feel really good about this one. I'm helping young kids from the same neighborhoods I came from, and that means more to me than anything" I replied.

"If you say so. I just don't think this school and the people that fund it cares. We haven't made much progress here since I've been here" Mr. Maxwell said.

"So it's safe to say that you're just here to collect a paycheck. I replied.

"Whoa....don't judge me Mr. Silas Jones. I care about my students, I just know reality. You're still new here with bright ideas, which is good. But let's see if they go through and get implemented. Then and only then could you judge me on what I say" Carl said.

I knew I struck a nerve when I said that. And his reaction was just what I thought it would be. I didn't know Carl Maxwell well at all, actually just met him. But I did know from his reaction that he wasn't the type to stand up for what was right. As long as he was getting his paycheck, he didn't care either. And that's why I said what I said. That was just me as a person. Very honest.....sometimes brutally honest.     Page 48

Wasn't no malice intended towards him, it was just honestly how I felt about it. After that our conversation stopped, and I'm guessing he felt some type of way about what I said. But I had no control over that so I continued on with my day and left the Teachers Lounge and went back to my classroom. As I was sitting at my desk, I of course got a visitor. It was Miss Summers, she said she needed to talk to me about something. So I told her to pull a chair up and she did near my desk. And we started a conversation about what was on her mind.

"I'm curious to know how Deshawn Williams is doing" ? Miss Summers asked.

"Well he's been doing ok, still has his flashes of feeling entitled. And that's when I have to remind him that I and his classmates and school owe him nothing. If he wanted to learn he has to work like the rest of the students. He got a C on his quiz last week. Was my first weekly quiz, so I didn't read too much into it. I'm hoping he improves and doesn't underachieve. But we shall see. Why do you ask" ? I said.

"I was just wondering if he had improved after coming to your class. Obviously his behavior has improved enough for you to keep him in class. Maybe it was me. I guess I didn't know how to handle the ego of a star student athlete" Miss Summers replied.

"Don't make it so much about you, and what you couldn't do Miss Summers. Maybe Deshawn just needed a man to show him that the show would go on without him. If necessary. Some kids need that, because some kids don't have that father figure at home. So I don't think it was about your inability to connect with him on a level to teach him. You just keep being you Miss Summers" I said.

"Thanks Mr. Jones, I appreciate that. And enjoy the rest of your day" she said walking out of my classroom.

I knew that I was very different than the rest of the teachers in my school. And despite the fact I knew I was, I still never acted like I was better than any of them. And wouldn't hesitate to help any of them out if I could. It was just my nature and how I was raised. It goes back to what I said about my parents, and how despite the fact they got divorced. They still instilled great morals and values in us. Kindness and helping people. Me being a teacher and my sister being a nurse. Anyway my day was over, so I gathered up all my things and went home for the day. It was another productive day, and another day with our new textbooks. The students were starting to get used to them, it was still too early to tell the impact they would make. But I was remaining positive and continued to teach my ass off. It was the only way to make my vision a reality.

Page 49

Got home that day and my Queen Fatima was home before me. She was sitting on the couch reading a book. As I entered our home I greeted and embraced my lady with a kiss and hug.

"Hey babe, how was your day? I got home earlier today, my boss said I could work from home. So I was on my laptop earlier doing some things" Fatima said.

"Oh ok....and my day was ok. My students are getting used to their new textbooks, and everything is going according to plan as of now. How was your day beautiful" ? I replied.

"It was fine. I have to meet up with my sister's to make sure all our dresses fit the way we like. You know how my sister's are, their dresses have to fit perfectly" Fatima said rolling her eyes.

"Yes I know" I replied smiling.

Our wedding was getting closer and closer, and we were both excited about it. And both couldn't wait to be officially Mr. and Mrs. Silas Jones. That always sounded so amazing to me. And when I met Fatima, it felt even better. Fatima Jones sounded amazing to me. For the most part, I had been like most men about the wedding planning. I let Fatima and her sisters handle a lot of it. Even my sister Savannah stayed clear and didn't involve herself in the planning. Maybe giving a few ideas here and there, but it was mostly Fatima. And as long as my family felt I was happy with that, we collectively were happy with that. We both picked the colors, and we stayed away from all traditional colors. Well....somewhat. We picked White and Peach. Fatima would wear a Peach dress, and I would wear a all White suit and a Peach tie.

The bridesmaids, Fatima's two sisters and my sister Savannah were to wear White dresses with Peach lining. It was different colors because we wanted to be different. That was something we had discussed after we got engaged, we wanted to be a little different. Fatima had planned to finalize the dress sizes with her sisters later that day. So while she was gone, I was going to go over some paperwork I had to do from class. And set my lesson plan for the next day. Those were my evenings. If i wasn't grading tests or quizzes, or setting my lesson plan for the next day. I was spending time with my Queen at home. And now that she wasn't here, I was watching a sports channel. And highlights of the Bears game. And I loved the Bears, so I was enjoying every moment of the highlights. And plus they won, so I was in a good mood.

As much as I loved Fatima, I also loved spending time alone. Alone in my thoughts, I was a thinker so my mind was always racing. That could be a good or bad thing depending on the situation. But I wouldn't trade it for the world.   Page 50

The next day was another school day as I got up early and got my coffee. My Queen Fatima got up right before I left, she had an early start at her job on this particular day. We said our goodbyes and have a great day like we always did. And ended it with a kiss. And went on about our days. As I was driving to work, I felt good. It seemed like as each day passed I felt that way. And the main reason for that was, I felt I was making progress each day. I finally got to the school and headed straight to my classroom. Got to my classroom and got my lesson plan and classroom ready for my students. Today I had something different I was going to do. I would tell my students after they all had arrived. Fifteen minutes went past and my students started entering the classroom, I could hear them coming.

I let them all enter and get seated and then I got their attention.

"Ok settle down class.....settle down. I have an announcement to make. You all will have a project to work on. And for the first time this year, you will be paired with a classmate. You will be assigned to who you will be working with. Each of you who are paired together will BOTH put forth the same effort towards your final grade. This project will account for twenty five to thirty percent of your grade for the marking period. So make it count, you both will be monitored throughout the process to ensure that BOTH of you are working hard. What's the saying....team work make the dream work. Well here's a chance for all of you to prove it. I will make the project fun and interesting. But this project is about being able to work hard with another individual as a team, and still be successful. Also about you motivating your fellow classmate" I said.

That's when one of my female students raised her hand for a question. "So are the projects all the same ? Or does each pair have a different project"?  she said.

"That's a good question. And the answer is yes each pair will have a different project. Each pair is assigned a project to do. And when I give you your project, the instructions of what you both are to do, will be with it. Any more questions ? Ok....come up and look on this paper I'm about to post on the blackboard to see who you are teamed with and what your project is" I replied.

I posted the paper on the blackboard and they all went up curious to see who they were teamed with for their project. I knew they all were going to be intrigued by that, that's exactly why I didn't tell any of them who they were teamed with. After looking at the paper I posted on the blackboard, you heard the initial reactions. Some happy some not so happy. Either way that was who they were teamed with and they had to make it work. That is......if they wanted a passing grade on the project and in my class.

"You all could get started on these projects ASAP. You can use some of your new textbooks for research, along with your old textbooks. Ok....let's get to it" I said as my students began work on their projects I assigned them.

In the meantime I sat at my desk and put together the weekly quiz my students would be taking this upcoming Friday. I hadn't even mentioned that to them yet. I wanted their minds to stay focused on their projects, it was a nice chunk of their grades for the marking period. But I also knew how a teenager's attention span was. Most of them had probably forgot about the weekly quiz. And that was fine too, because I wanted their minds to be able to focus on one thing. And be able to switch their focus to another situation without missing a step. Because in life, that's something they would have to learn how to do to survive. It wasn't just about me being a History Teacher, but also about me preparing my students for life. I felt that responsibility since I decided to be a teacher, and I took that responsibility very seriously.

My students would have the rest of that day to work on their projects while I prepared their quiz. Later that day at the end of the day, I was gathering my things and putting them in my briefcase. That's when Principal Hunt came strolling in my classroom.

"Mr. Jones I see you got your new textbooks, how's that coming along so far" ? Principal Hunt asked.

I got up from my desk and was ready to walk out when I walked over towards him and stood in front of him.

"Its going well so far, but it's too early to tell how much better it may get. But trust me, when I am able to tell. You will be able to tell also, and you're going to love it. That is if your interest is in seeing these students improve and become successful" I replied smiling.

He just looked at me with a somewhat disgusted look on his face. I knew deep down that pissed him off, because I challenged him. That was always the thing with superiors in levels of employment, they always felt it was their job to tell you what to do. Rather than lead you on the job. I knew what I had to do, and I knew my vision. I challenged Principal Hunt because I knew deep down inside that he didn't care about any of the students. He was just doing a job as a Principal in a school that he didn't know much about or related to. He was just collecting a paycheck, which some really do in school systems across this country. And then there were teachers like me. And Miss Summers that really did care about the students and their futures. As long as I was there, I was going to make the most of it.

## Chapter Three "Being Held Accountable"

As the day came to an end and I was heading home, that was always my time to think about whatever was on my mind that particular day. This day I was thinking about the short conversation me and Principal Hunt had. And how as time went on I saw his true colors. And it was becoming more clearer that I couldn't count on him to see my vision through. If I wanted anything done, I would have to use a creative way to go over his head. Like I did with the new textbooks. It was just going to take time, and I was certainly patient enough to wait for it. I went home that night feeling good and with my head held high like always.

I got home before my Queen Fatima so I was preparing dinner for us tonight. I was making Baked Fish, Rice, and Corn on a Cobb. Fatima and I had great communication, when one of us were working late the other would prepare dinner. That worked for us on nights we didn't want to eat out. Plus I enjoyed making dinner for my lady.

An hour had passed and Fatima had made it home as dinner was done. As usual we sat together and had a quiet dinner at home just the two of us. And as usual we had an interesting conversation about our jobs and our family....and of course the wedding.

"Oh my God, making sure our dresses were to our liking with my sister's. They're a trip Silas, and I know you know. They were both stressing me out with their petty back and forth. You would've thought they were the ones getting married. Mia talking about she didnt like her dress at first and then Destiny talking about she wasn't that happy about the colors. After a while I just told both of them to just shut up and wear the dresses" Fatima said sounding a little frustrated.

"You can't let your sister's stress you out baby, this is our day not theirs. Just remember that. They both should be making sure you're good before anything" I replied.

"I know and you're right they should, but they didn't. Either way we got it squared away. So everything is fine now" Fatima said.

I mean I generally liked Fatima's sisters Mia and Destiny. They were both beautiful black women who had great careers. And were both older than Fatima. So they both often had a lot of influence on Fatima's mind. And they also at times would stress her, she always felt she needed to impress her older sisters. Something I quickly checked her about. And it would sometimes be the subject of arguments between us.

"I had an interesting conversation with Principal Hunt today, actually just before I came home. He questioned me about the effects of my new textbooks with my students. I told him it was too early to tell, but when I could tell he would be able to tell. He's banking on me being wrong and I'm not going to be. My students test scores will indeed improve. I just can't wait for my students to prove him wrong. Principal Hunt is the kind of people we DONT NEED being Principal's of schools. You have to care to lead, and believe me when I tell you. He doesn't give a damn about those kids" I said.

"That's sad, really sad someone would be able to be in such a position and not really care. It just goes to show you how bad the evaluation process is. He cares enough to keep his job, I know some people like that. There's a lot of those kind of people within all areas of the workforce" Fatima said.

I knew Fatima understood how it was working with individuals who didn't put forth a certain effort when it came to their jobs. Whatever those jobs may be, even in the educational system. As well as in the social services system that she dealt with on daily basis. Our dinner was great and our conversation even greater. But that was just how great our relationship was. No we weren't perfect, we fought just like every couple does. But our communication was so much on point that we could talk things out before they got bigger than what they actually were. Any differences we had we were able to communicate through them. That's when the fact we were best friends showed in our relationship. We often times learned from the mistakes of our friends. Mitchell and Kendra, and Angelo and Lauren. Not that we were in their business, but they were our friends so we knew things that BOTH couples went through.

We watched how they handled it. That gave us insight. Especially Mitchell and Kendra, because they were married. They were where we wanted to be, and where we would be in less than three months from now. Angelo and Lauren gave us a look at what we had now. So both couples educated us on how to be and how not to be. We valued both couples the same.

"It is sad Fatima, but you know this isn't surprising at all. And that's why I'm here baby, to straightened all this out. To make good on my vision. He's just someone in the way right now. Another obstacle to hurdle. I have bigger things to think about than Principal Hunt" I replied.

"Just keep in mind he is someone you have to go through or get around to get things done. I'm sure you have a plan, just be weary of that" Fatima said.

Page 54

"You know I am. And just like I went around him with the new textbooks. If I have to do it again, I will. Of course initially I will respect his authority, I don't want to lose my job. But there's ways to get around him" I replied as Fatima nodded her head in agreement.

I always had a plan when it came to my vision for education, it was something I dedicated my life to since I came home from the Marines. As I said before, I did a lot of research before even applying for any teaching positions in the area. So I was well aware of what I was dealing with.

A few days later it was Thursday and my students were on their third day of working on their projects. So I decided to give them a refresher course on what they would be quizzed on the next day. So they took a break from their projects and focused solely on their textbooks.

"I need you all to turn to page 160 in your textbooks and read until you get to page 165. That will be what you all will be quizzed on tomorrow. So focus and read very carefully, you have the rest of class to read and study that portion of your textbooks. You can also take them home if you want, but do remember to return them when you return tomorrow" I said.

As I sat down at my desk after giving my students instructions, my hoops star student. Deshawn Williams raised his hand and asked could he come talk to me about something. So I waved him up to my desk.

"Mr. Jones I've been giving better effort in class and my grades are improving.....slowly but they are. I've really been working hard, but I have this problem at home" he said as I listened intently.

"What's the problem Deshawn" ? I asked.

"My little brother has been running with these gangs in our area, and I been trying to keep him away from it. And in the process I'm getting into beefs with some of these gang members. I can't let the streets take my brother Mr. Jones. I just can't. Basketball is my dream and what I want to do. But it's hard trying to concentrate on school and basketball when my little brother is running wild in these streets" Deshawn said.

"Son you have a mother and father right" ? I asked.

"Yeah...well my mother mainly. My father comes and goes. I'm the oldest so I feel like I have to protect my siblings" Deshawn replied.

"I can understand that Deshawn, but you can't be in the streets chasing your brother and trying to get your education and improve in basketball all at the same time. Have you talked to your parents about your brother" ? I asked.

"My mother works a lot and can't keep up with him. My father....I guess I could say something to him. I been able to keep him away from it when I'm home. But when I'm gone, he's in the streets" Deshawn said.

"You know I have talked to your aunt Mrs. Williams about you. She said that you're a good kid, and I believe her. Have you ever thought about talking to her and your uncle about this" ? I asked.

"Are you kidding me ? They don't give a shit about me Mr. Jones. All they're concerned about with me, is what they can get off of me in the future. They see dollar signs, they know I'm being highly recruited by major colleges. And they figure within a few years I will be going pro" Deshawn replied.

"And your aunt.......never mind. That's sad to hear Deshawn, it really is. But since you really don't have anyone that can help you, I will see what I can do. Just keep your mind on your education and your craft son. That's thee only way you're going to be successful. Your education will always take you further than the basketball will ever take you. Always remember that. Now get back to reading your lesson and studying for this quiz tomorrow. Its important" I said.

Deshawn got up and went back to his seat. I didn't necessarily know what I was going to do about Deshawn's problem just yet, but I was going to do something. Now I knew why Mrs. Williams asked me to look out for Deshawn. I did find it strange that I never seen them two ever talk to each other during school or after school. They obviously wasn't as close as Mrs. Williams had led on. According to Deshawn, they hardly talked. Which explains why Deshawn never spoke of his aunt or uncle. The only reason I even knew that Mrs. Williams was his aunt by marriage, was because of her. Not him. I wouldn't bring it up to Mrs. Williams at all. I would just rather move forward and try to help Deshawn out with his problem. But maybe I would use Mrs. Williams and her husband to try and help Deshawn with his problem without telling him. I would think of a way, I had an idea in mind. But for now I wanted all my students to get themselves prepared for the quiz that was coming the next day. And they did just that until the bell rang and ended the day. I reminded all my students that they could still get together and work on their projects at home to be ahead of the game if they wanted.

So as class ended and the day not long after. I decided to go in the Teachers Lounge, something I did rarely because I really didn't like sitting in there. But I knew that Mrs. Williams and the rest of the staff would be in there. Even as I walked in there, I got stares from other teachers. Not that I cared, but I knew me going in there would bring about an reaction from my peers. They weren't used to seeing me in there, although some of my fellow teachers were happy to see me and greeted me. I walked over to where the coffee and donuts were and Mrs. Williams was standing over there.

"Hey Mrs. Williams, can I have a word with you in private" ? I asked as I stood next to her.

"Yeah sure, what's going on" ? She said.

"Were you or your husband aware that your nephew Deshawn has a younger brother that runs the streets with gang members" ? I asked.

"I mean we're aware of Deshawn's little brother Corey, yes. But as far as him being around gangs, we had no knowledge of that. And why would it matter anyway, we aren't his parents. He has a mother and father. There's very little we can do. Is he in trouble" ? She asked.

"I just came to you because I remember how concerned you were before when you asked me to look after Deshawn and all. I figured you would also be concerned about his little brother's well being. He IS your nephew too" I replied.

"What are you implying Mr. Jones" ? She asked.

"Nothing Mrs. Williams, nothing at all. I just wanted to inform you what has been going on. Deshawn came to me with this, and now I'm bringing it to you. Maybe you can inform your husband and he could talk to his nephew. Have a nice evening Mrs. Williams" I said as I walked away.

She just looked at me and watched me walk away. I was also going to honestly see what I could do to help. Gang activity was always in existence in Chicago. Ever since me and my siblings were kids. And even before that. Some kids avoided and escaped it, others embraced the gang culture. Deshawn hadn't even gave me his brother's name to even try to help do something about it. But Mrs. Williams did, she said his name was Corey. So now I knew, but I did want to notify a member of the family about the situation. And maybe I didn't do it by the book, in notifying his mother first. But I was planning on calling her also. You could tell I didn't think or do things conventional, I had my own way of doing things.

When I got home that night, I called Deshawn's mother. Or at least the number he provided for his residence. So I was hoping and praying that Deshawn's mother would answer the phone. I knew she worked a lot, but I was hoping she would be home on this particular night. I wanted her to know what was going on, if she didn't already know. I just waited patiently as the phone continued to ring, after about five rings I was about to hang up....until. A woman's voice answered the phone on the other end.

"Hello". The woman said.

"Yes hello. I'm Silas Jones, Deshawn's History Teacher. Am I speaking to Deshawn's mother" ? I asked.

"Yeah this is Deshawn's mother. Why ? Has he gotten himself into some shit ? Is that why you're calling me" ? She said in a somewhat hostile tone of voice.

"No ma'am this is about your other son Corey. Deshawn came to me...." I said before being interrupted by the female on the other end who said she was Deshawn's mother.

"How do you know my son Corey ? He doesn't go to Deshawn's school" she said.

"I didn't get your name Miss" I replied.

"My name is Roberta...and how do you know my son Corey" ? She said.

"Well Deshawn came to me yesterday talking about his little brother had been around gangs and gang activity. And that he has to look after him, and it's affecting his work and his dreams. He's worried about him. Look Miss Roberta, Deshawn is a very gifted athlete and could be a very gifted student if he could focus more on his studies and his craft" I replied.

"Yeah well it's good to have dreams, but around here we're living reality. Which means I'm a single mother and Deshawn has to help out with his younger siblings. He has two little brothers and a little sister, he's my oldest. I trust him more with my other children rather than trust anybody else out here. I'm not giving you no sobb story, I'm just giving you the truth. I'm a proud hard working single black mother, living in a major city whose murder rate is sky high. And I try my best to keep my children out of all the shit that goes on around them. But I can only do so much, that's why Deshawn has to help me. Now does that answer your question Mr. Jones" ? She said.

"Yes it does Miss Roberta. And I didn't mean anything negative towards you by calling. It was simply to inform you on what I was told. I also mentioned it to your sister in law Mrs. Williams" I said.
Page 58

"Why would you be informing another person about my child's issue? I'm the one you need to be informing Mr. Jones. Maybe I need to talk to someone more professional about this situation" she said.

"No I apologize Miss Roberta. I went to Mrs. Williams because she informed me that she was Deshawn's aunt. So that's why I said something to her, I'm very sorry for doing that. I just wanted to let you know, because Deshawn is concerned about his brother. If there is anything I could do to help out, just let me know" I said.

"No Mr. Jones, thank you. You have done enough" she said before hanging up on me.

I can't lie, I felt bad for the way I handled that. But I was proud of my honesty, for letting her know that I messed up. And I was man enough to say I handled it the wrong way by bringing Mrs. Williams into it. Especially after Deshawn told me she didn't really care about him or his siblings. Deshawn didn't know that I had spoken to his mother yet.  Just like I was honest with his mother, I was going to be honest with him. So the next day came, and as soon as Deshawn came into class I pulled him to the side to tell him what I did.

"Listen....I made a mistake by telling your aunt about the situation with your little brother. I figured since she was a family member that she might've been able to help. But I realized by law I made the wrong decision. I did notify your mother about it, the whole situation. And I apologized about it like I'm going to apologize to you. I'm sorry son, don't know what I was thinking. But I still want to help you" I said.

"I just can't believe that you got my aunt involved, I told you she has nothing to do with us. Her and my uncle both think they're better than us. It's just another thing she can talk about to her uppity friends. It's cool Mr. Jones, I know you meant well. My mother was really pissed off. But I was able to talk to her and keep her from filing a complaint against you. Because I told her I knew you meant well" Deshawn replied.

"Well I'm happy we could get past this, and thanks for telling your mother that. Because I did mean well by it" I said as Deshawn and I shook hands and he went to his seat so I could start class.

Lucky for me, Deshawn helped smooth things over with his mother and she didn't file a complaint. That would be the last thing I needed at this point. I had gotten off to a great start at the school, getting the kids new textbooks and all. I didn't need that on my record. That would be all Principal Hunt needed to put the restraints on me, as far as how far I could push my agenda.

And I wouldn't forget what Deshawn and his mother did for me, by not filing that complaint. But I had to get past it and move on. And so I did. And what better way to move on, then to pass out the weekly quiz to my students.....it was Friday. Oh the look on their faces were priceless. But they knew from before that I was a man of my word. So as they all took their quiz, I sat at my desk and went over paperwork.

After they finished their quizzes, I began my lesson for the day. I went over my lesson which was the other half of the class. As the first half of class was the quiz. My students didn't get to work on their projects in class today. That would be their homework. They had another week before they had to turn in their projects for their final grade. And the kids were getting more and more interested in their projects as time went on. Some students were motivating their classmates that they were teamed with, which was exactly what I wanted to see. I wanted some of my more consistent and smarter students to motivate my often inconsistent students. They could be shown different ways to study and prepare themselves for lessons, quizzes, and tests. Not just by me, but also by their peers. That was what working together on this project was all about.

The kids finished their quizzes, and I would make them wait over the weekend and until Monday to let them all know how they did. Class was over and the students were filing out. I decided to stay a little late after school to grade their quizzes, and finish up the paperwork I had to finish. I loved my weekends. And if I had a chance to leave my work at work where it belonged, I would. Too many times I took my work home with me literally. So this particular weekend, I had plans to go over the final plans for our wedding coming up soon. I had told Fatima I would make time for it this weekend. So it would be an exciting weekend with my Queen.

I finally got home on that Friday night and was surprisingly tired. So I took a nap on the couch. An hour and a half went by when I felt a soft kiss against my cheek when I was half a sleep. That woke me up right away. I opened my eyes and the first thing I seen was my beautiful Queen Fatima. She had just gotten home from work and decided to surprise me with a kiss.

"Hey babe, tired I see. I guess we should order takeout. Chinese food sound good" ? Or maybe some Sushi" ? She asked.

"Why not both. I could go for both" I replied smiling.

Fatima and I ate a lot of different things. From Deep Dish Pizza to Soul Food to Sushi.

We even tried to go on a Vegan diet for a few months, that was tough for the both of us. So that didn't last that long. We were currently eating as healthy as we could. But of course we still cheated every once in a while with the foods I mentioned previously. This night we decided on Chinese and Sushi. Yeah we got both. I went and got takeout. And we sat together watching TV and enjoying some delicious food. Those nights were special just the two of us. We were enjoying each other's company in the comforts of our own home. That alone made it special. You add the Chinese and Sushi, and the night was perfect.

"Are you nervous now that the wedding is approaching babe" ? Fatima asked.

"Not at all woman, I been wanting to make you my wife since the day I met you. And I can't wait till it's official baby" I replied smiling.

"You know how a lot of men are about marriage, and the fact of it approaching fast. Hope you aren't getting cold feet" Fatima said.

"Of course not. Maybe I should be asking you that, the future Mrs. Fatima Jones" I replied.

"I'm ready to marry my King" Fatima said as I grabbed her and pulled her close to me as we kissed and things got hot and heavy.

That started the both of us into some wild passionate sex.....right there in the living room. As I said before, Fatima and I was very spontaneous. The more spontaneous the better for us. We just loved the thrill of it. After that we managed to make our way to the bedroom and fell asleep across our King Size bed. The next morning I woke up and Fatima was still sleep. Went to the bathroom, washed my face and brushed my teeth. I went to the kitchen and got myself some coffee brewing. By that time I guess the noise I was making woke Fatima up. She came in the kitchen with just her night gown on and looked as beautiful as she did the previous night....yes even in the morning.

"So I see you beat me up. I'm surprised, I'm usually up before you. That must mean you're eager to finalize these wedding plans. Isn't that right Mr. Jones" ? Fatima asked smiling.

"You know it baby" I replied as we both laughed.

I made some toast and we had coffee and toast. Fatima watched the news while I read the paper. Something I rarely did. Yes....a History Teacher that didn't watch the news that much. Or read the paper much. It was all negative most of the time anyway. Plus there was social media. Anything you needed to know was on there.

Page 61

A little later that day, we had a meeting with the Wedding Planner in Downtown Chicago. Fatima and I had saved for over two years for our wedding, we wanted it to be special for everyone involved. We finally decided on our honeymoon, we were going to Punta Cuna. But we weren't going to go after the wedding, we would wait until the summer to go because of me teaching. Either way we were excited about going.

After meeting with the Wedding Planner and finalizing everything, we decided to eat lunch Downtown at Shaw's Crab House. I had a great day with my lady, and by night I was planning on hanging out with Angelo. He wanted to have a few drinks, and just hang out. So after spending the day with my lady I got in the shower and changed to meet up with Angelo. We went to Delilah's Chicago on North Lincoln Ave. And had a few drinks. And as always our conversations were candid.

"How's things going at the job bro ? Haven't talked to you since the last time we kicked it" I asked.

"You know the same ole same Silas, a lot of meetings and managing a lot of people. I love the benefits of my position, but the stress is a bitch. It always is when you dealing with people. I had to learn and get better with that over the years" Angelo replied.

"Try being a teacher, although I love what I do. And I'm more of a people person than you A. That's why I was surprised you ended up being a manager. But I know when you need to be around people you can co exist with them. That's important in your line of work" I said.

"Exactly....its not something I'm thrilled about it but I do what I have to do. Are you ready to tie that knot playboy? The time is coming quickly" Angelo said.

"Oh yeah, I'm ready man. More ready than I'll ever be. Can't wait to see my Queen walking down that aisle. And see you and Mitch dressed up" I replied laughing.

"Whatever....I'm doing this for you chump" Angelo said.

"I would hope so, we been boys since we were kids. It's only right. And if I didn't have a brother, you would be my best man. But I did the next best thing, you're one of my groomsmen" I said.

"You already.....you know we go way back. And it's an honor and a pleasure being in you and Fatima's wedding. Wish y'all both the best" Angelo said.

"Thanks bro, love you. Let's get something to eat, a brotha is starving" I replied as we ordered some food from the bar.
Page 62

It was Sunday the next day and I had told my mother that I would go to church with her this particular Sunday. So I got up out of the bed and got in the shower. After showering I got dressed in one of my many suits. I decided to wear my dark blue suit with a matching tie and headed to da South Side to pick up my mother. We still attended the same church we did as kids. It was my mother's home church and she was a faithful member. Wasn't a Sunday I could remember that she missed. My mother usually went with my sister and her children. This particular Sunday my sister was working. And my brother, who knows where he was. I didn't even asked my mother. As soon as she called the previous day and said she wanted me to go with her. I agreed.

I wasn't really doing anything and I hadn't been to church in a little while. And my mother always had a soft spot in my heart, to where she could get me to do just about anything. I was definitely a mama's boy. Me and my mother had a great relationship and open dialogue. She listened to me and didn't judge, she let me be me. But she also told me when I was wrong and when I needed to re-evaluate myself and my decisions. That's how she was with all of us. I know she had that same relationship with my brother and sister. So after picking her up and on our way to church, my mother and I had one of our conversations.

"So how you been Mom ? I know I haven't came by in a little while, but I'm glad you asked me to go to church with you this morning" I said as I was driving.

"I been ok Silas, just enjoying life and watching my grandkids get big. Savannah's children are so adorable. They with they father now, they spent the night over there last night. Savannah worked a double. Your sister really works hard, I'm so proud of her. And I'm glad you came to church with me this morning too son. The Lord needs to see you in his house sometimes. Giving HIM some of YOUR time. You been off base lately with that huh ? I think I'm going to have Sidney Jr. come with me next week. And you can come when Savannah can't" my mother said.

I laughed a little. My mother always had a way of convincing us to do things her way. Don't ask me how. I guess because all of us really respected her to the fullest. And we would do anything for her. Because growing up, she did whatever she had to do for us to have the best upbringing we possibly could. We all appreciated her for everything she did for us. My mother was a fun mother also. She joked and laughed and had a good time. But she was also serious when she needed to be. A woman of strong faith. As I said, my mother loved her church. She loved everything about it. And she loved when her family was with her. Especially her children and grandchildren. That's why this Sunday was so special to me. Seeing my mother smile.    Page 63

    After a great church service, I took my mother to lunch slash dinner at one of my favorite Soul Food spots in the city. Pearls Place Restaurant on S. Michigan Avenue. Sitting there enjoying our food, and of course we had another one of our conversations.

    "Son are you ready to get married ? It's not that far away now" my mother said.

    "Yes ma'am, I can't wait to make Fatima my wife" I replied.

    "That's great son, that's great that you're happy and you're ready. That's very important. And Fatima is a beautiful and bright young woman, you both are very lucky to have found one another. And I'm happy that one of my children are finally getting married" my mother said.

    "Thanks mom" I replied as we continued eating.

    "Have you spoken to your brother lately ? He called me a few days ago and told me he was working a second job" my mother said.

    "We went to a Bears game a few weeks back, him, I, and his son Chris. I talked to him I think one time since then, but I did go see Pop. We had a good conversation, and I really wanted to bring up Sidney Jr. But I felt like I should just stay out of it. They're two grown stubborn men that need to talk out their issues. I tried in the past getting them together" I replied.

"You did the right thing Silas, by staying out of it. Your brother is his father's son. They're both very much alike and they both need to be men enough to put their differences behind them. And in due time they will make it happen. No matter what me and your father went through, he always loved y'all kids....always. Knowing that, just know and trust that they will get it together one day" my mother said.

"You're right mom, and I know. It would just be nice to know that we could all get together more than just at weddings and funerals. I mean everybody gets together for the kid's parties. But we need to plan a family thing. Maybe a cruise or something, in a few years" I replied.

"God willing we're all still here and healthy son, we could do that. I'm open to it" my mother said.

It was great to know that my mother was at peace with the past she had with my father. I'm sure their marriage had its ups and downs. The main thing was it didn't seem like my mother still had any resentment towards my father. She knew when I said "the family" I meant everybody.                    Page 64

Having my family together was important to me because we were all local, there really wasn't no reason why we shouldn't be close. I know people had their differences, but above all we were family.

Monday had arrived and I was happy to be back doing what I loved, teaching. I knew my students would be eager to know how they did on their quizzes from Friday. So I started class off by passing them their graded quizzes. The reactions were mixed but my students who were a little below the line were improving. And my students that always shined continued to shine. The class wasn't necessarily where I wanted them to be just yet, but they were improving as a whole. And that was all I could ask for. The class had came a long way since the beginning. That was the real way to look at it, instead of the statistic driven way that the country measured progress by in schools. To the country these kids were just numbers, to me they were everything. And that's the way I approached my job everyday. Me seeing the overall progress of my classes was the measuring stick for me. It let me know if I needed to improve myself as a teacher or the way I taught my class.

After giving my students the results of their quizzes. I began my lesson for the day. And for today I would spend the majority of class teaching, physically standing in front of the class. Something I did in bits and pieces since the beginning of the year. As I said before, I liked changing things up in my class to keep things interesting for my students. Today was no different, and as class went on and the end of the day was near. I had them read from their textbooks until the end of class. At the end of class Deshawn came up to my desk and asked to speak with me.

"What's going on Deshawn ? I see you got a B on your quiz, very good. Much improved, I'm proud of you" I said.

"Thanks Mr. Jones. I was wondering, we have a home game tomorrow night and I wanted you to come watch me play. So you can see ya boy ball out" Deshawn said smiling.

"Hmmm....I don't believe I have anything planned. Maybe my fiancée Fatima and I will come watch you play. I've seen you play before, very talented young man. How's things going with your brother Corey" ? I asked.

"Well you definitely got my mother's attention. She talked to him, but I don't know how much it will do. I always worry about him in these streets, sometimes I can't even concentrate when I'm at practice. I been really trying in class. And I hope to see you later today at the game Mr. Jones" Deshawn said.    Page 65

I was happy that Deshawn wanted me to come to his game. I had been meaning to get to one this season. But I was always busy. After he mentioned it, I realized I was free that day. So I text my lady Fatima and asked her if she wanted to go. She did and we made our way to the game that night. The gym was packed as I seen some of my students as Fatima and I entered the gym. Finally finding some seats right before the game started. As we were sitting there, you could hear some kids yelling my name "Mr. Jones" !! I just waved as the game started. Fatima just smiled after hearing the kid's calling me. She thought the kid's calling me was cute, and she admired that her man was admired by his students. She felt that showed how much the kid's looked up to me as a teacher and mentor. She knew that meant a lot to me, and that I was a born leader. That's what I loved to do.

The game was just like I thought it would be, loud and exciting. The fact that Deshawn was a local and now national basketball star. There were many scouts in attendance to watch him play. Anywhere our school played across the city, it was always a packed house just to see Deshawn play. I guess you could call Fatima and I his personal guest. We watched as our team took a five point lead into halftime. Deshawn played well in the first half with 15 points and 8 rebounds. As we were sitting there I also seen some staff members and a few teachers that were in attendance. The second half started and the energy level raised even higher. After a thrilling second half, our school won in a nail biter by three points. Deshawn finished with 27 points and 14 rebounds. It was a great game, Fatima and I both enjoyed every minute of it. I didn't get to talk to Deshawn. And I'm not sure if he seen me, but I would let him know I was there. It was a lot of people at the game. On the ride home, we had a conversation about the game.

"Deshawn did what he told me he was going to do tonight, he balled out. Proud of the team they had a great game" I said as we drove home.

"Yes....exciting. I haven't been to a game like that in years, glad I came with you. And yes Deshawn is very talented" Fatima said.

We finally got home that night and went straight to bed. It was a school night and we both had an early start the next day.

The next morning came and as always I got up early and showered, got myself dressed and headed out to the kitchen to make some coffee and ate me some toast. Fatima was just getting up as I was about to leave. We said our goodbyes while embracing one another before I left for work. And then I was out the door.

After getting to school, I entered my classroom and got to my desk. Did some paperwork I had to do and prepared my lesson for the day. I always got to school pretty early. I wanted that time to get myself prepared so when my class all got in and settled, I could start class. Usually its about ten to fifteen minutes before most of my students would get into class. But today was somewhat different. As I was sitting at my desk making sure my lesson plan was the way I liked, and Deshawn came into class....early.

"Mr. Jones, was you at the game last night? Did you make it" ? He asked sounding excited.

"Yeah Deshawn, I actually did make it. You guys played a great game, proud of y'all. It was nice going to a game, Fatima and I both enjoyed the game. And you're a very talented ball player. And you know that you can be the most talented ball player on Earth, but you still need an education. And not just ANY education, a great education. Always remember that" I replied.

"No doubt Mr. Jones, I will. I'm glad you and your lady enjoyed the game, and we have some more home games still on the schedule. So whenever y'all can, come out and watch us play again. I would really appreciate it" Deshawn said.

"Will do son, will do. Now its time to get ready for class" I replied as some of my other students were entering the classroom.

"Ok class settle down.....today we will go over a lesson. Within that lesson you all will need to take notes. Because as sure as time keeps moving, you all will have a quiz on Friday. So let us begin with you all getting out your textbooks and turning to page 217. Today we're going to talk about different times in history of chaos and confusion. Different times in history when this nation had to rise up" I said.

I continued teaching for another fifteen minutes until I let my students work on their projects for the last ten to fifteen minutes of class. They enjoyed class and they were very interested in the lesson. Them being interested is exactly what I wanted. Kids react well and do well when learning is fun and interesting. I was glad they reacted well to the lesson. I often times went over my lessons at home, sometimes even going over them with Fatima. To see what she thought. I always felt good about the lessons I chose, but I did value people's opinion. I could never imagine a student sleeping in my class. That's why the project I had them work on, would keep them all engaged. They were all teamed up, so all of them had work to do. And I made sure each student was doing their part. Another day was in the books, and another step in my journey. I didn't know what lie ahead, but whatever it was I was ready for it.    Page 67

A month and a half had passed and my classes were preparing for midterms. They had completed their projects they had teamed up to do. And we were still having quizzes every Friday. And my wedding was a week away.....yes a week away. And this weekend Mitchell and Angelo had planned a bachelor party for me. They even invited my brother Sidney. So after going through another week of teaching and preparing my students for their midterms. I was ready to enjoy myself, it was Friday. So I decided to go to the movies with Fatima, since Saturday was my bachelor party. Going to the movies was another one of our favorite things to do together. This was going to be a great weekend and I could feel it. But it wouldn't compare to the following weekend, our big day would be epic. But for now I would enjoy a nice Friday night at the movies with my soon to be wife.

We took in the movie and it was a great movie. As me and Fatima walked out of the theater hand and hand.

"So you excited about your big bachelor party tomorrow night" ? Fatima asked smiling.

"Just as excited as you are about your bachelorette party. I will be more excited about next weekend. When we become one my Queen Fatima" I said as I kissed her on her forehead as we continued to walk until we got to our car.

"Well I'm sure you'll have a great time. And you should babe, you deserve it. And you even get to hang out with your brother, I know you're excited about that" Fatima said.

"Yeah it's going to be nice, haven't seen my brother since we went to the Bears game. I'm just surprised Mitchell and Angelo were able to get along enough to put this together. I'm proud of them" I said as we were driving home.

"They better had got it together, because it's not about them. It's our day. And I hope you all have a good time tomorrow night. Just don't get too wild Mr. Jones" Fatima said.

"No worries the soon to be Mrs. Jones, no worries baby. I will behave" I replied smiling.

After getting home, we went straight to our bedroom and laid in bed watching TV. Until we ended up falling asleep. We had a great night, and the next night would be even crazier for the both of us. My friends and brother were having my bachelor party, and her sisters and friends were having her bachelorette party. We would both have to sleep good to be ready for the next night's festivities.

It was Saturday, exactly a week til the day of one of the biggest days of my life. I would marry my Queen, my best friend, my everything. But tonight would be all about the fellas, I was looking forward to seeing what my friends Mitchell and Angelo had in store for me. Along with my brother, it could be a wild night. But I did promise Fatima that I wouldn't get too wild. I was definitely going to have fun and enjoy this last weekend as a single man. And that didn't mean that I had any intentions on cheating on her or doing anything to jeopardize what we have. I knew what we had was special, and I wouldn't sacrifice that for anyone.

So early in the day, I had plans to go play golf with Mitchell. Yes...Mitchell and I were two black men who enjoyed playing golf from time to time. Well it was really Mitchell who got me into playing golf. Being a kid from da South Side, we didn't play any golf at all growing up. I would see it on TV and thought it was the most boring sport I had ever seen. But then one day I went along with Mitchell to watch him play in a tournament. Let's say it grew on me. And the next thing you know I found myself playing it and enjoying it.

"So you ready for tonight soon to be married man? This is the last weekend as a bachelor my brotha" Mitchell said smiling as we were playing a few rounds of golf.

"I'm definitely looking forward to tonight, to see what y'all wild boys got in store for me. But I did promise Fatima I wouldn't get too wild, so y'all don't get me in no trouble now" I replied laughing.

"Don't worry, I like Fatima. So you'll be fine" Mitchell said smiling as I took my shot and swung to hit the golf ball.

We stayed out there on the golf course for another forty five minutes before leaving. And yes we golf in the Fall/Winter. Well not in the dead of Winter, and especially not in Chicago. Me and Fatima wanted a Fall/Winter wedding, something different as where most weddings were in the Summer. After playing some golf, I went home and took a shower ate some lunch and watched some TV. Fatima, her sisters and friends had a whole day planned for her. They were out so I was home alone and enjoying the time to myself. After watching a little TV, I went over some paperwork. I know.....I said I didn't bring my work home with me often. But for some reason I felt compelled to do so today.  The day of my bachelor party. Teaching was my passion now, so I always felt I had to do something along those lines. Even if it wasn't actually work. I had a few hours before the fellas were coming to get me to go out for my bachelor party. So I decided to take a nap, because something told me it was going to be a long night.

A few hours had passed and I finally woke up after taking a nice nap. And started to get dressed for the night. Of course I had to brush my teeth and decide what I wanted to wear out of a few outfits I had picked out. I kept looking at all of them before I decided which one to pick. That's when I got a text message from Angelo asking if I was almost ready. I replied back that I was getting dressed. And as soon as I sent the message, my doorbell rang. I looked out the peep hole and it was my brother Sidney.

"Its me bro, open the door. What's going on, I'm ready to party. I hope y'all are" he said as I opened the door.

"Hey Sidney, how you been" ? I replied.

"Bro you know me, I'm always going to be alright. How bout you, you ready for tonight ? I know I'm ready to see some beautiful women. YOU may be getting married, but your big brother is still single" Sidney Jr. said.

Yeah I'm ready to have a good time with y'all crazy dudes. And I'm sure you are bro, and I'm sure Mitchell and Angelo will have plenty of beautiful women around us" I replied.

"Sounds like a party to me. It's been a while since we partied together anyway. You're a teacher now, I know this ain't your thang no more. Proud of you for what you're doing though. And tonight, send all the beautiful women your brother's way" Sidney Jr. said smiling.

"You got it bro, have a seat. Want something to drink ? Get what you want out of the fridge. I'm going to finish getting dressed" I replied going back to my bedroom to finish getting dressed.

I finished getting dressed and came out ready to go. My brother and I were waiting on Mitchell and Angelo to come pick us up in the Hummer Limousine that they reserved for us. It would just be us four on this night celebrating my last weekend as a bachelor. Just me, my best man, and my two groomsmen. I was looking forward to the night ahead. After waiting for another ten minutes, the Hummer Limousine was heading up the street as we were waiting outside. The plan was to drive around the city in the limousine and hit a few strip clubs. So after they picked us up, we headed to our first spot. First stop was the Pink Monkey on South Clinton Street, then we went to The Admiral Theatre. All the while having a great time, watching the strippers dance and throwing ones at them. After enjoying those two spots, we were headed to my bachelor party over at Polekatz Chicago Gentlemen's Club in Bridgeview, Illinois. A twenty seven minute drive outside the city.

Page 70

Upon arriving, all four of us in the Hummer Limousine. We stepped out the limo like we were superstars. We all were feeling ourselves that night. All dressed and clean we stepped into my bachelor party. The fellas went ahead of me to surprise me once I got in there. As soon as I stepped in the club, they had me sit down in this seat that was in the middle of the stage where the women danced. The pole directly in front of me. And one of the most beautiful women I have ever seen. She was exactly like I liked my women. Beautiful, thick, sexy, and very classy. Even though the women that were there were strippers, they were indeed classy. When I first sat down, the first woman just gave me a private dance. Well....It wasn't private, the fellas were sitting there watching and cheering me on. I played along with them and had a little fun with the women, but I kept it respectful like I had promised my lady.

After the first woman came out, it was another one right behind her. The first one then went over to the fellas. And just like my brother Sidney Jr, he pushed Mitchell and Angelo out the way to get the first private dance with the first stripper. All I could do was laugh a little and shake my head. As I had another stripper giving me a lap dance. The fellas were amped up, I guess because they wanted me to be. But I knew like they knew, we were all used to this. We all had been to plenty of strip clubs in our lives, but it was my bachelor party. So I wanted all of us to have a good time, not just me.

And boy did we. There were five strippers there at the party hanging out with us. We had the pool table there, open bar. Just enjoying ourselves with beautiful half naked women walking around us. Most would think that would get a raise out of me. I must admit. When I was single and younger, it most certainly would get a raise out of me. But what Fatima and I had wasn't worth risking for no one. I knew that I was going home after tonight, going home to the woman I would marry that next weekend. But for now, me and the fellas were acting up like we always did. And the fellas were pretty hammered, even Mitchell.

"Yo who put this together for my brother ? I know Angelo called me and told me about it" Sidney Jr said clearly drunk.

"I came up with the idea Sidney, and then I told Angelo. I have some business partners that used these strippers before. They're beautiful aren't they" ? Mitchell said taking a sip from his drink.

"Oh hell yeah. I'm trying to take one of them home tonight. Like I told my brother, y'all all booed up. But I'm not. Shit....they can all come home with me" Sidney replied still drinking

"Bro you crazy, you know they're not going home with you" I replied as me, Mitchell, and Angelo laughed.

"Y'all laugh if you want, don't be surprised if one of them do though" Sidney Jr said.

"So you enjoying yourself soon to be married man" ? Angelo asked.

"Oh indeed. With my boys, and my brother. Bunch of beautiful women everywhere, which none is mines. But yeah, I'm having a great time Angelo" I replied smiling as we both laughed.

I know that sounded sarcastic and all, but I really was having a great time. Just laughing at my brother and getting a kick out of the way Mitchell and Angelo were getting along. The whole night was fun. I ended up getting home at damn near three in the morning. We had gotten hungry and had the limo driver take us to a Chicago Diner early that morning. We ate and headed home. After finally getting home and making it to our bedroom. Fatima was sound asleep. I'm guessing her bachelorette party didn't last as long.

A few days later it was Monday, and I was back to my classroom. Where I was so comfortable yet focused. This week I would go over my lessons and we would still have our quiz on Friday. As class started, one of my students shouted out "I heard Mr. Jones is getting married this Saturday. Congrats Mr. Jones!! No invite" ? That's when the rest of the class started congratulating me on my upcoming wedding.

"Thank you guys and girls, I really appreciate it. And you all know I can't have the whole class attend the wedding. Y'all going to get me in trouble with my fiancée. But I will say, my top two students who work the hardest throughout the week. I will see if my fiancée will agree to add two more people to the guest list. I'm not promising anything, this is her wedding also. So if she agrees, then my top two students can attend if y'all want to. Deal" ? I said. And the class replied back that it was a deal.

So it was set. Maybe being able to go to the wedding, would motivate some of my students. Only time would tell. Either way it was time for me to get into my lesson plan for the day. And just like that, my day started. And I began doing what I grew to love, teaching.

As I was sitting there at my desk finishing up some paperwork, I got a knock on my door. It was Carl Maxwell the Science Teacher. I waved him to come in and he did.

"How you doing Mr. Maxwell, what can I do for you" ? I said sitting at my desk.

"Mr. Jones. I wanted to ask you if you think Principal Hunt would let me get new textbooks like you and your class has. I think it would really help. Our textbooks are really old" he said as I stared at him.

"Well Carl. Can I call you Carl"? I asked.

"Sure why not" he replied.

"The plan eventually is for us all to get new textbooks, improved components in our classrooms and all. Better tools to teach which makes you teach to your full potential, and makes the learning experience for your students so much better. Just be patient Carl, the rest of the teachers here are. Their time will come as well as yours. Just be patient, you have my word" I said. Even though I'm not sure I should've said that to him.

"But why you ? You're the lowest tenured teacher in this school, and they pick YOU !! I've been here at this school for over seven years and they don't even give me that shot, to improve my class first for all the time I've been here" he said sounding disgusted.

"Listen man, I understand how you may feel. But this isn't about me, this is about these kids that walk these hallways" I replied.

"Yeah....we'll see about that Mr. Jones. And oh yeah.....there's going to be the local news here in a few days. I'm sure you'll try to steal that spotlight from the rest of us. Good afternoon Mr. Jones" he said before leaving my classroom.

I didn't even have a chance to ask Carl why the local news was even coming to the school. He seemed so much in his feelings about the textbooks, he wouldn't let me ask him why. Either way it was the first I had heard about it. I guess they were going to tell me when they told me. All I knew was, I was ready to get out of here and go home to my soon to be wife. This weekend I was getting married. It was four days away at the time and I was so anxious. But I had to keep my mind on my job, and now maybe also being ready for a camera crew. Who may or may not come into my classroom. Either way I would be ready. After that encounter with Mr. Maxwell, I was beginning to think that I may be on this journey the whole time by myself. And I was prepared to if I had to, that's how passionate I was about improving education.

As I was leaving school that day, Principal Hunt flagged me down. And something told me he was finally going to tell me about the local news coming to the school tomorrow. But who knows, I could be wrong. Wouldn't be the first or last time.

"Silas....I'm glad I caught you. I wanted to tell you if you see news cameras here tomorrow. It's the local news doing a segment on inner city Chicago schools. Not sure if they will interview anybody or anything. But they did say they would like to go in a couple of classrooms. So just a heads up. Sorry.....it was kind of short notice" Principal Hunt said.

"No problem Principal Hunt, thanks for letting me know. I overheard some other teachers talking about it anyway" I replied.

Well I was right that time, and more than likely I was the last person he told. It didn't matter, I was going to be me regardless if the cameras were there or not. Besides, that was the last thing on my mind. Because this weekend I was finally getting married to my Queen Fatima. Speaking of her, I was on my way home to see her. As I get in the house, Fatima was in the kitchen preparing dinner. She had text me earlier saying that she would be home early today.

"Smells good baby....smells good. What are we having" ? I asked after embracing Fatima with a hug and kiss.

"Baked chicken, asparagus, and some cheese mashed potatoes. Does that sound good enough for my man ? And soon to be husband ? And you already been getting the benefits of being my husband and we aren't even married yet Mr. Jones" Fatima replied smiling as I kissed and hugged her again.

"And that's why I know I'm making the right decision by marrying you. Can't wait for Saturday" I said.

"Me too babe. Well the food is done, so let's eat my King" Fatima said as we both sat down and ate.

Everything smelled so good, and looked good also. Fatima and I were both good cooks. We both came from families that could cook. My mother Lucy was an incredible cook, although over the last few years she hadn't cooked as much as she used to. My sister Savannah and my brother Sidney Jr. were also great cooks. So was my father. Fatima's mother Frances was a great cook. We've been over her house plenty of times over the years for dinner. Very nice and beautiful woman, I could see where Fatima and her sister's got their beauty from.          Page 74

As we were eating, we had a conversation about our days. Like we normally do each day. I guess you could call Fatima and I a textbook couple. We basically did the things couples were supposed to do for their relationship to work. Communicate, listen to each other, and care for one another. Understanding about one another's feelings. Not only did we communicate very well, but we understood each other.

"I got some news today. The local news will be coming to my school tomorrow to do a segment on inner city schools in Chicago. Principal Hunt told me, but deep down inside I don't think he actually wanted me to know" I said.

"Why wouldn't he want you to know" ? Fatima asked.

"I just think since him and I made that agreement with the textbooks and all, he's been on my head and waiting for me to fall so he can stomp on me. And say I told you so" I replied.

"That's just ridiculous, you're one of the best teachers in the school. If not thee best. He should be glad you're there and that you genuinely care about those kids. That you want to improve education in a whole" Fatima said.

"I think Principal Hunt is there for the check. And he really doesn't want these kids tests scores to improve because he doesn't want the school to fit the bill. It would hurt his budget. It's all about the money and numbers with people like Principal Hunt, they just want to pass these kids through their flawed school system. And into a world lost and misled. The same old story baby. But that's why I'm here, and that's why I'm glad I'm at that school with him. It's going to be even sweeter rising above him and exposing him as one of many that were the actual problem in the educational system" I replied.

"I think following your vision of what you want to do. And how you want to improve education in a whole will expose all the ones who don't care about these kids. If they see that it's working and they're not on board with you, then you know who really cares and who doesn't. And hopefully the powers that be see it also" Fatima said.

"Exactly baby. I know he's the Principal and he gave me my shot there. I wouldn't blatantly expose him for my gain, because it's not about me. And it's definitely not personal. It's about these kids. Like my mother always used to tell me, the truth will always come out" I replied as we finished eating dinner.

After a very delicious dinner prepared by my Queen. I went and took a shower. We then decided to watch a movie together. Just Fatima and I . As we were cuddled up on the couch just enjoying each other. Page 75

The next day had arrived and I awoke early like always and went through my daily routine. My Queen Fatima had off the rest of the week, so she was still sleep when I left. I got to school and entered my classroom and got started on my lesson plan. I would use my blackboard today for this particular lesson. So I began writing what I wanted the class to see when they first entered my classroom. Each day I taught different ways, using everything I had in my classroom that was a source for learning. It kept my students intrigued and very much interested in their lessons and their work.

Today was the day the cameras would be rolling in the school. Not that I thought that the news cameras were coming to my classroom or anything. But I thought maybe they may at least get a shot of one of the teachers who really cares in action. But then again, I thought about how I rubbed some of the teachers the wrong way because I bet on myself that the textbooks would work. And improve my students test scores. Principal Hunt was leading the local news crew around the school. There was no way they would come to my classroom and hear what I had to say. So I went about my day like I always did, and was sitting at my desk getting things ready before my students arrived. A lot on my mind and a lot going on this week and weekend, with me getting married and all. So it was hectic, but I remained focus on the job at hand. And that was teaching.

As I was sitting at my desk looking over paperwork, I could hear some people coming through the hallway and my door was closed. It was somewhat loud. I figured it couldn't be anybody but the local news crew or some students in the hallway at the same time. Then all of a sudden, there's a knock on my classroom door. I got up to answer the door and looked at my watch. It was still a little early for my students to arrive. Opened the door and it was Principal Hunt with the local news.

"Hello Mr. Jones, they picked your classroom to interview you and to film you teaching. So here we are. Where can they set up at" ? Principal Hunt asked.

"Ok that's fine. And they can set up over here if they want" I replied as I directed them to where they could put their cameras at.

I can't lie, I was shocked to see Principal Hunt and the local news walk in my classroom. It really caught me off guard, because I really had in my mind that it would never happen. But here they were, and I was going to take full advantage of discussing my platform for education if they asked me. I was just glad he said they were also going to film me teaching. Most people would be nervous, but I was far from it. I felt like this was my opportunity. It was now or never. I didn't know if I would ever get another chance to push my platform and agenda on such a huge stage

The news crew got set up as I watched off to the side, and they wanted to interview me. Which was fine with me, I had a lot to say. But I would keep it short and to the point. Didn't really know what questions they would ask, but I was ready. This was my shot, and I had to take it. So after watching them set up, I was asked to sit back at my desk so I could be interviewed.

"This is ABC7 News Chicago and we're here today at one of the local Chicago High Schools for another installments of our visits to inner city schools to talk to different people within the staff about education and their goals for their students. I'm here with History Teacher Mr. Silas Jones. Tell us a little bit about yourself and your goals and aspirations for your students" ? The man asked.

"Hello I'm Silas Jones as you said and I'm from da South Side of Chicago. I served in the Marine Corps for eight years. Before that I went to college locally at DePaul University where I got my Bachelor and Masters Degree in Secondary Education and Teaching. After coming home after my eight years of duty, I applied and was hired at this school that I currently work at" I replied.

"Very impressive, very impressive resume. What are your goals and aspirations for your students as a teacher" ? He asked.

"Well my plans for not only my students, but education as a whole is to revamp it entirely. Put our money where our mouths are as regards to education. This country and its politicians talk a whole lot about education and how important it is. But as far as first and secondary education, we are way below the line in this country. Our supplies and  resources to teach aren't up to par. I personally pushed for new textbooks that I felt would help improve my students test scores. And I honestly believe they will. I believe education is very important and that as a country we should act like it is through our actions. The textbooks were just a start for me and my school. And thanks to Principal Hunt who gave me the opportunity to come to this school. I want the very best for my students. And I believe we as not only a city here in Chicago, but as a country in a whole can provide that for our children. If we invested more into first and secondary education. With better funding nationwide" I replied.

"That's amazing to think about, and hopefully things will improve on those levels of education. It was great talking to you Mr. Jones, and good luck on the rest of your school year. This has been ABC7 News Chicago. Signing off" the man said as the interview wrapped up.

Principal Hunt just stood off to the side staring at me the whole time. And knowing him, I'm sure he didn't like what I said. But I did give him a shout out.   Page 77

For giving me a shot at the school. I mean I knew if I couldn't get on at this school, I had other offers. My resume was impeccable, so I could have gotten a job basically anywhere. But I chose this school because it felt right to me. And now after being here several months, I had already gotten new textbooks for my class and an interview I had hoped would influence and change some minds. Minds of the powers that be. Minds that could directly effect inner city schools across this country. That could financially effect these schools and improve their resources for learning.

Having that stage of being on a local station was big because it was broadcast all over the city of Chicago. And with social media being as popular as it is, there was a great chance it could go viral across the country. I mean at the time it was only wishful thinking. But you never know. After my interview my students were allowed to enter my classroom.  Many of them arrived in time to catch the last part of the interview. After entering, class went on like any normal day. But it wasn't just any normal day, we had cameras inside our classroom. I tried my best to ignore the cameras and teach. And for the most part I did. The news crew didn't stay filming inside the classroom long, only about fifteen minutes and they were gone. But they were able to film me teaching and my students, I was proud of that. And glad they could catch me in action teaching my students.

Principal Hunt left with them without saying a word to me and I continued teaching.

After class Deshawn came over to me and asked to speak with me. I always had time for my students. And especially Deshawn, because I knew what he was dealing with. I always told my students they could come to me whenever they had a problem, my door was always open to them.

"Mr. Jones I see the local news as here, that's what's up. And they interviewed you, that's a good look. Your one of the best teachers here, glad they interviewed you" he said.

"Thanks Deshawn, I try my best. Yeah the local news came through to do a segment on inner city Chicago schools. I guess it was our turn, but I was grateful for the opportunity" I replied.

"Yeah....I've gotten some letters and offers from some big time colleges the last few weeks. I'm really excited about it" Deshawn said.

"That's great, keep your focus on your craft and your school work and you'll be fine Deshawn. Just don't lose focus on your goals" I replied.

"Deshawn....what I'm going to say to you, you may not like. But I'm saying this to you because I truly care about you son. And I don't want you to be another statistic in these streets. With the talent you have on the court, and you using your mind to excell in school like I know you can. You can get your mother, brother, your whole family out of your circumstances. But all that takes sacrifice. And apart of that sacrifice is letting your brother go if he doesn't want to do right. It's called tough love son. I'm not telling you to go against your mother's wishes by not looking after your brother and other siblings. What I'm saying is, you can only do so much. You have to look out for yourself. You can't let this opportunity you have go to waste because of your brother. Your potential is limitless Deshawn, and if you waste it. You will never forgive yourself for it.....trust me" I added on.

"You're right Mr. Jones. Thanks for listening to me and helping me, I appreciate you. And oh yeah, I think I did well enough to attend your wedding this weekend. Remember....you promised a few of us that did well this week could attend" ? Deshawn said.

"Oh wow. Thanks for reminding me Deshawn. And I didn't even mention anything to Fatima yet. She's going to kill me. Yes you're right. I believe you are and I gave you kids my word. So you can count on it. Thanks again for reminding me. I guess with the local news coming and all, it must've slipped my mind. Enjoy your night son, and be safe out there" I replied.

I can't believe I really forgot about the promise I made to my students. There was a lot going on this week with the wedding and all. Then the local news coming in my classroom interviewing me and filming me teaching. Slipped my mind, but today I would definitely tell Fatima as soon as I got home. It was two days before the wedding, and telling her I was adding more people to the guest list probably wouldn't sit well with her. But it was my students, and more than anything I had promised them. Fatima knew how I felt about my students and my passion for teaching. So giving my students some incentive by inviting them to our wedding, she would ultimately be ok with it.

I finally got home and Fatima was out running errands. I had to soften her up, so I could tell her about the added guest. I prepared a nice dinner for us. And it worked out great. Because it was about an hour and a half gap between the time I got home and the time she got home from running errands. So I was able to have dinner ready by the time she walked through the door. And just as I spoke, Fatima was home and I was happy to see her.

"Hey baby, how did your day go" ? I asked as Fatima walked in.

"It was cool, had brunch with a few of my girls earlier and then we did a little last minute shopping for the wedding. Food smells good babe" Fatima said.

"I got something to tell you. And please don't be too mad at me. I promised two of my students that if they did well this week, that I would allow them to come to our wedding.....I know its short notice and all. Baby it slipped my mind with the wedding coming and the local news being there today. But Deshawn reminded me today about it. So now I'm telling you" I said sounding sincere.

Fatima just looked at me and shook her head. One of those looks like, "Boy you lucky I love you".

"I guess that's fine, even though now I have to order how many more plates and reserve how many more seats for the reception" ? Fatima asked.

"Two more people baby....only two more. That's all I promised them" I replied.

"So how did the day go with the local news and all" ? Fatima asked.

"It went great baby, actually they interviewed me and all. They chose my classroom to film, and filmed me teaching" I replied.

And just as I said that, my cell phone rang. It was my boy Angelo.

"Turn on the news bro, you made the news!! You on TV right now !! I'm watching you"!!! Angelo said sounding exciting.

"Ok hold on. Turn on the TV baby, Angelo said I'm on now" I replied telling Fatima.

Fatima and I sat quietly and watched my interview with the local news and watched them film me teaching. We both just smiled at the TV screen as we watched. It was great seeing myself on TV. But it was even better that I was able to get my message across to the public. An important message about education, and I hope people heard loud and clear what I was saying. And more importantly, understood what I was saying. It was the beginning of me putting pressure on the powers that be to make a change. A change for the good, no matter the costs. If education was the keys to our future, then I wanted the country that stressed that to stand by their word. According to one report, the country's educational system ranked fourteenth in the world. Another report said seventh in the world. Regardless. Either ranking was unacceptable for a country that claimed it was the best in the world.     Page 80

"You look good baby, look at my soon to be husband !! I gotta call my sister's" Fatima said sounding excited.

All I could do was watch the TV screen, I was focused on the screen and making sure they got everything I meant to say. And they didn't cut me off. There was a message behind what I was saying, and more than anything that's what I wanted people to notice. After watching the interview and them showing me teaching, my baby Fatima came and gave me the biggest hug and kiss.

"So I guess this means you liked the interview" I said smiling and laughing.

"Of course I did, and I taped it. Plus I think they will show it later on the news. So proud of you baby" Fatima said still hugging me.

"What a weekend right ? Appearance on TV and we're getting married in two days" I replied.

It truly was shaping up to be a great weekend, a memorable weekend for the ages. And I was more than ready for it. Fatima and I enjoyed the rest of our night by having a nice glass of wine marked by a toast. A great way to end a great and memorable day, and this was only the beginning of an epic weekend. But first I had class the next day, which was Friday and also the day we have our weekly quiz.

That morning I woke up feeling happy. My wedding was the next day and the interview I did representing the school the previous day went well. I couldn't hide the fact I was happy, and in a great mood. It was going to be an epic and monumental weekend to say the least. And I was all so looking forward to it all.

As class began that day I was teaching with such a swagger and such confidence. I felt good doing what I was doing. And my students were congratulating me throughout the day about being on the local news. And my upcoming wedding tomorrow. It seemed like the day went by so quickly, my students did their quizzes and I did some instructional teaching before the weekend was officially here. I left school that day an engaged man, and would return that Monday a married man. That Friday I went home and got my clothes and my tux because I was staying over my brother's apartment. Fatima and her sister's were staying at our house, they were going to stay there for the night. And get ready for the wedding there in the morning. I was staying at my brother's tonight and the men would all meet at the church in the morning and get ready there. But before that, me, my brother, my mother, and sister all were going out to dinner that night. Our place of choice ? A Jones family favorite, Dan's Soul Food & Bakery on W 79th Street. We all loved that restaurant.      Page 81

After finishing my day I headed to my brother's and then we met our mother and sister at the restaurant. As I said before our whole family loved that restaurant, my father was the one that put us onto Dan's years ago. My father couldn't make it tonight, he had a prior engagement he had to attend. But he would definitely be there tomorrow at the wedding. I was just happy that the rest of the family were all having dinner together before my big day tomorrow.

"My big bro getting married tomorrow, I'm so happy for you and Fatima Silas" Savannah said.

"Thanks sis, we appreciate it" I replied.

"Yeah bro, congrats to you and Fatima. I saw that interview too, you did real well little bro" Sidney Jr. said.

"Thanks bro. I felt like if they were going to give me the opportunity to speak, I was going to use it wisely. By actually saying something. I was actually surprised they interviewed me and filmed my class. I have rubbed some of my peers the wrong way I guess, because I've been shaking things up with the textbooks and all. But I tried to explain to them all that it isn't about me, it's about these kids. And all of us will ultimately have new tools to teach our students, if all goes according to plan. And now with me doing this interview and them filming me teach, it's only going to get worse. But I have to be me and do things the best way I see fit. I guess in the end we'll see if I'm right" I replied.

"As long as you're doing the best job you can do, and staying true to yourself. That's all that matters Silas. And I'm sure you are" my mother Lucy said.

"Yeah bro, them haters are always going to be around doubting you. If these kids education improves because of you. They'll be thanking you later" Sidney Jr. said.

"Silas just keep doing you. We're all proud of the job you're doing with your students. And I know I'm ready for this wedding and getting done up. It's been a while since I really got dressed up. Almost like your sis needs a makeover Silas" Savannah said laughing a little.

"You're beautiful sis, the make up will only add to your beauty" I said smiling.

"Thanks big bro" Savannah replied smiling.

"So nice to see my children showing love for one another and supporting each other. I'm just glad I got you three together for once" our mother Lucy said.     Page 82

My mother always loved when we all were together. And I personally wished that my father could've made it this evening, but he had plans prior to me asking him. Him being at the wedding tomorrow was good enough for me though. That's when everybody would be together, helping Fatima and I celebrate our big day. We continued eating and enjoying the delicious Soul Food from Dan's. And of course having our crazy family convo.

"So Sidney what you been up to ? Where are you working right now bro" ? I asked.

"Working two gigs at the moment. Part time at the ship yard and fulltime at this restaurant. Just trying to get some extra money with Christmas coming and you know my kid's want everything under the sun" Sidney Jr. said.

"Speaking of my babies, you haven't brought my grandkids over in a while Sidney Jr. I hope to see them soon" my mother Lucy chimed in.

"Oh no doubt mom. I just been working a lot, basically working seven days a week. I haven't even seen them much. But when I get them both next time I will stop by" Sidney Jr. replied.

"And how's your relationship with their mother been like lately ? I know y'all were bumping heads a lot in the past. And I had to almost beat that ass a few times" Savannah added in.

"Savannah" !! My mother Lucy interrupted.

"I'm sorry mom, but I did a few times. I'm just being honest. The woman gets loose at the lips sometimes" Savannah replied as my mother just looked at her.

"Mom wasn't supposed to know that Savannah" my brother Sidney Jr. said shaking his head and laughing a little.

"Y'all both should be ashamed....my children. Yall know I raised y'all better than that. There's other ways to handle those type of situations. Now if a person puts their hands on you, then you have to do what you have to do. But I hope y'all wasn't looking for trouble" my mother said.

"Of course not mom. Now maybe Silas and Savannah, they're more like the troublemakers of the family. I'm the innocent one" my brother Sidney said laughing.

"Boy you better ask the good Lord for forgiveness for telling that bold face lie" my mother replied. As she had beat us both responding to him.        Page 83

Savannah and I just sat there and laughed. My mother even started laughing. We had a great time enjoying each other's company and enjoying a great dinner. After having dinner, Sidney Jr. and I went to his apartment and Savannah and our mother went to their house. We were all looking forward to seeing each other the next day.....my big day. My brother and I got back home to his apartment and played some cards and just talked about a few different things. And I felt as I was sitting there, that this was the right time to bring up our father. And him and my brother's relationship. Being that I was trying to help mend their relationship for some time now. I just had to bring the situation up.

"Sidney Jr. when was the last time you talked to Pop" ? I asked.

"It's been a while Silas. And are we going to get started on this again" ? My brother replied asking.

"Yeah why not ? Listen man. I'm getting married tomorrow bro. This is going to be one of the biggest days of my life, and I need to know if my father and brother are good. Y'all used to have a great relationship, you wanted to be just like Pop. The past is the past bro, our parents are getting old. We need to come closer as a family. I know you and Pop are both stubborn men and just alike. I'm asking you to make that first step to talk to him tomorrow. And have a great time celebrating our union. But not just for the wedding, for our family. Take the first steps to mending yall relationship is what I'm saying bro" I said.

"I guess you're right. And I do miss the old man. But you know this whole process is going to take time. It's been a long time since we actually talked one on one. But for you, and because it's your big day. Consider this your wedding gift, I'll get my sister in law Fatima something myself" Sidney Jr. replied.

"Hey if that's what you want to call it, that's fine with me bro. As long as you both are on good terms. Now let's get back to these cards and me taking your money" I said as we continued playing cards.

My brother and I stayed up til damn near midnight playing cards and drinking a few beers. Almost felt like we were in our 20's again, staying up late and all. It was good hanging out with my brother, we didn't get to hang out as much because of our schedules. So talking to him about not only our father, but life in general was interesting. Even though we were brother's, we were definitely different. I knew that Sidney Jr. was somewhat of an outcast in the family being that Savannah and I went to college. We never looked down on him for it. My brother was smart despite not going to college. College didn't make you smart, it only added to the knowledge you already had. My brother taking that step in mending his relationship with our father was great.  Page 84

Chapter Four "Still A Ways To Go"

My brother Sidney Jr. set my alarm pretty early the next morning. How early ? How about seven thirty in the morning early. And our wedding wasn't until one o clock. I got up briefly and fell right back asleep. Two hours later, I finally got up for good and got in the shower. But before I got in the shower, I passed my white tuxedo with my Peach bow tie and thought about me standing at the alter waiting for my Queen Fatima to walk down the aisle. I was truly overjoyed about marrying this woman. Fatima had been not only my fiancée over the last few years, but also my rock. We were meant for each other and we both knew it. I had went to the barbershop earlier in the week. But I had my barber come to my brother's apartment and sharpen us both up before the wedding. After that and looking in the mirror, I felt good I looked good and I smelled good.

My brother Sidney Jr. was dressed in his tuxedo. Peach jacket with Peach pants and a White shirt with a Peach tie. My brother Sidney Jr. was my best man, and my groomsmen were my friends Angelo and Mitchell. They would be dressed the same. I was already dressed and pacing back and forth in my brother's living room. Yes I was a little nervous, and I couldn't understand why. I was very sure about marrying my Queen Fatima and couldn't wait to see her walking down that aisle. I guess it was normal to be a little nervous about one of the biggest moments in your life. Another two hours had passed and my brother and I made our way to the church. We met Mitchell and Angelo over there. I was already dressed, Mitchell and Angelo were getting dressed. My brother was outside smoking a cigarette.

"So you ready? Won't be long now my friend" Mitchell said to me smiling.

"Ready as I'd ever be. Ready to be like you and Kendra, enjoying the married life" I replied.

"Marriage is a lot of work everyday, but I'm definitely glad I married my wife Kendra. She's one of the best things that's ever happened to me. Gave me my two kids man, you two will experience that one day soon. I'm just happy to be here to share this moment in time with you and Fatima. Good luck friend....to the both of you" Mitchell said embracing me with a handshake and hug.

"Thanks man, I appreciate you and Kendra for celebrating this moment with us" I replied.

Just as I said that. The Reverend came and told us it was time. My brother and I made our way back inside the church. And we came out into the sanctuary. Seeing all our guests had my stomach in somewhat of a knot. This was really it, I was finally marrying my Queen Fatima. Fatima's cousin Renee sang a beautiful song as the Bridesmaids and Groomsmen made their way down the aisle. I looked over at my mother Lucy, she was teary eyed as she sat with my nephews and nieces. Glanced over at my brother Sidney Jr. He just smiled and nodded his head in agreement. I couldn't see if my two students Deshawn and Claudia were in attendance. I'm sure they were, they were excited about coming. And lastly I looked over and located my father Sidney Jones Sr.

After my sister Savannah and my homie Angelo came down the aisle. Fatima's friend Sophia, the matron of honor made her way down the aisle. I waited patiently as everybody rose to their feet. I was about to see my bride for the very first time. As soon as the music started playing, I could feel my heart drop in my stomach. I was a little nervous, but anxious at the same time. Fatima was led down the aisle by her father Johnny. She looked absolutely amazing, I couldn't keep my eyes off of her as she came down the aisle. I had a smile on my face the whole time, as me and Fatima's eyes stayed locked on each other's. As she made her way to me and the Reverend stood at the center. I turned as me and her father had each of Fatima's arms. That is until the Reverend asked who is the man giving this woman away. Fatima's father Johnny spoke and gave me her hand. I nodded in agreement as me and her father's eyes locked. I was saying I got this from here Mr. Malone with my eyes, and he knew it. Me and Fatima's father had a great relationship.

The Reverend then began the service. We stood in front of each other, our guests, family, friends, and God. It was the biggest day of my life. And Fatima and I couldn't have been more happier. She was so beautiful, and after saying our vows. The Reverend finally gave me the green light to kiss my Bride. I took Fatima's vail and moved it over her head and gave her the sweetest kiss. As our guests, friends, and family erupted in cheers. We stood in front of our guests hand and hand in front of everyone, with our hands joined in unison. And raised them to the sky, before walking down the aisle and out of the church. We stood outside and greeted everyone, thanking them for coming and looking forward to the reception.

Our reception was at City View Loft, nice venue that was set up amazing. They treated everyone with class. We had a nice dinner and was enjoying our guests and family at the reception. And as usual. Me, my brother, and friends Mitchell and Angelo were acting up and having a good time with each other and the guests.     Page 86

"You're married now Silas, you can't go out for wings and drinks no more bro. You have to ask my sister in law Fatima before you can go anymore from now on" Sidney Jr. said laughing.

"Man you can't be serious, nothing is going to change bro. My Queen trusts me, she knows what we have. Nobody is paying you any mind Sidney Jr. " I replied laughing.

"My man Silas done finally tied the knot. Once again, congratulations my brotha. Wish you and Fatima the best" Angelo said giving me a handshake and hug.

"Thanks bro, and thanks for sharing this moment with us. Means a lot" I replied.

"Wouldn't have missed it for the world, time for me to get on the floor. That's my jam....excuse me my brotha" Angelo said grabbing his lady Lauren and heading to the dance floor.

That's when I got a tap on my shoulder, it was my two students Deshawn and Claudia. The two students that I had promised if they had the two highest quiz scores, they could attend my wedding.

"Hey Deshawn and Claudia, thanks for coming" I said.

"Thanks for inviting us Mr. Jones, this place is really nice. Are we still having a quiz this week ? I hate to ask you now, but I just had to know" Deshawn said smiling.

"Why would you ask that now Deshawn ? Oh my God. Anyway congratulations Mr. Jones" Claudia said.

"Thank you Claudia. And to answer your question Deshawn, of course we're having a quiz this week. Just like any other week. Plus you guys have to get ready for midterms soon. It's very important for you guys to be ready, we have a lot riding on this. We must improve our test scores District wide. And I'm not going to go on my honeymoon until the summer so I will have plenty of time to help you guys get ready. Well I have to mingle with some more of my guests. Thanks again for coming kids, I will see you Monday" I replied.

As I was walking through the crowd, I saw my brother and father talking. That was a welcome sight. And meant that Sidney Jr. was doing what he said he was going to do.  As I looked around the room, from my wife Fatima talking and having a good time with her sisters. To my sister Savannah and my mom sitting down eating with my nephews and nieces. Mitchell and Angelo were actually talking over by the bar. I was glad Fatima and I could bring all our family and friends together.      Page 87

After mingling with some more guests, I made my way over to my father. Who was talking to my father in law Mr. Johnny Malone at the moment. My brother had went over and mingled with other people.

"What you two old timers up to" ? I asked smiling at them both.

"We're over here doing what us old timers do, relax and talk. Congratulations son, to you and Fatima. Proud of you both" my father Sidney Sr. said shaking my hand and giving me a hug.

"Yes...congrats to you both. I'm sure you both will make each other happy. Just know it won't be easy. But if you truly love each other, you'll get through it" my father in law said.

"Indeed......it's always good to get some advice from people who've been married. Trust me, I will definitely listen to any advice you two have to give me. And thanks to the both of you for everything you've done for Fatima and I in our lives" I replied.

"Well that's good son, then you and my daughter will be fine then. If you keep listening to me that is" Mr. Malone said as we all laughed.

"That's right, don't listen to me Silas. I'm no longer married" my father Sidney Sr. added on laughing a little.

It was a joke all around. Don't know if my brother Sidney Jr. would've thought what my father said was funny. But me, him, and Mr. Malone had fun with it. After that I pulled my father to the side and asked to speak to him one on one. I had to ask him how him and my brother's conversation went. I was curious....and of course a little nosey.

"I saw you and Sidney Jr. talking, that was great to see Pop. Really was. I know how y'all both were going through what y'all were going through. I just hope everything is fine now" I said to my father sounding curious.

"Yeah we talked for a little while. Your brother always had a hard time with me and your mother splitting. You all know that. He just still held resentment towards me all those years and we never really got down to talking about it. I figured your brother would eventually get over it. As he got older, I didn't feel it was necessary to talk to him about it. And to be honest with you, we didn't really tonight. We just asked how each other were, and what we've been doing in our lives. I love all my kids, I've always have. I stayed away at times because me and your mother weren't getting along. We stayed together as long as we could hold it together. And I still love your mother and care about her. And I know she still loves me, she just has a strange way of showing it" my father said.    Page 88

"I just want us to be able to be a family again. Regardless of the past. But I'm happy that you two got to talk, that's a start. Hopefully Sidney Jr. can get passed the past. And I'm sure he will Pop. Him reaching out said a lot Pop. You know he's stubborn like you" I said.

"That's my son......and I know he is. I'm getting older and I want to spend as much time as I can with my children and grands. Happy for you and Fatima, this is really nice son. And I'll be looking forward to my grandchildren from you too" my father replied smiling and winking.

"No doubt Pop, Fatima and I got you. Glad You're here to share this with us....thanks again Pop. Love you" I said.

Around that time, it was time for me to dance with my bride Fatima. She was soooo beautiful. We joined hands and I led us to the middle of the dance floor, as we danced to our favorite song "When I Said I Do" by Chante Moore and Kenny Lattimore. As our guests watched us smiling at each other and kissing each other every once in a while. We were in marital bliss at the moment, and enjoying our day with the people that meant the most to us. After we danced, it was Fatima and her father Johnny's time to grace the floor. I watched from a far smiling and enjoying the moment. I don't believe there had been a day in my life that I had smiled more than the present. We were finally married and everything turned out perfectly. It was unbelievable.

Before I could get even more deep into thought about the day, it was time for my mother and I to dance. And boy would it be a memorable dance. I went over to my mother Lucy and took her hand and helped her to her feet. Led her to the dance floor as we danced. I was so overjoyed that I was overcome by emotion. I thought of all those times my mother was my rock. I was that happy that we both shed tears. She could feel the energy. But thank God it wasn't a bad time, and they were tears of joy. I believe my whole family felt it. Because as we were coming off the dance floor, I could see my sister Savannah and my brother Sidney Jr. a little teary eyed. After that emotional dance, it was time to turn up and start to really dance. And we had a great DJ on hand to get us started. One of Chicago's best local DJ's was in the building, and blessed us with some 90's Hip Hop and R&B.

We were all dancing. Even had a Soul Train line and all. And of course it wouldn't be a Chicago wedding reception without "stepping". Fatima had her shoes off....of course by now tired of her heels. The night wore on and it began to wind down. We all had a great time. And Fatima and I couldn't have asked for a better day. After the reception and getting home late that night. We had a conversation about it.      Page 89

"What a day and night huh Mrs. Jones" ? I said as Fatima and I lay relaxing on our couch.

"Yessss....what a day Mr. Jones. My fine ass husband" Fatima replied giving me a kiss.

"My father and Sidney Jr. got a chance to talk at our reception. While I was talking to some of our guests I saw them talking. I spoke to my father about it, and he's willing to be more understanding about how my brother felt. I mean that's all any of us can ask for, I'm just glad their on good terms now. I would've liked to have had them squash all this year's ago, but if it took our wedding to do it. Then so be it, I'm happy with that" I said.

"That's really great to hear babe. I'm glad they was able to put aside their differences, I mean they're father and son. And I know a father and son relationship is different than a mother and son relationship. Or a father and daughter relationship. Men are normally closer to their mother's" Fatima replied.

"Yeah it was really good to see. My sister Savannah was saying the same thing at the reception. And I want to tell you. You did a great job with picking out everything, because I did very little. I want to thank your sister's too, they were a big help. Filling in for where I was lacking, when I was busy with my school stuff" I said.

"Thanks babe. You know that's a woman's dream from the time we're little girls, is to one day plan our weddings. I enjoyed every minute of it. And hoping and praying to God that this is the first and last time I'm doing this" Fatima replied.

"Oh it will baby, you aint going nowhere. And neither am I" I said bringing her closer to me.

Everyone that was invited to the wedding, attended the wedding. Fatima and I appreciated each and everyone that came and shared our moment with us. I didn't invite anyone from the faculty at school to the wedding. Because basically I didnt feel like I was that connected to anyone. Or on a level with them to invite them. I felt more connected to my students, that's why Deshawn and Claudia were there.

Maybe it would take some time to get closer to some of the staff. Either way with or without them, my mission stayed the same. I was always open to developing relationships with people I didn't know. That was IF I felt connected to them on an intellectual level. Most people think educators are smart, not all are. They may be gifted and knowledgeable in their fields of teaching. But not logically smart. On a level as to want more for their students, and realize that we as a Nation are way below the line as far as education. Page 90

I knew most of the faculty were tow the line type, they wouldn't dare bend the rules. But why not ? Why not bend the rules for a greater good. The greater good was preparing these kids for life and being successful. Because I had already bent the rules by possibly increasing the budget. Most of the faculty distanced themselves from me regularly. But I seen early on that they wouldn't have my back, unless they could get something from me. I was fine being the bridge to fill the gap between the District and these kids. Because basically that's what it was. The powers that be were the people that controlled the money, the people that could really make a difference but chose not to.

If they didn't know who Silas Jones was, they would eventually. Because I was going to fight for a better educational system. That Monday after my wedding weekend, I was feeling recharged and ready to get back to my passion of teaching. I was happy to see my students. This past weekend felt like it last forever, obviously because of the moment. I had the greatest weekend of my life, but now it was back to business. My students all came in and congratulated me on my marriage. And Deshawn and Claudia were telling their classmates how nice the wedding was. After that I told them to open up their textbooks and we went over a few lessons. We needed to get on task with midterms coming up. Although it wasn't finals, they still very much mattered. And I wanted my students to do well.

As I finished my lesson and told my students to read a chapter out of their textbooks. Principal Hunt knocked on my door and asked me to come out in the hallway, he had to talk to me. I had no idea what it was about, with Principal Hunt it could've been anything. So as I stepped out in the hallway, I was curious to know what Principal Hunt wanted to talk to me about.

"So I see you made the most of your opportunity in the spotlight, when the local news was here the other day" Principal Hunt said.

"It wasn't about being in the spotlight Principal Hunt, had nothing to do with that. I was asked a question and I answered it" I replied.

"I see. Well I hope you're on the same page as the rest of us here at the school. We're all here to help these kids. And we don't need you trying to outshine the rest" Principal Hunt said.

"Outshine ? That's where you guys as a faculty and I seem to differ. I'm not here to just be the status quo, or outshine anybody. I'm here to make a difference, because the status quo hasn't worked Principal Hunt" I replied.          Page 91

"Mr. Jones it's not about how YOU think, or what you think about our educational system. We have a curriculum to follow in this District and being that you work in this District. That means you should follow them also" Principal Hunt said.

"I do follow the rules. And my thoughts on education when a person asks me I must answer them honestly. As honest as I can. I do work in this District, but that doesn't mean I agree with everything this District does. This country for that matter. I do everything I'm told within the rules of the District. I have respected you as one of the leaders within this District. And I haven't ever crossed you. Challenged you....yes. But I haven't crossed you. See you and most people that have been in this District has settled for the norm for so many years. And the norm has been reflected in these kid's grades and test scores. You hired me to do a job, and I'm doing it. I'm doing it in a way, that's away from the norm. And it will eventually pay dividends. I promise you that. That's why I was willing to put my paycheck on the line for those textbooks. To prove to you and everyone else. That I could improve our students grades and test scores with better resources for them to learn" I replied.

"I understand that Mr. Jones, just be careful. I have people over my head that calls the shots. Especially when it comes to funding" Principal Hunt said before walking away.

I knew Principal Hunt was a puppet, and his strings were getting pulled by the District. But as long I showed numbers of improvement throughout my students, he couldn't touch me. I was confident that those numbers would be where they needed to be by midterms and finals. It would be a challenge for me as a teacher to get my students on par with what was ahead of them. Getting them to buy into the lesson plans and keeping them interested in learning. That was all on me, and I was more than up for the challenge. After talking to Principal Hunt, I went back inside my classroom and finished teaching my class. My students had finished reading what I had them read and by that time there was little time left in the period.

After my students left after class, I sat at my desk to do some paperwork. It was something I did often after class. I liked to be ahead of the game as the next day was approaching. I had a routine down and I stuck to it. It worked good for me from day one. I hadn't been in the Teachers Lounge in a while, so as I was leaving I decided to stop in there. Miss Summers, Mrs. Williams, and a few other teachers were there.

"Hey there, there goes the movie star. Getting interviewed by the local news and all. Hello Mr. Jones" Miss Summers said as I entered the Teachers Lounge.

"Far from a superstar or movie star. But hello Miss Summers. How are you" ? I asked.

"I'm fine. Back in the Teacher's Lounge huh ? I thought you didn't like coming in here. How do you think your students will do with Midterms coming up" ? She asked.

"My students will be ready. I decided to stop in here, it's been a while since I was in here last. Plus I wanted some coffee" I replied.

"Well it's good to see you" Miss Summers said.

"Thanks Ms. Summers, good to see you too. And good luck on Midterms coming up in your class" I replied before exiting the Teachers Lounge.

I knew that some of the teachers in my school envied me and had some sort of jealousy when it came to me. Because I got things done, and of course the textbook legend. The fact that my class was thee only class to receive new textbooks, naturally rubbed some fellow teachers the wrong way. I knew that would stick with me for the rest of the year, if not my whole teaching career. When anyone mentioned Silas Jones, me and those textbooks were connected. I was ok with that, because if it helped improve my students grades and test scores. It was all worth it. But they hadn't seen anything yet. I was going to do more than just ask for new textbooks. I wanted to change part of the structure of education in this country. I went home that night and did some research, read a little and thought a lot about my next move. My next move meaning, what challenge would I present to my District next. The textbooks were just the beginning. It was way bigger than that, and I was about to prove it.

As a class we had a week before Midterms, and my job was to prepare my students for just that. I continued having quizzes each Friday, to keep my students sharp. I knew it would take time for my students to get used to the way I taught. And that was a good thing.

Because the school's test scores over the last few years before I arrived were really bad. It wasn't about me, it was about doing something different to help these students improve. We all knew how the country viewed inner city schools. Everything was set up for us all to fail. But if we had evidence that change to our educational system, would improve our city schools for the better. They couldn't deny us funding to make even more improvements. That was the overall goal. Not really changing the perception of inner city schools, because some people were ignorant and going to think what they wanted to think. We wanted to improve our school system for US. To give US better opportunities in the world. In any inner city in America, we all knew the odds were stacked against us. But it would never stop us from becoming great. I believed in all my students that wanted to learn, and I was going to fight for each and everyone of them. If it took everything I had inside of me.     Page 93

The next day came and I arrived early in my classroom like I do most days. I always liked to get an early start. So I got my lesson plan in order and wrote a few things on the blackboard before my students arrived. My students came in the classroom energetic as always. I loved the energy they always had, it really made me want to teach.

"Ok settle down class. We have Midterms in less than a week and we need to be prepared and do well. We will start with our lesson plan for today, I suggest you all take notes each day this week leading up to our Friday quiz. You can then use these notes to study for your Midterms next week. So let's get down to business" I said as I officially started class with my lesson plan.

After going through class that day, I was hopeful by the end of the week to have all my students ready for Midterms next week.

Deshawn and Claudia were still my top two students. I was especially proud of Deshawn, after being transferred into my class. He had came in my class as a self entitled student athlete. I was happy to say that now he was a hard working student athlete that didn't take anything for granted. He worked just as hard, if not harder than the rest of my students. And it showed in his grades. So after class later that day, I pulled him aside to let him know just how proud I was of him.

"What's going on Deshawn ? I pulled you aside to tell you that I'm proud of the progress you've made in my class. You're doing really well, keep up the good work" I said.

"Thanks Mr. Jones. It hasn't been easy with the distractions at home. But I'm doing my best. To be honest with you, I don't know how much longer things will be good. My brother isn't listening to no one. I've roughed him up a few times trying to get through to him. It hasn't worked....nothing has worked" Deshawn replied sounding down.

"Son I've always been real with you, and I'm not going to stop now. Your brother is old enough to know right from wrong. I know that you're concerned and I know your mother is concerned. But you can't ruin your future trying to keep your brother out the streets. All you can realistically do is pray for him, pray that he changes for the better. I know that's a hard thing to do, let go of a loved one that is headed in the wrong direction. But Deshawn you have so much going for yourself, so much potential. You have a chance to get you and your family out of the neighborhood and area that you're in. That's if you're successful with your education more than anything. That degree you can fall back on if your basketball career doesn't work out. Not saying that it won't, I seen you play and you're very talented. But it starts here Deshawn, don't let the streets or nobody ruin that for you. That includes family" I said to him.

"I understand what you're saying Mr. Jones. I don't know if I can just leave my brother behind like that. My mother counts on me to look after him. I will do the best I can, I have to get going Mr. Jones" Deshawn replied leaving.

I knew a lot of kids like Deshawn, who I grew up with on da South Side. I was one of them kids growing up. But with me it was my older brother Sidney Jr. who was in the streets for a while. Yes I worried about him too, but I couldn't stop my life because of it. My mother wouldn't let me. No matter what my brother was doing, she made sure that I kept my focus on my education. Because she knew that I loved learning. The point I was trying to make to Deshawn was, no matter what him or his mother did. It ultimately was up to his brother to leave the streets alone. Deshawn had so much potential, I didn't want to see him waste it. Not even for his brother. I worried about Deshawn more than I worried about any of my other students. Because I knew his situation.

Later on that night at dinner. Fatima and I had our usual conversation about work and our day's. While enjoying a quiet evening at home

"So Midterms are coming up. I know your students are ready, are you excited about them" ? Fatima asked.

"I've done everything possible to make sure they're ready. I've been going over things that will be on the Midterms with them this week. Having them take notes. And of course we have our weekly quiz on Friday" I replied.

"They're blessed, they're getting taught by the best teacher on the Planet" Fatima said smiling and giving me a kiss.

"Thanks my Queen. So how's things going at your job Mrs. Jones"? I replied asking.

"Everything is ok. I mean in my profession days could be up and down at the drop of a dime. Lately things have been steady" Fatima replied finishing her dinner.

Fatima and I always had good conversation. We were newlyweds, but you couldn't tell. Because we were best friends and lover's before we even got married. So not much changed in that sense. We were just now officially married with the license. Which felt great because I loved saying Mrs. Fatima Jones. That meant we were really official. After having dinner, we relaxed and watched some TV. In between I was looking at a few papers I had to look over. There were times I was at home and wanted to do some type of school work. From grading papers to looking over lesson plans. It was one of those nights, and my wife knew about those nights. And she let me be me. It was nothing about her, she knew my passion and she let me give it life.     Page 95

The next day came and it was a day closer to Midterms. The clock was ticking and I was up for the challenge to have my students ready for them. As I was sitting at my desk, Mrs. Williams walked by my class and asked to speak with me. Of course my doors were always open to any of the faculty. So as Mrs. Williams entered my classroom, I didn't necessarily know what she wanted to talk about. But I was ready for whatever.

"Hello Mrs. Williams how may I help you"? I asked sitting at my desk.

"I just wanted to say that I'm happy with the job you're doing with Deshawn, he seems to be really focused on his school work. And I'm sorry if it seemed like we got off on the wrong foot when I first approached you about him" Mrs. Williams replied.

"It's cool Mrs. Williams I didn't take it personally, and I know you meant well. You just misled me when it came to just how close you were to him. I know you're related to him by marriage, but you have little to do with his life. And I wish you would've told me that before I spoke to him. Because Deshawn did tell me" I said.

"I care about Deshawn....I really do. And that's not really for you to judge how close I am with him or not. The point is I care for his overall being, that's why I came to you about him. I want him to do well" Mrs. Williams replied.

"I understand Mrs. Williams. Have a great day, I have to start class soon" I said.

"Good day to you too Mr. Jones" Mrs. Williams replied walking away.

It was clear that Mrs. Williams and I agreed to disagree, when it came to Deshawn. On the surface it didn't seem like Mrs. Williams and her husband were that close to Deshawn. Deshawn and his mother both told me they weren't. They both told me that Mr. and Mrs. Williams had very little to do with Deshawn and his siblings. One would think Mrs. Williams interest in Deshawn had more to do with his potential earning power if he made it pro. There was no doubt that he was a very talented High School basketball player. And was sought after by every major college in the country. The only issue with Deshawn was making sure he kept his focus throughout his distractions at home. He and his mother worried a lot about Deshawn's little brother Corey being in the streets of Chicago.

As much as I tried to keep him focused on himself and his goals. I knew deep down inside that he was worried about his brother. And that's natural. I didn't tell him not to. I just didn't want him to waste a golden opportunity to potentially better his family. And have a bright future. He was a smart kid, and being Black in America is hell. Page 96

There wasn't a whole lot of opportunities for young Black Men in this country, so I wanted Deshawn to reach his full potential. My students made their way into class a few minutes after Mrs. Williams exited. And I welcomed them with open arms. I was eager to teach today, and with Midterms coming up I was really excited. Excited for my students. I really felt since I had arrived up until this point, that I had prepared my students for the moment they were about to face. Today I would continue to prepare them. I had a lesson plan that would go over some of the things that were going to be on the test. When I started class, I noticed that Deshawn was absent. It caught me off guard at first. Because since Deshawn had been transferred to my class, his attendance was perfect. He hadn't missed a day in my class. I had to continue teaching, and just hoped he and his family were Ok.

Class ended that day with no trace of Deshawn. I even asked Claudia had she seen or heard from him, she said she hadn't. After class ended I sat at my desk and finished up some paperwork I had. After that my day was over and I was ready to head out the door. Eager to get home to my wife. We lived for those hard working days that turned to great nights between us. And this particular night I was preparing dinner for my wife and I. Decided to cook some Barbecue Ribs Mac N Cheese and some Corn On a Cobb. It was one of our favorite meals. I had gotten home before Fatima so I could prepare dinner for us. While I was preparing dinner, I couldn't help but think about Deshawn. I wasn't going to call his home just yet. Especially after I had called before, and his mother wasn't too happy about it. Either way, if I had to call again I would. I know Deshawn wanted more for himself and his family.

But for now I was ready to enjoy another night at home, and dinner with my wife. Fatima got home just as I was finishing up dinner. She entered our home looking tired after another long day. I immediately went over to her and greeted her. I grabbed her briefcase and took her coat off. As she walked in the kitchen and immediately smelled the food.

"Oh my God babe, it smells soo good in here. I can smell those Ribs cooking....ummmm" Fatima said opening the oven and checking out the Ribs.

"You know your husband is nice in the kitchen. So how was your day my love" ? I asked.

"Tiring long day as usual. But smelling these Ribs have woke me up. Thanks to my husband" Fatima replied giving me a hug and kiss.

"Ok well let's eat beautiful" I said after serving her and myself food.

"So how's things going at school ? Are the kids excited about this upcoming week" ? Fatima asked.

"Yeah they have been, they've gotten more excited as it's approaching. But I'm more concerned about the fact Deshawn didn't show up to class today. I mean it's just a day, but it's unlike him to miss class. Every since he's been in my class, he's never missed. Just seems strange. But I will wait another day before I call" I replied.

"You did say he was having some issues with his little brother right" ? Fatima asked.

"Yeah that's what worries me. His brother be in the streets. Deshawn is street smart and all, but that isn't the life for him. He has way too much potential for that. I just hope he doesn't make a bad decision because of his brother. It's already hard out here for us Black Men already. We hardly get any opportunities, and Deshawn could have anything he wants if he keeps his head on straight. He knows it starts in that classroom. He's already a great talent on the court" I replied.

"Well as much as you want him to succeed, that's out of your hands once he leaves your classroom. All you can do is your part. He knows he has a great role model and male figure in you. He knows you care Silas.....he knows. You just have to let things work itself out" Fatima said.

"You're probably right. If he doesn't show up tomorrow, then I'll call and see where he is" I replied.

As always a great conversation with my wife. She not only supported my passion of teaching, but she was interested and knew things about my profession. We listened to each other about our respective days. I shared the same interest about her profession. That meant a lot when it came to spending the rest of your life with someone. I couldn't ask for a better person to be my life partner than Fatima.

The next day would be Friday, and our weekly quiz. But this wasn't just no ordinary Friday. This was the Friday before Midterms. It was very important that my students do well on this quiz, heading into Midterms on Monday. After getting up early like I normally do, I made my way to school. Entered my classroom and prepared to get my quizzes ready to hand out. I was really hoping to see Deshawn here today because it was important for him to be there. So I was hoping for the best. Twenty minutes later my students started to make their way into my classroom. I watched one by one as they entered. Claudia, one of my top students. Was amongst the students that were making their way to their seats. I waited as they all found their seats, and I was about to start class with no Deshawn in sight.          Page 98

I had to start class regardless of him not being there, and I did. I taught the kids that were in attendance. And I had a stern message to them before I had even got started.

"Class this is not only Friday the day of our weekly quiz, but this is the last day before the first phase of our testing. Important testing. As you all know we have Midterms next week. This is your moment of truth and your time to shine. Starting with this quiz, which is a mixture of all the things we've learned thus far. I'm confident and have faith in everyone of you doing well. Let's concentrate and do our best. This quiz is the start, let's get to work" I said as I passed out the quizzes and my students got started.

I sat quietly at my desk and let my students focus on their quizzes. As my students were taking their quizzes, I was reading a local Chicago paper and reading about the many shootings that happened the previous night and over the weekend. That was a daily thing, the shootings. Being from Chicago, sadly to say you were used to it. Picking up a local paper in Chicago and reading that they weren't any shootings the previous night would be a shock to our system. Not that we wouldn't want that as Chicago natives. Most people from Chicago wanted peace within the city and community. But we also knew how dangerous the city was. And I feared that for some of my students. I knew some would fall victim to the streets. I tried my best to keep all my students focused and off the streets. But I knew in reality that I wasn't with my students every minute of the day. I only had them in my class for about forty minutes a day, five days a week. And I used that time wisely. I had hoped that I made enough impact on my students, that my words held weight. Only time would tell if I really did.

I let my students take their time on their quizzes this particular Friday, as opposed to a normal Friday when they were timed. I really wanted them to focus their minds on not only the quiz, but on Monday also. So after they took their quizzes, the rest of class I instructed them to look over their notes. Monday morning would be huge. So at the end of class I had a clear message for my students. Study hard this weekend, and come Monday morning. Be prepared to use their minds for Midterms. After my students left that day, I felt real confident that they were more than ready to do well on their Midterms.

As I was leaving I thought about Deshawn, and wondered if there was something terribly wrong. He had missed his second consecutive day. Not only that, he missed his weekly quiz the Friday before Midterms. Which was very important for preparations before the tests. I had to pay a visit to his home to see if he was ok. I knew once again I was taking a chance, especially the way his mother was the first time I called. But it didn't matter to me at that point. I needed to know if he was good or not. So I left school that day en route to Deshawn's home on da South Side.     Page 99

Deshawn lived in the Fuller Park section of da South Side of Chicago. A very dangerous area, but a place I had been before. When we were younger, our parents had some friends who lived out there. It was dangerous then, but a lot worse now. Either way, I needed to see how he was. So I finally made my way to his home and knocked on the door. Amid numerous people outside doing anything from shooting dice, to playing basketball on make shift baskets from milk crates. Kids were out playing despite it being basically Winter time. It was definitely cold. And as I approached Deshawn's house and knocked on the door, a young man answered which I believe was Deshawn's little brother Corey.

"Who are you ? And what do you want" ? The kid said as he stood in the door.

"Hello I'm Silas Jones, Deshawn's History Teacher. Is he home" ? I replied asking.

"What the fuck do you want with my brother" ? The kid asked looking agitated.

Just then Deshawn came from behind the kid and saw me. He then told the kid to go back in the house as he came to the door.

"What's going on Mr. Jones. What are you doing here" ? Deshawn asked.

"Deshawn you haven't been to class the last two days. You missed the weekly quiz today, which is important to your preparations for Midterms. What's going on Deshawn ? Are you ok" ? I replied asking.

"I'm good. Just been dealing with some family stuff. You got some balls coming to this neighborhood Mr. Jones. You know how crazy it is out here" ? Deshawn said.

"Yeah I know. Deshawn I'm from da South Side, I know all these neighborhoods. And the point is, your falling behind at a crucial time of the year. This will certainly effect your grades. You have to be there Monday to take your Midterms. Since I know your situation, I brought your quiz with me. And here are some notes to study for your Midterms. Make sure you study, and be there Monday to take your Midterms Deshawn. Don't waste your future for no one, not even your family. You hear me ? Don't waste your future for no one....not even FAMILY" I replied walking away and back to my car. And then left.

Deshawn just stood there with everything I gave him in his hand. I believed he would listen to what I told him. I understood that he was very much influenced by his family. And they had somewhat of a hold on him. But more than that, I know he wanted better. And to get out of Fuller Park. We both knew how dangerous it was and how it was influencing his brother. I'm sure that was his little brother Corey who answered the door. I assumed his mother was working. Either way I was glad I talked to him.   Page 100

Later that night I got a call from Mitchell, he wanted to know if I wanted to shoot some pool. I was a little tired after the twenty three minute drive from Fuller Park back to the Near West Side section of Chicago where Fatima and I resided. But it was Friday night, I figured why not. So I told Mitchell we could meet up and shoot some pool.

After getting home taking a shower and a little nap. I met up with Mitchell at our usual spot.

"So what's been going on ? How's teaching on the High School level" ? Mitchell asked.

"Its kind of hectic right now with Midterms coming up on Monday. Had to go to Fuller Park to check on one of my students. You know Deshawn Williams. Great basketball talent, and a smart kid. But he's been dealing with some family issues. His little brother is heavy in the streets, and he worries a lot about him. His mother works a lot, and I believe she wants the best for him. She just has her hand's full. A single mother you know.....I can relate to that a little. After my parent's split, it just being my siblings and I. We were older at that time, but still home. My brother moved out the following year and I was about to go to college. I just hate to see this kid waste his potential because of his circumstances. Too many black men have that happen to them, we have to change that trend man" I said.

"Definitely. And him coming from where he comes from, it's rough. I know he wants to get out of there. Hopefully you going to his neighborhood will make him realize just how serious this is" Mitchell said.

"Yeah he was surprised, told me I had balls to come to Fuller Park. I told him I'm from da South Side. And I had been in that neighborhood when I was a kid" I replied.

Mitchell and I continued to shoot pool and chop it up about any and everything. It was always cool to hang out with Mitchell. He was a smart man and a very successful businessman. He reminded me of the other side of where I came from. He was a role model. He was also very active in church. One of the leaders in our Men's Group at church. He was a religious man, but not too religious where he associated everything with religion. He knew reality being from the West Side of Chicago. That's why him and I got along so well. Plus his wife Kendra and my wife Fatima became pretty good friends.

Matter of fact it had been a while since Fatima and I had been to our church. Mitchell had reminded. So I would definitely mention it to Fatima. I'm sure Fatima would be thrilled to go. We hadn't been since we had gotten married. It was a fun night shooting pool with Mitchell. Afterwards I returned home and called it a night.    Page 101

Two days later Fatima and I were in our church enjoying this Sunday's church service. We both enjoyed the Pastor's sermons, he was a Pastor that wasn't too much older than us. We felt like he could relate to us both better. As I said before, Mitchell Bates my good friend held a pretty important position in the church and was a leader in our Men's Group. He also was a Deacon in the church and stood next to the Pastor before his sermons. We once again enjoyed a great church service and afterwards returned home. My wife Fatima was cooking as I enjoyed the Bears game. We were having my boy Angelo and his lady Lauren over for dinner today. After about fifteen minutes, Angelo and Lauren had arrived. Fatima and I greeted them. Angelo and I sat in the living room watching the game. While Fatima and Lauren were in the kitchen.

"So what's going on my brotha Silas" ? Angelo asked.

"Nothing much man. Fatima and I went to church today. Came home and waited on y'all. Big day tomorrow, Midterms. How's things going with you bro ? You want a beer"? I replied.

"Same ole same Silas, work is work man. About to go on vacation soon. Lauren and I are going to Jamaica for a week, can't wait. And hell yeah I'll take a beer" Angelo said.

"Nice....yeah I can't wait til the summer. Fatima and I will finally go on our honeymoon to Punta Cuna. I hope y'all enjoy y'all selves.

For now everything is riding on these Midterms man. Hoping my students do well, I did my best to prepare them" I said.

"As long as you know you did, that's all that matters. I'm sure they'll do well, I got faith in you bro. I heard you was on TV too. Just in the short time you've been at that school, you've made an impact. A positive impact. Getting those kids new textbooks, that's huge. Just keep building towards your goal, make your vision become a reality. I've known you all my life damn near, you always was a leader" Angelo said.

"Thanks bro, I appreciate you brother" I replied.

Angelo and I had a unique and different friendship than Mitchell and I. Just because Angelo knew me a lot longer. Angelo has been around since the beginning, us both being born and raised on da South Side. Angelo was the other brother I had besides my own brother Sidney Jr. One thing was always true, we both supported each other in our respective careers. We both came from nothing, and were both successful in our own right. And whenever we were together, we always chopped it up about the old days growing up in da South Side. It was always a good time, and it was a pleasure having Angelo and Lauren over our house for dinner on this Sunday. Page 102

After dinner was served, all four of us sat down and enjoyed the delicious meal my wife Fatima prepared. And of course always a fun and interesting conversation between us.

"Angelo told me that you two are going to Jamaica soon for a week. I can't wait til the summer and Fatima and I finally go on our honeymoon to Punta Cuna" I said smiling.

"Yes and I heard, she told me. I heard Punta Cuna is beautiful. Angelo and I have to get there one day. But yes we're definitely excited about our vacation, this is actually the second time we've been to Jamaica. Still exciting though" Lauren said.

"Yes I would love to go to Jamaica. We picked Punta Cuna after looking at pictures from there out of a catalog with our Travel Agent. We figured we'll get to Jamaica one day too. I'm just ready to get my tan on girl....well a little at least" Fatima said smiling.

"I'm sure after this year and dealing with them High School kids, my boy Silas will be more than ready for that honeymoon" Angelo said as we all laughed.

"Yep...you got that right bro" I agreed as we all continued to laugh and enjoy each other's company.

We continued to talk after we finished dinner. Sat and had some wine and just talked about our lives and what was currently going on in all of them. That's how we were with our friends, they understood us because they knew us. They had met us in the dating phase, seen us in our relationship. And now seeing us as a newly married couple. That was the main reasons Angelo and Lauren, as well as Mitchell and Kendra were our close friends. Both these couples shared a lot of special moments with Fatima and I, and that meant a lot to the both of us.

"Good luck on Midterms this week bro" Angelo said.

"Thanks bro. Had to go to Fuller Park to see what was going on with Deshawn. First time I been over there since we was kids. He had missed two days of class, missed his quiz. So I took his quiz and work over there. I can understand what he's going through with his family. His mother works a lot and he has to look after his younger siblings. But the kid is so talented and smart. It would be a damn shame for me to watch him waste it all, even for his family" I replied.

"Typical story for many kids growing up in inner cities across this country. And we both know how rough Fuller Park is. Just remain hopeful that he understands how talented and smart he is. Maybe once he realizes that, he will get more focused on making that happen for him and his family" Angelo said.     Page 103

"I really hope he does realize it, because he's came a long way since the beginning of the year. I guess I will see if he's there Monday. Anyway man, y'all enjoy y'all vacation. I'm sure it's going to be a great time" I said as Angelo and Lauren were about to leave.

Another great evening with some of our good friends. After Angelo and Lauren left, I helped my wife clean up the kitchen and we relaxed the rest of the night. Tomorrow was going to be a huge day. Midterms were the start of my journey and mission for a better education. My students doing well on their Midterms meant everything to me right now. It wasn't about me, never was. It was about someone stepping up and showing the country and powers that be. That if we put our efforts and finances in education for ALL, we would have a better and smarter world. Less crime and poverty. If we really believed that education was the key, we should act like it. Find ways to improve it. It was just my passion to be one of those people to lead the fight.

I knew what education meant to my siblings and my close friends. I knew if I didn't have an education and went to the Marines, I probably would've been dead or in jail. It was just a fact. I was Deshawn Williams when I was younger growing up on da South Side. That's why I related so much to him. I got up earlier than I did on a normal Monday morning. I was anxious I guess, and couldn't hardly sleep the night before. And I wasn't even taking the test. Regardless I got up and showered, got dressed and made myself some coffee. My wife had also got up a little after me, she knew how much this day meant to me. As she entered the kitchen.

"Good morning babe, and good luck today. Your students are going to be fine. They will do well, I have faith. And I know you do too, I love you" Fatima said giving me a hug and kiss.

"Thanks beautiful, love you too. And I appreciate you" I replied before walking out of the door and heading to school.

The drive over to the school, I felt good. I felt good for my students, and I was really hoping to see Deshawn in class today. So as I pulled up to the school I was also feeling optimistic about it too. I had faith that I would see Deshawn today and all my students would do well. Entering the school and getting to my classroom, I sat down at my desk and the Midterms were already on my desk. I just sat and looked at them for a little before I even picked them up. I just wanted to let it sink in, and enjoy this first big moment for me as a teacher. After doing that, I picked the tests up and carefully passed them out. Putting them on every students desk, so when they arrived they could get started right away.

Ten minutes later my students made their way into class. Their Midterms were already on their desks. I didn't say a word. They knew once they came through that door that day. It was time to get down to business. And that's exactly what they did, I was impressed. And happy to say that Deshawn made it to class, with his quiz from Friday in hand and his other work.

I let my students get to work while I just paced around the classroom watching them take their Midterms. It was complete silence in the classroom for the first time this year, that showed me that my students were focused on their tests. I had a great feeling about today. As they continued taking their tests I went and sat down at my desk. It would take each student the entire period to complete their tests. I just sat patiently and waited for them to finish. As the day wore on, the tension eased up a bit. As each student finished their tests before their classmates, they were to continue sitting there quietly until their classmates finished.

After all this particular class had finished their Midterms. I collected each test and my students were dismissed to their other classes, to take their other Midterms in those respective classes. There would be a difference with Midterms, a computer would grade each of them. Unlike quiz and tests within the classroom that us teachers graded. So in a sense it was easier and quicker to find out the results. After all my classes had completed their tests, and what seemed like an incredibly long day. I was a little exhausted, I hadn't gotten much sleep the night before. I was really anxious about the whole experience. My first experience as a teacher during Midterms, I could only imagine how I would be once Finals got here. It was just an exciting time.

Later that day it would get even better, as I got home and my wife Fatima was home already. I was surprised that she had got home earlier than me. I mean there were times she did, but most times she got home after me. Either way, I was glad to see her.

"Hey baby, you home early today huh" ? I said coming in the door and giving my wife a kiss and hug.

"Yes, wasn't feeling good so I came home" Fatima replied.

"Oh....really? Wow sorry to hear that baby. You need me to get you some soup or something? Medicine? What's wrong" ? I asked feeling concerned.

"Well I really don't feel like eating anything right now, but maybe later. I've been especially sick in the morning" Fatima said before I quickly interrupted her.

"Say what ? In the morning ? So you telling me that ....."? I asked sounding excited.

"Yes babe, I believe I'm pregnant....but. I took one pregnancy test, and it came out positive. So I'm going to make a doctors appointment first before we really know if its official" Fatima replied.

"Wow.....I'm trying to hold my excitement for when it's official, but I don't know if I can. This is so great baby. With Midterms here and all too, and now we may have a new addition to our family. Starting our family, this is priceless" I said with the biggest smile on my face.

I was very happy to hear that Fatima may be pregnant. We definitely wanted children, we just wanted to wait until after we got married. Fatima loved her career and I loved mines, but we both understood that our lives would change once we were married. And once we decided to start a family. We both knew it was only a matter of time. It would be a welcomed sight, and our families would absolutely be overjoyed. For now I would contain my excitement for the official announcement. Since Fatima wasn't feeling that well, I decided to eat something light myself. We relaxed that night and watched some TV. The next day I would learn my students Midterm results. That alone had me excited about getting to school that next morning. As usual I got up early and got myself together with my usual cup of coffee. Glanced at the local paper to see the usual and consistent violence that plagued the city.

Just shook my head and grabbed my briefcase, then headed out the door. The whole drive over to school I thought about being a father. Going through the whole process. I had nephews and nieces, and my friends had kids. But for us this would be our first experience as parents and having our own baby. But I had to keep that in the back of my mind for now. At the moment I was curious to see the results of the Midterms. And I was actually hoping they would be on my desk waiting for me when I entered my classroom. After the short drive, I was finally at school. Got out of my car and headed to my classroom. As I got in my classroom and turned on the lights. I noticed my graded midterms were on my desk like I had hoped. All I could do was smile as I sat down and immediately went through them.

Looking through them, each test result and smiling all the while. I was loving the results I was seeing. And very proud of my students. Most of my students had passed their Midterms. And even some of my students that were at the bottom of my classes did better than expected on the tests. I was proud of their efforts.     Page 106

I took my time to go through each test, after going through each test. I was reassured how well my students did. And I couldn't wait until they all got there so I could give them the good news. I'm sure they would be just as excited as I am. I know all my students wanted to do well, not just for me but themselves. Because that's what it was all about. Fifteen minutes went by and my students started to make their way into my classroom. I waited until all of my students were in class and seated, and then I got their attention.

"Ok young men and ladies, let's settle down. I have a huge announcement concerning all of your Midterms. I have the results" I said as my students started cheering.

"I know we did well Mr. Jones, I know we did. We worked really hard and studied hard" my student Claudia said.

"Oh.... is that so ? Well I hope you all studied hard because I definitely prepared you all for this moment. So without further a do, I will pass out your Midterms with your grades on them. I will say as a class we did really well, and I'm very proud of you all for your efforts. This is just the beginning, as you all know we still have Finals at the end of the year" I said passing out their Midterms.

As my students got their Midterm results you could hear each reaction, they were mostly happy and excited. Some students felt they could've done better. I reminded them that they still had a chance to do better on their Finals later in the year. But in the meantime they had to do well in class. And do well on my weekly quizzes leading up to the Finals. There had to be optimism in my student's minds. This was the best that this school had done on Midterms in quite some time. I had did my research on previous years test scores for Midterms and Finals. As soon as I got the job there, I was able to look it up. I was just curious like I always am. My mind was always starving for knowledge of any kind. So it was just me, many of times I would be at home and research something I was interested in knowing. There was no doubt I would research the school I was employed at.

"As you all can see, you all did very well on your Midterms. And once again I want to say how proud I am of all of you. But this doesn't mean we can't strive to do even better on your Finals later this year. We will get better, it's my job to make sure that happens.

How do we get better? Well we'll start by going over our lesson plan everyday and complete our lessons. Continue to take our quizzes each Friday. That will prepare us for Finals like they did for Midterms. So today we are going to celebrate how well you all did by having a day of just celebrating. I have some authentic Chicago Deep Dish Pizza on the way and a cake. Enjoy students, you guys deserve it" I said as the pizzas were delivered. Along with the cake.
Page 107

I didn't tell anyone that I was surprising my students with Chicago's finest Deep Dish Pizzas. And a nicely decorated and catered cake. It was my appreciation for them buying into and being receptive to my plan on a better education for them. And the many that would come after them. And my students loved me for it. I wanted to show them that I was not only stern on discipline when it came to learning. But I was also appreciative of their efforts and rewarded them. We had a great time that day, and in a sense I gave my students a break from actually working. All we did was celebrate that day.

As the day ended I got a text from my wife Fatima. She said that she had a doctors appointment scheduled for today. I was excited to hear that. It would be icing on the cake of an already great day celebrating with my students. So after the day ended at school, Fatima and I found ourselves at the doctors office. As he confirmed what Fatima had already thought after taking a pregnancy test prior to the doctors visit. She was pregnant, about six weeks pregnant. We both were of course very happy. After leaving the doctors appointment, I convinced Fatima that we had to drive to my mother's to give her the news. And thats exactly what we did. On the drive over we were all smiles. I couldn't wait to tell my mother and sister. My whole family for that matter.

So as I got to my mother and sister's home, I opened the door for Fatima to get out. And we rung the door bell and my mother answered.

"Hey y'all, how y'all doing? Come on in" my mother Lucy said letting us in the door as Fatima and I gave her a hug and kiss.

"Hey momma, we've been good. Where's Savannah" ? I replied asking.

"She's in the kitchen. Savannah" !! My mother said calling my sister as we made our way to the kitchen.

We got in the kitchen and my sister was in there sitting down reading this magazine and having her dinner.

"I'm here mom. Hey Silas and Fatima, how y'all doing" ? She asked as we came in the kitchen.

"We're good sis. We came by to give y'all the good news. Fatima is pregnant, we're expecting our first child" I said proudly.

"Awwwww....that's so nice. Congrats bro and sis, love you guys. So happy for the both of you. You both are going to be great parents. So excited for yall" my sister Savannah said.
Page 108

"Thanks Savannah, and thanks Mrs. Jones. I told Silas the other day because I took a pregnancy test. It came out positive, but I still wanted to make a doctors appointment. Y'all know he wanted to tell everybody, but I made him wait until we went to the doctors appointment to make it official" Fatima said as my mother and sister laughed.

"I bet he did, I can only imagine how excited he was. Bro you know you have to wait until us women make it official before you start bragging soon to be daddy" Savannah said messing with me smiling.

"Hey....as a first time father, y'all should know I'm going to scream that to the world. My wife is pregnant, and I couldn't be any happier. I will be at every doctor's appointment and visit. I've dreamt about this moment all my life.....we both have. It's an exciting time. And I have some more good news, while I have the three most important women in my life with me right now. It couldn't be a better time. I'm proud to say that my students did well on their Midterms. Most of my students passed the test. I believe for the first time in many years" I said sounding proud.

"That's great Silas, to God be the glory. I knew you were a leader since you were a kid, I'm proud of you son" my mother Lucy said giving me a hug and kiss.

"Thanks momma, means a lot. And I love you more" I replied.

"Yes, very proud of you bro. I remember you telling me a while back when you were on the job hunt that you could feel the place where you felt you fit. I guess your feeling was right on. Happy for you bro, love you too" Savannah said giving me a hug.

"Thanks sis, love you" I replied.

"Yes my wonderful husband told me the news before we came over here. Well some of it. Proud of you baby, I told you they were going to do well" Fatima said smiling as she hugged me.

It was a great time sharing my new accomplishments with the three women who meant the most to me in my life. With the baby officially now on the way, and everything slowly going the way I had envisioned at school. Things were really falling into place. Upon

Fatima's request I didn't tell anyone besides us telling my mother and sister. They were the first two people that knew besides us. And we were both happy with that. After leaving my mother and sister's home. Fatima and I would visit her parents that lived on the North Side. Which was also where my father lived. My father lived in the Wicker Park section of the city on da North Side. Fatima's parents lived in Rogers Park, and that was where we were headed. We were on a tour to tell our loved ones.

As we got to Fatima's parents home in Rogers Park, they both greeted us with hugs and handshakes. It was always good to see Mr. And Mrs. Malone. Johnny and Frances Malone raised their three daughters. Mia, Destiny, and Fatima in the Rogers Park neighborhood and still lived in the same house til this day.

"Fatima and I have some great news to share with you Mr. And Mrs. Malone. We're expecting our first child, Fatima's pregnant" I said as we both smiled.

"Well congratulations you two, that's wonderful. Our baby girl is finally having a child of her own. Well you're a great aunt to your nieces and nephews, I'm sure you're going to be a great mother baby. So happy for you and Silas" Mrs. Malone said.

"Thanks Mom, we're really excited. So what do you think Dad ? You're going to be a grandfather again" Fatima said smiling.

"Yes I am baby girl, I'm happy for you two" Mr. Malone replied hugging his daughter.

Johnny and I had a great relationship, I truly loved and respected my father in law. In part because like me, he served in the United States Marine Corp. That was something we both had in common and could relate to. He had many stories for me and I had many stories for him. With that being said, Fatima went in the kitchen with her mother Frances. And my father in law and I preceded to head down into his man cave. Oh yes, my father in law had a man cave. Equipped with every Chicago Pro Sports team memorabilia you could think of. Much like my brother and father when it came to local sports in the city period. Mr. Malone knew his stuff, and was well connected within the city sports scene.

"So you and my daughter are finally having y'all a little one. It's great timing too, y'all just got married and are practically newlyweds. Its great for you two. I know for me when I had my children, I wanted at least one boy. But after seeing my three daughter's born, seeing them grow up and become the incredible beautiful women they are. I'm glad I had my girls. They mean the world to me, all three of them. They gave me life when they were younger and they give me even more life now. Watching my grandchildren grow from them. And now I have another grandchild on the way by my baby girl finally" Mr. Malone said.

"Yeah Mr. Malone, it's an exciting time for all of us. Fatima and I are excited and ready to be the best parents we can be" I replied.


Page 110

Chapter Five  "Time To Make My Mark"


After paying Fatima's parents a visit and sharing the great news with my in laws. We were off and heading back to our home. It was late in the evening and we both had an early start the next morning. On the drive home, Fatima and I had a conversation about our interesting and exciting day sharing the news with our loved ones.

"What a day right babe "? Fatima said.

"Yes indeed. A great day it was, and our families are excited. Although you haven't told your sister's yet. And I haven't told my father and brother yet. But we need to make that happen ASAP" I replied.

"Yes I know. And I hope my sister's don't feel some type of way because they didn't find out first. They probably are going to cuss me out" Fatima said laughing.

"Yeah I'm sure you'll get the business from them. But hey you have a great excuse, your parents found out first" I replied.

"Silas you know they don't care about that. Remember they had to know first about our engagement. My sister's are a trip" Fatima said laughing.

And that they were. Don't get me wrong, I loved Fatima's sister's. Mia and Destiny were Fatima's two older sister's. Fatima was the baby of the family and her sister's treated her as such. They were both very protective over her. Trust me, when I first started dating her it was hard for us to ever be alone. Over time and her sister's getting to know me, they became more comfortable with me. They would always tell me the reason that they were so protective over one another. Was because they didn't have any brother's to defend them, so they had to have each other's back. And growing up in Rogers Park, they knew that all too well. I loved Fatima's family, and she loved mines. Both coming from three children homes. But with somewhat different family dynamics. In my family of course there were two boys and one girl. Fatima came from a family of all girls.

Either way we were meant for each other and were enjoying the news of being expecting parents. From that day forward I treated

Fatima different as far as her responsibilities around the house. I made sure I did most of the work around the house. I wanted her to relax and have a smooth pregnancy. I was indeed a first time father, worried about any and everything. And doing my best to make things as comfortable as possible for my wife.

That next day in class I had a new lesson plan to familiarize my students on what they were going to learn in these next few weeks. We had done pretty well as a class on our Midterms. Now it was time to step it up and take on a new challenge. And thats exactly how I explained it to my students.

"Ok class we're starting what will be a few different lesson plans over the next few weeks. As we move into our next phase of our learning experience. So we need to open our textbooks and turn to page 105 and read til 115. That's eleven pages I need you guys and gals to read. Afterwards we will talk about what you all have read. Ok let's get started" I said as I let my students get to work.

I sat back down at my desk and read something I needed to read. I also sat and watched my students work. I liked doing that from time to time. To try to gauge each student's focus level. We had came a long way as a class, but we still had a ways to go. We were moving along and we were definitely progressing. For the first time in several years, most of the class passed their testing. My first year here. If I could help make that much of an improvement, I had to keep going. It was time to make my mark.

Class ended that day and as my students all left for the day. Principal Hunt came in my classroom. Which was and wasn't too much of a surprise. But like any day when it came to him, I was ready for whatever came my way.

"Mr. Jones, I would like to congratulate you on a great job with the Midterms once again. I was impressed with a high percentage of the students passing, it's been a long time since that's happened around here" Principal Hunt said.

"Yes.... thanks Principal Hunt. As long as we invest in these kid's and believe in these kids, the skies the limit. Such a small invest like new textbooks. Have improved and made these kids learning experience so much more interesting. It's not just about investing the money. It's investing the time and resources also, keeping their interest so they're hungry to learn. I'm not done at all Principal Hunt, I'm just getting started" I replied.

"Mr. Jones I have to admit you're quite the dreamer. And I like a lot of your ideas, you just have to be careful and realize you're just a teacher. There's only so much you can do. There's so many people above us, and I have to explain to them and my superiors about these new textbooks if the school has to fit the bill. Within the budget that is. Good day Mr. Jones. And like I said, be careful" Principal Hunt said before walking away.

Page 112

I just looked at him and nodded my head as he left. I wasn't concerned about Principal Hunt or any of his superiors. My concern was and always would be with the students. I always believed that your students would let you know what type of teacher you were. From the standpoint of you getting them and motivating them to learn. And more importantly you leading them. It was almost like coaches of sports teams. Your players had to have loved to play for you. With teaching, it was about if your students wanting to learn and being motivated by your teaching. If kids weren't interested in your class, they weren't going to apply themselves. And it started with something as small as paying attention to detail. I knew that it started with small improvements throughout the District. That would in turn improve the kid's education across the city, then hopefully expand into the state. And lastly nationwide.

It started with our school, but we still had to keep pushing. Because we were far from done. The improved test scores could open doors for bigger and better things in my eyes. To me that's what I was chasing, while being the best teacher I can be. I knew where Principal Hunt stood early on when we first got to know one another. So it wasn't surprising to me that he was timid when it came to challenging the powers that be. Challenging any authority for that matter, but his own. That's why I would always push Principal Hunt to the limit, and challenge him. Plus nobody else amongst the faculty would dare to challenge him. They all talked behind his back, and smiled in his face. Me on the other hand, have been honest with him since day one. It was one of the reasons he was always somewhat uneasy around me. He knew with me he would always get my honest answer on everything.

At the time I didn't know what I was going to do next, to challenge the District. But I was definitely thinking about doing something. Later that day I met up with my brother and father. Yes you heard it right, my brother and father have put the past behind them. And just in time for my great news. So we decided to meet up for dinner. Where else but one of our favorite Soul Food spots. We met on the North Side so we decided to go to Luella' s Southern Kitchen on North Lincoln Avenue. A spot that was one of my father's personal favorites. So as we sat down and was about to order, I decided to finally tell my brother and father the great news.

"I met y'all here to tell y'all some good news. Fatima and I are expecting our first child, she's pregnant" I said sounding happy about sharing the news.

"Congrats bro, I'm happy for you both. And it's about time too, ain't Pop" ? My brother Sidney Jr. said looking over at my father.

"I've been waiting for a grandchild from you two, congratulations son to you and Fatima. I know you both will be great parents" my father Sidney Sr. said.

"Thanks Pop and Sid, we appreciate it. And now you don't have to wait no more Pop, because the time is now. Your grandchild is coming. Besides that what y'all both been up to ? Haven't seen either of you since the wedding" I replied.

"Son you know I don't get out a lot. Just in and around my neighborhood. Got a few guys I hang out with and gamble with from time to time. And of course play Chess. Other than that I'm home, you know where to find me when you need me. Just like today" my father Sidney Sr. said.

"That's true. And we need more time like this, just the three of us. And you know when Tremaine can come through and get together with us. He's apart of the family too, being him and Savannah have been together for a while now. What you been up to Sid" ? I asked.

"Just working Silas, trying to stay on the straight and narrow. Trying to make the best of my life and hoping to spend some more time with my kid's" my brother Sidney Jr. replied.

"That's great Sid. And hug my niece and nephew for me too man. We all have to get together soon with the kids. Besides the great news of Fatima and I expecting our first child. My students all passed their Midterms and the class is really improving. It feels great because I believed in this when no one did. Aside from my family of course, and now my students. It just inspires me to do more, to push myself beyond limits. Make education interesting and fun again. My students passing their Midterms meant everything to me. But I know we have so much more to do with Finals coming up towards the end of the year" I said.

"And you're the man to do that. This is your passion, and this is why God put you here. This is your calling, so why not chase it. I knew when you told me about Midterms that your class would do well. You're from Chi Town, so you know the city. You can relate to those kids because you was one of those kids years ago. Follow your vision son, you know we're always a hundred and ten percent behind you" my father said.

"Thanks Pop. I definitely know. I love the challenge of teaching my students everyday. Those kids inspire me to bring out my best for them. I was able to get Deshawn back on the right track. But I sense that his situation at home is going to get a lot worse before it gets better. There's only so much I can do as a teacher. I've already been to his house in Fuller Park. And his mother is a little rough around the edges" I replied.     Page 114

"She's a parent, and more importantly she's a single Black mother. From the experiences you two had after me and your mother split, those are the experiences your student Deshawn may be going through. Or worse. Its a lot of pressure on that young woman to make ends meet. And living in Fuller Park isn't easy. I'm sure she works hard trying to take care of her family" my father said.

"Oh it's worse Pop. Fuller Park is more dangerous now than it was when we was coming up Pop. Remember you and mom had some friends over there when we were younger. Y'all went over there and played cards this one night. Remember Sid" ? I said.

"Hell yeah, rough area. I remember" my brother replied.

"Yes Frank and Virginia lived over there. Silas it's obvious you care about Deshawn and want him to do well. Some kids need that extra push to get motivated. With his family life the way it is, school life may be his break from the drama. Stick by him if you believe in him" my father said.

"I believe in all my students until they show me otherwise Pop" I replied.

Talking with my brother and father was always enlightening. It had been a while since we were together like we were today. Just the three of us. Not even at my wedding were we in an atmosphere like this. But just the fact my brother and father were getting along was a great feeling to me. Their relationship was getting back to where it once was, and things in the family were going great. My sister Savannah had gotten promoted at her job at the hospital, which meant more demanding hours. My mother was retired. So between her and my sister's boyfriend Tremaine, they would hold down the fort when my sister was working those long hours.

A few days later it was Friday, and our first weekly quiz since Midterms. We had a great week of work, and I was curious to see how my students would do on this first quiz since their testing. If their focus was still there and remained. That was important for them moving forward. As I said before, I never looked at myself as just a teacher. My students looked at me more than just their teacher. They knew they could always talk to me about anything they felt they needed to. That was what I was there for. It was my passion to teach and lead. And that also meant listening to my students and not judging them. I had several conversations with several of my students about serious and personal things that were going on in their lives. Deshawn was far from the only kid that was dealing with tense situations at home. Everyone knew him because he was a basketball star. Speaking of that, Fatima and I had planned to go to another game. Which would be that following night. It was a home game, and I knew the gym would be packed. It always was.

Page 115

Later that evening we made our way to the game. And like the last time I seen a bunch of my students. Fatima and I heard "Hey Mr. Jones" and "Hi Mr. Jones". As we walked through the crowd to find our seat. After finding our seat we enjoyed a very intense and competitive game. Between our school and another city rival school. Deshawn shined like he always did, having another great game. It was good to get out and support one of my students that needed the support the most. I knew what Deshawn was dealing with at home. So I felt I needed to be there to show him support. He didn't ask me to come to the game at all this night. I went on my own, and I'm not even sure that he knew I was there.

The fact of the matter was I believed in him and I wasn't going to give up on him. My father knew that I cared about my students. And he also knew if certain students needed me more than other's, I would do my best to be there. I was just different in a sense when it came to things of that nature when dealing with my students. I had conversations with my students about their concerns. And of certain teachers not treating them like they cared. In those conversations I explained to them that. Like any other profession, there were those that truly cared about their job and their students. And others didn't. I never paid too much attention to teachers and staff who I felt wasn't in it for the love of teaching. I only paid attention to the teachers that did care, and there wasn't a whole lot of us. After watching a great game and Deshawn play well like always, my wife and I were driving home.

"Great game wasn't it baby ? Haven't been to a game that good since the last game. And we beat our rival in a nail biter. Deshawn is definitely ready for college ball, he looked like a man amongst boys out there" I said still excited about the end of the game.

"Yes it sure was. I had a great time last time we came to the game too. Before that, I hadn't been to a High School basketball game since I was in school. But it was good to get out to another one tonight" Fatima replied smiling.

"How you feeling baby ? You need anything" ? I asked her.

"I'm good babe, stop worrying. It's still early in my pregnancy. And yes I'm taking my prenatal pills and everything, so don't worry" Fatima replied.

"I'm just checking on my Queen. Baby you know I'm a first time father so I'm going to worry.

"I know babe, everything is going to be fine. Just think positive. I'm so excited, about being a mommy" Fatima said smiling.      Page 116

"And I'm just as excited about becoming a father. I had a good conversation about that with my father and brother the other day. I'm glad that they're in that space now, and we could all get together. I was smiling the whole time baby" I said as I was driving us home.

"I bet you were babe, I know how much it means to you all. That's great and important. I thank God everyday that my immediate family has remained intact. My parents and my sister's, we're all still very close. That means the world to me" Fatima replied.

That was one thing that was important to us both, our families. From the day we started dating, it was a subject that was brought to the table from day one. Were either of us family oriented ? The answer was an emphatic yes !!! We both loved and valued our families greatly. From our parents to our siblings. We finally got home and after getting out of the car. I went over to the passenger side and opened the door for my wife, like I always do. We settled in at home and called it a night.

The next week at school another one of my top students as far as grades are concerned, Claudia Henderson. Said she needed to speak to me. As always I was willing to talk to my students about anything they needed to talk about. They all felt comfortable coming to me about anything. So we went out in the hallway away from the rest of my students to talk.

"So what's going on Claudia ? Everything ok" ? I asked.

Claudia just looked at me and started crying. I quickly tried to console her and waited for her to tell me what was wrong. She kept crying before she replied to what I had asked her.

"I don't know if I can really talk about it, I'm scared" Claudia replied as she continued to cry.

"Here sweetheart, wipe your tears. And calm down, you know you can talk me. Whatever is said is between us, and will stay between us if that's what you want" I said after giving her some tissue to wipe her face.

"Mr. Jones I was raped.....I can't believe he did this to me" Claudia said as she started to break down again.

I was shocked at what Claudia had just told me. She was raped.....wow. I must admit this was the first time that I had to deal with something like this. At first I didn't even know what to say to her. I was definitely caught off guard.         Page 117

I didn't even want to ask her who raped her. I was that much in shock. I just held her while she cried, but I knew I had to not only say something. But I had to do something also. So I continued to try and calm her down.

"When did this happen Claudia ? If you don't mind me asking" I said.

"It happened this past weekend. I went on a date with this guy and everything was going good until he started to force himself on me. I told him to stop Mr. Jones, but he wouldn't....he just wouldn't" she said starting to cry again.

"Its ok....It's ok. Do you want to tell me who did this to you" ? I asked.

She paused and started to shut down, which I was hoping she wouldn't do. But I could understand why being the circumstances, so I let her have a moment. And if she wanted to tell me, she could tell me. I just didn't want her to feel pressured. For her to come to me with this, that meant something in itself. She felt that comfortable with me, to come to me. Rather than her going to one of her female teachers or classmates. Or even a family member, like her own mother. Either way, now that I knew I had to do my best to get her to open up about it. Without making her feel pressured. I felt like when she was ready she would tell me. I didn't have to wait that long, because after a long pause she decided to tell me.

"It was this guy name Dak Hollis, he's a Senior and plays football for the school" Claudia said.

"Yes....I know who he is. He's a great football player. Seen him play a few times. He has a lot of colleges after him. So you two were dating" ? I asked.

"Not really dating. We had went out one time before, and this was the second time. I thought he was nice, so I decided to go out with him again. And this is what happens" Claudia said still sobbing a little.

"It doesn't matter how many times you two went out, it doesn't justify what he did. I know this is a dumb question, but I have to ask you this. Are you telling me the truth about Dak raping you" ? I asked looking directly at Claudia.

"Yes that's what happened. I told him to stop, and he wouldn't. I wouldn't lie about something like this Mr. Jones. I didn't even want to come to you with this at first. I wasn't going to tell anybody. But after thinking about it, I felt I had to. So he wouldn't do it to anyone else. I just can't believe he did this to me, he was so nice all this time" Claudia replied.                    Page 118

"Sometimes that's how it happens Claudia. So what do you want me to do with this ? I mean we need to take this to the Police, so he doesn't do this to another young woman. Are you prepared for that ? Because you may eventually have to appear in front of him in court. So I need your permission to go to the Police with this....well I don't need it. But I would like your permission" I said to her.

She looked at me with some tears still in her eyes, and nodded yes in agreement. So that was my green light to go to the Police. As a teacher and just as a person that cared about Claudia, it was the only right thing to do. But before I did that, I had to get her together so we could go back into class. And her classmates wouldn't be nosey trying to guess what was going on. Dak wasn't one of my students, and if this was true I'm glad he wasn't. But I was going to speak to him, just because I wanted to. I wanted to get his side of the story. After talking to Claudia outside my classroom, we had to both get back to class. So she got herself together and we entered the classroom, I was still able get my lesson plan in for the day. Which was important, because we were still building on our results from Midterms.

I can't lie, I was thinking about what Claudia told me all that day. It was hard not to think about it, something so serious. I didn't want to believe it, but I couldn't just let it go without finding out the truth. So after teaching that day with that on my mind, the day had came to an end. After leaving my classroom for the day, I decided to make a trip to the weight room at the school. In search of Dak Hollis who was known to spend a lot of time there. And just like I thought, I arrived in the weight room to find Dak was there. He was on the weight bench doing some reps when I came in.

"Hey Dak how's your workout going" ? I asked.

He just looked at me and kept working out. Didn't say anything at all.

"You know a young lady by the name of Claudia Henderson ? She says that you two went out and while you were out, you forced yourself on her. Which led to you eventually raping her" I said as he stopped working out.

"I didn't rape her, that bitch wanted it just as much as I did. If not more. She's just mad that she's not my girlfriend. I haven't been out with her in a while. I wasn't ever trying to be serious with her" Dak said.

"Well it's your word against her's, and you may have to explain this in a court of law. Lets hope you're not one of these star athletes that thinks because you're a star athlete. That you're going to get away with anything. If this is true, you being who you are won't matter. Because I'm not going to let you get away with it" I replied. Page 119

"And who are you supposed to be ? You wasn't there to know shit, so how do you know what happened ? You're only taking her word....I gotta get back to my workout" Dak said walking past me and going over to the other free weights.

"You're right I wasn't there, but we will find out what happened that night. One way or the other" I replied before he walked off.

Dak was somewhat of a typical star student athlete, similar in the mold of Deshawn when I first met him. They both were stars in their respective sports, and knew each other pretty well. Just from being student athletes that were on top of their games. One thing I was going to do before I went to Principal Hunt like I was supposed to do according to the District. Was talk to Deshawn about Dak and see just how well he really knew him. I know my first impression was a somewhat arrogant kid who sounded like he was hiding something. I'm no Detective, but it just seemed like he was. So to get a better understanding of who Dak was, I wanted to talk to Deshawn.

So the next day after class, I pulled Deshawn aside to talk to him about Dak Hollis.

"I understand you and Dak Hollis are pretty cool. The other star on campus here. Y'all two cool Deshawn" ? I asked.

"I mean he's cool, we talk from time to time. He's from the West Side. We've gotten closer after coming to this school. Other than that its business as usual, a mutual respect so to speak" Deshawn replied.

"Oh ok.....I see. Well does he seem like the type to be quick tempered or anything" ? I asked.

"I haven't been around the man that much to know that. I just know he's a hell of a football player. Where's all this coming from Mr. Jones" ? Deshawn replied asking.

"Dak may be involved in something that was not good at all. I can't speak on it any further right now. And this conversation stays between us. I just wanted to see how good you really knew him. Because I had heard you two were pretty cool, but I see now it's more like you two know of each other. And that's fine. Thanks Deshawn, have a nice evening" I said before we both walked away.

I now needed to speak with Principal Hunt about this, so after talking to Deshawn I headed to his office. I was following the rules of the District with a situation like this. It was the first time I had ever had to deal with something like this, it was all new to me. So I had to tell the head of the school, which was Principal Hunt.
Page 120

I got to his office and knocked on the door. Principal Hunt was expecting me because I told him I needed to talk to him about something.

"Have a seat Mr. Jones. What did you want to talk to me about" ? Principal Hunt asked.

"A student may have raped another student Principal Hunt. That's why I'm here speaking to you. And it's one of our more popular students. Dak Hollis is the name of the student who may have raped another student" I replied.

"Dak Hollis ? Rape is a very strong accusation Mr. Jones. Whoever this student is that's accusing Dak Hollis must be sure that this actually happened. It must be the truth" Principal Hunt said.

"I agree Principal Hunt. And I wouldn't be here telling you this if I didn't believe it's true. I trust the student that told me this" I replied.

"Ok Mr. Jones. Who is this student" ? Principal Hunt asked.

"Her name is Claudia Henderson, she's a student of mines" I replied.

"I need to talk to them both, one at a time of course. Then we can proceed from there. Thanks for bringing this to my attention Mr. Jones" Principal Hunt said.

"Just doing my job Principal Hunt, good day" I replied before leaving his office.

I honestly believed that Principal Hunt was going to handle the situation from there. I did my job as her teacher and told my Principal. But I wasn't going to give up afterward. I would keep an eye on the situation from a distance, with hope that it would be handled correctly. That's all I could do at this point. I know I felt for Claudia, she was very distraught when she was telling me what happened. And if you was a man in your right mind, you would feel for any woman who had claimed to be raped. It was a very serious crime. I felt once I told Principal Hunt who the person was that may be responsible for this, that it sent a shockwave through him. Much like Deshawn was a star around school for basketball, Dak was the man for the football team.

Either way, if he did something wrong he needed to face the consequences no matter who he was. That was something I felt very strongly about. And I would hope that Principal Hunt would feel the same as I did. I guess only time would tell if he did. I know I believed that my student Claudia was telling the truth. And it wouldn't have mattered if I knew both or one of them. Rape is rape, and that's something I didn't condone as a man that had a mother and sister, and aunts. And a wife.

I went home that night with a lot on my mind. Did Dak Hollis really rape Claudia ? Was Principal Hunt really going to handle the situation ? And how was this going to all turn out ? I didn't know, but I knew I was going to stay involved. Because I told Claudia I would.

After getting home I didn't really feel like cooking. And I didn't want Fatima to have to cook, so I decided to order out. Since finding out about Fatima's pregnancy, I've tried my best to keep as much pressure as possible off of her. And more on me. I was prepared to take it all on. But I did want to talk to her about the situation with Claudia. She knew Claudia and Claudia attended our wedding. She was one of my top students, and I cared about her a great deal like I did about all my students.

"What's going on babe ? You seem a little down, it's not like you" Fatima said looking at me as we sat and ate dinner.

"Well something happened with Claudia baby. She told me she was raped by one of the star football players. In particular Dak

Hollis, the All-State linebacker. I seen him play a few times, great talent. But if this is true, I definitely won't ever look at him the same. I trust that Claudia is telling the truth. She was brave enough to come to me and tell me herself what happened. So I feel responsible in some part to do something about it. I approached Dak about it......and before you say anything, I know I shouldn't have. I guess I was that disgusted that I had to" I said looking at Fatima.

"Oh my God, that's so awful. I feel for Claudia, she's a very nice young lady. And babe you were just being you. Silas being Silas, caring and helping people out. That's one of the reasons I married you. Maybe going to Dak with it wasn't the smartest thing to do, but I understood your intentions as a respectable man. As a man that would defend a young lady from a coward" Fatima replied.

"Thanks. Means a lot because I've been having mixed feelings about the whole situation. In a sense that this isn't going to end well for either of these kids. You have a very talented young man that could one day go pro. And a beautiful young lady that is very smart and could eventually go to any college in this country. For her, this could affect her for years to come. Him....it could end his career before it even gets started" I said shaking my head.

I hated the fact that as a teacher I had to deal with something like this at my school, but we were here now. And I was eager to see what was going to happen after Principal Hunt talked to them both. And more importantly, was this going to be a priority.

A few days later it was Friday and we had our weekly quiz. I loved the weekly quiz, it was a staple in my class. It always let me know how much my students paid attention and learned throughout the week. As I previously said, it keeps their minds focused and sharp. Claudia despite dealing with what she was currently dealing with, still continued coming to class. I felt like that was very brave of her and took a lot of courage. I kept an eye on her since the day she informed me about what happened. Sort've like the way I've kept my eye on Deshawn. I saw the potential in them both.

Benjamin Evans who was the Superintendent for Chicago City Schools at the time was making headlines of late in the local news. Announcing budget cuts within the schools, schools that were already in need of major improvements. The buzz surrounding it all had me angered, along with the other things that were going on with my students. The anxiousness and excitement of becoming a father for the first time. It all was weighing heavily on my mind. Teachers amongst the faculty were talking about the budget cuts. And when I would come in the Teacher's Lounge they would get quiet for whatever reason. I could guess what they were saying. That now because the Superintendent announced budget cuts, I wasn't going to get the necessary new things I needed for my classroom. To them it was all about me, to me it was about us all. And mainly the students. I was just the first teacher to step up and demand more. I bet my future and my money on my students improving, and I got part of that back with Midterms.

I was here for way more than just improving on a yearly basis, I was here to change the course of education. Or at least one of the people that sparked the change. I as well as other parents and teachers across this country weren't happy with the educational system. I myself personally would be up against a battle between all the men that were above me in job rank. It was clear Principal Hunt and I didn't see eye to eye, and now Superintendent Evans joined that list. I had never even met the man before, but people around the District seemed to fear him. It was said that he was a brash man who wanted things his way. It didn't matter to me, because with my passion no man would stand in the way of my journey. Not even the Superintendent. Although I had never met him, many of his views on education I didn't agree with. And him cutting our budget even further didn't sit well with me. To me Superintendent Benjamin Evans was very similar to Principal Hunt. Two men that were happy with their job titles and paychecks, but really didn't care for the students like they should have. I liked the fact that I did my job and was at arm's distance from Principal Hunt. It was like I was in my own world, even though he was there. And I loved it.

Page 123

After another long week of ups and downs, it was finally the weekend again. And on this particular Friday night Fatima and I were just enjoying a quiet evening at home. We were both enjoying the early stages of pregnancy. Minus the morning sickness of course. Fortunately Fatima didn't have a lot of it, and she was now moving along. It was a joy to see her each day, growing with the baby. We rented a movie to watch, but before we watched it. Fatima had turned the TV to the local news. Watching the news and who comes up ? None other than Superintendent Evans. He was being interviewed by the local news about him announcing earlier about the state's plans for budget cuts. And he also said that he would be visiting a few High Schools in the District. He named about five schools. One of which was the High School I taught at. Our school on the North Side.

As Fatima and I was watching it, I kind of smirked a little. My mind started thinking about how I was going to engage in a conversation with this man. Not because I was a fan of his, but because I wanted to pick his brain and put pressure on him like I did Principal Hunt. Unlike Principal Hunt, Superintendent Evans had the ability to actually make changes to improve education. I was hoping the Superintendent was the man he was proclaiming to be. A concerned Superintendent that really wanted his students to succeed. All I know was, I couldn't wait to see if he was willing to change once I talked to him. And then there was the situation with Claudia and Dak that was ongoing. And was Principal Hunt going to proceed in doing something about the whole situation. I would find out sooner rather than later. A few days later, at the school. Dak Hollis was arrested and charged with rape. A lot of the kids at school looked out their third floor windows to see Police escort Dak out of the school and into a Police car. One of those people looking out the window was me.

It was almost like I just watched a person's life and dream potentially end abruptly, it was sad to see. If Dak really did rape Claudia, it would follow him for the rest of his life. I felt bad for them both in a sense. They were two talented kids that had a ton of potential in different aspects of life. Dak was a football star and Claudia was smart enough to be anything she wanted to be. It was a bad look for the both of them. And now he was arrested. It was something I eventually expected, but actually seeing it made it that much. Dak wasn't my student, but I did care about him as a young black male growing up in inner city Chicago. And just as a young black male living life and chasing his dreams in this country. Like many of the kids in the school, we could relate because some of us were from the same streets. Or at least adjacent neighborhoods. After it was announced that Dak was arrested and a few local Chicago News stations got a hold of the story. Claudia began getting threats from other students. She felt almost guilty that she would be known as the girl that claimed rape at the hands of the school's best football player. And one of the most talented kids in the country.    Page 124

   Our school on the North Side was getting a lot of attention lately with this recent story. There was the good attention, when the local news came out earlier in the year and did a great story on the school. I was even interviewed. Then just this week the Superintendent announced that our school was one of the schools he would visit. And now the story that has dominated the local news. Dak Hollis the local football star was being accused of rape. Having these situations happen towards the weekend gave me a chance to just sit back and reflect on everything that was going on. I had to get my mind off things so me and the fellas got together to shoot some pool. Yes Mitchell and Angelo, my best friend and associate. And the person that filled in the gap between them both when they were around each other. Me.

   "How's Fatima been doing with the pregnancy ? And how are you handling the changes with the pregnancy here now" ? Mitchell asked.

   "Fatima has been fine, and we been cool, no hormonal stuff going on. But it's early, she may be letting me off light right now" I replied as we all laughed.

   Mitchell and I was talking about him teasing me about the first trimester of pregnancy, when a woman is hormonal and it could test the will of a first time father. Ever since I shared the news with him, he's teased me every chance he's gotten. We had a good time with it, as we all continued to shoot pool.

   "So do y'all want a boy or girl ? Or should I say, what do you want first, a boy or girl" ? Angelo asked.

"We just want a healthy baby, I mean that's all we can ask God to bless us with. Just excited man. But like anything else, with good news and God blessing you. The Devil is right behind trying to steal your shine. I know y'all seen recently about my school and everything happening with Dak Hollis" I said.

"Yeah I saw that, I was going to ask you was he one of your students" ? Mitchell said.

"No he's not one of my students, but the female accusing him of rape is. I know her and she's one of my best students. She actually came to me first with it. I took it to Principal Hunt. And here we are now, the story has broke" I replied.

"That's crazy because the kid is a great talent, I've seen him play. Hell of a player and athlete. It's a shame that he could potentially ruin it. I could seriously see him playing in the NFL one day" Angelo said shooting a shot.

"That's what's so disappointing. Both kids I believe deep down inside are good kids. I know the potential both of them have" I replied.    Page 125

"Rape is serious Silas, especially for a young black man with potential. Whether he did it or not, just him being accused. It could follow him for the rest of his life. Five to ten years from now if this kid makes it to the pros, they'll still be talking about it. You know how the media is" Mitchell said.

"Most definitely, and I've been thinking about that the whole time. He could really be ruining his future. And I'm in part responsible for taking this to the Principal. And I don't regret it at all, I was doing my job as a teacher. Plus I know Claudia, she is one of my brightest students. And as you both know I have the upmost respect for women. I have a wonderful mother and sister, and a wife that means the world to me. There's no way I was just going to let that slide because of Dak being a star football player at the school. And you're right Mitchell, rape is serious. And that's why I went to the Principal with it. Obviously we now know he went to the Police with it, which was the right thing to do" I replied.

"Indeed it was Silas, it was the right thing to do" Mitchell said agreeing.

"Ok fellas, I didn't come out here to talk about work. Let's get some more rounds in. I'm sorry for both of them kids, but it's Saturday and I'm trying to shoot some pool. And have some male interaction with yall brothas" Angelo said as me and Mitchell looked at each other laughing and shaking our heads at Angelo being Angelo.

We had a good time playing countless rounds of pool and just hanging out. It was something we did from time to time. Just to get out of our normal routines. We loved our wives, girlfriends, and family a great deal. But hanging with the fellas was my escape from everything else. However long that was, it was an escape for all of us. We needed it to somewhat recharge so we could get back to our respective careers. We were all successful men that had careers that we loved. It was good for me having a great circle of people that lived similar lives that I lived. We had things in common. One thing I didn't have in common with them was being a father. That is until recently when Fatima and I found out we were expecting our first child. So soon we would have more in common, all being father's.

After shooting pool with the fellas, I returned home where Fatima was sleep in our bedroom as I opened the door and looked in our bedroom. She was laying on her side of our King Size bed. I went back in the living room and sat down on the couch and watched some TV. While sitting there watching TV, things were going through my mind as usual. Mostly things that had to do with life in general. And of course the visit from the Superintendent, which I wasn't really thrilled about. But I did want to pick his brain so to speak, so I was looking forward to that.   Page 126

   The next day was Sunday and I was once again going to church with my mother, which I enjoyed. But this time Fatima and I were accompanying my mother to her church. Most times when my sister worked her shift at the hospital, my brother Sidney Jr and I would take turns accompanying our mother to church. My brother went with her last week. It was the one Sunday that Fatima and I didn't go to our own church. We were both happy to go with my mother, and she was excited about us going. So after I picked my mother up, we were off to Sunday morning service.

   "So glad that you two are coming to church with me this morning. My son and daughter in law, and my soon to be grandchild in her belly. Nothing like continued prayer and worship in the Lord's house" my mother Lucy said.

   "We're glad to be going with you too, on this fine Sunday morning" my wife Fatima replied smiling.

   "We all enjoy accompanying you to church momma, and we love spending time with you as well" I said as I was driving us to my mother's church.

   We all truly loved going to church with our mother because we knew she was at her happiest when she was serving the Lord. When she was surrounded by the many in her congregation that she held dear to her heart. She had told us all recently that she wanted the whole family to attend church with her sometime soon. Of course we all agreed, we all wanted nothing but to put a smile on our mother's face. As we finally arrived at my mother's church and I got out. I opened the door for the two women that meant the world to me. And walked arm and arm with them into the church, smiling from ear to ear.

After an uplifting Sunday morning service, we were on our way to eat lunch/dinner. Neither of us felt like cooking so we decided to eat at one of the many nice restaurants in the city. This time we decided to eat something else besides Soul Food like we normally ate. Me, my mother Lucy, and my wife Fatima went to Drawl Southern Cookhouse & Whiskey Room. Now my mother didn't drink. Plus it was Sunday and I didn't drink around her. Fatima was pregnant so I ordered some sweet tea with my dinner. We sat and talked about a lot of different things from the baby coming to the family in general. I was with two of the most important women in my life so you know I was all smiles the whole day. My mother was just as excited as us about the baby coming. She has wanted a grandchild from me for a while now.

After a nice afternoon with two of my favorite ladies, we headed to my mother's home on da South Side and dropped her back off at home. My nephew and niece were waiting for her as soon as she came in the door. It was a great day.    Page 127

The next day was of course Monday and I was energized and ready to go. I felt good about this week, and I just felt good period because I had a great weekend. So driving to school that morning I was feeling great. Actually jamming on the way to school listening to one of many Chicago radio stations banging that 80's and 90's Hip Hop and R&B. I finally got to school and was eager to get in my classroom. When I finally got there I entered and turned on my lights and get to my desk. But before I could get to my desk, something told me to look at my blackboard. And I did. To my surprise my blackboard had in big letters "SNITCH ASS LYING ASS TEACHER".

To say I was shocked was an understatement, my students for the most part loved me. They knew how much I cared for them, and how I would fight for them. They also had heard about Dak Hollis being arrested. They didn't know what female had accused him of rape, because that wasn't disclosed to the media and local news outlets. Something tells me that the fact someone may have found out that I told Principal Hunt. And that was the reason for the message on my blackboard. Either way I was going to get to the bottom of it, some how some way. I left it on my blackboard so my students could see it when they walked in. And I proceeded to get myself prepared like I always did for my students. Many students were talking around the school about Dak's arrest, and others speculated on who the female might be.

Fifteen minutes went by and my students started to enter my classroom. I was sitting at my desk when my students arrived and were talking. Then they noticed the blackboard. Some of them whispered to one another and pointed to the blackboard. I just continued sitting at my desk. That is until all my students were seated. That's when I got up from my desk and got their attention.

"Ok class. As you all can see one of my students or a student from this school decided to decorate my blackboard with garbage and nonsense. Would that student be in attendance today in this class? If so please stand and face the music. Don't be a coward. You won't even get in trouble. You have my word, and you all know my word is bond. So what's it going to be ? Is the student going to remain the coward he or she is.....huh" ? I said looking in each of my student's eyes.

The room grew silent as my students were looking around at each other. No one said a word. I just stood there in front of my class looking them all in their eyes. These kids couldn't break me, I was a former United States Marine. And then all of a sudden a voice spoke up.

"I did that shit. And you are a snitch ass bitch for saying my boy Dak raped that bitch, she's lying" !! My student Lance Fields said. Page 128

"No Lance, I never said Dak raped anyone. What I did do was help a young lady that came to me and was scared. Obviously something happened that frightened her. As a teacher and leader in this school and community, I was doing my job. You and everyone else need to let the law handle it. And let the process play out" I said.

"No you and her. Yeah fucking Claudia accusing my boy of raping her......you lying bitch !! You could ruin my boy's future" !! Lance yelled.

"Lance !! Get out of my class !! Now" !!!!! I yelled interrupting him.

Lance got up and stormed out of the classroom, and Claudia just put her head down sobbing. I felt bad for Claudia, as the news was circulating since Dak's arrest. I knew Dak knew who accused him of rape. Because he basically said it when I talked to him. Anyway Lance was out of line and I wasn't having that energy in my classroom. He had to go, and I couldn't tell you at this point if or when I even wanted him back. For his blatant disrespect towards me and his classmate Claudia. I understood it was his friend,  but he should've been angry about his friend putting himself in that situation. Dak knew what he had on the line. So in a sense I didn't feel sorry for him, if he did do it. I just know the whole situation had the school on edge, and I could only imagine how it affected Claudia.

I had to start class and that's exactly what I did. After the distraction I began class, and although it would be a rough day for Claudia. I was hoping she would remain brave and get through it. By this time I had erased the garbage of a message off my blackboard. My students regained their focus and the day went on. After class that day, I held Claudia back in class as everyone left. I needed to have a conversation with her to see where her head was at.

"Claudia I know this is a rough time for you and people may be talking. Trying to doubt you and assassinating your character. But you need to remain brave like you were the day you brought this to me. I'm in your corner and a lot of other people are in your corner. More than you think. And if he did this to you, he deserves to be punished regardless of who he is. I just want to let you know that I'm here for you and I'm on your side" I said.

"Thanks Mr. Jones, I appreciate everything you've done for me. I'm just scared to go anywhere. I'm scared here at school sometimes. People have been saying a lot of cruel things about me thinking I'm lying. I have no reason to lie, like who wants to be raped. I just can't believe how some people can be because he plays football. What about my future ? Shouldn't that matter too" ? Claudia replied.      Page 129

"Of course it does, that's why you have to remain brave throughout the adversity that you're dealing with. This process is definitely not going to be easy. But just stay the course and justice will be served. I expect you in class all week, and if you need me to drive you home I will. I need to get going. You have a great night Claudia" I said.

"Ok. And thanks again Mr. Jones, I will see you tomorrow" she said as she was leaving.

I felt for Claudia, but I also knew she was brave enough to get through it. She had came this far with it. Two of my brightest students were going through some serious trials and tribulations. Through it all, I was by their sides. And I continued to be. And I would do the same for any of my other students as well. Before I left that day, Principal Hunt knocked on my door. It was to be expected, with what happened earlier with Lance. I was sitting at my desk finishing up some paperwork when he came in.

"Mr. Jones I'd like to talk to you about what happened earlier today, in regards to Lance Fields. I have no clue what happened. So I'll ask you" Principal Hunt said before I interrupted.

"He wrote on my blackboard calling me a liar and a snitch. Those are two major and serious accusations to pin on a person. Especially when the young man doesn't hardly know me. The point was he disrespected not only me, but Claudia also by calling her a bitch" I replied.

"I understand Mr. Jones, but he needs to get back into class at some point. This is a sensitive situation for him, as well as other students that are close to Dak. And yes that's definitely disrespectful. And he will apologize" Principal Hunt said.

"Give it some time Principal Hunt......give it some time. I can get his work together and he can do his work in another room. Just not in my classroom right now. Think how sensitive of a situation it is for a young woman who may have been raped" I replied.

"Silas I just think it's in both our best interests, to let Lance back into class tomorrow. He'll apologize, and we'll move forward. Please " Principal Hunt said.

Principal Hunt had no clue about what happened. And he also had no clue about how to deal with the kids in this school. The fact that a young woman may have been raped, and more and more of the kids being against her. Should tell you a lot about the young minds of America. And how we as adults in this society still had a ways to go in teaching and preparing our youth. To do the right things and believe in the right things. Having ambition, great attitudes, and work ethics. Wanting to be successful, and working towards that goal. Dak and Claudia's case was a prime example.   Page 130

After my almost useless conversation with Principal Hunt, I called it a day and was heading home. I wanted to get home before my wife Fatima, I had planned to prepare us a nice dinner. So on the way home I stopped by the store to get a few things for dinner. After that I headed home and started to prepare dinner for us. Even though I worked and was tired myself, I took on a bigger role once Fatima was pregnant. I told her that the day she let me know we were expecting, and I stood by my word. So as my wife entered our home, she could smell the delicious meal being prepared.

"Hello babe I'm home, ummmm....it smells so good. What are we having tonight" ? Fatima asked.

"Lemon and pepper chicken with rice and fresh collard greens. Almost done beautiful, have a seat and relax. Get ready to eat" I replied pulling her chair out as she sat.

"I've been reading the paper about Dak Hollis arrest, I can only imagine the effect it has been on the school and other students" Fatima said.

"You don't know the half baby. I arrived at my class this morning to find the words "SNITCH ASS LYING ASS Teacher" on my blackboard. I left it there until all my students were seated. Then I asked who was the coward that did it ? Would he or she come forward and speak up ? After about another ten minutes a voice said that they did it and I am a snitch and liar. Believing that bitch who told me that she had been raped. And potentially trying to ruin my boy's future. Yeah Dak has a good friend in my class, Lance Fields. I immediately told him to get out of my class. He ended up leaving. Later that day Principal Hunt comes to see me, and says Lance needs to be back in class. I told him he could IF he remained respectful and apologized to me and his classmates. And all this happened right in front of Claudia. I felt bad for her, but I talked to her after class and told her to remain brave like the day she brought this to me. It's important that she does as this moves forward" I replied.

"Oh babe I'm so sorry you had to go through that. That's just ridiculous. Friend or not, that young woman was raped. No need to act that way. These kids nowadays, this culture and generation. Sometimes it frightens me thinking that we're bringing a child into this cruel world" Fatima said.

"This world was cruel when we came in it too baby. All we can do is do our best. I'm not wavering, as long as Claudia stays strong I will continue to support her no matter what. And if its proven that he did rape her, then it will all be clear. The truth will be out for the world to see. I have great faith that she's telling the truth" I replied.

Page 131

"Its just a shame that people seem to look past the real issue here in all of this. It's such a tense situation. Half of the city is on Dak's side, and the other half pulling for Claudia" Fatima said.

"I just want my students to remain focused on their studies. The case will take care of itself" I replied.

The next day would be eventful, Superintendent Evans was coming to visit our school. It was just another day to me as I woke up early the next morning. Drove myself to school like always and got to my classroom. I was introducing a new lesson plan for my students. And I was excited about it, I really felt my students would be interested in it. That was the main thing to my teaching curve, keeping my students interested in our lessons each day. That prepared them for what lie ahead..... Finals. So I got my lesson plan together and ready just in time as my students began entering the classroom. Amongst those students were Lance, as he returned to class the day after I made him leave class because of his disrespect. He had better come back to class with a better attitude and respect towards me and his classmates.

Whatever opinion he had on Dak being accused of rape, was his and his own right. But being disrespectful towards others wasn't the answer. All my students made their way to their seats and I started class. I was teaching for about twenty minutes before someone had knocked on my door. It was Principal Hunt accompanied by Superintendent Evans. They told me to continue teaching and they would observe from the back. As they walked to the back of class after entering my classroom. I continued to teach. It was a good and productive day for my class and no distractions. After class and my students cleared out, the Principal and Superintendent were waiting to speak to me.

"Hello Silas, you know Superintendent Benjamin Evans. Superintendent Benjamin Evans this is Silas Jones. One of my History teachers here at the school" Principal Hunt said introducing us two.

"Hello Superintendent Evans, nice to meet you" I said shaking his hand.

"Likewise Mr. Jones. I've heard some good things about you, and I've seen the improvements in the student's test scores from their Midterms" he replied.

"Yes I was very proud of my students, they worked really hard. As I told them hard work pays off. I think they will all do well when Finals get here also" I replied.

"Confidence is always good Mr. Jones. I know you are well aware of the case involving this school that's been all over the news lately. Plus the young lady came to you first with the accusation before you brought it to Principal Hunt am I right" ? Superintendent Evans asked.

"Yes she told me she was raped. And after talking to her and making sure that's exactly what happened, I brought it to Principal Hunt. I didn't want to bring anything to Principal Hunt, that I didn't believe was true. I wouldn't ever make a situation bigger than what it really was. I trust this young lady and I know this young lady" I replied.

"Nothing has been proven yet. I think you're jumping the gun a little bit Mr. Jones. And that's something you have to be very careful with being a teacher in this District. You can't show bias towards another student because you have a relationship with them. Dak is innocent until proven guilty, isn't that how it works in this country ? We'll let the judicial system handle this" Superintendent Evans said.

"Yes you're right, Dak is innocent until proven guilty. That I agree with you. And my relationship with the young lady is a student teacher relationship which is based off strictly education. The young lady is one of my brightest students and has a chance to go to any school in this country. And Dak does too, he's a talented young man and I wish them both the best. But I find it hard to believe that this young lady would lie about something like this. All the negative attention they're both getting, it makes no sense to make any of this up. But we all will see when the truth comes out. So I'm not showing bias to either student, I just know rape is a serious accusation" I replied.

"I also hear you were one of the only teachers to receive new textbooks for your class. Courtesy of the District, consider yourself lucky. We haven't had new textbooks in this District in a very long time" he said.

"And maybe that was part of the problem Superintendent Evans, as you witnessed since my class got those new textbooks. My student's Midterm scores rose considerably since a year ago. I'd say it was a much needed improvement. And I believe that the rest of the teachers should get the same. The textbooks are just the beginning, we can improve on other things as well" I replied.

"I think this conversation is over Mr. Jones. You're going into a whole other realm when you're talking about buying all kinds of new things when I just announced our budget cuts within the city and state. That was passed down to me from the local and federal government. Those are the guidelines WE have to follow, and that includes you Mr. Jones" he said.

I just looked at him, and shook my head. Not that I was surprised. I saw the news conference when he announced the budget cuts. I just wanted to hear it up close and personal. Look in his eyes as a man, to see that he was just as much a puppet if not more than Principal Hunt. After he said that, Principal Hunt just looked at me. He should've known I wasn't going to agree with no Superintendent about anything regarding our school or education period. So his reaction to me didn't matter at all. I was glad that the Superintendent came and talked to me so he knew exactly how I felt. My peers at school would've been shocked to know, that I had their backs in this fight for a better education for our students. It was never about me, as I've always said. I was just the only one that had the guts to speak up, even if it meant me losing my job. I knew I wasn't happy with the state of education.

"I understand Superintendent Evans, but I can't honestly say I'm happy with it. It's my job and I will follow the rules as always. But I won't stop or give up on a better education for all students who want to learn....never" I replied.

The Superintendent and Principal Hunt just walked away. I had faced both men that were above me in the chain of command. They were the two men I had to answer to according to my job. They both now knew how I felt. And I'm glad they both did, so from here on out there would be no misunderstandings. As to where I stood with the case or education in a whole. I knew I had to do all I could for my students in spite of those two men that were more worried about their job titles, salaries, and budgets to do anything.

Somehow some way I was going to see my vision through. I was committed to it, and the more I showed results from my vision. It would validate change in my favor for a better educational experience. If the students did well, there was no way that the Superintendent or Principal Hunt could deny me what I needed. Or any of the other teachers for that matter.

I knew I would have a fight on my hands. And most people would be against me. But it didn't matter to me, because when all this is over they would all be thanking me. After that conversation with the Superintendent and Principal I was done for the day. I got my things together and exited the school in route to my home. It was a good but challenging day, and I needed it. Finally getting home I was a little tired, we were eating some leftovers so I had a break from cooking tonight.     Page 134

After she got home and finally got her bath, I sat by the bathtub and washed her back for her while we had a conversation.

"The Superintendent finally made his visit today. Him and Principal Hunt of course came to my classroom. Watched me teach the second half of the period. Afterwards we had an interesting conversation. He congratulates me on my students doing well on their Midterms. And without him even saying anything, you know I had to tell him how I felt" I said.

"Well of course, you wouldn't be Silas Jones if you didn't" my wife Fatima said interrupting being sarcastic and laughing.

"Hey...it's not everyday the Superintendent comes to your school. You have to take advantage and seize the moment baby. And that's what I did. And he goes on to say that basically we all got rules to follow, including me. Which is true, but I told him that I won't stop or give up on improving education any way I can" I replied.

"I wouldn't expect anything less from you Silas, I know the type of man you are. I love the type of man you are. You've taken over a lot of the house duties since I've been pregnant. After work each day I can just come home and relax. I really appreciate this babe, I love you" Fatima said.

"No doubt baby, you know it. And I love you more" I replied.

My wife and best friend, it was always a joy just being around her. I would hope our communication skills would remain great throughout our marriage. Fatima and I were just great for each other. After taking her bath, I helped dry her off and we relaxed the rest of the night in bed watching TV until the TV watched us.

Later that week, on that Saturday. My father and I decided to get together. So we got together at a North Side neighborhood bar to chop it up. So as we sat in the North Side Bar & Grill, I was having an always interesting conversation with my father.

"So how you been Pop ? You talk to Sidney Jr. lately" ? I asked.

"He called the other day wanting to borrow a hundred dollars. You know your brother, always got some type of scheme and hustle going on" my father replied.

"So did you give it to him" ? I asked.

"No I told him I didn't have it. I had it, but I just didn't feel right giving it to him. Sometimes it's not good to open the flood gates in terms of money. When he REALLY needs me, I'll be there like always" my father replied.     Page 135

I always listened intently while my father spoke, he was a man that had a way with words. Sometimes hearing him speak had you mesmerized, amazed, focused, completely bought in. Because you honestly believed what he was saying. Because it all made sense. I remember when my brother Sidney Jr. and I were growing up and our father was in the home. He always took time out of his day to talk to all of us kids. But especially me and my brother, because we were his boys. My father had a brother, my Uncle Charlie. He still lives on the West Side of Chicago. Not far from the same neighborhood he and my father grew up in. It was just my father and Uncle Charlie on my father's side of the family as far as my father's siblings were concerned. We would see our Uncle Charlie from time to time growing up.

I had heard stories about my Uncle Charlie growing up. How he used to be a big time hustler and numbers runner in Chicago back in the day. I even think my father had a hand in it also, but we as kids never knew. He never brought any of that around us. Just being with my father in the present time was great. Like I said, conversations with him were always interesting.

"Its only right Pop, I'm sure by now you know how to deal with your oldest. I know we do need to get together again soon. I enjoyed us all being together last time. Was a great time" I said.

"It was nice. It's always nice getting together with y'all kids and my grands. I know we haven't done it as much as we should have over the years. But better late than never, we're all still here and alive. Which reminds me, I have to call your sister later. And you and I. When it gets nice out towards the Spring, we have a date in the park to play Chess. Don't forget" my father said.

My father's favorite thing to do with almost any male in the family when it was nice out, was to play Chess. In one of many Chicago city parks. We always had competitive games between one another. My brother Sidney Jr. played my father a few times in Chess. But my

Uncle Charlie was another person that gave my father a battle in Chess. And it was something else my father and I could do while we hung out together. So you know I agreed.

"Yeah Savannah has been working a lot of crazy hours. Did she tell you about her promotion ? She's doing really well at the Hospital. And of course we can get together when it gets nice for some Chess" I replied.

"Yes she did tell me. So proud of my daughter. I knew when she was younger walking around the house pretending to be everything from a doctor to a singer. I knew she was going to be successful in life" my father said.    Page 136

That was something my father always did was encourage us as kids and now as adults to be the best we can be. He wanted so much for my brother being the oldest and a boy. My brother disappointed my parents in his early twenties, he had strayed off into the streets for a period. That hurt my father a great deal because he had fought so hard to keep us all on the straight and narrow. I believe that's when him and my father's disconnect started. It was evident with my father just telling me he told Sid that he didnt have the money he asked my father for. My father had mended his relationship with my brother, but he still didn't fully trust him.

"Yeah Pop I'm proud of Savannah too. You and my mother were blessed with some great kids" I said smiling.

We finished having some drinks and went on about our way. My father got in his car and I got in mines. Another great time with him. As I was driving home, I got a text from my wife saying that a reporter called and wanted to speak to me. At the time I had no idea what a reporter wanted to talk to me about. Not a clue. The only thing I could think of was, the case against Dak Hollis. But who knows. I quickly made my way home from the North Side and entered our home.

"Hey baby. So a reporter called ? That's crazy, I wonder what he wants to talk to me about" I said sounding curious.

"Well call him and see Silas" Fatima replied handing me the number.

I didn't waste any time taking the number and calling the reporter.

"Hello this is Silas Jones, you called to speak to me" ? I asked.

"Hello. And yes I did. How are you Mr. Jones ? I'm Roger Hamilton from The Chicago Spin and I wanted to talk to you about some comments you made to us earlier in the year when we came to your school" the reporter said.

"Oh yeah, I do remember that now. You guys did a piece on Chicago Public Schools. Can't remember exactly everything I said. But what about my comments" ? I asked.

"Yes that was us. And your comments were very insightful and we wanted to continue interviewing you for this piece we're doing on teachers" the reporter said.

"Oh really ? Ok. Yes I would be honored to talk about my comments and anything that has to do with education" I replied.

"Great. Let's say we meet somewhere low key and talk. Are you free in like an hour"? The reporter asked.

"Yeah that will work. Let's say we meet at The Bar Below in an hour" I said.

"Sounds good to me, see you then" the reporter replied.

I really thought I was in for the night, but this was an opportunity I couldn't pass up. It was a tool to be heard by the masses in the city. I would be heard by some people who thought similar to me and wanted a better education for the kid's of Chicago as well. The kids of this country. I had to seize the moment and do the interview, I knew there would be a lot riding on this too. With all the adrenaline going through my body, you would've thought I was nervous. But I wasn't, I was more anxious. So on the drive over there, all I could think about was this being my opportunity and how I wasn't going to disappoint. I knew what I wanted to say and in my mind I was ready for whatever question the reporter was going to ask me.

So after the short drive I arrived at my destination. And as I pulled up and got out of my car. I walked in the bar with a confidence and swagger like no other. As I approached the table where the reporter was sitting, he got up out of his chair as I reached the table and he shook my hand.

"Hello Mr. Jones, I'm Roger Hamilton" the reporter said.

Chapter Six  "My Impact Is Being Felt"

"Hello Mr. Hamilton, nice to meet you again" I said as I sat down.

"Call me Roger. I brought you here because I remember how passionate of a teacher you were from interviewing you the first time. It was actually a breath of fresh air to hear a teacher like yourself that really cared about the kids. The first interview actually stuck with me. I was eager to interview you again, but I only work for the local news. I don't call the shots. But now that I talked my bosses into doing a story on some local teachers, you were the first one I had in mind" the reporter said.

"Wow that's great to hear, and I appreciate the opportunity. Thank you. And yes I am one of those teachers that care. There's a lot more of us around than you think. Like any other profession, there's good and bad teachers. Just like they're good and bad cops. Sometimes it's hard to tell at first. But like my father used to say, the cream always rises to the top. So any questions you have for me, feel free" I replied.

"Sounds great. Lets start by asking what got you into teaching ? What made you want to teach" ? The reporter asked.

"Well after I got out of the Marines after eight years of serving in the Marine Corp. I knew I had my Masters Degree in Teaching and Secondary Education. I had great leadership skills from my time in the Marines, so I decided why not teach. I mean when I looked at it from that standpoint, it was a challenge to me. And I love challenges. I had a few interviews after I came home and applied at several schools. At first it seemed like I couldn't find a place where I knew I could fit for a while. And then I seen the school I'm at now, and heard they needed a History Teacher. So here I am" I replied smiling.

"Interesting. The fact that this is your first teaching job, and to have the impact you've had on your students is special. After we were here the first time, I had requested to see some of the results from the time we were here before. Of your students test scores. And then I got the current ones after your latest Midterms. Your class was one of only a few classes from that school that showed tremendous improvement in just one year. That's quite an achievement Mr. Jones, especially for a first year teacher" the reporter said.

"Thanks. I owe it all to my students, they worked really hard. And I'm proud of them. I just tried my best to prepare them the best I could" I replied.

" It's about these kids man, and their futures. If you're from Chicago you know how hard it is to make it out. And be somebody besides what society deems you to be. These kids are smart and some very talented in other things besides education. And we should never look down on any of them because of the environment they come from. I'm one of those kids, being from da South Side" I added on.

"Speaking of that. And knowing now that you come from the same neighborhoods that some of these kids come from. Have you had personal relationships with some of your students" ? The reporter asked.

"I've been all over the city and I know these kids that come from different neighborhoods. It was one of the main reasons I took the job at my school, the diversity of all the kids coming from all over. I love this city and I wanted to help as many kids from different backgrounds as I could. And yes I have some personal relationships with a few of my students. Nothing more than the normal teacher student relationship. I'm a very honest person, and my students know they can talk to me about anything that's going on with them. My door is always open. And I believe that's one of the reasons some of my students are fond of me" I replied.

"There's a case right now that's got your school in the spotlight for all the wrong reasons. It's been alleged that a local football star was accused of rape by an unnamed female. Any thoughts on that case while I have you here" ? The reporter asked.

It was a moment that would in part define me moving forward. And if the world would take me and my vision seriously. I really didn't know if the reporter had knew much about the case because it was still fresh in the news. He didn't say anything about it at all when we first met. But that's how slick the media is. I seen it happen too many times to pro athletes to let it happen to me. So I was already ahead of him and was ready when he asked the question.

"Well the case is still fresh, all I know is what everyone else knows. So I will not rush to judgement on the case. I have to sit back like everyone else and let it play out. But I will say, rape is a very serious crime. And when someone accuses another of that, you don't know what to think. You hate to think that this happened at all you know" I replied.

"What ways do you think that education can be improved in this country overall" ?

"I think first this country's government needs to actually do what they say they're doing. And make education a REAL priority on every level in this country. Not just on the collegiate level, but on the elementary level, the middle school level, and of course the high school level. And that starts with funding" I replied.

"All great ideas Mr. Jones. How long do you plan on teaching" ? The reporter asked.

"I never really thought about it, considering I'm just getting started. Who knows, as long as my school will have me. And as long as my students are buying into what I'm selling" I replied.

"Very interesting talking to you Mr. Jones, and a pleasure. Thanks for giving me this opportunity to interview you" the reporter said.

"And thank you for the opportunity to be interviewed. I appreciate the platform that allows teachers like myself and others to voice their concerns about the educational system. It's really important that you gave us this voice" I replied.

We shook hands and went our separate ways. It was an interesting interview and enjoyable to me because I was able to speak my mind. And get out most of the things I wanted to say. It was an unexpected encounter with the reporter. When Fatima said that the man called and wanted to speak to me. I immediately thought it would be all about the pending case of Dak Hollis. And of course he was aware of the case, it had dominated the local Chicago news. Besides the daily shootings of course. I felt I answered the question as best that I could, without showing my overwhelming support for Claudia. I couldn't do that within the media, and I couldn't legally without the process following through. And without me knowing the absolute truth.

So I decided to answer the question politically correct. And of course mixed with some truth, I got my point across. All and all it was a great day. That next week school was in full motion. I was introducing new lesson plans and my students were catching on. Deshawn was still having his issues at home, but was in class everyday. Much to my encouragement. I made sure Deshawn knew that I wanted him in class, even if I had to go pick him up in Fuller Park. Claudia was still doing her best to avoid the already negative attention she was getting from the case. A lot of people were still riding with Dak Hollis, mainly because he was a local star. And a lot of people were rooting for him from around the city. Hoping that it wasn't true.

I just wanted the truth to eventually come out, and I knew eventually it would. I still believed Claudia, and would stand by her side if needed. It was yet another day in the books at school. After my students left class I was finishing some paperwork at my desk when Mrs. Williams came to my door. And knocked on it as she stood outside.

"Can I help you Mrs. Williams" ? I asked.

"Nice to see you too Mr. Jones. Did you see the paper yet today ? Well you're in it, along with your interview with a reporter from The Chicago Spin" Mrs. Williams replied.

"Oh yeah, I was expecting that. Just didn't think it would be in there this quick" I said.

"Oh so you're doing interviews on the side without the school's consent ? That's not good Silas. It's definitely not a secret now, it's in the local paper" Mrs. Williams said.

"This school doesn't control my life. And the reporter contacted ME, not the other way around. He asked me to do an interview about education, which is my passion. So of course I wasn't going to hesitate to talk about that. Check the article out and decide for yourself. It was a great interview. And trust me Mrs. Williams, I'm not trying to keep it a secret" I replied.

"Well it sounds like you know what you're doing. I just wanted to let you know it was in the paper. Enjoy your night" Mrs. Williams said as she was leaving.

"You enjoy yours also" I said as she walked out.

Mrs. Williams always tried to stir things up with me. When she felt I was going out on a limb or against the grain. When it came to the school and District. And their rules. I always followed the rules, and I didn't feel like I did anything wrong by doing the interview. But I'm sure some of my colleagues and peers thought I was. Especially being that none of them had stepped up and put themselves out there like me. This is my passion and my destiny, this is what I was supposed to do. So my decisions only affected me not my colleagues and peers. But whatever I accomplished to further reach my goals, it would eventually benefit all. That was what being a leader was all about.....sacrifice.

I knew this. And I also knew how far I could take my agenda without obviously overstepping the boundaries but still pushing them. That was me. And that wasn't the only visit I got before leaving that day. But this visit I was expecting, and actually it was a little late. Of course none other than Principal Hunt. Right before I was about to walk out of my classroom, Principal Hunt got my attention as he was walking in the hallway. We went back inside my classroom and had a conversation.

"I just read your comments in the paper. Seems like you really enjoyed the interview, was this planned Mr. Jones" ? Principal Hunt asked.

"Actually it wasn't planned. The reporter that was here earlier in the year that did the segment on inner city schools, asked to interview me again. So I said, why not. I wasn't doing anything, and you know I'm always willing to talk about bettering education nationwide. It was a great opportunity" I replied.

"Mr. Jones you never cease to amaze me with your persistence. But what you don't realize is, funding and bettering education isn't solely on our hands. In most cases our hands are tied. Ultimately the decision comes down to the local, state, and federal governments" Principal Hunt said.

"I do realize that, and I mentioned them too. I know they all control the cash flow. And we do have some say in it Principal Hunt. By putting pressure on them. Parents, teachers, and students collectively. If we want better, we have to fight for it. And it's not going to be easy. Doesn't the saying go, nothing worth having is ? It's the truth Principal Hunt. I'm sure you know that" I replied.

"I'm all for the fight, but at what price ? My job ? I still got two kids in college, I can't lose everything over something that I have very little control over. I can't do it. And I know you may look at me like I don't know much about the inner city. But I've been in some of the toughest neighborhoods in Chicago. I knew guys that were from Cabrini-Green Homes, State Way Gardens, and Robert Taylor Homes. Believe it or not I grew up in the Wicker Park area. And now reside in Lincoln Park. So I know the city more than you think I do. And I want more for these kids also. As I said before, just be careful Silas. As much as you think I'm against you. I don't want to lose a teacher like yourself. I know you care. But there's other ways besides the way you're handling this" Principal Hunt said as he got up and was about to leave.

"I'm good Principal Hunt, I can take care of myself. And you enjoy your evening" I replied as he walked out.

I knew I was going to hear from Principal Hunt at some point, I was waiting for it. I even learned something about him I didn't know. And he finally realized that he wasn't going to determine if I was going to give up my fight for a better education. He realized that day how determined I was, and how serious I was. I wasn't expecting anyone to join the fight with me at first. I had said that previously. What was transpiring wasn't anything surprising. First Mrs. Williams, and then Principal Hunt. They both knew I wasn't the type to give up on what I believed in. They saw that for the little time they've worked alongside me. But once my vision would become more clearer for the world to see, I believed others would join me. Because they too would realize it wasn't just about me, but about the kids we were teaching.     Page 143

Later that night as I sat home. Fatima and I were relaxing on the couch watching TV. As we were sitting there I just stared at my pregnant wife admiring her beauty from head to toe. I told her recently that she looks just as beautiful as she always has. Of course her being a woman and pregnant, she didnt think so. But I honestly did feel that way, I really thought she looked sexy pregnant. I would often remind her that she was beautiful. I might've had my school work and everything else going on, but I was very much apart of this pregnancy. Every step of the way, like I had promised my wife.

"One of my fellow teachers, Mrs. Williams. Deshawn's aunt. Let me know that my interview with the reporter from The Chicago Spin was in the paper" I said.

"It was ? !! Did you get a paper babe ? Let's see it" Fatima interrupted.

"Calm down baby, let me finish" I said laughing.

"So she tells me and I guess she felt like I didn't know that the interview would be in there, but I knew that was already agreed upon. Anyway she goes on talking all this nonsense sounding fearful like always. And I told her yes everything in that article I said. Then after she leaves, Principal Hunt comes in. Almost sounding the same. Saying him and the Superintendent's hands were tied. All the funds had to be approved and distributed by the local, state, and federal government. Blah..blah...blah. Which I knew. So I told him, we have to fight for what we need. Put pressure on them. Teachers, parents, and kids collectively. It has to be a collective effort, that's the only way it will work" I said.

"And what did he say after that" ? Fatima asked.

"Well then he told me that he really did care about the kids, and he didn't want to lose me. That I should be careful. Said he knew people from all over Chicago, in the projects. And that he knew about the city, and the kids that come from this city. I didn't know what to believe from him, he's not someone that I trust. I appreciate the opportunity that he gave me to teach at the school. But I don't trust him as far as in my best interest" I replied.

"As you shouldn't, they're only co-workers. And as far as Mrs. Williams is concerned, we know she's a hater. She was probably thinking you were going to go back on the comments you made in the paper. Speaking of that, where's the paper babe? I want to see it" Fatima said sounding excited.

I smiled and gave her the newspaper, I had it in my back pocket the whole time.

Dak Hollis hearing was coming up in a few days and Claudia had to be present. She had her support system, her family. But she did ask me to be present. I had no problem being there for her. For now we had class and we were going over another new lesson plan I was introducing for the second straight week.

"I know you all are wondering why we're getting yet another lesson plan for the second straight week. Well we're in a race against time so to speak. We want to be as prepared as possible for Finals. You guys and gals need to finish up strong. Most of you are Seniors and are about to start a new journey in your lives. Some to college and others in the workforce. Some even in the Armed Forces. Either way finish strong, its very important for you all moving forward. Our new lesson plan is on page 105, so please open your textbooks and turn to that page" I said as I got class started.

It was yet another productive day in class. And after class and after everyone left, Claudia had said she needed to talk to me. So now was the chance for us to talk.

"Thanks a lot for agreeing to come to the hearing with me. It means a lot. Thanks for supporting me period, it hasn't been easy but I'm getting stronger each day" Claudia said.

"That's great Claudia, and you're welcome. You're one of my brightest students and a very nice young lady. Of course I will support you. And I'm glad that you're getting stronger. You will need to be strong for the trial, because that will be when you have to revisit that night. I'm proud of you Claudia for being brave and strong, it takes a lot of courage to come forward in a case like this" I replied.

Claudia knew that she was up against a lot of people locally in Chicago. Some who thought she was just another girl trying to derail a promising young career for a young black man. But Claudia was also a person of color, so it definitely wasn't about race in this particular situation. Some thought maybe she was a girl that really wanted to be with Dak and he didn't want to be with her like that. And so she got bitter and screamed rape. I completely disagreed with that theory because Claudia was a beautiful brown skin young woman, who could've been with any guy she wanted to be with. I seen plenty of young men try and get her attention in the hallway throughout the school year. But me being a teacher at the school. I couldn't show as much bias in the public eye. Including when and if I would be interviewed again.

Another day in the books and it was productive, it was all I could ask for from myself and my students. Progression being shown each day, until we got to where we wanted to be. I wanted my students to do better than they did on their Midterms. I think doing that. It would further cement our claim that all our inner city schools needed more funding and improvements. A better education period. Page 145

That next day came and as always on Fridays, I was energetic because the weekend was amongst us. But Friday itself was special to me because those quizzes let me know where my students were with their learning. By this time, my wife's belly was growing and getting bigger. And I was admiring the whole process. Each morning I would wake up after getting out of bed, and just stare at my pregnant wife sleeping so peacefully. To me that was so beautiful. Being a first time father I wanted to experience it all.

I stepped out of our home in the midst of a bunch of cameras out of nowhere. I had no clue that a news crew were outside our home. As I was trying to get into my car, I was approached by three reporters.

"Mr. Jones could you explain your comments about the District and the country in regards to education" ? A reporter asked.

"Excuse me. I need to get to my car. My comments that were made in the article was how I felt about the state of education in this District and country. So whatever you guys read in the article, is what I said. Now if you'll excuse me, I have a job to get to" I said getting in my car and driving off.

I was shocked that the news media was outside my home. I wasn't expecting that and I wasn't expecting that interview to be that big of a deal. But to be honest I'm glad it was. Now maybe it would open eyes not only in this District but in this country. With the news cameras in my face, I could only imagine how things would be at school. On my way to school, I got a call on my cell phone. It was Mitchell.

" Hey Silas, we need to talk. I was in a meeting and I was pulled out of a meeting and watched you on TV. These people Downtown have been talking about you and mentioning your name. Asking questions about you" Mitchell said.

"And all this is supposed to mean what Mitchell ? I'm not doing anything illegal. I'm not no criminal, I just said what I felt and thought was right. We live in a country that proclaims to have freedom of speech. Well I'm only practicing it" I replied.

"Silas you can't say everything you feel in your profession. You have people that work above you. You can't show them disrespect by questioning their decisions and how funding is being dispersed. By no means are they perfect, nobody is. But just be careful what you say. They appreciate your efforts as a great teacher, but some want you gone for how you talk down the District and this country" Mitchell said.

"Mitchell do you hear yourself ? Is this the man I grew to know talking right now ? Or you letting the pressures of your job get to you ? I'm just being the Silas Jones you grew to know brotha" I replied.

"Silas theres ways to get things done without going about it the way you are. All this attention your getting from the media isn't good. It's making the District look bad. You still work for the School District you know" Mitchell said.

"Mitchell I think we need to end this conversation, it's clear we're not fighting the same fight. There isn't much more to talk about. I will continue to put pressure on the powers that be to do what they need to do. Make education a REAL priority. Politicians talking about putting education first, and education is the key to our future. But they never put the country's money where the country's mouth is. I'm a teacher that cares about my students, and my students know this. So if the District feels like firing a teacher that actually cares, so be it. I'm not afraid Mitchell, I have no fear with my agenda. About anything" I replied.

"Ok Silas, suit yourself. I'm only being a friend, and giving it to you straight. Don't say I didn't warn you" Mitchell said.

"A friend ? Good day Mitchell" I replied laughing a little and shaking my head.

Like the saying goes, pressure busts pipes. And it was clear Mitchell was feeling the pressure from his superiors. They knew we knew each other and probably told him to talk to me. It had to take this to know that Mitchell was only going to go so far with me. It was actually something that my boy Angelo had warned me about. Despite the fact him and Mitchell didn't always get along, Angelo kept the peace out of respect for me. After that day I knew us as associates would never be the same. He knew my vision more than anybody. I talked to him and Angelo plenty of times about the improvements I wanted to see with education.

I knew that I would be in this battle alone when it came to the professional level. But I always believed the people closest to me would be in my corner personally. I knew that Mitchell's bosses were putting pressure on him to try to keep me in line. Because they knew that he had referred me for a job in the District before. But Mitchell or anyone else couldn't control me or my thoughts when it came to education. If you didn't agree with my vision, that was fine. But you wasn't going to stand in my way either. I knew now where Mitchell stood.

I finally got to school and was relieved to get into my classroom. It seemed like it took forever to get to school. The reporters outside my home, and my not so cool conversation with Mitchell. I was finally here and focused on my day. It was Friday and it was our weekly quiz. After class had started and my students took their quizzes, in which I had my students take their quizzes at the beginning of class right away. I waited for each of them to finish one by one.

After class that day Deshawn asked to speak to me. He had been doing well after being distracted a little by his home life. His attendance had been perfect ever since, and I was proud of the turnaround. So after class Deshawn came up to my desk after my other students had left.

"I just wanted to say thanks a lot for believing in me Mr. Jones. I've never had a teacher like you in my life before. You didn't let me go and give up on myself because of my circumstances. You stuck by me, and I will never forget that. Can I ask why you didn't give up on me" ? Deshawn said.

"I would never give up on any of my students unless they gave up on themselves. And you especially, I seen the potential in you. Not only on that court, but in this classroom. I see your drive each day, your progress each day. I know you want to be successful for you and your family. I know you can have it, that's why I wouldn't let you give up on it. Don't let no one come between you and your dreams Deshawn, not even your brother" I replied.

Deshawn just looked at me and shook his head agreeing. I knew no matter what I said, Deshawn was always going to be worried about his brother. I was just glad he understood how to deal with it better. By not letting it distract him from his goals and dreams.

"I got some offers from a bunch of colleges, from all over the country. Part of me wants to go far away from Chicago, and another part of me doesn't want to move too far away from my mother and siblings. The important thing is, they're all full rides. Full scholarships" Deshawn said sounding excited.

"Think long and hard about it, and go where your heart and mind tells you to go. What place will you feel home at ? There's a lot of things to think about when making that decision. I mean to be honest with you, I stayed close to home and went to DePaul University in the city. But that doesn't mean you have to. Go where you feel it's right for you" I replied.

Page 148

"Was there a particular reason why you stayed so close to home" ? Deshawn asked.

"No reason at all, I actually liked DePaul a great deal. When I went to visit it just felt right to me. Being that it was in my hometown made it even better. It was an easy decision for me, but I'm not expecting you to do the same. Maybe you want to get away from Chicago, and the distraction of furthering your education in your hometown. It's a lot of pressure on you Deshawn. You're going to be a college athlete that has a chance to one day possibly go pro. Your situation is different than mines" I replied.

"It's like I really don't know what to do Mr. Jones. Part of me wants to leave Chicago, get away from everything that's been going on. Just wish I could take my family with me. The other part of me doesn't want to go too far away because of my mother, I help her a lot with my younger siblings. She counts on me a great deal. Especially with my brother still running the streets from time to time" Deshawn said.

"Well you have a decision to make son. If you stay here and do nothing with that talent of yours, where do you think you will end up ? You think you'll ever get your family out of Fuller Park if you stay here ? Don't go to school and become a working man ? You have to take that chance Deshawn, if you want better for your family. You can always come back home and visit. But you have to want to get out of here, so you can focus. Be the best student athlete you can be. Just know either way you decide you have my support if you're doing something positive with your life. I can't support negativity, and I would be telling you wrong if I did. And I don't want to ever do that" I replied.

Deshawn knew he could talk to me about anything, and he knew I knew his situation. I was the only one he would talk to at school. Not even his aunt Mrs. Williams he would open up to like he did with me. He also knew I understood him. All the kids from my classroom were from all over the city, and I loved it. Different areas and different backgrounds, they kept me on my toes. Not only did I make things interesting for them, they made things interesting for me. At first things were rocky, and that's what I expected. Naturally Chicago people didn't trust you to lead until you proved yourself. It was a show and prove town, and I wouldn't have it any other way.

"Thanks Mr. Jones, I always get a better understanding of things after talking to you. Definitely going to think long and hard about it. Not sure what I'm going to decide. But whatever it is I'm going to consider everyone I care about and mean the most to me" Deshawn said.

"As you should Deshawn......as you should" I replied as Deshawn was leaving.

After leaving that day, I peaked out the door before I left to avoid any reporters or cameras. Thankful to say there wasn't any reporters or cameras. But by the time I got home that night, another local Chicago paper had inflamed my comments into criticizing the District in a whole. As soon as I walked in the door, Fatima had it sitting on the table with my dinner.

"It seems one of our local papers made your comments out to be against the District. I was watching TV earlier and they were talking about it. I finally turned it off because I knew what you meant by your comments and I didn't want to watch that nonsense any longer" Fatima said sounding irritated.

"Baby don't let that garbage bother you. Let them think what they want. My students know the teacher I am and that's all that matters to me" I replied.

"Trying to destroy a man that's doing something positive within the community. Being a teacher and wanting more for his students. I guess it would be cool if you was out here doing something negative. What a sick backwards twisted society we live in" Fatima said sounding frustrated shaking her head.

"Yes we do baby. It don't matter what they write about me, it's not going to stop me from being who I am" I replied pulling my pregnant wife closer to me and giving her a kiss.

"I know, you're always going to be you. That's why I love you" Fatima said smiling as I was giving her a ton of kisses.

I dealt with the outside world when I dealt with it. But when I was home, I was indeed at peace with my Queen. And as the days turned to weeks and the weeks turned to months. My Queen was filling out and I was so excited at the maturation of the pregnancy. Watching our baby grow. And going to every appointment, and enjoying every moment with my wife.

After another great dinner together and a nice relaxing evening, my Queen and I were off to bed. Most nights I would be cuddled up holding Fatima from behind while she lay on her side. And I did the same tonight, holding her as we slept. We both loved and felt comfortable sleeping in that position. It was relaxing and we both slept like babies.

That next week came and Monday had arrived once again. I got up early as usual and made myself some coffee like I did most mornings. My wife had took the day off. I made my way to my car and off to school I went. No reporters or news crews as I got in my car unbothered. Made it to school and parked my car, but something was strange. I couldn't park in my usual spot. Most if not all the faculty knew I parked there. The spot was taken for some reason. After getting out of my car, I was a little confused. But proceeded to walk in the school. When I did, Principal Hunt was waiting for me at the entrance to the school.

"Mr. Jones you've been put on Administrative Leave" Principal Hunt said.

"What ? For what ? That interview ? You've got to be kidding me" I replied in disbelief.

"Just go home Mr. Jones, you will be notified when you can have a meeting with the Superintendent and School Board" he said.

I just stared at Principal Hunt and shook my head. Turned around and walked right back to my car. I sat in my car for ten minutes trying to make sense of the whole situation. Administrative Leave sounded too much like what corrupt cops got who killed unarmed people of color. That word or term just didn't sit well with me. In my heart I know I didn't do anything wrong to deserve any leave from my job. I was still shocked driving home. I couldn't go home, not now. Fatima would know something was wrong, and I didn't want her to find out just yet. I didn't want her to worry, especially with her being pregnant.

So I called my brother Sid and seen what he was up to. Didn't know for sure if he was working or what shift he was working at the time. He happened to be working at that moment, so then I called my father. He was at home so I made the short drive to his place. My father was surprised to see me at that time of day himself. He knew I was a teacher and at that time of day I would be teaching. So he had to know something was wrong.

"Son it's mid morning, why aren't you at work" ? My father asked.

"Have you been reading the paper ? Watching the local news ? I had an interview with a reporter from The Chicago Spin and he asked me some questions about education. How I felt about it locally and in general. I answered the questions as honestly as I could. You know how I feel about education Pop. I just told it like it was, and as a result of that. The District thought I was at odds with them, and I guess in a way I am. I get to school this morning to find out that I was put on Administrative Leave because of what I said" I replied.                    Page 151

"I guess freedom of speech doesn't matter in this country when you're being honest. Sometimes the truth hurts, but I think the District took it too far by putting you on Administrative Leave. It's not like you had sex with any of the students, abused any of the students, or disrespected your superiors. And still you're put on leave. I just don't understand it son, but either way I know you did what was right to you in your heart. And thats all that matters" my father Sidney Sr. said.

"I have no regrets Pop, no matter what happens. I know what I'm here for. Them putting me on Administrative Leave, will not stop me or my vision. This is just a bump in the road on my journey" I replied.

"Well while you're here, and while you have time. Let's get a round or two of some Chess in. I can't wait till the weather gets warm again, and we can go out to the park" my father said taking his Chess set out.

It was one of my father's favorite games. He enjoyed playing Chess and he loved when me or my brother played with him. So I decided to play with him, as we continued to talk about any and everything.

"How's my daughter in law and soon to be grandchild doing" ? My father asked.

"Oh they're doing great Pop. I'm at every doctors appointment, going through the whole process with her. And I'm enjoying it all" I replied.

"And you should son. It's a great time in a man's life when he's expecting a child. It can also be stressful. But I'm sure you and your wife have things under control. How's your sister ? I called her the other day, she hasn't returned my call yet" my father said.

"Yeah sis is busy, the hospital keeps her busy. I mean we are in Chicago as crazy as that sounds. But it's the truth, her job keeps her busy. I hardly speak to her myself Pop" I replied.

It was good seeing and spending time with my father as always, even though it wasn't planned. And considering the circumstances, it was a bright spot in an otherwise dark day. After leaving my father's home and heading to my own house. I had some time to think. And all I could think about was my students and how they would be affected by this. I didnt regret what I said at all, but I was disappointed that I was put on leave. For now all I could do was wait and be patient until I heard something different. With my time off I would be as productive as I could be, and help my wife around the house.

Page 152

But before I could do that, I had to get home and let her know what happened. I had stayed away from my home and went to see my father for the day. But now it was time to return home. And it wasn't that I was ashamed of coming home and telling my wife the news. I just wasn't ready to go home after Principal Hunt told me my immediate fate as a teacher at the school. Even getting home early, my wife was in our bedroom sound asleep. So I decided to prepare dinner for us.

As I was preparing dinner I had some more time to think. Even though I was a man of my word and would stick to my comments until my demise. I missed teaching and I missed my students. BUT I wasn't backing off of any of my comments because I felt strongly about them. After being home and preparing dinner, my wife had gotten up from her nap. I guess she smelled the food cooking in the kitchen.

"Hey babe, dinner smells great. How was your day ? You got home early huh" ? My wife Fatima asked.

"I'm glad you asked. I was put on Administrative Leave because of my comments in the interview I did about education" I replied.

"What ? You have got to be kidding me. You didn't do anything wrong. That is just ridiculous" Fatima said in disbelief.

"I said the exact same thing. But now it's something I have to deal with. I don't regret it at all, I meant everything I said. But I do miss teaching and I do miss my students. The District has taken away something that I love to do. They knew what to do to hurt me. And with this trial coming up with Dak and Claudia. Deshawn's situation. I need to be there for my students. And it hurts me that I can't be there right now" I replied.

"I can only imagine babe, I know how much you love teaching. But just take this time to reflect, and get energized so you can be ready when they do call you to come back. Having you home some of this these days will be nice anyway" Fatima said smiling at me.

My wife was getting further along in her pregnancy, so she started working from home more. Actually part of her day was at her office, and the other part she worked from home. And now with me being home, she loved having me around. And to be honest it was nice seeing more of my wife. Doing things for her from rubbing her feet to rubbing her belly. I was enjoying the whole process that was pregnancy. I felt almost as connected to our baby as Fatima was. Although I know there is nothing more stronger than a mother's bond with her children. I knew that because I knew the bond that me and my siblings had with our mother.      Page 153

After a relaxing evening with my Queen, the next morning came. And to be honest, I dreaded that next morning. Because it was the realization that I was still on Administrative Leave. It was hard for me, especially being that I had developed great relationships with my students. But I was here now, at this point and I had to deal with it like I dealt with everything else in my life. Take it in stride and keep moving. So with that being said, I got up and went to the gym. There was no way I was going to stay home all day. While I was at the gym on the stationary bike, I was watching the Tv's when I seen what looked like my school and a bunch of students standing outside with picked signs. They were yelling something but I couldn't hear because it was loud in the gym.

I walked closer to the Tv's and looked up to see that the signs read "Bring Back Mr. Jones". I was in somewhat disbelief, watching my students outside the school like that. And I was also touched at the fact they did all that for me. It really made me feel like I had served a purpose and made a difference in their lives. I just stared at the Tv's and smiled. Unbeknownst to the rest of the people at the gym, who had no idea that those kids on TV were talking about me. After the news cameras stopped filming, I went back to my workout.

Later that day I returned home and was about to prepare dinner, when I got a call on my cell. It was my sister Savannah.

"Silas what's going on ? I was watching the news earlier and they had your school on there and some kids outside with signs saying "Bring Back Mr. Jones" Savannah said.

"Yeah. Well sis I was put on Administrative Leave because of a interview I did on my thoughts about education. A reporter from The Chicago Spin wanted to interview me, he was the same reporter that did a piece on our school earlier in the year. So I said why not and did the interview. I definitely don't regret it, I stand by what I said no matter what" I said.

"As you should. And obviously your students feel the same way too, because they're out there protesting for you. So proud of the impact you've had on these kids bro, it's truly amazing" my sister said.

"Thanks sis, I appreciate it. In the meantime I've just been helping Fatima more around the house and just trying to keep myself active.

You know I'm not the type to just sit around doing nothing. And I'm trying to be patient throughout this process, but it's tough I'm not going to lie" I replied.

"I'm sure it is Silas, but you're standing up for what you believe in. And what you believe in is right. I admire you for that bro" Savannah said.

"I went to see Pop yesterday, he asked about you. Said he called you but you didn't return his call. Is everything ok between you and Pop" ? I asked.

"Yeah everything is fine. I will call him later today. Things were hectic at the hospital. I'm just now finally getting a breather. I better get going big brother, the kids will be home soon. I'm going to call dad after that" Savannah replied.

"Ok sis, give mom and the family my love. And I will tell her about what happened with me, if she doesnt see it first. But let me tell her" I said.

"Will do bro. Give Fatima and the baby my love" Savannah replied before hanging up the phone.

It was always good talking to my sister. She was a hard working woman and great mother to her children. Great person period. And even though she was my baby sister, she was wise beyond her years. I was glad to hear that things were still good between her and my father. Savannah and my father always had a great bond and relationship, even through my parents eventually splitting. They still kept a pretty close bond. And with my brother and father repairing their relationship, my family was coming together in a crucial time in my life. A time when I needed them. I had my first child on the way, and I had just been put on Administrative Leave at my job. Things looked like they were spinning out of control, but to me it was a test of my will.

They would reinstate me in a heartbeat if I went and apologized. But what was I apologizing for ? I didn't regret or wouldn't regret what I said. So it was either they were going to realize they made a crucial mistake and reinstate me. Or I was done being a teacher. As much as I feared that reality, I knew that it could be a reality for me. I loved teaching it was my passion, something I had thought about doing before I left the Marines. Once I did my eight years in the Marines, I knew teaching was what I wanted to do. Here I was only teaching for several months before they stripped me of that. I would continue to wait patiently. Enjoying my time at home and watching my wife go through her pregnancy. Watching our baby grow, and spending time with people that mean the most to me. My time off was very productive so far, but I was getting anxious about getting back to doing what I loved.

A few days had passed and Mitchell must have got wind that I was on Administrative Leave, because that morning he called me on my cell. At the moment I wasn't in the mood to talk to Mitchell. Because something told me I knew what he was going to say, and what he was calling for. So I saved myself the aggravation of hearing it. Mitchell would still be an associate of mines, but not necessarily someone I wanted close to me. We would still hang out from time to time with our wives like we did. Fatima and Kendra were pretty good friends and got along well. I wasn't trying to drive a wedge between them two, I knew they both enjoyed being around each other.

I would just keep our situation between us. Wasn't no need to get our wives involved. I just knew after that day, that my vision didn't include Mitchell. He had a different take on things, and I respected it. But I didn't agree with it. Mitchell was the tow the line kind of guy, I was a step outside the lines type of guy. I wasn't going to agree to something that I didn't feel strongly about or believed in. No matter what the District said. And I knew I was treading on thin ice, because I was pushing the District so to speak. I did an interview that pretty much exposed them and the country to things they already knew. But didn't want to face. Problem was, being in my position as a teacher. The District felt I had no right to express my feelings about the job they were doing, or the job the country was doing as regards to education.

I was born and raised in a country that has freedom of speech, and I was the type to speak my mind. Always was and always will be. The District was happy as ever when it came to me helping my students and our school improve our test scores on our Midterms. About 77% of our students passed their Midterms. Which was a great improvement from 56% the previous year. A 21% improvement in just a year was a great achievement, especially in these times. When some kids hadn't been to school all year. You had some kids that came to school when they wanted, which was something that bothered me but was essentially out of my control. You had some female students become pregnant and drop out. These were things I had witnessed since teaching at the school.

If I could go all around Chicago and get every kid that I knew had potential, that was troubled but just needed to be pushed and guided. I would. To me I always summed a child's support system up like this. 30% was the parents 20% was the teacher, and the other 50% was the student. The parents had a bigger responsibility because it was THEIR child. They could discipline them more than a teacher ever could. The teachers owned that 20% because they taught the children. The child holds the biggest share because it's their life. And they had to want to learn to be successful. By applying themselves. That's why I always said, I love teaching kids that want to learn.  Page 156

My students were still doing some protesting, as the local news was giving the city of Chicago play by play. My name was starting to circulate beyond the city, because of the main reasons I taught. My students. They made me proud. And not just because they were fighting for me, but because they did it without breaking the rules at school. They protested before school, some did it on their lunch and non-school hours. I knew because I watched it live at home. I definitely didn't want them to jeopordize their futures for me. Not for something I did. And then I realized that they were doing it more because it was the right thing to do.

That next day I was at home and my cell rang, it was Principal Hunt. I didn't know what to think about him calling me. I guess you could say I was ready for whatever it was.

"Mr. Jones this is Principal Hunt. I would like you to come to the School District offices to have a meeting with Superintendent Evans and the School Board. To discuss everything that's went on, and your job at the school" Principal Hunt said.

"Principal Hunt if Superintendent Evans and the School Board are going to fire me, let me know now so we don't waste each other's time. I don't want this to drag out any further than it has" I replied.

"Mr. Jones just come to the meeting. If they were going to fire you, they wouldn't be meeting with you. So I will see you tomorrow, I will also be there" Principal Hunt said.

"Yes....tomorrow" I replied.

I agreed to the meeting with the thinking they weren't going to fire me, especially after Principal Hunt told me himself. I knew what the meeting was about, I guess you could say I was disinterested. I wasn't apologizing for anything I said, and my philosophy as a teacher wasn't going to change. My fight for education wasn't going to change. So I had no idea what they had for me in regards to that. But one thing was for sure, they knew deep down I was a good teacher and I cared about my students. And all of Chicago saw that my students cared about me too. So whatever they was going to come up with, it better be on point. I felt confident, and I felt I should be confident.

In the short time I was at the school, I had done pretty good for myself. I was able to get things done that wasn't done before I had arrived. I was hoping after this meeting tomorrow, I could go back to doing what I loved. For now I would enjoy my night. I would pray on it before I laid my head on the pillow. And sleep peacefully feeling like tomorrow was my day for redemption.

Page 157

That next day I was to meet with Superintendent Evans and the School Board at the School District offices. I got up early although the meeting was at nine. Got my coffee and sat down to watch some TV. I was dressed as if I was going to school to teach. A few hours had passed and I was on my way to the School District offices. When I finally got there and got out of my car, I headed straight into the building.

"Hello Mr. Jones, have a seat. We called you here to the School District offices in front of I and the School Board to discuss your comments made in an interview with The Chicago Spin. It was certain comments made about the District and the way we do things. You do understand you are employed by the District ? We can't have you making those comments when we're trying to do our best with the kids in this District" the Superintendent said.

"With all due respect Superintendent Evans. I didn't say anything that was wrong or untrue. You may disagree with me, but I know what I see everyday when I teach my students. I know the resources that we have to teach with. When I received my new classroom textbooks, I knew that they were going to make some type of difference. I didn't know specifically at the time, but I knew it would make a positive difference somehow. And it did. The students in this school did well on their Midterms for the first time in a long time. As the saying goes. Men lie women lie, but numbers don't. The results didn't lie, those new textbooks helped improve test scores. My students protesting because they know I care, and their protesting for whats right. I'm one of the teachers that really cares about his students. And if all of you members of the School Board really value the students in this District, then you would understand my fight for education" I replied.

"Its not about you Mr. Jones, not at all. We're running a District with what we have, and you need to think about if you want to still be employed in it. We do what we can with what we have. So I will give you another day to think about it. When and if you return, there will be no more interviews referencing the School District. You can feel the way you do if you choose to, but here you must be on the same page as everyone else. I know you may not agree with everything the School District does, but you must follow the rules.

And not talk down and undermind the School District because of your own beliefs" Superintendent Evans said.

"Give me time to think about this. The only reason I would come back is for my students. And if I do come back, be rest assured Superintendent Evans. I will follow the rules like always. One thing I won't do is apologize for caring too much about my students education. Not only do I think this School District is below the line, this entire country is also. It's not just about what I believe, it's the facts" I replied.    Page 158

"You have two days to let us know what you want to do. We'll be expecting to hear from you. Good day Mr. Jones" Superintendent Evans said as Principal Hunt sat on the other side of the desk just watching with the rest of the School Board.

Only a good teacher that truly cares could talk like that in front of the School Board. I knew I had leverage because my students had put pressure on the School District to give me my job back. Their protesting was getting a lot of news attention around the city of Chicago. And it was starting to go National. With social media being as relevant and popular as it is, my students were able to spread the word on their pages. I was getting mail sent to the school for me, supporting me. It was like I had became a star overnight. And I believe that was the only reason that Superintendent Evans and Principal Hunt even considered giving me my job back. They knew I was one of the best teachers in the school. And they knew my students loved me, which would make it difficult for them moving forward.

I had to think and think hard if I could continue tolerating the Superintendent and Principal. I knew they were my two biggest critics, I felt like they both were waiting for me to fail. And it was good that I knew it, so I would know how to deal with them. I missed teaching my students, but I wanted to take a few days to get myself together. Get my mind back on the positive aspect of the situation. And that was being able to teach my students again. That meant more to me than anything.

A few days had passed and I let the Superintendent and Principal know that I wanted to return to teaching. They agreed to let me return and I was ready to go back to what I loved. Three days later I agreed to return to school. I was excited that morning, and ready to get to school. I woke up so early that I woke Fatima up.

"I'm sorry I woke you baby, I'm just anxious" I said sitting up in the bed.

"It's ok babe, I know you've been waiting for this day. I'm glad you're going back to what you love. Of course I'm going to miss having you around the house more, but I know it was killing you that you couldn't teach" Fatima said.

"It was. But I knew I had a great reason why I couldn't teach, I had to stand by my words as a man like I was raised to. I told the Superintendent and School Board that very thing in the meeting. I wasn't going to apologize for anything I said, because I know what I said wasn't wrong. It was the truth. And more than anything, I was a man of my word. It crossed my mind that I would never teach again, that could've been a real possibility. I'm glad it wasn't the end of my teaching career, but it did cross my mind" I replied.

Page 159

"Its always a possibility, but I'm glad it's not an option in this situation. Your students want you back and you want to be back. So it's all good" Fatima said.

Fatima as right. As I was returning to teaching, all that mattered was I was back. And I was happy to be back. An hour had passed and I was up and ready to go. On the drive to school, I thought about a few things. Where were my students in their lessons ? I hadn't been to school in over a weeks time, it was almost two weeks. Getting my students up to speed would be a challenge I was up for. The whole time I was off, I still had my lesson plans put together as if I was still teaching. I guess you could say that was one of the ways I was coping with the situation.

I finally got to school and entered my classroom for the first time in nearly two weeks. As soon as I entered I got a feeling I couldn't explain, it was almost like I was home again after being away for so long. I got chills all over just looking around at my classroom. I finally made it to my desk and sat down, still looking around in amazement of being back where I belonged. After that I had to get myself together and ready for my class that would be entering soon. Not even sure if the District told my students that I was returning. Either way, I would be excited to see them and I'm sure they would be excited to see me also.

Fifteen minutes went past and my students started to enter my classroom. They were very excited to see me, each one coming up to my desk and welcoming me back. Telling me how hard they were fighting for me. It meant a lot, especially coming from these kids. These kids were from the city of Chicago, all over the city. You had to be great and be able to relate to all of them for them to be able to show this much love to you. It definitely wasn't easy in the beginning. I had to stand up to some kids that probably could've plotted to kill me. There were some kids that went to our school that were gang affiliated. But instead, me standing up to them in turn garnered their respect. They knew at that point, if I was crazy enough to stand up to them they knew I cared. Once I was put on leave, my students had to deal with a substitute coming in while I was gone. They were used to me and my teaching. The way we did things as a class, and last but not least my Friday quizzes.

Since I had been gone, my students missed a total of two quizzes, even though it's passed and they missed them. I had a plan to integrate them in my lesson plans now that I was back. As the rest of my students made their way into the classroom, I saw Claudia walk in. She smiled and welcomed me back also. But I didn't see Deshawn at all. I even waited a few minutes after everyone else had made their way to class. But still no Deshawn. For now I couldn't worry about it, I had a class to teach and I was going to do it.
Page 160

"Hello class I'm happy to be back. And I would like to say, I thank all of you for your support of me while I was out. It meant a lot to me and my family. I watched you all from my home on TV. And I was proud of you guys and girls for fighting against something that was clearly wrong. I care about this School District, I care about you students. And I care about the city of Chicago. I care about this Nation, but we have to do better as a whole. As humanity, no matter your interests, the color of your skin, or the background you come from. I'm here because I believe in a great education for all. Not just in this city, but across this country. And it starts with us, with all of us. Now let's get started from where we left off. Turn your textbooks to page 148" I said as I started class.

As I said what I said, I looked all my students in their eyes. They knew I meant every word. I had to thank them for doing what they did, and let them know I appreciated it all. But I also I wanted to let them know that they had to remain focused, and our fight was far from over. As they read out of their textbooks, I sat at my desk and reflected on my time at the school. Don't ask me why, but it was what I was thinking about at the time. I thought about the conversation I had with Superintendent Evans and the School Board before being reinstated. I was going to try my best to follow the rules, but I wasn't giving up my fight.

As class ended that day, I thought about Deshawn and if I should go back to Fuller Park to check on him. He hadn't been in class for a few days I was told. Me being out for two weeks, it may have triggered a down spiral in the young man. I was concerned, because I knew his situation more than anybody else. I had to go see what was up with the kid, I didn't want him to waste his future. So I headed to Fuller Park. When I got there, it was some people standing outside Deshawn's home. Including his brother Corey.

"This teacher is back again y'all. Can y'all believe this shit ? What the fuck you want" ? Corey said as the other guys looked at me.

"Is Deshawn here ? I need to speak to him" I replied.

"And if he is what ? My brother ain't worried about no school. Don't even know why you keep bringing yo ass around here for. He ain't here, and don't come around this bitch again" !! Corey said walking towards me.

He went to swing on me, and I side stepped it and grabbed him from behind in a choke hold.

"You think shit is sweet huh ? You think you going to disrespect me you little punk ass kid !!! Stay the fuck back y'all before I choke his ass to death !!! Now you go in the house and get Deshawn punk" !!! I said pushing Corey into the door.     Page 161

I didn't know if Corey was going to get a gun or get Deshawn, but I was willing to take that chance. I stayed where I was. Five minutes had passed and I was still standing out there. The door then opened and it was Deshawn.

"Mr. Jones what are you doing here man ? I thought you was on leave"? Deshawn said.

"Never mind what I'm doing here. Why haven't you been in class ? I know I've been on leave, but that's no reason for you to skip class. You knew eventually I would be back. What's going on son ? This is the second time I had to come get you. Even had to rough your little punk ass brother up. For coming at me. What's going on Deshawn" ? I asked.

"Shit is complicated Mr. Jones. It's not like I don't want to come to class. I'm just confused right now with what I want to do" Deshawn replied.

"You gotta be kidding me Deshawn. After all we talked about, I thought you understood that this isn't about you or me. This is about the people that come after us. This is about your family having a better life Deshawn. You're not ever going to have that hanging around here and not going to school. This is the last time I'm coming to get you. If you don't want it, I don't want it for you. Good day Deshawn" I said as I walked away and got back in my car. And then left.

I wasn't giving up on Deshawn, but I was done going out of my way to make his dreams come true for him. Especially him acting like he really didn't want it. If he was serious he would be in class the next day. And remain in class from here on out. I went home that night a little frustrated with Deshawn, but happy my first day went well. When I got home my beautiful pregnant wife was preparing dinner.

"Hey sexy woman, it smells great in here. And you look beautiful as ever" I said giving my wife a kiss.

"Thanks babe, I appreciate you. How was my favorite teacher's first day back" ? Fatima asked.

"It was a good day. I thanked the kids for everything, the support and all. Me being back at school, let me know how much I missed it. It was great seeing my students again. But Deshawn wasn't there. So I went to his house in Fuller Park again. And before you say it, yes I was fine. Had to rough his little punk ass brother up though, disrespectful kid who needs his ass whooped. But I eventually got to talk to Deshawn, he told me he was still confused about what he wanted to do in life. After all we talked about. So I told him, I wasn't coming to get him anymore. It was all up to him now. His future that is. I'm done pushing the issue" I replied.     Page 162

"Silas if he doesn't want it, you can't make him want it. Those are your words. But I hope for his sake, that Deshawn really makes up his mind. And get away from here and further his education" Fatima said.

"I believe he will. Maybe me falling back, it will teach him to make that decision for himself like a man should. I guess we shall see" I replied.

I really did have faith that Deshawn would make the right decision and would get his life together. And eventually would return to school. I had almost lost thought about me and my wife's bundle of joy. Which was still in her belly, but on the way. At this point we were only a few months away from her due date. And the excitement was building. With everything going on as of late, I didn't have time to sit and think about the arrival of our gift from God. Now that I was back at school and teaching, I could concentrate on getting everything ready. We had a good amount of things already. But there was one thing that I had to do, and that was get with Fatima's sisters to plan the baby shower. That was the next thing on my list. I had called her sisters Mia and Destiny, and we had planned to meet for lunch one day to discuss them helping me plan my wife's baby shower.

To be honest, they were going to do most of the planning. I was just there to help out, I knew practically nothing about planning a baby shower. Her friends were pretty much busy, so that left it up to me and her sisters to plan it. So that's what we were aiming to do. So a few days later without Fatima knowing, I met her sisters Downtown for some lunch. I arrived after them at a Downtown Chicago restaurant. As I walked in, they were sitting there as I approached them both. They then got up and greeted me with hugs.

"Hello ladies, sorry I was a little late. Had to go over some paperwork from school. You both look great, and thanks for helping me with this" I said as I sat down at the table.

"Hey Silas, and it's no problem at all. You know we would've wanted to be involved with our sister's baby shower anyway. Mia and I were discussing some ideas before you came. Right Mia" ? Destiny said.

"Hey Silas. And yeah we were discussing some ideas. And since you two don't want to know what you're having. We were thinking a mix of both colors" Mia said.

"It sounds good to me ladies. Whatever y'all feel is right, go for it. Just tell me what I need to do, and I'm on it" I replied.

Fatima and I didn't want to know the sex of the baby, we wanted to keep it a mystery. Enjoy the pregnancy for everything it was. Page 163

"I guess we'll leave you in charge of getting some things we need for the shower. We'll text you a list. And if you have any ideas that sound reasonable, let us know and we'll hear you out brother in law. Sound good" ? Destiny said.

"Sounds good to me Destiny, y'all both got my cell so hit me on there and we'll go from there" I replied.

"Ok brother in law, it was nice seeing you again. Keep taking good care of our baby sister. And we'll keep in touch" Mia said.

"Will do ladies" I said giving them hugs before I left.

Fatima's sister's always were a big part of her life. Much like me and my siblings, Fatima and her sister's were close. And as her husband I always wanted Fatima's family as well as my family involved with all the important things that were going on in our lives. Our marriage was between just the two of us, like it should be. But now that we were having our first child, we wanted both our families involved. I knew Fatima's sister's would take the wheel when it came to the baby shower. I would just do what they needed me to do, that way everybody would be happy.

As the weekend was coming to a close, that Sunday my wife and I decided to take in a movie. Something else we liked to do together from time to time. We enjoyed the movie, watching as I had my arm around her like I did when we first started dating. It was a great movie and a great time with my wife. After the movie driving home, I got a call from Mitchell on my cell. I looked at it and let it ring for a little, not knowing if I wanted to answer it.

"Who's that babe" ? Fatima asked.

"Mitchell. I'm not answering it right now, not trying to talk. I'm spending time with my wife" I replied.

Fatima just smiled. She didn't ask anymore questions, and I'm glad she didn't. I believe she could feel that I wasn't trying to talk to Mitchell. It seemed like he had distanced himself from me after I did that interview. Which was fine, but I wasn't going to front like we were friends. The next day came, the beginning of the school week. As I got to school and to my classroom, Deshawn was standing in front of my door.

Page 164

Chapter Seven  "A Fight Like This Is Worth Fighting....And We Won"

"What you doing here Deshawn ? I thought you was undecided about your future" I said looking him eye to eye.

"I decided I wanted to come back, I don't want to waste my future. I decided I'm not going to let my family distract me anymore. My little brother distract me anymore" he replied.

"Why should I even believe you Deshawn ? I mean we been down this road before man. I've heard you give me this same speech when I came to Fuller Park last time.....remember" ? I asked.

Deshawn paused for a little as if he didn't know what to say at the particular time. It was the first time that I had seen him shut down in front of me. I was patient and let him get himself together because I wanted to hear what he had to say. I wanted to see just how serious he was about doing what he said he was going to do. Was he really going to be able to block out the distraction of his little brother whiling in the streets? Would he be able to handle balancing his school work, playing basketball, and helping his mother ? He had done it before, but he had gotten off track. He was coming to me at a time when I no longer felt an urgency to push him. Which was a strange and bad space for our relationship as teacher and student. There was a time not too long ago that Deshawn and Claudia were my top two students. They both attended my wedding because of their grade point averages. After I had promised them.

Since then, Claudia was a victim in a high profile rape case against a popular Chicago High School football star. And Deshawn, since I was given my leave of absence missed over two weeks of school. All our lives had changed in a matter of weeks.

"I remember Mr. Jones, and I'm serious this time. I really am. Just give me a chance to prove it to you. And I need another favor Mr. Jones. I need you to get me back on the basketball team. It's the only shot I got Mr. Jones, I'm begging you man. I need to get back on track. And I promise I won't let you down this time" Deshawn said.

"Because I like you as a person Deshawn, I will see what I can do. I'm not promising you anything. And I'm sure there will be some sort of consequences for your missed time with the team. IF and when you get reinstated, you can discuss that with the coach. Now you can get yourself to class, see you later today" I replied.

I didn't know for sure whether Deshawn was serious as he said he was this time. But the fact he did make the effort and came to school, made me give him the benefit of the doubt. But regardless of me liking Deshawn as a person, this would be the last time I would go to bat for him. This was his final chance to prove to himself, that he was really serious. I wanted him to prove it to himself first, before anyone else. Including me.

Later on that day, I was happy to see both Claudia and Deshawn in class. As well as the rest of my students. Things were getting back to normal. And that meant getting back to our weekly quizzes on Fridays. It was something that I reminded myself of when I started class that day.

"Ok you guys it's time to get down to business. Did you all read those chapters I told you all to read in your textbooks" ? I asked the class.

Of course most of them said they did and others didn't say much. Either way they would be quizzed on some of that material this coming Friday. I balanced out the way I taught my students. There were times that I gave my students more in class work, as opposed to homework. And then as of late, I've been giving them more homework in the second half of the year. Changing things up kept things interesting, and in my opinion kept my students on point. They knew they couldn't just relax in my class. I challenged their minds and work ethics. I loved my students who worked hard, even if they didn't necessarily get it. I was always open to helping any of my students, their efforts meant a lot to me. After class that day, Claudia said she had to talk to me.

"Hey Mr. Jones, I'm glad you're back. I didn't know if you were going to come back or not, but we were definitely fighting for you" Claudia said.

"And I appreciate that. It really meant a lot. And of course I was coming back. Y'all aren't getting rid of me that easily" I said as we both laughed.

"You know the trial is coming up. I'm still a little nervous about testifying in court and being in the news. Just seeing him again. And being judged by people from all over this city. It's not a good feeling Mr. Jones" Claudia said sounding concerned.

"I can only imagine Claudia. But you're here now and you've came this far. You've been this brave for so long, you can't turn back now. The reason for you telling me, and eventually coming out with this was to get justice. So this kid doesn't do this to any other young women like yourself. So finish strong and get your justice. I'm sure there's pressure on you because Dak was a star athlete. But regardless of that he did something wrong. These are the consequences of his actions" I replied.   Page 166

The more I talked to Claudia the more at ease she became. But I knew that would change by the day. Her being threatened by some students about her case against Dak Hollis. Dak was real popular amongst students naturally because he was a student athlete. Besides being one of the best High School football players in the country. Dak was also very charismatic, and popular with women around the school. So just about everybody was against Claudia. And the School District knew it. So they kept a close eye on her safety. Many people threatened her, but they knew she was being watched and guarded being involved in a high profile case.

I personally felt good that she was safe. She was a brave young woman for stepping up and revealing what happened. I always told her that I admired her for that. Besides her parents, a few friends, her family, and me. Was all she really had in her corner.

"Thanks Mr. Jones, you always make me feel better about things. Thanks for talking to me. I feel good about the case, it's just sometimes I have my moments of doubt. On whether I should go through with the case or not. But I will be ok. And you're right, I've came a long way. And I'm not turning back....I want justice" Claudia replied.

After talking to Claudia, I finished some paperwork and was about to head home. When I got a call from Mitchell again. I was tired of avoiding the situation so I answered the phone finally.

"Silas, what's going on man ? Look I know you're not too happy with me, but I need to explain myself. Let's meet for a drink and I will explain my stance" Mitchell said.

"That's cool man, where are you trying to meet up at" ? I replied.

"You can come over to my hood at Money Gun" Mitchell said.

"West Side, Ok. I'll Be there" I replied.

Mitchell was someone that for some reason I kept around. I knew we had different views on things, and I felt some type of way about how he handled my interview situation. He suggested some things that didn't sit well with me. But I knew that he knew he had made a huge mistake when dealing with me. I didn't know if our relationship would ever be the same. I know I didn't trust him anymore. But I was willing to hear him out and have a conversation with him about it. I was always fair with people, sometimes too fair.

Anyway, I was headed to da West Side to meet Mitchell so we could have a conversation about everything that went down.

   When I got there, Mitchell was already there. He was sitting at a table when I came in. He got up to shake my hand, as I arrived and sat down.   Page 167

   "So what's going on Mitchell, you got me here.....now what" ? I said.

   "Silas I just wanted to let you know I wasn't against you, I just had to do what my job asked. You were making a lot of noise within the School District" Mitchell replied before I interupted.

   "And they thought since you knew me, that you could calm me down. Shut me up and silence me about issues that need to be addressed. What happened to honor and respect amongst men. No matter what the powers that be say, we as men have to think with our own minds. If the roles were reversed, I would've told them that it was none of my concern. They had you do their dirty work for them. I lost a lot of respect for you Mitchell. I always thought of you as a leader, being how you lead our Men's Group at church" I replied.

   "Silas it's my job, you should know how it is being a teacher. And I am a leader my brotha. And you have no right to question that" Mitchell said.

   "Naw my brotha I dont, I can only go by what I see. And I don't conform to no system, I tend to go against the grain. I just know where you stand with it now, and I can respect it. Even though I strongly disagree with you. And I felt you should've let me know that from the beginning" I replied.

"I just wanted to clear the air Silas. We were cool before all of this, no need for us to be at odds because of our different views. Plus our wives are very good friends, let's put this behind us man" Mitchell said extending his hand for me to shake it.

I shook his hand and we continued talking for a little while longer before we both left. On the drive home, I thought about our conversation. And I just chalked it up as something that I already thought, Mitchell was an associate. He wasn't a person I could depend on to help with the fight. He didn't know how to do things his way but still stay within the rules of the School District like me. I knew because I knew my rights. Mitchell and I would never see eye to eye. I would keep our relationship strictly for couples night with our wives. And keep our relationship at a distance as a whole.

"Mitchell, the only issue I have with you is pretending to be a person that you're not. All the conversations I had with you since meeting you, you came off as a person that believed in the same things as I did. And you not being that person isn't a problem for me, but I would've appreciated you being the real you from day one. The person you really are. We could've still clicked and been the best of friends. I respect people from all walks of life Mitchell, you know that. I coexist with different people with different views and backgrounds everyday. We all do" I replied.    Page 168

"Silas I know who I am. And I'm the same guy that you met years ago. Nothing has changed, just being in my position I can't be as opinionated as you are on such issues. So I stayed away from your comments in the interview. Some things I agreed with you, others I didn't. I have that right. I've been the same person Silas, I'm not here to deceive you man. Our wives are close, and Kendra and I have tried our best to be the best friends we can be to you and

Fatima. It's real man, there's no motive with me.....with us" Mitchell said.

"I hear you man. I gotta get outta here, get home to my pregnant wife. Tell Kendra Fatima and I said hello. You have a good night" I replied as I got up and left.

It was a productive meeting between Mitchell and I. We were able to iron things out, and better understand each other. Although I still didn't necessarily trust him. As I said before, our relationship would strictly be through our wives moving forward. Anyway I was headed home. Things were getting a little more difficult for Fatima as the pregnancy went on as expected. We were less than a month from her due date, which meant the baby could come any day now. We were both beyond excited about having our first child. So as I got home, my Queen Fatima was sitting on the recliner watching TV when I came in.

"Hey baby, how was your day? How you feeling" ? I asked coming into our living room.

"Hey babe. It was ok, I worked from home again today. Didn't really feel like going into the office. And I'm feeling ok. Was trying to take a nap earlier. It was a little uncomfortable with this belly being so big but I tried. I can't wait to deliver this baby" Fatima replied looking visibly tired.

The later pregnancy months had took a toll on her physically. That was the main reason I started doing a lot more around the house. We were thinking about hiring a Nanny, but after discussing it with our families. Our sister's agreed to help Fatima when they could. Fatima's sisters Mia and Destiny, and my sister Savannah. Plus our mother's were around. So both families would come together to help us, I wouldn't expect anything less from both families. Fatima and I loved them all dearly.

"I bet baby. You need anything? You hungry ? I could order out, since I came home so late. I had a drink with Mitchell on da West Side" I said.

"Yeah I could eat something. And how is Mitchell doing ? I talked to Kendra a few days ago" Fatima replied.

"Ok I will order out, how about some Deep Dish Pizza" ? I replied asking.

"That sounds great babe" Fatima said.

After ordering the pizza, I got in the shower and then came out into the living room to wait for the pizza to arrive. While sitting there, Fatima and I continued our conversation.

"Mitchell and I just talked about the misunderstanding we had about the interview. I know you and Kendra are pretty good friends and all. And I respect that, I really do. But Mitchell and I aren't on that level. And probably never will be baby" I said.

"As always babe, I trust how you feel. I'm not expecting you and Mitchell to have the friendship Kendra and I have" Fatima replied.

At that time the door bell rang, it was the pizza. So for the moment our conversation was interrupted yet again. I got the pizzas and paid for them, then took them to the kitchen. After getting us both some pizza, I served my wife and myself. And then we went back to our conversation.

"When I was dealing with everything that came with doing that interview. I felt like Mitchell fronted on me when he could've just been himself. At that time it wasn't the most popular thing to be friends with Silas Jones. I agreed to meet him to clear the air, only because of your relationship with Kendra. We both didn't want to come between you two, we both knew what y'all friendship meant to each other. I mean you two were friends and introduced us two anyway" I said.

"That's true. I just figured after I met Kendra and then Mitchell. That they were a nice couple to be around. They were both so nice and welcomed us with open arms when I met her. Everything seemed fine to me. I'm sure it wasn't personal Silas, Mitchell more than likely folded under the pressure of his job. I'm not saying it was right by you, but at least now you know where he stands" Fatima replied.

"I thought the same thing baby. It is what it is. It's not going to stop me regardless. Let's eat, this pizza smells great" I said as we started to eat.

After another great conversation with my wife and best friend, we enjoyed our dinner. The next day would be Friday, and our weekly quizzes. And my students were finally getting back on track after my over two week leave of absence. So that morning I got up early as usual, and got started on my day. Shower, got dressed, and had my daily morning coffee. After that I was out the door and in route to school.

I got to school and upon arriving at school, I had sensed something had happened. Police cars were outside the school. It was a weird scene, and I had no clue what had happened. As I drove up, I was instructed to go around to the back parking lot. And not where I normally parked at, where all the other teachers parked. As I was driving to park, some students were giving me dirty looks. I had my nine millimeter handgun in my car as always. I had a license to carry, although I had never attempted to take it into the school. It stayed in my car always, I mean I did live in Chicago.

Getting out of my car, I walked to the entrance to the school and was stopped by local law enforcement.

"Hello sir, may I help you" ? The cop said.

"Yes I'm a teacher here trying to get into the school so I can teach my class. What happened here" ? I replied asking.

"What happened was some classes were vandalized, totally trashed. Not sure if you'll be teaching today" the cop said.

Just then Principal Hunt came out in front of the school, and seen me talking to the cop.

"Silas...come in" Principal Hunt said motioning me to come inside the school.

And so I did, as we were walking in the school and through the hallways you could see the destruction. As I was walking with Principal Hunt, classroom after classroom was trashed. And the more we walked the more I came to the realization that my classroom was sure to be destroyed also.

"I just can't believe this, these kids that we help everyday are the ones who've done this? What's it all worth Silas ? Us doing this ? Being here day in and day out. Dealing with the crap these kids put us through. And you say fight for education ? These kids don't even want to fight for the school and people that's helping them !!!

There's days I feel like giving up, just saying the hell with it. You know who has to pay for all of this Silas ? The School District. The same School District that you've criticized" Principal Hunt said.

"Hold up Principal Hunt. The fight and importance of education has nothing to do with some knuckleheads vandalizing the school. And yes it is all worth it. For the kids that want to learn. And hell no we can't save every kid, but we can save some. And that's why it's worth it. No matter how small that amount is, they're why I'm here. No one ever said it was going to be easy, we'll get through this" I replied.          Page 171

"There's a lot of work to do. Look at all this, this is completely unacceptable. Thousands of dollars of damage, maybe in the hundred of thousands of dollars of damage. I can only imagine. How can you or any of your colleagues teach in this" ? Principal Hunt asked.

"Don't worry Principal Hunt, I'm definitely going to teach. And I have ten minutes to get to my class and get my class started. I will help you with the rest of the school later, we need a team of volunteers to clean up. Talk to you later" I replied walking away in route to my class.

"Silas....where are you going ? There's still some things we need to talk about....." Principal Hunt said as I was walking away.

"Later on Principal Hunt.....later on. I have a class to teach soon" I replied.

I knew my class was vandalized, but it wasn't going to stop me. Whoever did it would've loved for the school to be shut down. And our students to have no class at all, but I wasn't going to let that happen. Not only was I going to have class, but I was going to have my students help me clean up in the process. I got to my classroom, there were things thrown everywhere. I stepped over things and got to my desk, looked up at my clock in my classroom. Which was cracked as if someone had threw something at the clock. I could still see the time and it was working. I had about ten minutes before class was supposed to start. So I did my best to clean up as much as I could clean up, quickly washed my blackboard off and got it ready for class.

"Wow....oh my God Mr. Jones what happened" ? You could hear my students saying as they entered my classroom. I just acted as if I didn't hear them until I had them all present. Then I would address my class about what happened. Another fifteen minutes went passed and all my students were finally present, all looking around the room at the destruction.

"As you all can see, some cowards have vandalized our school. In an effort to distract us from getting the best education that we can. That effort will not go unnoticed, but it also won't be successful. It will fail because WE are all stronger than the cowards that did this. I know I am, and I know you all are stronger also. We have some cleaning up to do. And yes I say WE because this is both our fights. These cowards are trying to destroy us all. But look at us. We're all STILL here and ready to learn. For today's class. We will all get some trash bags that I have up here in the front of the class with me. And get all this trash up and clean up our classroom. With the time that's left, I will allow you guys and gals to relax for the rest of class. Socialize if you want...but we have to clean up" I said passing out trash bags.          Page 172

I along with my students began cleaning up the classroom. With everyone helping, it didn't take as long as the mess looked. A half hour later, most if not all the mess was cleaned up. As we were cleaning, Principal Hunt walked past my classroom and seen the work we put in cleaning. He was proud to say the least. I believe that day is when Principal Hunt had a new respect for me as a teacher and leader. And my ability to get my students motivated to do positive things. I myself was proud of my student's resolve in this situation.

After class ended, Claudia wanted to speak to me. I knew she was concerned seeing the classroom being in the shape it was. And something told me she was blaming herself and the case for the whole situation.

"Mr. Jones who do you think could've done this ? Claudia asked sounding concerned.

"To be honest with you Claudia, I have no clue who could've done this. And I wouldn't want to assume. I'm just glad we got this cleaned up so we can move on from this. Thanks again Claudia" I replied.

"You welcome Mr. Jones. I don't think you would've gave us a choice, but I was glad we helped" Claudia said smiling.

"You're right about that, its you guys and girls classroom also. So it's only right that y'all helped clean up. We live in turbulent times Claudia, people will do anything nowadays. Just know that you're safe. I'm sensing that you may be blaming yourself. I can see it all over your face. Don't worry Claudia, everything will be fine" I replied.

I knew with each action leading up to the trial, Claudia would be concerned. It was natural for a young woman being in her position. At school all she had was me for her support system, and every chance I got I made sure to keep her encouraged to stay strong.

Because I knew she would need that, especially at school where kids could say things to her. I also knew I had an effect on the way she thought about things. After talking to Claudia and her leaving. I decided to stay a little later than usual to finish cleaning up my classroom. My students and I had got most of it cleaned, I was going to finish up. As I was finishing up, I got a text on my phone. It was Fatima's sister Destiny saying that Fatima's water broke and she and her were headed to the hospital. I immediately dropped what I was doing, got my things and left.

On my way to the hospital, my thoughts. First....was this really happening ? Was I really about to be a father for the first time ? I was excited and nervous at the same time. And in a little disbelief. I knew her due date was approaching, but now the time was here. And I couldn't be any happier. So as I raced through Chicago streets en route to the hospital, after a fifteen minute drive I was finally there. I quickly parked and ran inside the hospital. After going through the annoying front desk, I was escorted back to my wife's room.

"Hey baby, I made it as fast as I could. How are you feeling" ? I asked immediately going to one side of her bed side. With her sister Destiny on the other side of her.

"Hey babe, I'm Ok. They have me on something right now to help with the contractions. Destiny was home and brought me to the hospital" Fatima replied sounding basically out of it.

"Yeah I see baby. Thanks and hello Destiny. Thanks again for bringing her in" I said looking over at Destiny.

"Of course Silas, I wouldn't miss my sister giving birth for the world. Mia and I both said, and promised her. That whoever was home at the time would be here for her. When the time came. This is our baby sister, that's how it's always been between us" Destiny replied.

That was one thing Fatima definitely had, was great relationships with both her sister's. They had a great bond between the three of them, I admired their bond. And even with her and her sister's being so close, it never had any negative effect on her relationship even before we were married. But as I said before, her sisters made it hard on me at first. Once they got to know me, we were good. In some cases people's relationships and marriages may have been affected by friends or family members. Male and female. But Fatima and I were able to separate that when it came to our relationship, and now our marriage. This situation being the birth of our first child was definitely different, we wanted our family members involved. It just so happen that the same hospital Fatima was having the baby in, was the same hospital my sister Savannah worked at. And as we were sitting there in her room, in walked my sister Savannah.

"Hello sister in law, how are you ? Hope you're doing fine. Hello big bro, and hello Destiny. How are y'all doing" ? Savannah said coming in the room.

"Hey Savannah I'm doing ok. Just on these meds" Fatima replied.

"What's going on sis" I replied.          Page 174

I knew that the women were going to make fun of my first time being in the delivery room. They were waiting on me to break, get real nervous and pass out or something. But I had other plans. I was really interested in the whole pregnancy, since day one. I never missed any appointments. I was able to be flexible with my schedule. Around lesson plans, grading quizzes, and just teaching in general. Encouraging my top two students, who were going through difficult times in their lives. But now at this moment. It was all about me, my wife, our families. And the precious gift from God that was soon to arrive.

I sat bed side with my wife and watched her reaction to each contraction, while holding her hand. Kissing it from time to time to let her know how much I loved her and how much I cared. Fatima was everything to me, she had been everything to me since the day I met her. And now she was helping bring the greatest gift of both our lives to us finally. I told myself that I wouldn't get emotional, but honestly I didn't know how I would feel. I had never experienced this before. But I was focused on the whole process, I just sat by my wife's bed side and watched everything. From the nurses coming in and out of the room every once in a while, to watching my wife sleep. I soon had to make a decision if I was going to teach the next day. The day had turned to evening. And this being Fatima's first pregnancy, labor could be very long. I was prepared to spend the night with my wife. I told Destiny that she could go home.

"Get some rest baby sis, love you. Call me if you need me Silas, love you brother in law" Destiny said giving me a hug and her sister a kiss before leaving.

Fatima was sleeping off and on, every once in a while moaning a little from the contractions. I sat in the chair, after a while trying to get some sleep myself. But before I did, I called Principal Hunt and told him that I wasn't going to be in the next day. After sleeping for a few hours, I was awakened by Fatima screaming in pain from a contraction. The nurse re-entered the room and she started timing the contractions. I immediately got up and was wide awake. After about ten minutes the nurse called the doctor in, and I knew it was time. I picked up my cell and called Destiny. She was on her way.

I was about to witness something I had waited all my life for, I was so excited and still holding my wife's hand. She was in pain and I felt for her, doing anything I could to ease her pain and comfort her. At the same time I was watching everything that was going on, I didnt want to miss any part of the experience. I was all in. The doctor had arrived and him and the nurses were getting ready for delivery.

I was there to help any way I could, but I was definitely hoping that Destiny would return in time enough. As they propped Fatima's legs in the air the time was coming. It was time for her to push. I was coaching my wife on like I was teaching my last and final class as a teacher. Her sister Destiny suddenly arrived and got on the other side of her where she was before she left. Fatima pushed for, it seemed like forever before I looked down and seen hair. It was the baby's head as I looked in amazement.

"Keep pushing baby, you got this. Keep pushing" !! I said sounding excited.

And she did keep pushing, she pushed until I heard our baby let out a strong cry. That's when I knew our baby was strong and healthy. The doctor reached down and pulled the baby out as she pushed.

"Its a girl, congratulations to the lovely couple" the doctor said.

My eyes lit up looking at our daughter as the doctor handed her to Fatima.

"Oh my God sis, she is so beautiful" Destiny said as we both were on either side of Fatima and the baby.

A beautiful healthy baby girl who weighed in at seven pounds and six ounces. She was indeed beautiful as Fatima was holding her and just smiling with tears of joy rolling down her cheeks. And I can't front, I was crying tears of joy myself. It was one of the biggest moments of my life. The birth of my first child was something I thought about my whole life, I didn't know when it would be. But now that it was here, I was beyond overjoyed. After the baby was finally delivered, I immediately went to call my mother, father, and brother. My sister Savannah was still inside the hospital somewhere working. My mother was so excited to hear that she had finally got a grandchild from her baby boy. Something she had hinted at for years to Fatima and I.

My father was also excited for Fatima and I. He knew this pregnancy meant everything to me. I wanted to tell any and everybody, tell the world. I was so excited. I finally got back to Fatima's room and Fatima was sleep, her sister Destiny was holding the baby. As I came in the room, Fatima's sister Destiny said the words I wanted to hear.

"Brother in law, come hold your daughter" Destiny said smiling as I got my daughter from her.

She hadn't even been name yet, and I was still holding her. Rocking back and forth in the rocking chair that was in the room. As I watched my wife sleep. I knew she was tired, so I held my daughter as long as I could before the nurse came in and got her. And returned her to the nursery. I just sat there and watched my wife sleep.　Page 176

Before I knew it, it was the next day and I awoke and opened my eyes to my wife feeding our daughter. By this time our daughter still didn't have a name. That is until my wife and I had a conversation.

"Hey good morning baby. How are you feeling" ? I asked.

"Hey babe, I'm Ok. Just feeding our hungry child. You do know we need to name this little girl right" ? Fatima replied smiling.

"Yeah I was just thinking that. How about the names we thought of for girls" I said.

"I like Jezell Marie Jones. Remember you liked that name too" Fatima said.

"I do like that name baby, sounds great" I replied.

"Well Jezell Marie Jones it is, so beautiful our baby girl" Fatima said holding our daughter still feeding her.

I just looked on admiring two of my favorite females in the world, I would give my life for the both of them without hesitation. I had another reason to live and love life. My baby girl had made her arrival in this world. As we sat there, our family members one by one made their way to the hospital. Fatima's parents were at the hospital first. Johnny and Frances, Mr. and Mrs. Malone arrived and immediately congratulated Fatima and I on our first child. And then wanted to hold their granddaughter Jezell Marie Jones.

"So how does it feel to finally be a father young man" ? Fatima's father Johnny asked.

"Feels great Mr. Malone, she's beautiful like her mother" I replied.

"Great answer son, great answer" Fatima's father said putting his arm around me and smiling.

It was a great time for Fatima and I, and a great time for our families. Not long after Fatima's parents were there and left. In came Mitchell and Kendra, who brought a pink balloon and teddy bear with some flowers for Fatima.

"Congratulations to you and Fatima bro. Happy for you both" Mitchell said shaking my hand.

"Thanks man, we appreciate it. How's things going on down at the office"? I asked being sarcastic as I could be at times.

Mitchell just looked at me and shook his head, he knew I was being somewhat sarcastic. But he deserved that from me.    Page 177

Mitchell asked me to come out in the hallway for a little. He had to talk to me.

"To answer your question. Things are going as they always have at the OFFICE. I would hope you have enough respect for me than that Silas. You may not agree with me being on the corporate level, but at least respect it. Remember I tried helping you get in this District before you actually did" Mitchell said trying to whisper so our wives couldn't hear.

"Fatima knows Mitchell. That's my best friend in there, you know I was going to tell her how you sold me out about my comments in the interview. But don't worry, it's all good. Fatima and Kendra are close, we can always remain cordial. No hard feelings brotha, I just had to let you know that. The time felt right, so I did it" I replied.

Mitchell didn't know what to think or say. After that we both returned to the room with our wives and my baby. And saved face for the rest of the time Mitchell and Kendra was there. That was all the visitors we had for that day. I was preparing myself to return to school, even though I hated to leave my wife and daughter. I had to get back to my students. I had already missed some time from my leave of absence, it was crucial that I remained consistent with my students. As Finals would be coming up shortly. It was something I didn't even have to discuss with Fatima, she knew I had to get back to teaching.

"How's the new beautiful mother Mrs. Silas Jones doing ? I just love the way that sounds" I said smiling at my wife.

"I'm doing good Daddy. Our daughter is soo beautiful isn't she" ? Fatima replied asking.

"Yes she is, just like her mother" I said as I kissed my wife on her forehead.

We were two extremely happy first time parents. We had heard all the stories from our family and friends, now we had our own child. And two days later I was picking my wife and daughter up to go home for good. It was so nice finally having them both home. Fatima's mother Frances. And her sister's Mia and Destiny would take turns staying with her and the baby while I was at work during the day. My sister was busy working at the hospital to help us. And my mother had her hands full looking after my sister's kids while she worked. So I was indeed grateful for Fatima's mother and sister's helping us out. But I also knew when we needed my family they would be there when they could. So all in all, we had a great support system to raise our daughter in. Fatima would be off work for about six to eight weeks. So I had to hold things down for us. And it was an honor to take care of my family, it was my job as a man.      Page 178

The next day I was ready to return to work and return to my students. It was the first time we had slept in our bed in a few days.

Each time Fatima got up to feed our daughter, I got up with her. It didn't matter to me that I had to get up in a few hours. I was fascinated just watching my wife feed and care for our daughter. Our daughter's crib was right next to our bed. I went back to sleep off and on for the next three hours, and was back up and ready to start my day. It was one of those days that I definitely needed my coffee. I got up early enough to make myself plenty before I left for school.

On the drive there I was feeling great, just thinking to myself and realizing I was a father. That I had a beautiful baby girl that was counting on me to give her the best life possible. That alone gave me a renewed sense of being the best teacher that I could be. My students got my best everyday, and I expected them to give me their best. So as I walked into school that morning, with a swagger like always. And a smile on my face, as I greeted faculty and students alike walking through the hallways. I got to my classroom. Once I got in my classroom and closed the door. I sat down at my desk and was appreciative of the job my students and myself did cleaning up. When it first happened, it didn't look good at all. They were things thrown everywhere, and trash everywhere. A lot of classrooms were trashed throughout the school, and the investigation was ongoing. At the moment the local Police had no leads at all. In a big city like Chicago where daily shootings dominated the headlines. Our school being vandalized wasn't the highest priority on law enforcement's to do list. But all in all, we as a school overcame it all and moved forward. I was happy about leading the charge to move forward.

My students made their way into class and I was ready to start class. But before I could, one of my students Myra stopped me.

"Mr. Jones we heard that you just became a father to a beautiful baby girl. So on be half of myself and my classmates, we got you and your wife a gift" she said.

She then went outside the classroom as I looked on. And came back in with a box, it was a brand new car seat. I was surprised for sure, and so grateful. My students really cared. And although we already had a car seat, we could always use another one. One for my car. So it was very much appreciated.

"Thank you all very much, I speak for my wife and myself when I say thank you all very much. We appreciate you all. Now open your textbooks to page 190 and read the first two chapters" I said smiling as I returned to my desk. Car seat in hand.

My students never ceased to amaze me, the gift was very nice and meant a lot. But I knew we needed to get down to business. Finals were approaching.　　Page 179

After I gave my students the first half of class to read out of their textbooks, I began a new lesson plan I wanted to partially put in. I had my students read the first half of class on purpose. I only wanted them to get a part of this new lesson plan I was putting in. It was another part of the lesson that would appear on their Finals. I would cover the rest that next week. I wanted them all to be as prepared as they could be. I had a mix of Seniors and Juniors in my class, mostly Seniors. These Finals would be everything for them. It would help them decide what direction they would go in furthering their education. In recent years our school hadn't had a high rate of our Seniors going to college. It was something I had read about when I first got to the school, as apart of my research. Of course this was my first year at the school, and I was hoping I could help improve that ASAP.

That was for the kids that wanted to go to college. I never believed college was for everyone, because it's not for everyone. The ones that had that drive to go to a four year college, and after pursue successful careers could lead several paths. But I also believed you could do the same by going in the workforce with some sort of skill. Possibly a Technical School to obtain a trade, something nobody could take from you. That was something my brother Sid thought about at one point in his life. I just wanted all my students to succeed in some form or fashion in their lives....LEGALLY of course. For Deshawn I was hoping he would get out of Chicago and focus on himself. It was too many distractions here in the city for him to succeed. I didn't want him to completely leave his family, but I knew in order for him to focus on being successful he had to leave for a while and just get away.

Claudia would have a difficult transition. First she would have this trial that was coming up, and then she would have to try and get back to herself. I would continue to support her now and throughout the trial. I believe once she gets past this, she'll be fine. Claudia was a very intelligent young woman, with a bright future ahead of her. I naturally saw the change in her since this all happened. I was the only one she would talk to at school. There were times I suggested that she see the School Counselor, she went a few times but never opened up to anybody. Just me and her family, and I never took that for granted. And that was with any of my students that felt they could open up to me, about anything they were going through. I wasn't no Guidance Counselor, but I was a realist. And I had experienced a lot in life. They knew whatever they told me, they were going to get my honest opinion on it. Whether they liked it or not.

I guess that's why they told me things they were going through. Plus I never judged them. I went home that day still feeling good and excited about going home to my wife and daughter. Coming home after work felt even better now.

It was really tough being around my sexy wife and not being able to make love to her. But I tried my best to be patient. Plus she promised me an amazing night once she fully healed from the birth of our daughter. As soon as I got home, I washed my hands and immediately went to get my daughter so I could hold her. Fatima was relieved because she wanted to make us something to eat. And I was glad to take my daughter off her hands. As I sat on the couch holding my daughter and looking in her beautiful brown eyes with her long eye lashes like her mother. All I could think about was giving this little girl the best life that I possibly could. My wife and daughter were everything to me. They were the reason I faced the world everyday and strived to be the best teacher I could be.

"So how was your day babe" ? Fatima asked from the kitchen as she was preparing dinner.

"It was cool, had a great day. Got a gift too, from my students. They got us another car seat baby. Now I have one for my car, instead of us switching it between cars. And I introduced a new lesson plan, well half of it. I wanted to ease it on them. It's to prepare them for Finals of course" I replied.

"Oh ok. Sounds interesting. And it's always good for them to be prepared, because I'm sure Finals will be challenging" Fatima said.

"Yep, especially when you're not prepared. But they did well today. They've been getting better with getting their lesson and learning it at a good pace" I replied.

"That's great babe, they have an amazing teacher. Our daughter and I slept all day today" Fatima said.

"Say mommy, I'm daddy's little girl. And good looking like him too" I said speaking to my daughter while holding her in my arms smiling.

Fatima just rolled her eyes and smiled. We always had fun together, way before we had our daughter. And now we were having fun with her as a family. Those were the times I cherished so much. After holding my daughter and feeding her. I laid her down for her evening nap and by that time Fatima had dinner prepared. As we sat there eating and watching some TV. Fatima was flipping channels until she got to a channel which said "breaking news".

"Hold up baby, let me see this" I said watching as I was eating my dinner.

Fatima kept the channel on, and I couldn't believe my eyes. It was unbelievable, but I can't say I was surprised that this would eventually happen.          Page 181

Corey Williams, Deshawn's brother was accused of shooting a man in the chest twice and killing him. He was now on the run from local law enforcement. At that moment the first person I thought about was of course Deshawn. And what was he thinking ? Was he going to give up on his dreams now because of this ? I figured something was going to happen with Corey, because of the type of kid he was. He had little respect for anyone. Regardless of it all, I was hoping he would turn himself in. Before the cops caught up with him. In this world we live in now, it would be open season on another young black man if the cops caught up with Corey. The smartest thing for Corey to do, would be to turn himself in. I was really eager to see if Deshawn would show up to school the next day. I could understand if he didn't, considering the circumstances.

But for now, I discussed it with my wife as we watched the details of the case being reported by the local news.

"So that's Deshawn's little brother ? Wow" Fatima said shaking her head.

"Yeah thats his little brother. The punk ass kid I had to snatch up when I went to their house in Fuller Park. For his total disrespect" I replied.

"Deshawn's such a nice kid, it's hard to believe that's his younger brother. That's a shame" Fatima said.

"I feel sorry for their mother more than anything. I know in her heart that she loves her kids. She just came off a little on the rough side at me. And to be honest, coming from Fuller Park you have to be. I hope Deshawn continues to come to school and let law enforcement handle the situation with his brother. I mean it's out of his hands at this point" I said.

"Yes. Him even being around his brother right now wouldn't be good for him or his mother. I really feel bad for him and his family" Fatima replied.

"Yeah....I do too" I said still sitting there watching TV.

A lot was going through my mind, and I was hoping to see Deshawn tomorrow at school. I was even thinking about moving Deshawn in with us just to finish his Senior year, until he went off to college. That was what I was thinking the whole time Fatima and I were talking. I didn't necessarily say anything to her then, because I wanted to run it by Deshawn and his mother first. So for now I would keep that thought to myself. In the meantime I went to bed that night feeling optimistic about the next day, and moving forward period. I watched my wife put my daughter to bed and then we were both out, I had an early start the next morning.

Getting up that next morning, and getting to school. The only thing on my mind at the moment was Deshawn in his situation with his brother being on the run. I really felt for him and his mother. But I was also hoping he would remain strong through all this, for his mother more than anyone. As I entered my classroom like always I turned on the lights and got my class prepared for my students to arrive. I wouldn't find out if Deshawn was at school until last period. Well I could go into the attendance office, but I rather keep the mystery until last period. Because that's when I had Deshawn in class.

As I taught my first period class, and my other classes throughout the day. I felt like everything that I was doing and going through up until this point, was meant to be. It was my destiny so to speak. And I meant the positive and negative things, that went with teaching. It all had brought me to this point. Right back in front of my students like I have been the last month in a half. Since being put on a leave of absence. The time had came, and it was last period. The class that had Claudia and Deshawn apart of it. As that class was entering my classroom, I sat at my desk until everyone was there and seated. Unfortunately Deshawn didn't make it to school that day, and I can't say I was surprised. I completely understood why he wasn't there. I was concerned for him and his family, but I was going to let him have his space. He knew I cared, and he knew if he needed me I would be there for him. But now just wasnt the time. I'm sure he had enough things to think about. And I had a class to teach.

While I let Deshawn deal with his situation. The local D.A. announced that the trial for Dak Hollis would be after the school year. So for the moment I could put that situation in the back of my mind for now. Claudia was improving emotionally, although she was still damaged a lot mentally. Which was to be expected. She had developed tough skin from all the negative attention in the beginning. And she still had her moments, but she remained brave and strong. And every chance I got, I reminded her how much I admired her for her strength and bravery.

After teaching my last period class that day, I was finishing up some paperwork when Miss Summers came to my door and knocked.

"Hello Mr. Jones, haven't had a chance to chat with you in a while. You haven't been in the Teacher's Lounge lately" she said as I sat at my desk.

"Yeah I've had a lot of things going on. Became a father for the first time almost a month ago. And as you know I just came back from being put on leave not too long ago also. So I'm just getting back to the swing of things so to speak. How have you been Miss Summers" ? I replied.

"I've been good. And I heard about the birth of your daughter, congratulations to you and your wife. I know you two are overjoyed. Children are a gift from God and always a blessing. And I heard about your leave of absence. I also seen the interview with the local news. I just wanted to say that I totally agree with you on all the comments you made on education. I know it may seem like some of us are against you, but I know it's bigger than you. You're just leading the charge, and as a teacher I admire and appreciate you for that. I had to be honest with myself, and say. If a man is this passionate about teaching and leading these kids. Then I can't be against him" Miss Summers said.

"Thanks Miss Summers, I'm glad someone is seeing the bigger picture here. It's something I also tell my students. It's not about me, it never was. And I'm hoping soon after Finals, it will all be proven. That's the only way to get ahead and make things happen in this world Miss Summers. Is to show and prove. Show them that your vision on how you see things. Will make not only your students successful, but the school system in a whole. With my vision, the federal government would have to start actually doing their jobs and accurately fund first and secondary education. That's where it starts. I never said my methods are conventional to what this country is used to" I replied shrugging my shoulders.

"They don't have to be Mr. Jones, as long as they're right. And in the best interests of the students. And your ideas are, so I can't help but to support you. I like what you have to say and think that you're a very smart man" she said.

"Thanks. Look I have some things I have to do, but it was nice speaking to you Miss Summers. And thanks for all your compliments, and I'm glad you're seeing that I'm not out to hurt. But to help. Enjoy your day, and if you ever need to speak to me again. You know my door is always open" I replied as she left and I got back to what I was doing.

It's always good to be thankful and appreciative of any support. Whether some or none of the faculty supported, it didn't matter. Because it wasn't going to detour me from my goals that were set. But it was good knowing that at least somebody figured out what the actual purpose was. And that the outcome just didn't affect me. In the end, it was for all us teachers. To not only be valued more for our work, but to be treated that way by being afforded the best resources to teach. Financially and also through overall support. Any teacher that truly cared wanted all his or her students to succeed. Some worked tireless hours trying to come up with the best lesson plans and ideas for teaching. Just not with the curriculum, but with each teacher's style. When things got better for us, things would get even better for our students that wanted to learn. Because sadly enough, we knew everyone didn't want to learn. But for those that did, we wanted to give them the best learning experience they could ever have.     Page 184

As I was leaving school that day, I got a text from my wife saying that someone was at the house that wanted to see me. She wouldn't tell me who it was, but she said for me to get home as soon as I could. You could only imagine all the things that were going through my mind. I tried to get home as fast as I could without getting a speeding ticket and trying to avoid Chicago traffic. Driving and weaving in and out of traffic. I had to get home. After about almost twenty minutes later, I was finally home. I immediately went into my house wondering who was there to see me. As I came into my home, in the living room sitting on the couch. While my wife was on the rocking chair trying to put my daughter to sleep. Was none other than Deshawn Williams.

"Hello Mr. Jones. Look I know it might've not been good for me to come to your home" he said before I interrupted.

"How did you find out where I lived" ? I replied asking.

"I looked you up, and I found the address. Look I'm sorry, but I needed to talk to you. I didn't want to come to school, with everything that's going on with my brother" Deshawn said.

"Because I know you pretty well and I've been to your home. I guess it's only right. Normally I wouldn't want anyone knowing where I lived. I have my family here. Let's go in another room and talk" I replied as Deshawn got up and followed me in another room.

I always kept my personal life and my school life separate. I was the same person, but I didn't want my family involved with anything that had to do with my job internally. Yes I let Deshawn and Claudia attend our wedding, and that was incentive from their performance in class. And it was something that Fatima and I had discussed beforehand, and was agreed upon. We didn't mind sharing our big moment with the world. But knowing where I lived was something different, but in a way I was glad Deshawn was here. So I could finally find out where his head was with all that was happening right now.

"I can understand that you couldn't make it to school because of the circumstances and all. But showing up at my home isn't helping either. So I assume you have something to talk to me about. I know what's happened with your brother. But I need to know where your head is at. And what you plan on doing with your future now that this has happened. What happened with your brother is unfortunate, but I don't teach your brother Deshawn. I teach you. So what's it going to be" ? I asked.

Page 185

"That's why I'm here Mr. Jones, I want to come back to school. But I don't have no place to live anymore. I can't go back to Fuller Park, I fear that someone would retaliate because of what they say my brother did. My mother and other siblings had to leave too. I've been staying with a friend. My mother and younger siblings are with my mother's aunt on da West Side" Deshawn said.

"Damn Deshawn. This is really bad, and I truly feel for you.....I do. Right now I can't do much for you but get you something to eat if you would like. You are welcome to stay for dinner with us. Beyond that, I will let you know if I can do anything else moving forward.

You know I will do anything in my power to help you if I can. You just have to give me some time with this one. Continue to stay with your friend, and if you need a ride to school. I will give you one. But I need you to be in class, you're falling further behind missing class. So as long as you're committed to getting your education, I will help you. If you're aren't and lose focus, I'm done helping you for good Deshawn. I can't help anyone that doesn't want to help themselves. From here on out, you have to prove to me that you really want this. You can't control what the outcome will be with your brother. You can only support him from afar like any brother would, I understand that. But don't lose YOUR focus because of it" I replied.

"You have a deal Mr. Jones. I never wanted to leave class, and I never wanted all this shit I'm going through now to happen. I can't believe my brother did this. You know Corey wasn't always like he is now. When we were younger, he was a fun loving kid. Always laughing and making us laugh. Making fun of people. But in a loving way, not to deliberately hurt them. He just always liked to have fun. Then being where we came from, he started hanging around the wrong crowd. I always had basketball as my escape, Corey never found his true talent. I know he was very smart. That's why at first it surprised me when some guys from around our neighborhood said he was involved with the gang culture. I tried my best to keep him off the streets. Anything from starting fights with him, to hunting him down in some of the roughest Chicago neighborhoods. You name them, I've probably been through them looking for my brother. But I'm ready to get down to business Mr. Jones" Deshawn said.

"Only time will tell with that son, here's my number and remember what I said. If you need a ride to school, don't hesitate to call. Now if that's all you need to talk about, if I could drop you off somewhere or anything ? Or do you want to stay for dinner with us" ?

I asked not knowing what he wanted to do or exactly where he was staying.

"No I'm fine Mr. Jones, my friend can pick me up down the street. And I'll get something to eat. Thanks again Mr. Jones for hearing me out. I appreciate you sticking by me through all this" Deshawn replied.     Page 186

I didn't really know how Deshawn's life would end up, at this point it was all up to him. I just knew this was his final chance with me, and I let that be known. All I could do was hope the best for him. After Deshawn left, my daughter was just waking up and I couldn't be more happier to see her. As soon as I came back in the room, I immediately picked her up from out of her crib and gave her the sweetest kisses. As Fatima looked on smiling.

"A father and daughter's love is priceless. So nice watching you two connect and develop that bond. I know she's going to need that as she grows up" Fatima said.

"She will always have plenty of love and support from daddy.....isn't that right my sweet Jezell" ? I said looking at my beautiful daughter as I was holding her talking to her.

The rest of the night was as always special. Spending it with two of my favorite girls, my wife and daughter. But before I went to bed that night, I had to finish up my lesson plan for part of the day the next day. It would be Friday and part of class would be our weekly quiz. But I did want to put the other part of my lesson plan in tomorrow. So I stayed up a little late to get it done as Fatima and Jezell slept.

That next morning Friday was here, and I was always excited about Fridays. Our quizzes and it was the start of the weekend. Later on that night I was supposed to meet up with my boy Angelo and go shoot some pool. It had been a while since him and I got a chance to talk. I got to school that day and got myself prepared to teach. Deshawn did make it to school that day, although you could tell he was going through a lot. He wasn't the same Deshawn Williams I grew to know. But I was happy and glad he had made it to class anyway. The day went according to plan. My students took their quizzes and I was able to put in the other part of the lesson plan like I wanted. I told Deshawn I wanted to see him after class. And after class he came up to my desk as all my other students left.

"I wanted to see you after class to give you the work that you missed. And you missed quite a few assignments. It's important that you make all these assignments up and get them turned in before the end of the year. A lot of them have been due, but because of your circumstances I will give you a chance to make them up. So get to work ASAP so you can get caught up" I said.

"Ok thanks Mr. Jones, I'll get right on it. Did you get around to talking to my coach about letting me come back to the team" ? Deshawn replied asking.

Page 187

"You prove to me that you're really serious and focused. AND your progress is consistent then I will do that" I replied.

"But Mr. Jones, it may cost me scholarship offers" Deshawn pleaded.

"Deshawn just handle what's in front of you, stay focused on what you have to do and the offers will be there. Trust me" I replied.

Deshawn shook his head in agreement. I realistically could've had him back on the team instantly. Deshawn was by far the best player on the school's basketball team, and the coach would've accepted him back with open arms. But I wanted to see how focused Deshawn really was. I had heard the same story from him since I had met him. He was a kid with no ceiling, meaning his potential was endless. But there was always something holding him back. Most times it was his own family, and the people he decided to surround himself with. I needed to see more of a reason why I should continue to help him. Like I told him, only time would tell.

I was happy that the week was over, and I was ready to unwind a little and hang out with my boy Angelo. It was a while since we kicked it last. So of course we got together and did one of our favorite things to do when we hung out. Shoot some pool. With Angelo, I knew what friendship we had. I knew with him I didn't have to ever think he would switch up who he was because of his profession. Or anything else. The only person that was closer to me besides my boy Angelo, was my brother Sidney Jr.

"Angelo what's good playboy ? How you been bro" ? I asked as I arrived after him.

"You know the same shit man. Congrats again bro on the birth of baby girl Jezell. I know you can't even sleep at night, watching baby girl sleep and all. I been there, that's a monumental moment in life my brotha" Angelo replied as we both greeted each other with a handshake and hug.

"Thanks bro. And you know it. Every time Fatima gets up with her, I'm up. It's a joy watching her grow each day. I hate leaving the house in the morning. But enough about me, how's things going with you and Lauren" ? I asked.

"We're good. Just both working and thinking about going on a cruise this summer. Maybe you and Fatima can go. Since you said y'all had to postpone y'all honeymoon and all" Angelo replied.

"Yeah we postponed once we found out she was pregnant. Not sure if we can bro, I'll have to discuss it with Fatima. Jezell is still somewhat of a newborn, and will still be young. Not sure if Fatima wants to leave her with anybody" I said.     Page 188

"That's understandable, Lauren was like that after our son was born. So I can dig it. But if y'all change your mind, let us know" Angelo said.

"Yeah no doubt, I definitely will bro. Thanks for inviting us. Now rack them up, so I can whip you again" I said as we were about to start another game.

"You ain't whipping nobody. You so confident in those skills, put some money on the table" Angelo replied.

"You aint saying nothing but a word. But in all seriousness though. You were right about Mitchell, he was doing a lot of fronting. You know when I did that interview he distanced himself from me. And his bosses had him talk to me. I guess they thought he could silence me or something. We all know that wasn't going to happen. We talked since then, after I let him know how I felt about it. When it first happened, I wasn't trying to even speak to the man. But I cooled down and heard him out. I just let him know he didn't have to be someone else to be around me. Going to college and being in the military. I've been around, and got along with people from all walks of life. And most if not all didn't agree with my vision. I don't need no co-signers, but if you said you was going to ride with me. Then ride with me til the wheels fall off" I said.

"I can't say I'm surprised, and as much as you think I'm going to say. I won't say I told you so. I learned over my years of life. That having associates isn't a bad thing, just never confuse them with your actual friends. In my line of work, it's good to have a lot of associates. Not that they come to your home, just that you hang out from time to time. Maybe because of business, maybe because of your line of work. Whatever that may be. I never confuse any of those people with what we have. What we have goes back to da South Side" Angelo said.

"Indeed bro.....indeed. At least I know where the man stands now. And we're still cordial. And you know Fatima and Kendra are close. We're both in a Men's Group at church. So I still deal with the man on some levels" I replied.

"And you should Silas, I mean he has a voice Downtown. You may need that at some point. He knows you didn't appreciate what he did, he may feel like he owes you a favor. Something to think about bro" Angelo said.

Angelo was right. And that's why I loved him like a brother, man we are brothers. He always kept it a buck with me. And he could've been bitter towards Mitchell because of what I told him. But he made me take my own advice when I tried to convince him to co-exist with Mitchell. When they first met and Angelo got bad vibes from Mitchell from the start. Angelo always seen the bigger picture. Page 189

I guess those vibes proved right, because it seemed like anybody that dealt with Mitchell eventually got bad vibes. Including me. As we were talking and continuing our game of pool I happened to look up at the TV that was sitting above us on the wall. The headline on the TV said. "Fugitive Standoff Live".

"Yo man, turn that up. Hold on Angelo, I gotta see this" I said turning my attention to the TV.

I watched as it was Corey Williams. He was inside a store and the local Police had it surrounded. The whole lounge where we were playing pool at and having drinks, were glued to the TV like myself. I'm sure at this point the whole city of Chicago was watching. Corey's face was all over the news, and a ten thousand dollar reward was put up for his capture. I could only imagine what Deshawn and his family were thinking. The little brother he always worried about and was distracted by, was now in a standoff with Chicago Police. A very dangerous standoff, considering he was accused of murder. Angelo and I watched in shock as we could see everything live on TV. All you could see was the store, and the Police across the street with one officer with a bullhorn talking to Corey. Then all of a sudden, you seen Corey come running out of the store gun in hand. As the officers yelled for him to drop the weapon, Corey clutched his gun in his hand and raised it towards the Police.

After that act, all you heard was multiple shots from every gun all the officers out there had. As they fired numerous times, over and over until Corey dropped to the ground. Even hitting him with more while he lie on the cold Chicago streets. In just over seven to eight seconds, it was all over. Corey Williams, the younger brother of star basketball player Deshawn Williams was dead. Killed by Police in a standoff. It seemed like the whole city was watching. We all watched it unfold live on TV. I could only imagine how Deshawn had to feel watching his little brother die right before his eyes.

"Damn....what was the story on this kid Corey man ? I mean this kid was this wild that he was in the middle of a Police standoff" ? Angelo asked a little bugged out at what he just saw live on TV.

"He was a punk ass kid who got caught up in the gang culture. When I went to Fuller Park to check on Deshawn, him and I had a situation that turned physical. Something I really don't care to mention to too many people. Because I felt bad about the whole thing. Despite the fact he came at me and forced my hand. I had to defend myself. After that, I knew that the kid had no respect for anyone. Anytime you disrespect your elders, you will disrespect anyone. I really can't say I'm surprised at what just happened. I just didn't think it would come to this necessarily" I replied.     Page 190

"Its sad regardless man. That's why I'm glad we got brothas like you Silas, that's trying to make a difference in the community. And you have these kids around you up close and personal being in the school system. Hopefully seeing Corey's story, will help other kids in the Chi that may be wanting to follow the same route. I've even thought about doing some volunteer work myself. Me and Lauren" Angelo said.

"Yeah....and what's even sadder is there's kids like Corey walking all around the city right now, that you can't tell a damn thing. No matter what you do to help them and be there for them. It falls on deaf ears. That's probably what happened with Corey. As much as that kid was disrespectful towards me and any other person in sight. I still would've tried to help him if he really wanted to be helped" I replied.

"I guess that's too late now. What do you plan on doing about Deshawn ? You know this is really going to hurt him. How close you say he was to his brother, this really has to shake him to the core. I know it would for me" Angelo said.

"Yeah I plan on talking to him. He was at my house the other day, he and his family couldn't go back to Fuller Park. Because of Corey shooting that kid" I replied.

Angelo knew like I knew the potential that Deshawn had, he seen Deshawn play ball before and knew he was a smart kid. And he knew I was the one person that stuck by him through everything he went through. He also knew that I was the only person that Deshawn would really talk to about things going on in his life.

A few days passed and the weekend was over. It was back to business. And today would be the day I would go back to Fuller Park, that would be later on that day. Deshawn and his family was finally able to return to their home after Corey was killed. Earlier that day I had my classes as usual. Kids were talking about what happened to Deshawn's brother Corey. Those that knew Deshawn that is. They were really worried about him, and felt bad for his family. Over the weekend I had bought two sympathy cards for Deshawn and his family. One that I would have all his classmates sign, and one from Fatima and I.

For this day I would stay on the same lesson plan as I had introduced on Friday. I had my students read a few pages in their textbooks. And did some in class teaching before the day was over. I didn't waste any time getting my things done after class so I could head to Fuller Park. On the drive over I didn't know what to expect, Deshawn and his family had no idea I was coming over. But I'm sure they had other visitors in the wake of Corey's death.
Page 191

I finally made my way to Fuller Park and after making my way to Deshawn's house, there were a good amount of people standing out front. I was of course in my suit just leaving school, as each person stared wondering who I was. Once I got inside the home, I immediately saw Deshawn standing over near his mother. She was sitting in a chair quietly sobbing holding a tissue in her hand. Deshawn was standing behind her rubbing her shoulders trying to comfort her. When he saw me, he immediately came from behind his mother and over to me.

"Mr. Jones, I didn't know you were coming here. But I shouldn't be surprised, you been here before. Thanks for coming, we need all the support we can get" Deshawn said looking mentally drained.

"I'm sorry Deshawn, I really am. I know how you felt about your brother. And I'm really sorry that you, your mother, and other siblings have to go through this. But I'm here if you need me as always. How's your mother doing" ? I asked.

"She's a mess man, really broken. As bad as Corey was, my mother loved the shit outta him. He caused her a lot of stress over the last few years but she still wanted me to look after him. I had to sometimes fight my brother for him to act right. Corey wouldn't hardly listen to anyone, let alone me. We actually heard from him before he decided to take a shot at those cops and get himself killed. He told us he wasn't going to jail. He knew what he did, and he knew he wasn't getting out of it. But he wasn't going to jail. Honestly Corey was terrified of jail. Although he had never been, just the idea of being in jail scared him" Deshawn said.

"That's interesting but not surprising I guess. Listen I know your mind hasn't been on school work or anything with everything going on. But I don't want you to get too far behind on your school work. It could limit your chances of returning not only to school but to the team. So whenever you get a chance, do some of this work. Don't worry no due dates, as long as you get this done before the end of the year" I replied.

As we were talking, Deshawn's mother came over to where we were.

"Hello Mr. Jones it is right ? Thanks for coming. I know the last time we spoke I wasn't the nicest person to talk to. After seeing your interest in my son Deshawn, and your fearlessness of keep coming back to Fuller Park. I can tell you truly care for my son. My son Corey meant just as much to me as Deshawn and my other children. No matter what his choices in life were, he was still my baby. It hurts like hell to know I tried my best to give all my children the best life I could. And it just didn't work for Corey" Deshawn's mother Roberta said sounding upset.     Page 192

"Miss Williams I can't say I know how it feels, I would be lying to you. But I do care about Deshawn, he's a great kid. Not only is he talented in basketball, but he's also a really smart kid. Even if he never picks up a basketball again in his life, he can use his mind to be successful in life. I know many used to think that the only way any of us African American males would make it out of our neighborhoods. Was either playing sports or being an entertainer. You know as well as I do, that we can be anything we want to be. One of our own that has done a lot of work in this city, became the first African American President. But Miss Williams I have to tell you what I honestly think, Deshawn has to get out of here. Let Corey's death be a wake up call for all of us. I know it is for me. After seeing this, I'm going to push Deshawn even harder to succeed. To make a better life for you and the rest of your children. You have my word on that. As long as this is something Deshawn really wants. And it would help greatly Miss Williams, if he has your support" I said.

Deshawn's mother Roberta looked at him and nodded in approval with tears rolling down her eyes. She knew that I was right, and she knew that Deshawn had to get away from his environment. The pain of Corey's death finally made her realize how much this was true. Roberta was a strong black mother, who was a very proud woman raising her children in the inner city. It was hard for a man to just come in and tell her how she was to raise her children. Especially after she had done it for so long by herself. Roberta had four children. Three boys and a girl. Her three boys had the same father, and her daughter which was the youngest had a different father. Her ex boyfriend was her daughter's father. He wasn't apart of her life for the most part. And Deshawn and his two brother's father was in and out of their lives.

The only consistent presence in Deshawn's life was his mother Roberta. He cared very much about his mother. It's exactly why he often times listened to her and looked after his younger siblings. Rather than come to school and handle his own responsibilities. He knew how it was for his mother, working two jobs to support him and his siblings. So he felt like he had to be there, which was understandable. And now with Corey gone, who was only a year and a half younger than Deshawn. His mother would need him even more to look after his little brother and sister.

"Mr. Jones I want my son to succeed, I really do. I know there isn't anything in those streets but trouble. Chicago is dangerous, it always has been. I've been here all my life and want better for my kids. I seen a lot of horrific shit growing up in this city, that I don't ever want my children to have to deal with. It's too late for my son Corey, but I have a chance to save my children that remain. I will make sure Deshawn gets to class each day and gets his work done" Deshawn's mother Roberta replied.     Page 193

"Thank you Miss Williams, it means a lot that he has your support. I know we didn't necessarily hit it off at the beginning, but I always respected you as a woman and mother. I admire and see how hard you work to provide for your children. If there's anything I can do, or the District can do. Don't hesitate to ask. I'm going to get going, my condolences once again to you and your family. I told Deshawn he could take some time off, and I will send his work home. Hopefully after the funeral, I will see you in class Deshawn. Y'all stay strong" I said before I left and headed home.

I was so glad I was finally able to get through to Deshawn's mother Roberta. We didn't get off to the greatest start, she seemed like she had a bad attitude towards me. Or anything with positive potential in Deshawn's life. I truly believe Deshawn was her security blanket from herself and her son Corey. She knew Deshawn was smart and talented. And he could very well leave the entire family behind, on a ride to success. Not that he would. But he could if he wanted, he had that much potential. Once Corey was killed, she realized she no longer had to worry so much about her and her children's lives. And she also realized she could no longer hold Deshawn back, she had interrupted his growth long enough. With her support, I now knew that Deshawn would be in class everyday. And NOW I could go to his coach to seek reinstatement for the final seven games of the season.

The next day class was as normal as it could be. Of course Deshawn was home with his mother planning his little brother's funeral. His work was given to him so he was in the loop and knew what was going on in class. That was one of the conditions of me helping him. Getting his work done with the rest of his classmates. Later on that day, I decided to go in the Teacher's Lounge. I walked in and I saw Carl Maxwell, the Science Teacher. He was someone I talked to from time to time, he seemed like a decent dude.

"Silas what's going on ? Haven't seen you much lately, I guess our schedules have us in the wind" Carl said as I came in and sat down after getting a drink.

"Mr. Carl Maxwell, I'm good man. Just going about my day. How you been" ? I replied.

"I'm fine Silas. That kid Deshawn Williams, he's a student of yours I believe. Well I know you seen his brother Corey was killed by Chicago Police. That kid Corey was nothing but trouble. The kid that he murdered was a good friend of mines nephew. My friend loved his nephew dearly, shit is killing him inside. I didn't know Corey personally, but I was around him a few times and he wasn't a respectable person. He never showed respect to anyone that I know of. He took a person's life, so he deserved for his life to be taken. Just my thoughts on it, not sure what your thoughts are" Carl said.  Page 194

"Does it even matter what I think Carl ? I mean what you think is enough. Yes Deshawn is a student of mines, and all I could do is be the teacher and mentor I am. And support him through this difficult time. What happened between Corey and your friend's nephew was between them. Although I don't condone anyone killing anybody. I can't judge Mr. Maxwell" I replied.

Carl just looked at me, as if he was disgusted at my response. It didn't bother me one bit, because I didn't trust any of the teachers or faculty. The last thing I needed was them to have anything to use against me. I walked to the beat of my own drum. And despite the fact I didn't say anything negative about Corey to Carl, I knew Corey was very disrespectful. I dealt with that first hand. When I had to snatch his ass up on one of my many visits to Fuller Park. But Carl didn't know that, and he didn't have to know. After that brief conversation and a drink inside the Teacher's Lounge. I was back to my classroom and then called it a day. I finally got home that day and all I wanted to do was play with my daughter. Seeing her face when I got home always made me smile.

As I entered our home, my wife Fatima was preparing dinner. And much to my disappointment, our daughter was lying down taking a nap. So our daddy daughter time would have to wait. But I also was always happy to see my beautiful wife. After entering our home I came behind her while she was cooking.

"Hey baby. Food smells delicious as always. I see our little girl is sleeping, taking her late afternoon nap. It's great to be home" I said kissing my wife on the back of her neck.

"Hey babe, yes she is. I just put her down not too long ago. Don't worry, she'll be up in a little. How was your day babe ? And how's Deshawn ? Fatima replied asking.

"My day was cool, and Deshawn is grieving as expected. But me and his mother have a better understanding. I think since Corey's death, she's realizing that she can't hold Deshawn back anymore. So she agreed to make sure Deshawn's focus would be on his school work. It's sad it's took this long, but maybe Corey's death will bring about something positive. And maybe this is it. The fact that his mother is finally letting go and letting him reach his full potential. It's great for him, I believe Deshawn is going to be just fine baby" I replied.

"That's great, I'm glad things are coming together for him. Still sorry to hear about his brother though. So sad" Fatima said as we both sat down and ate.

After we ate our daughter woke up, and I finally got my time to spend with her. The highlight of everyday for me. I was in Heaven playing with my daughter, tickling her and making her laugh. And plenty of kisses for daddy's little girl.     Page 195

Several days later Fatima accompanied me to Corey's funeral. The family had very little money to bury Corey. So there was some fund raising across the city trying to help the family pay for the funeral. After about four days, the family finally came up with the money to give him a proper burial. There was some controversy about the city raising money for the funeral of a killer. Being that Corey was on the run for murder when he was gunned down by Police himself. But regardless of any opposition, the city came together and raised enough money to bury the young man.

Deshawn sat arm and arm with his mother, and his little brother and sister sitting right next to them on the front row. Fatima and I also saw Mrs. Williams and her husband. Deshawn and Corey's uncle, Roberta's older brother Larry. It was quite a few people at the service, which was held at a local funeral home. Deshawn was strong for his mother and siblings, I was proud of him. His mother was overcome with grief, Corey like all her other children meant the world to her. After the service outside, Fatima and I ran into Mrs. Williams and her husband.

"Hey Silas, how are you ? I wanted to introduce you to my husband, Roberta's older brother Larry" Mrs. Williams said introducing Fatima and I to her husband.

"Hey...nice to meet you considering the circumstances. Sorry about your nephew Corey, I'm your nephew Deshawn's History Teacher" I replied.

"Yes my wife has spoken of you before. Nice to meet you also" Larry said.

"Mr and Mrs. Williams I'd like to introduce you two to my wife Fatima" I said introducing them to my Queen.

After we all exchanged greetings after the service, Fatima and I were on our way home. During the drive we had a conversation about the whole day.

"So that's the Mrs. Williams that acted like she cared so much about Deshawn ? And that was the first time you met her husband" ? Fatima asked.

"Yes and yes. According to Deshawn his uncle has very little to do with his or his siblings lives. So I never really needed to know her husband. He was never at the school or anything. I was proud of Deshawn today though, he stayed strong for his family. I know it had to be tough" I replied.

"I could only imagine losing one of my sister's, knowing how close we are. It would be devastating. So yes I know it has to be extremely hard for him" Fatima said.

"That's why I told him to take his time. I will send his work home so he doesn't get behind. It's going to take some time for him to get past this. As long as he makes an effort to continue to learn, I got his back on everything else" I replied.

We were heading down the home stretch to the year, and Deshawn after a few days decided to return to school. He knew how much he had at stake. He wanted to get back to work and get back on the court. After I talked to the coach, it wasn't hard for the coach to reinstate Deshawn back onto the team. The team welcomed him back with open arms. Just before the regular season was coming to an end. Fortunately for Deshawn, the team was playing in the League Playoffs this year. They played pretty decent in Deshawn's absence, enough to earn a playoff spot. And now that Deshawn was back in the lineup, the team was back to getting the national exposure they were getting when Deshawn was on the team.

They had a few important games coming up to cap off their season, which was Deshawn's first game back. My boy Angelo and I decided to attend the game. Fatima was home with the baby. Plus Angelo said he wanted to see Deshawn play. As Deshawn took to the floor to start the game, he pounded his chest with his fist and pointed to the sky. To acknowledge and salute his little brother Corey. It was something Deshawn would do the rest of that season. But that night, his comeback game. Deshawn would help lead the team to victory by scoring 26 points and grabbing 11 rebounds. The college scouts were all over our school gym watching Deshawn play for the first time in over a month. There were also local news stations everywhere, Deshawn's story was a highly publicized story. Especially with his little brother's recent death at the hands of Police being talked about throughout the city. As local civil rights groups were calling for an investigation in the Police killing of Corey Williams.

As much as I wanted to categorize Corey's death as another innocent black male murdered by Police. This clearly wasn't the case. Corey was a fugitive from justice and clearly didn't want to go to jail. He told his family that before he stormed out of that store that day, gun in hand pointing at Police. He knew it wouldn't take long at all for Police to kill him as soon as he raised his gun at them. It was the tragic end to an eventful and recently troubled life of

Corey Williams. The local news put two and two together to make Deshawn's comeback also about his brother. And a tribute to him. Regardless of how Corey was, Deshawn in the eyes of many in the city of Chicago was a good kid from the neighborhood. And the city was rooting for him. The family of the kid that Corey murdered wasn't too happy about the local news running a story about Deshawn and his brother Corey. Let alone running a story on him paying tribute to his brother, who happened to have murdered their loved one. Page 197

But like always the media needed a story. They knew Deshawn was in direct contrast to his brother Corey, and the way he lived his life. Deshawn had remained in school throughout the years. Corey hardly attended school, and basically dropped out after being in high school for a year and was supposed to be a Sophomore. He was also held back a year.

After the game and a great win by the team. Angelo and I had a conversation about the night, as we drove home from the game.

"I seen Deshawn play before way back when he was a Sophomore, I knew he was going to be something special then. Of course I didn't follow him like I do now, since I heard he was a student of yours. The kid has a high ceiling man. And it took a lot of courage to go out there and ball like that tonight. A week removed from burying your little brother. He's a strong young man and he's smart. I believe he's going to do really well bro. Possibly NBA material. Silas you did a great job of sticking with this kid man" Angelo said.

"Thanks bro. And yes he's everything you said he is. I've watched him come a long way since he was brought to my class. Each day I've seen him grow. I've gotten on him. Because like any teenager, you have to stay on their ass every once in a while. I never gave him special treatment because he was a star athlete. I've seen too many young men of color, get passed through the educational system like they were nothing because they could dribble a basketball. Or run track, and run and catch touchdowns. Something besides actually using their minds. Not saying in those sports that you didn't use your mind, but I was tired of us being looked at and stereotyped into certain careers. We were never dumb people at all, and we never will be. You look around this world everyday you see something that a person of color created. We're innovators, doctors, engineers, lawyers, judges, police officers, teachers. We're not just sports figures and entertainers. I knew even if Deshawn never picked up a basketball again in his life. He would still be successful because he was smart" I replied.

"I know that has to make you so proud bro. And the progress and relationships you've developed with these kids is inspirational. No bullshit man. And I know you're far from done. But I see the progress and I don't even work at the school. You even having the courage to support one of your students, who just so happens to be a rape victim. That a lot of Chicago thought was lying. Not every man is that courageous. Not every man gives a shit about some kids that he isn't necessarily invested in. Not every teacher wants to make a difference, they rather just collect a paycheck. Not my boy Silas, my boy Silas wanted to be the true leader he is" Angelo said. Page 198

"It's how we came up bro, you know it. You can't be weak coming from da South Side baby. We're all born leaders" I said smiling as Angelo and I exchanged handshakes.

"Remember back in the day, we used to catch the L to The Lake and Wrigley Field ? Even when we didn't have much money. We was some wild boys back then, but we used to have a lot of fun though" Angelo said smiling.

"Yes....those were the days. That's the difference between us and this new generation. Don't get me wrong, we lost a lot of people we came up with in these streets. But look at us, we're successful and beat the odds. Grant it, it's extremely dangerous in these streets these days. But these kids can still beat the odds if they really want to also" I replied.

After dropping Angelo off at his house, I headed home. It was always good hanging out with my best friend from way back. And we always found ourselves reminiscing about da old days. I finally arrived home and my wife and daughter were asleep in our bed. I didn't want to wake either of them, so I slept out on the sofa bed in the living room. Brought my alarm clock with me, so I could be up bright and early the next morning. That next day came and I got myself up and ready. Made my way to school and got my class ready for something different today. I had a lesson plan that my students would team up in groups of three to complete a group project. This was another project that would help prepare them for Finals. I let my students team up with who they wanted, as long as the work got done. The project would be similiar to the one I had earlier this year.

After I gave them their assignments I sat back at my desk and did some paperwork. I also watched how my students worked together. I made their grades not only about the work, but the way they worked together as a team. So in between the paperwork I was watching to see their interactions. While that was going on I got a visit from Principal Hunt. So I stepped outside into the hallway so I wouldn't disturb my students.

"What's going on Principal Hunt ? What can I do for you" ? I asked wondering what he wanted.

"I just came to say that it's good to see Deshawn back in school. I had a conversation with him on the day he came back. He told me that you had a lot to do with him not giving up and coming back to school. He said you basically saved his life. And that his brother's death really opened his eyes. It's unfortunate about his brother, but I want to thank you for having such a positive impact on our students" Principal Hunt said extending his hand to mines.

"I'm just doing my job Principal Hunt. I told you when I got here that I was one of the teachers that really cared about his students. And oh yeah. Doesn't the District owe me money for those textbooks ? I'll be expecting a check from the School District in the mail" I replied smiling.

"I believe you're right Mr. Jones, and I want to say that you proved me and a lot of other people wrong by making the progress you've made with our students. It sets a great example for what we want in a teacher when hiring in the future. I know personally we didn't always see eye to eye and agree on things, but I always knew that you would do right by these kids. And it shows man. They love you, as witnessed by the support they all gave you when you were on your leave of absence. I must say I was somewhat shocked at the overwhelming support you got from the student body. That let me know that you wasn't just a regular teacher, you're special and I appreciate you. Thanks again Mr. Jones" Principal Hunt said as he left.

I can't say I was expecting that but I was appreciative of the fact that he and the School District appreciated me for the work I had done with my students. In the short time I was at the school. I made some things happen that improved the school overall, starting with a considerable improvement of the percentage of our students passing their Midterms. It turned heads amongst the school and raised eyebrows and shook things up within the School District. I guess it was a good and bad thing. Because I had been recognized for my efforts. But I was also ridiculed for them and singled out enough that the District felt I deserved to be given a leave of absence. Something I felt was wrong til this day, but I dealt with it like only a real passionate and professional man would. Who believed in his vision, despite what the School District thought. Either way, it was always good to see that the Principal of my school was finally understanding my vision and appreciating me for it.

Having the School District endorsing a check to me for the purchase of the new textbooks was just evidence that I was right. As far as the many improvements that I felt we needed to make within our District. It started with us, but the plan was to go from local to state to federal with it. And because the year was coming to a close, it didn't mean the fight for a better education was over. A fight like this was worth fighting....and we won so far. But there was still so much work to do. To me, the textbooks weren't about the money. It was to serve a bigger purpose for eventually all of us teachers. And that was to prove that with improved resources we as teachers could teach and educate our students a lot better. And the students themselves would be more interested in our lesson plans. Which in turn would hopefully make our students more interested to learn.                    Page 200

After talking to Principal Hunt, I went back in my classroom as my students were finishing up working on their projects. I was impressed at the fact they got a lot done with the time permitted. My students had got accustomed to what I expected from them, even despite us not being together for a full year. You could say I hit the ground running when I got here, and been rolling ever since.

"Remember class, as always we have our weekly quiz tomorrow. You all have the tools to study, so I suggest you do so. Finals are a month away and we still have some work to do before you all will be prepared for them. You all be safe out there" I said as my students were leaving.

It was another productive day, and I was pleased with my students progress and how hard they worked. I didn't necessarily let them know today, but I would tomorrow. I believe it's always good to let your students know how much you appreciate their hard work and efforts. But at the same time keep them focused and on task. I was in a good mood as I left the school that day. And I was eager to get home as always. Finally getting home and stepping into my house, it was always exciting. Because I always missed my wife and daughter, and when I got home that was all I wanted to do. Was spend time with them both. My daughter was lying on her blanket on the couch. And my wife was sitting next to her, rubbing her back.

"Hey to the two most beautiful females in the world, Daddy's home" I said as I embraced my wife with a hug and kiss. And then I kneeled down to kiss my daughter Jezell.

"So how was your day Daddy" ? Fatima said smiling.

"It was actually a very good and productive day. And Principal Hunt pulled me aside and finally gave me my props. And recognized and realized the real impact my vision has had on the school. AND he told me that the school would be endorsing me a check for the new textbooks WE bought at the beginning of the year" I replied smiling.

"We ? Oh it's WE bought the students new textbooks now ? Ok....that's news to me" Fatima said with a smirk on her face being sarcastic.

"I know you remember the bet I made with the District. And you know Principal Hunt and I kept it between us. Baby I did what I believed in, and I was confident that it would work. And it did. So I guess we even" I replied smiling. As Fatima just shook her head.

"You better be glad it did work. Those textbooks aren't cheap" Fatima said looking at me. Before I got closer to her and gave her another kiss.          Page 201

"Your man came through again, like always" I replied as I got up and picked my daughter up.

As I picked her up, towards the ceiling. She just smiled and laughed, she always loved that. Just to see that beautiful smile on my daughter's face meant everything to me. I continued playing with her as Fatima prepared the leftovers we were having. Another great day, and now another great night had ended.

That next week Deshawn and his teammates would start their playoff run. And Deshawn was excited about the opportunity to just be able to play again. He had been back now for a few games, and seemed to be getting that chemistry back with his teammates. Earlier that day after class, Deshawn and I had a conversation about him and his future.

"Mr. Jones, I know you're coming to the game tonight right ? You can't miss the playoff game" Deshawn said.

"Yeah I'll be there. I mean these will be your final games in High School coming up. Have you narrowed down your college choices yet" ? I replied asking.

"I'm still at about eight schools. Indiana, DePaul, Connecticut, Arizona, Clemson to name a few. Still just waiting it out. But I know the time is ticking" Deshawn said.

"Yes it is young man. You have to make a decision soon, give it some thought. And I wanted to tell you again, how proud I am of you. For just being a strong and smart young man. Going through all you been through is remarkable. You never gave up, when you had every reason to give up. You should be proud of yourself for that. You been through a lot, and some people would've broke after going through what you went through. But you stood tall, thats admirable. Hows your mother doing" ? I replied.

She's doing Ok, still dealing with Corey's death. My mother is a strong woman Mr. Jones. I've seen her get through the roughest of times, but Corey's death is really breaking her down. I'm just trying to help her as much as I can before I leave for school in the Fall. I'm really excited about going where ever I decide to go. Just the whole college experience" Deshawn said.

"I'm sure you are son. Wherever you go, I want some tickets to the games too" I replied smiling.

We then went our separate ways. But I was definitely attending the game tonight. This time I was attending the game with my brother Sidney Jr. I hadn't seen my brother in a while. And he agreed to attend the game with me.     Page 202

After picking up my brother from somewhere on the North Side. We made the short drive to the school gymnasium. As usual the stands were jam packed, and plenty of my students in attendance like always. As my brother and I were walking through trying to find a seat. We could hear some of my students calling my name, just to say hello like always. My brother just looked in amazement.

"Damn these kids love your ass Silas.....I couldn't hardly stand some of my teachers when I was in school" Sidney Jr. said as we both laughed.

"Sid you crazy. That was because you was hardly in school at one time. I remember. Mom and Pops used to be on your ass, and you eventually got it together" I replied as we finally found our seats and sat down.

The game was just about to start as we took our seats. Our school jumped out to an early lead in the first quarter, as Deshawn had scored a few times. Including a dunk that made the crowd go wild. As I was watching the game, I looked over across from us at this woman that looked familiar. It looked like Deshawn's mom. I stared for a little, and it was Deshawn's mother Roberta. We finally noticed each other and waved. It was good to see Deshawn's mother at a game. I don't believe I had seen her at a game before. I thought it was nice, I could only imagine how overjoyed Deshawn was. He always wanted his mother to attend his games, but he knew she worked two jobs. So in reality he couldn't hold it against her, and he understood why she couldn't. With his mother in the stands, Deshawn and his teammates ran away with the game. Beating the visiting team by twenty five points.

Deshawn had 26 points and 13 rebounds. Another stellar game for him, as the schools who were vying for his services next year were all in attendance. And he didn't disappoint, a great game and the team was ready for a playoff run. With all the people there, I didn't get a chance to talk to Deshawn or his mother. But on the ride home, my brother and I talked about the game.

"You definitely wasn't lying bro, da kid got skills man. Where's he leaning towards going to college at" ? My brother Sidney asked.

"Him and I were talking about that earlier today. He's narrowed it down to some schools, but no clear cut choice yet. So I guess when he's ready, we'll all know. But what a great game though. Deshawn's mother was at the game, I was happy to see that. I know her being there made him extremely happy. That family has been through a lot, and I'm hoping Deshawn stays on the right path. He could get his family in a better position financially if he does stay on the right path" I replied.          Page 203

"Yeah getting out of Fuller Park would be smart. I see NBA in this kid's future, he was a man amongst boys out there tonight. So I would say his family has a great chance of getting out of there. If he keeps his head on straight. And I'm sure he will, he has my baby brother to keep his ass in line. So I know he's good" Sidney said.

"Thanks bro. But ultimately it's up to him, and I have confidence he will also" I replied driving.

I finally got to my brother's house and dropped him off. It was a good game, and it was cool hanging out with my brother like always. I got home that night and my daughter was sleep, but my beautiful wife Fatima was waiting up for me. And when I mean she was waiting up for me.......she was waiting up for me. She had this skimpy see through night gown on as she was laid across the couch when I came in. The lights were dim and some soft music was playing. I was definitely surprised, and Fatima looked so good.

"Damn baby you look so good" I said going over towards Fatima and embracing her with a hug and kiss. As we both sat down on the couch. There was a bottle of wine and two glasses with wine in them on the table.

"Thank you babe. I thought since my husband has been so patient and supportive, that I would surprise him by letting him know that....we can have sex now. And I'm ready" Fatima whispered in my ear as she kissed me on my ear lobe.

Fatima saying that was music to my ears, we both were so anxious to get back to our normal sex life. Of course we had to wait for a time period after our daughter was born. We were both glad that time was now here, and we wasted no time getting it in that night. Right there on the couch. Our daughter was sound asleep, as Fatima had the baby monitor in the room with us so we could hear her if she got up. We were alert for her, but so much into each other. It was a great night. After a great sex session and us both laying there naked looking up at the ceiling.

"So glad you had this surprise for me tonight, I needed this baby. You know we been wanting to tear each other apart since Jezell was born" I said as Fatima agreed with me right away.

"Oh my God yes" !! She chimed in.

We laid there for another fifteen minutes before Jezell made her presence felt and woke up. Fatima threw on her night gown, and went and got her. She then brought her in the living room with us, as I had finished getting dressed before getting a shower.

Page 204

It was late at that time, and my daughter was up. So I was up. I had to see her and spend some time with her before I went to sleep. So after I got my shower, I did just that. The weekend was here and we hadn't had Jezell out much because of the brutal Chicago Winter. But on this particular Saturday it was unseasonably warm. Warm enough that we could put Jezell in her stroller, bundled up of course. We wanted her to get some fresh air, see things. So we went Downtown to Millennium Park. A place Fatima and I would ride our bikes. We loved that park. And everything that came with it. And from the looks of it, Jezell did too. As she was wide awake looking around.

"Seems like she loves the park like Mommy and Daddy. Going to be nice bringing her here when she gets older too. Finals are coming up, so is this trial. How are you feeling about the both of them" ? Fatima asked as we continued walking pushing Jezell in her stroller.

"I feel good about my students being prepared for Finals. And I believe they all will do well. As for the trial, I have mixed feelings about it. Just because of the media attention I'm sure it's going to be a circus. Dak is a pretty well known athlete in the city like Deshawn is. I just hope Claudia gets the justice she deserves, no matter what" I replied.

"I hope she does too babe. She deserves it after all she's been through. So you and your brother had a good time hanging out together last night ? We were so wrapped up in each other when you arrived, that we didn't get a chance to talk about you and your brother hanging out at the game" Fatima said.

"Well of course not, when my beautiful sexy wife was in her night gown laying on the couch ready to give it to me. The last thing I was thinking about was hanging out with my brother. My mind was on you" I replied as Fatima was trying to hush me as we both laughed.

"Really ? Fatima said trying to sound innocent.

"You know I'm right, so don't even try it woman" I replied as we continued to laugh and smile at one another.

"Hey I missed my man and my man missed me. It was a great night babe. But I hope you enjoyed the time with your brother. I know you hadn't seen him in a while" Fatima said.

"Yeah we had a good time. And he got to see Deshawn play up close and personal again. And Deshawn gave us a show like always" I replied.

After being at the park with our daughter, it was time to return home.    Page 205

A month and a half later, it was the moment I had prepared my students for. Finals were here, and I couldn't be any happier. I woke up that morning excited to get to school. On the way to school that day, my short teaching career all played in my mind. From the first day I got there, and had to prove myself to some inner city Chicago kids who were fearless. Some had been in the streets most of their lives, and came to school occasionally. After I started teaching this class, those students started attending school more. It made me feel good that I had something to do with that. In just a little under a full school year, I had made some progress. And now was the moment of truth to see if all the hard work of my students paid off. I had got them to this point, and now it was up to them.

The mood at school was quiet and focused, other classes were taking their Finals also. I sat quietly at my desk and watched my students take theirs. I thought it was interesting being able to watch my students take their tests. I could get a sense how their focus may be. I had a lot of thoughts as I was sitting at my desk. Mainly hoping all my students did well. My last class completed their Finals and the day had came to a close. It was a day where I didn't do too much teaching, I did a lot of observing. But I did feel good about today. I couldn't wait to see the results of our Finals test scores. But for now I was headed home. On the drive home I got a call on my cell from my sister Savannah.

"Hey bro, I'm calling because Mom wants us all to go to church Sunday, and then have dinner here at the house. And Mom wants Dad to be there also. Yes you heard me right, she wants Dad to come to dinner" Savannah said.

"Ok....Pop ? Wow....well that's nice of her to invite him for dinner" I replied.

My mother and father had been around each other for family gatherings for years, but my mother never invited him to dinner. I wasn't so sure how my father's girlfriend would feel about it. He had a new girlfriend. Either way I hope he could make it, it was always nice when we all got together.

"Yes I thought the same thing when she told me to tell everyone. Hey they've been around each other for my kid's birthday parties. So why not have dinner with the whole family. I'm excited about it, it's going to be nice to have both our parents together for dinner. Haven't seen that since we were kids" Savannah said.

"It really is going to be nice Savannah. And oh yeah, what are we having ? Do I need to bring anything" ? I asked.

Page 206

"Mom says it's a surprise, and she says we'll all love it. Even my hardworking man Tremaine will be here. So it's going to be nice. I can't wait to see you, Fatima, and my niece baby Jezell. I'm really excited" Savannah said.

"Ok....mom is something else. I guess I'll see you then sis, love you" I replied.

"Ok big bro. I'm about to call our big bro Sidney Jr. Love you too" Savannah said before we both hung up.

It was good to know that the whole family would be together on Sunday. I was definitely excited about eating my mother's cooking, and spending time with my family. I believe this was the first time all of us would be together in a long time, if any time. I'm sure Fatima would be happy once I got home and told her about it. My wife loved my family, and I loved her's.

A few days later in school we got the test results from Finals. 75% of all my students in all my History classes passed their Finals. Which was a great number, up from only 42% the previous year. A 33% improvement in just a year's time was remarkable. I was very proud of myself and my students. No it wasn't a hundred percent like I wanted, but it was close. I had proved a point once again, that my teaching methods worked. And providing the kids with improved resources like new textbooks worked. I was hoping the School District recognized that because of these things, we were able to achieve improved test scores. And maybe that would bring about change. For now it was out of my hands, but it made our side of the fight stronger.

After getting home and telling my wife about the upcoming Sunday dinner at my mother's house for the whole family. My wife was so excited about it. And I can't lie, I was also. It was going to be a fun day with all of us being there.

"Did Savannah say if we need to bring anything ? And what are we having" ? Fatima asked.

"She said bring ourselves. But you know I'm going to take something. And she told me my mother said it was a surprise. And we would all love it. So I guess we shall see" I replied.

"I love my mother in law's cooking so I know we're going to love it" Fatima said smiling.

"Yep. And get this, my mother invited my father. You know they've been around each other for family gatherings before. But never really family dinners since they were together and we were kids. But I won't complain, I'm grateful. It's going to be nice having my parents together. As well as the rest of the family" I replied.

Page 207

After another productive week in school, and the good news of the Finals test scores. Another weekend was here and the highlight of the weekend was dinner at my mother's on da South Side. We were back home. And as soon as Fatima and I entered my mother's house after church. You could smell the food. She had been up late the previous night, my sister told us. Preparing dinner for the family. Everybody was there, as we all gathered around the dining room table holding hands about to say the blessing before we ate. My mother really out did herself this time. She made Baked Chicken, Baked Mac n Cheese, Collard Greens, a Roast with White Rice and Gravy. And some Cabbage. What a feast, and we were all starving. After saying the blessing, we all ate.

"I'm so happy and appreciative that you all came today. I wanted us all to get together as a family. First serving the Lord, and praising the Lord. And then enjoying dinner together. I'm happy all three of my children are here today together. I know it's tough for them to get together because of their busy schedules, but I'm glad I was able to get you all together. I'm happy that my daughter in law and my newborn granddaughter are here. As well as my other grandchildren. I'm happy my soon to be son in law Tremaine is here. I know you work a lot Tremaine, but I'm glad my daughter found such a good hard working man like yourself. And last but not least,

I'm happy my ex husband and father of my three children is here. Thank you all for coming" my mother Lucy said.

"Thanks Mom, for having us all" I replied.

"Yeah thanks Mom, the food was great as always" my brother Sidney Jr. said.

"When I'm telling yall she was up almost all night preparing everything....she was up almost all night preparing everything. I'm like Mom, aren't you done ? She's like, no girl just go to sleep. I got this" Savannah said as we all laughed.

"Lucy could always cook, that's one of the things I loved about her. She always took care of the home. Made sure you kids ate well and lived well. If I was ever gone, I knew she would take care of things" my father Sidney Sr. said chiming in as my mother looked on.

"She would hold it down huh Pop ? That's right, Mom Dukes held the fort down always" my brother Sidney Jr. said.

Sid...Silas. I wanted to eat some of that food last night when I came home from work, it smelled so good. But Mom wouldn't let me" Savannah said laughing.

It was always a good time when we all got together. It was no different this time. The food was great as expected, my mother was a wonderful cook.      Page 208

My family got to see how our baby Jezell had grown since they had seen her when she was a newborn. And boy did my family enjoy the new addition to the family. Holding her, kissing on her. The whole nine.

"Oh my God Fatima, my niece baby Jezell is so adorable. If I didn't have to work tomorrow, I would keep her here with me. You and big bro could have some free time for yall selves" Savannah said.

"Savannah I will definitely take you up on that when you're free. We love our baby girl more than anything in this world, but we could use the free time at some point. We still haven't went on our honeymoon yet. We had to postpone it after we found out I was pregnant" Fatima said.

"Yes I remember. You guys let me know, when yall decide to go on your honeymoon. I will help look after her while yall are gone, she's so adorable" Savannah said still holding Jezell.

"Hey Tremaine, I think my sister has gotten baby fever. You better be on point playboy" I said laughing and joking.

"No, no, no.....no more kids for us Silas. We're done. We got our hands full with the ones we have" Tremaine replied laughing.

"That's right, so hush Silas" my sister Savannah chimed in.

"Hey y'all, I have to get going. Have some things I need to do, but it was great seeing everybody and spending time with the family. We have to do this again sometime soon. Mom and Pop love y'all and thanks for having me over" my brother Sidney Jr. said before he left.

"Ok Sidney Jr. you call me later this week sometime. Love you too son" my mother Lucy replied as my brother gave her a kiss before he left.

"No doubt Mom I will, goodbye everybody" my brother Sidney Jr. could be heard saying as he walked out the door.

Not long after that, Fatima and I got our things together with Jezell and left also. It was a great Sunday and a great time with the family. My family was a big part of my life, and always would be. And it felt more like a family with my father and brother's relationship now repaired. And my parents getting along to the point now that we as a family, could sit down and have dinner together. Life was good, and as the school year was ending. There was still two important things that had my attention.   Page 209

Deshawn's big decision. He would be announcing where he would attend college today in the same school gymnasium that he's played in the last three years. And although he had missed some games this year due to personal matters. He still put in another great season averaging 24.3 points per game along with 11 rebounds and 4 assists a game. Solid enough numbers that only a few colleges had changed their minds about still wanting his services. Deshawn would announce his decision that morning in the gymnasium. And as I entered my classroom that morning, I was in my classroom for ten minutes when there was a knock on my door. It was Deshawn.

"Hey Mr. Jones, I came here because I want you to be there with me this morning when I announce my choice for college. You've been on my ass since I entered your class. And it was what I needed. I don't know where I would've ended up if you wasn't on my ass about my school work and my future. I might've ended up like my brother Corey. I just want to thank you for everything you've done for me and my classmates. You even came to my neighborhood in Fuller Park several times. I don't know too many teachers that would've done that, or were that brave. And this morning is apart of me showing my appreciation for all of those who remained by my side through all this" Deshawn said.

"Thanks Deshawn, I appreciate you wanting me to be there. And it would truly be an honor. I'm just glad you got through everything you went through this year. You showed a lot of courage. You're a smart and strong young man, you can go as far as you want to go. It's all up to you. Good luck son with everything you do. See you in a little. And I won't ask you what your choice is. I will find out when everyone else finds out" I replied shaking Deshawn's hand as he walked away and headed to the gymnasium for his big moment.

I was indeed happy for Deshawn, happy he had finally got focused and handled his business. Happy that his mother had finally understood that he needed her support, and not to hold him back from his destiny. I guess you could say Corey's death was a blessing in disguise of some sort, because it opened the eyes of a lot of people. Not only Deshawn, their mother, and other siblings. But also the community. Amongst all the other violence that was going on in the streets of Chicago. The community pushed for more Police presence in neighborhoods. And not necessarily stiffer laws like the local, state, and federal government had handled things. When those laws got stiffer, they more than likely affected only Minorities versus their White counterparts. And for doing the same crimes. And despite the Police killing Corey. The citizens of Chicago never claimed that the killing of Corey Williams was similar to all the other cases of Police killing unarmed Black Men. They all knew Corey was armed and raised his gun at Police, to in turn get shot. Because he didn't want to go to jail.         Page 210

As I stepped into the school gymnasium, there were students and local press everywhere as the gym was packed. Not packed like an actual game, but a lot of people was there. Deshawn was accompanied by his mother Roberta.

"Thanks for being here Mr. Jones. He really wanted you here, and I did too. Nice seeing you again. And I want to thank you again for sticking by my son. I know at times him and I made it rather difficult. Not to mention my son Corey" Deshawn's mother Roberta said as I walked up.

"Its all good Miss Williams, thank you for letting me guide your son on his journey. Deshawn is a fine young man that has a bright future ahead of him, I wish him the best where ever he goes. And I'm sure where ever he goes, he will shine" I replied.

Miss Williams just smiled as we both sat down behind the podium. Deshawn's aunt by marriage, Mrs. Williams his uncle's wife was also in attendance. After about ten minutes, Deshawn came out to the podium and began to speak.

"Hello students, teachers, faculty, family, and friends. I'm here to announce where I will be attending college next year. After a lot of thought, and going back and forth with my thoughts. I've decided to attend the University of Illinois" Deshawn said as the crowd cheered.

Deshawn decided to stay close to home, by remaining in state. He would be two hours and fifteen minutes from Chicago. After announcing where he was going, he embraced his mother. Then embraced me by giving me a handshake and hug.

"You did it man, I'm so proud of you Deshawn. Good luck" I said before I left to go back to my classroom.

I let Deshawn have his moment with his mother, he deserved all the shine he was getting. He had came a long way since I met him in the beginning of the year. And been through so much as a young man already. It was good to see his life turning around for the better. Claudia was one of the students who were in the crowd as Deshawn announced his choice. She herself had an important part of her life coming up. The trial of Dak Hollis. She smiled as Deshawn made his choice, her and Deshawn were friends. And two smart people, they both had bright futures ahead of them.

I got back to my classroom and prepared to began my first class of the day. And even though the school year was in its last days. I was still eager to teach like it was day one of a new year.

And I did, taught the last few days like it was the first day. Because it was my passion. And I have to be honest, I was sad to see the year coming to a close. But I was grateful to teach some amazing students I had. We got off to a rough start, but we eventually got it together. We learned what to expect from each other, it made for a very interesting and successful learning experience. A few days later it was graduation time. And me being apart of the faculty, I was in attendance for that also. As I got to see two of my best students, Deshawn and Claudia walk across the stage to get their diplomas. It was a great experience, as well as seeing the rest of the class get their diplomas.

I knew after graduation, the trial was looming. So I was preparing myself for everything that came with a high profile case. And me supporting Claudia, I would need to remain strong because almost everyone was on the side of Dak Hollis. School was finally over and I was cleaning out my desk and getting ready for my summer. A summer that was supposed to be our honeymoon, in which we were still planning to go. But we just didn't know when. I gave Claudia my word about my support for her throughout the trial, and

I wasn't backing out of it now. She deserved my support and she was going to get it.

The first day of the trial I came in the courtroom, as Dak's side of the courtroom was packed with people. Claudia had her family on her side and some school officials. I looked to my left and it was Mitchell. We looked at each other, gave each other a head nod and I kept walking to my seat. A few rows up from him on the other side. I didn't feel like I needed to deal with Mitchell any longer. What he said didn't matter to me anymore, because I had seen how he was when he was put under pressure. He broke, and that was all I needed to know.

Claudia entered the courtroom and looked nervous as expected. She glanced over at me as she walked by and I gave her a nod, as if to say I'm with her. From the very start of the trial, you could feel the tension. It was just like I had imagined it would be. Most of the people on Dak's side, and very little on Claudia's side. After the first few days of trial, it was a rollercoaster of emotions. As the courtroom heard Claudia's tear filled testimony of the night in question. Her mother who was seated a few rows ahead of me in the courtroom, she could be heard crying as her daughter testified.

It all made for major courtroom drama, and the media ate it up. Each day after court ended, they were trying to interview anybody they could. That they thought was important to the case. They tried to interview Claudia several times, and she never said a thing. She was always guarded by her lawyers as she left the courthouse each day. The same with Dak. He never said a thing, his lawyers always spoke for him. But it didn't stop the local news from covering the story day by day.     Page 212

One day during a court recess, I decided to step outside and have a cigarette. I hadn't had a cigarette in weeks, but this particular day I had one. Didn't even have a pack, I had gotten it from another person. So anyway I'm out smoking, and out walks Mitchell. Something told me he was going to come over to me. And sure enough, he did.

"Silas what's going on man ? Haven't spoke to you in a while. We used to be closer than this man. I know we've had our differences. But why the distance ? I thought we had a understanding" Mitchell said.

"Distance huh ? You know a lot about that my brotha. So it shouldn't be unfamiliar to you. I don't know what you want from me Mitchell" I replied before Mitchell interrupted.

"I just want your friendship !! The same friendship we had before you got hired by the School District. The same friendship you and I had when we met through our Men's Group at church. What happened to that" ? Mitchell asked.

"What happened is, you forgot how passionate I was about my craft. How much this meant to me and what I've been trying to accomplish. Why ? Because it isn't your vision, I wouldn't expect you to understand it. And you could have told me that you wasn't about this life from day one. But instead you portrayed that you were. I have no clue why, but you did. You should've been who you really were from day one. That's all I have to say. Good day Mitchell" I replied walking away. As Mitchell just stood there shaking his head.

Mitchell was wasting his time thinking that we were actually going to be friends. I remained in the Men's Group at church, and we would see each other there. And our wives still remained really good friends. But Fatima also knew how I felt about Mitchell. So she knew where I stood with it. And she tried not to have Mitchell and I together too much if any. Her and Kendra would just do things together on their own. And I was fine with that. Back to the trial and back in the courtroom. As the trial continued moving forward. And other people took the stand. From the medical examinator's office to some students who were at the party that night.

Dak Hollis sat quietly surrounded by his lawyers in a dark blue suit. Pretty much emotionless as he listened to testimonies from several people. Dak himself eventually took the stand, and when he did you could see his arrogance on the stand on full display. To him Claudia was nothing but one of his female groupie fans. That really wanted him that night. Claudia claims she went to the party with Dak as his date. No more no less. But that didn't mean sex. Either way, they were here now and after hearing both sides of the argument. And statements from the prosecution and defense. The jury would now decide Dak's fate. Page 213

The court would recess while the jury deliberated and came up with a verdict. In the meantime I went to a local eatery a few blocks away from the Courthouse in Downtown Chicago. As I was in the eatery, I looked up at the TV screen to see that the local news were on site at the courthouse reporting as we speak. As everyone was awaiting the verdict. I completely ignored it and sat down to have some lunch. I didn't want anyone bothering me or asking any questions about the case. I sat quietly in the courtroom all week hearing each side's case. My support never wavered, I still believed that Dak did rape Claudia. It was something that always ate me up each time I said it. Because in my mind either way this case wasn't going to end good. Even if Claudia got her justice, which she deserved. It would be another young black male with so much potential incarcerated for a major wrong doing.

Rape is a serious crime, and I had no respect for men who did it. But it was also a fine line. Because I also didn't respect women who lied about falsely accusing men of rape. Especially men with money, or potential to make lots of money. Like Dak Hollis, who definitely had the potential to make lots of money. He was a dominant force on the football field. Sure to excel on the college level, and a strong possibility on the professional level. This case was huge and the whole city was watching. After about another forty five minutes. We were called back to the courthouse, the jury had reached a verdict. At that moment I was texting my wife back and forth letting her know what was going on.

I can't lie, I was a little nervous taking the short walk back to the courthouse. I mean I felt strongly about Dak being guilty after hearing both arguments. But you never know in the court system. Anything could happen. So as I got back to the courthouse, amid all the cameras and press. I walked in unnoticed and glad I was, as I made my way back to my seat. After everyone got back to their seats, the judge started the court session as I looked on.

"So the jury does have a verdict" The judge said as he handed the verdict to the Jury Foreman.

The Jury Foreman then read the verdict.

"We the jury in the above case The State of Illinois vs Dak Hollis for the crime of rape find the defendant guilty on all charges" he said as the courtroom erupted.

"Order in the court !! Order in the court.....settle down" !! The judge said banging his gavel as there was clear frustration and anger on Dak's side of the courtroom. And cheers and hugs on Claudia's side.        Page 214

I looked up at Claudia, she had her head down on her table. I could tell she was crying. I know she must've felt a range of emotions after the verdict was read. People on Dak's side of the courtroom left very angry. When the verdict was read, and after watching Claudia's reaction. I looked over to watch Dak's reaction. He just shook his head in disgust and was clearly upset about the verdict. He was then led out of the courtroom. I let most of the people that were in the courtroom leave before I got up myself and left. Claudia passed me and looked over towards me, but didn't say anything. I wasn't expecting her to, being the moment.

On the drive home I was glad it was all over. I had kept my word to my top two students, who were also my students who had been through the most this year. I had fulfilled my responsibilities to them both and was happy I could. I went home that day feeling good.

"I seen the verdict on TV, I could only imagine how it was in the courtroom" Fatima said as I arrived at home.

"Yeah it was pretty tense. Especially on Dak's side after the verdict was read. I mean I feel good about Claudia getting the justice she deserves. But there goes another young black male's life essentially destroyed. Because of a bad decision made one night. A stupid and wrong decision mind you. That's how fast everything can just end for you" I replied.

"Yes babe, it's truly sad that the young man has destroyed his life. You never want to see that. Especially a person of color with very few chances to be successful. I just hope these young men and women learn from this case" Fatima said.

"I hope so too Fatima, because this is something I don't want to experience again" I replied.

I had to go back to school to get the last of my things for the summer that next day. I got to school and my classroom and got my things. But before I left, I just stood in my classroom and looked around. I envisioned everything from my first day here, to Midterms, to Finals. All the projects my students and I did. The weekly Friday quizzes. I envisioned everything that happened that year. As I was there, I got a knock on my classroom door. It was Claudia.

"Hello Mr. Jones, I didn't know if I would find you here or not. But I'm happy I did, I didn't know if I would see you again this year. But I wanted to say thank you very much for all your support throughout the trial. Thanks for believing in me, you're the best teacher I ever had. You're an amazing man Mr. Jones" Claudia replied.     Page 215

"Thanks Claudia, I appreciate that. It means a lot that my students feel that way about me. It truly does. I only ever wanted the best for all of you. You're a smart young woman Claudia, you can do anything you want to do. Don't let anyone tell you otherwise, best of luck to you Claudia" I replied.

"Thanks again Mr. Jones" Claudia said embracing me with a hug.

Claudia decided to go to The University of Michigan College of Pharmacy in the Fall. She always said she wanted to be a Pharmacist, I was proud that she followed her dreams. Despite their trials and tribulations throughout the year, they both showed courage and determination to want to be successful. And they were both well on their way to becoming just that. I was happy for the both of them, and wished them the best. But now it was about my wife and I, as we were about to go on our much anticipated honeymoon. Finally. Flying out of Chicago O'Hare International

Airport to Punta Cuna. We flew United Airlines and enjoyed the four hour and thirty one minute flight. Just the two of us.

Our daughter Jezell was back home with family. Cared for by both families, so we had no worries. If you're wondering if Fatima had mother daughter separation anxiety, nope she didn't. She was more than ready for our honeymoon, we both were. And as we arrived at our resort we were beyond excited.

"Babe as soon as we get settled we have to get in this beautiful blue water. Oh my God.....so beautiful. I'm in Heaven" Fatima said admiring the beautiful blue water as we walked along the beach.

"Yes....indeed. This is real nice, real nice. Away from the noise and hustle of Chicago ya feel me" I replied looking out at the water.

After settling in our room, my wife and I did what she said we should do. Got changed and got in the water. We got our drinks and sat in the water. After that we swam together and just enjoyed the scenery. It was so beautiful. By night we went back to our room got showered and changed. Then went to see a Jazz Band play, we both loved Jazz. It was truly a relaxing evening, and we enjoyed every minute of it. We both drank way too much the first night and paid for it the next morning. But we also enjoyed the cultural aspects of the Island also. Like the tours and boat rides.

After finally getting up, we ate breakfast as we sat at our table with only our robes on.

"Last night was great, well as much as I can remember I should say" I said as we both laughed.

"Last night was great babe, I remember what we did when we got back here to our room" Fatima replied smiling at me as we both laughed and kissed.

"Oh I do too baby, how could I forget" I chimed in.

Fatima and I just had that type of relationship, we were friends as well as lovers. It was that way since we first got together. And it remained that way, and probably was the reason we were still together til this day. Each day we spent in Punta Cunta was great. But before you knew it, we were back on the plane headed back home to Chicago. On the flight home, Fatima and I had a conversation about our honeymoon.

"An amazing time, really was. I didn't want to leave, but I miss my baby girl Jezell. Can't wait to see her" I said as I had my arm around Fatima and she lay on my chest the whole flight home.

"Yes I miss my baby too. But I definitely could've stayed another day or two" Fatima replied looking up at me.

"Oh hell yeah, no doubt baby" I said agreeing with her smiling and kissing her on her forehead.

Four hours later we were home and exhausted. I could barely keep my eyes open, so Fatima decided to drive us home from the airport. After that, everything was a blur. As I woke up the next morning in our bedroom in our bed stretched out. Fatima was in the living room feeding our daughter because I could hear her. I stepped in the living room and went directly for my daughter as my wife was feeding her. I just took her out of my wife's arms. I just had too, I missed my baby girl.

"Silas....I just started feeding her" Fatima said looking in disbelief that I took her from her arms.

"Baby, I missed my baby girl like crazy. Yes Daddy did, Daddy missed his baby" I replied talking to Jezell while kissing on her as I continued to feed her.

I held my daughter for a little while longer and continued feeding her until my cell phone rang and I had to answer it. As I gave Jezell to Fatima, I looked at my phone and it was my father.

"Hey Pop, what's going on" ? I asked

"Hey son, I see you're back from your honeymoon. I hope you and Fatima enjoyed y'all selves. I called to see if you wanted to get that game of Chess on in the park. We haven't played in a while. And how's my granddaughter doing" ? My father replied.

"Yeah Pop we had a great time. And Jezell is doing very well, laying here getting fed by her mother. Yeah we can get together and play, it has been a while. I'm on my way to come get you" I said.

"Ok son, sounds good" my father replied.

I went and got my father and we headed to the park. As I said before, it didn't matter what my father and I were doing. I was just happy to spend time with the man, as well as my mother. I realized my parents were getting older, so every moment to me was priceless. I made sure when they wanted to see me, I was there. When my mother wanted me to go to church with her, I was there. Those things meant a lot to my parents, and I loved to make them happy. So as I drove to pick my father up to play Chess in the park, I thought a lot about that. A lot about my life and how far I came. From a young kid who was born and raised on da South Side of Chicago. Went on to college, served eight years in the Marine Corps and came home to make a difference in my community as a teacher.

Leading minds and hopefully changing the course of education, like my vision sought me out to do when I started this journey. There was still a lot of work to do in regards to education, especially on the first and secondary level. But what I accomplished was a start. As my father and I sat in the park playing Chess, everything was put into perspective.

"You know Pop, I was happy with the progress I made as a teacher this year. And the progress we made as a School District. But I realize there's so much more to do. But getting the ball rolling was huge this year" I said.

"Son you did some amazing things. And everything wasn't done at your school. You were not only these kid's teacher, but also their mentor and confidant. You stood by these kids throughout their hardships. Not all teachers would've done what you've done. The world needs more teachers like yourself Silas, you care and you get it. You get these kids nowadays, that's saying something. I know what you've done and everyone at that school knows what you've done. I couldn't have asked for a better son. Man, soldier, veteran, husband, father and teacher. Proud of you son. Now it's time to kick your ass in Chess" my father replied.

"Oh you think so Pop? Not happening today old man" I replied as we both laughed and continued playing.
Page 218

Later that year. There were laws that passed that allowed for more funding in the city of Chicago for Chicago Public Schools. Strictly on the first and secondary levels of education. Which was huge in our fight for a better education for not only inner city schools in Chicago. But all over this country. In every major city in America. It would take some time to expand out, but eventually would. And I was name one of the top 50 Teachers in America, as I was recognized by my city for the work I did with our students.

I think being recognized by my own city was the biggest accomplishment I had as a teacher. Even bigger than being name one of the top 50 Teachers in America. Basically because no one knew me like Chicago knew me. It was my birthplace and where my family was. My wife and growing daughter. And the greatest parents a man could have, along with my siblings. They were all very proud of me. And that meant the world to me.

When I set out to make a difference in my community, it was never about me. It was all about the children of Chicago. I had been to college, I had seen the world as apart of the Marine Corps. When I returned home, I had a purpose. And I believe I made a pretty good mark in doing that. I was proud of myself. And now everyone knows the name Silas Jones. Not for being a statistic in Chicago streets. Not for being a career criminal, not for anything negative. But for being a positive force in his community, by leading young minds to become future success stories. I'm Silas Jones.......and this was MY story.


The End

Made in the USA
Middletown, DE
31 December 2019